FOUL

John Klawitter

FOUL

DOUBLE DRAGON

Dedication

For Lynnie,
a fubsy wench
in whose presence the flowers
blush and grow pale
unaccustomed to such
loveliness

AUTHOR'S NOTE

This is a work of fiction. All of the major characters are made up. Because the story plays against the historical backdrop of professional football, an avid fan may recognize that the Rams did take on the Vikings in a play-off game in 1969, a game in which there were so many controversial calls that sports reporters of the time questioned whether the refs had taken the game out of the players' hands and decided it for themselves. Where actual players are mentioned in the context of that game, their actions have been taken from the newspaper sports pages of the time, primarily from the Los Angeles Times and the Herald Examiner. It is my hope that none of these figures has been misrepresented. However, the fictional characters involved in that game and in the larger context of this story-including Ripper Brown, Lani Kazin, Loaf Ludder, Rand Burkle, Jeff Raymond, Nathan Paramis, Jimmy "Motorfoot" Teams and George Haslins-are purely fictional, as are their motivations and actions. There have been many colorful names for defensive lines; there have been at least three Fearsome Foursomes playing for various teams (although arguably the most famous was the Rams line of 1964-1974), to say nothing of The Steel Curtain, The Doomsday Squad, The Purple People Eaters, The Orange Crush and many others. "The Mighty Foremen" are a creation of this author for this novel, and represent a completely fictional defensive front four. On the other hand, there is a real Megan's Cafe in Aurora, Minnesota, run by a blonde lady named Gwen who has a sense of humor.

CHAPTER 1

Never mind my name; I promised the name-under-the-title (a vain and pompous little current day auteur) that I wouldn't tell. But I'll give you enough clues in passing that you'll get it before we're through. Let's just say I was the rough and ready Hemingway of my time. Well, Odd's Plut and her Nails, maybe not Hemingway, but at least something resembling a delicious combination of a higher-plane Nora Roberts and a Robert B. Parker with a better vocabulary..., that is, if they did cheap, two-penny novels. That said, will it 'freak you out', as you say in your own quaint dialect, 'devil your pleasantries' too much, if I reveal to you that I've been dead for over 200 years? Right. Your storyteller, your narrator, cold stone dead as a mackerel...bones ground and blown to dust, actually...but that's another story, and one that's never been told. Here's the thing—I'm the only bumfiddle who can actually tell this tale, this delightful little penny dreadful called FOUL. That's because our protagonist, one Brando Mahr, came back from the mental dead zone in 1980 by reading penny novels scribbled two centuries before—mostly by moi! Yea and verily, my friends. Yes, myself—the great, tattered bard! Allow me to take a bow, and that accomplished, I'll retreat ass-over-teakettle (swiftly but not humbly) into the background as a sort of translator, here for you whenever the going gets a little patchy. You see, Brando's returned to the 20th century, but he thinks like somebody just off the streets of London in the mid-1700s. So, with no further pleasantries, let us begin in the middle of his troubles.

As our story opens, it is August, 1984. Brando Mahr hadn't actually ever intended to *gather the acquaintanceship* of the famous football hero Ripper Brown, as he might have said in that quaint, cobbled-together English of his. That he had met Ripper at all—or Mister Doomsday, as the great footballer had been dubbed in his glory days of yore—was the result of a bit of well-meaning dirty work on the part of Brando's old studio pal Keith Lagosi.

It was a hot August in the summer of 1984. Lying with his back on the stained and dirty floor of an interrogation room next to Los Angeles Police Lieutenant Baker's scuffed black work shoes, Brando found himself bearing Keith plenty of ill will.

Wish you were here, pal Lagosi, his overworked brain thought, *that we might discuss the unpredictable mushroom manifestations of your foolish pipe dreams.* As I've said, Brando talks like that because, after years in a coma, he re-taught himself English—unfortunately, by reading my fantastico 18th century picaresques.

Brando stayed down on one elbow on the floor and felt the painful fires flicker through every joint in his body. He swallowed the thin trickle of blood from the inside of his torn cheek.

"Oh, yeah. Quite a mess, you're in," Baker commented, looking down at him while he took a laconic drag from one of those unfiltered Camels that he counted on as part of his drably anachronistic persona. Baker seemed to think he was Sergeant Friday of Dragnet. "How the hell did you think you were going to get away with it?" he asked in his quietly menacing way.

Brando knew Baker meant the murder of Ripper's wife, and that it was time to answer.

"Considering that, in your mind, I am the guilty party," he said, "it is a fair but complex question, and I require a moment to cognize."

Mulling over the situation seemed to deaden his physical pain, and after a few moments Brando was able to drag his reluctant frame semi-erect. He tottered for a moment and then sagged into the nearest chair.

And there, while Lieutenant Baker smoked and watched him, he tried to sort out his thoughts and recollect the scattered fragments of his recent past.

The morning the Ripper mess had begun, the sun was shining down on Lotusland, and Brando had been thinking he was a *bona fide* Hollywood eater, that is, a chap of substance and possibilities. He was relatively unrecognized in show biz, but he felt he had excellent prospects. There would always be his uncertain health, but on that day he'd convinced himself he was sputtering forward. Think positive thoughts, he told himself. Passible, Peppy, Perceptive, Perfect, Pleasing. His old learning techniques danced along at the back of his awareness. Ordinary humans don't usually think this way—in alphabetical order—but Brando, as you will see, is far from ordinary, and beggars cannot be choosers.

Here now, take a moment to look back: Here is what happened to him to make him the way he

11

was: Once upon a time, at the precise wrong moment for his well-being, Brando had been too close to the massive concussive force of a large artillery shell. It had left him catatonic, dumb as a stone for a number of years. After that duration, and against all odds, he had revived—only to find himself aphasiac and prey to epileptic seizures. Aphasia, of course, is a mental disconnect; it is knowing what a thing is even while your brain can't remember the word for it.

After a time, Brando had managed to gather enough of wit about him to sneak out of the Veterans Hospital on Wilshire in West Los Angeles, and then, after bumming around a bit in Santa Monica with the street people, to get a minimum wage job carting books back to the stacks in the UCLA library. It was there, deep in the bowels of bookville, that he re-taught himself words... and, incidentally, learned to think and speak in London street slang that hasn't been heard in ordinary conversation in nearly 200 years. As for the epilepsy, well, you know what that is.

Even in this, Brando is no ordinary garden variety tomato of an epileptic. Like some of the rarer strains, strange and deceptive delusions—visions, even—sometimes precede his seizures. He has given these visionary delusions the name *Zeemans*, because they seem to come from some unknown "z" dimension, perhaps like a rain of frogs from a clear blue sky. While not unpleasant, unless he recognizes the Zeemans for what they are, and is able to interrupt them, they invariably led to a fairly predictable series of mental and physical interruptions that can easily kill him.

12

Before he'd met Ripper Brown, Brando hadn't had the beginnings of a Zeeman in weeks, and he was infused with boundless enthusiasm. Captain Padrow had warned him this sort of euphoria generally came before a fall. Padrow? She was a practicing U.S. Army psychologist with multiple professional degrees and a career to protect. He saw her as a deep and fuddering yawn-bearer who scribbled papers and nodded with great authority at meetings of her peers. He'd also had her in bed, so their relationship was, if nothing else, complicated.

Don't get too accustomed to life, Brando, she'd warned, *you're not going to be here that long.* Brando shrugged her off, figuring her comments were the army version of tough love. Even if she was right, what did it matter? There was today to be enjoyed, and maybe tomorrow. It was what he had, so it had to be enough.

The day he met the Ripper, he was some years down the road from his bumbling early revival in the bowels of the library. Progress had been made, and he was stumbling along in a career of sorts in show biz, where people mostly couldn't tell who did and who didn't have their wits about them. On this particular sunny day, he was outfitted *tres chic militaire* in an old army shirt and a pair of fatigues so threadbare they'd gone beatnik. Ronald Reagan was running for his 2nd term against Walter Mondale, Cats was big on Broadway, and Brando was heading north, out of town, to get as far away as he could from the swarm and blather of the Summer Olympics He was scooting Fifi, his rumbly little brown Fiat Spyder, along in fifth, the gear that real sports car

13

aficionados hardly ever employ in L.A. due to freeway clog. Brando and Fifi were on their way to meet his old pal Lagosi, soon to be known as *master of treachery*.

Brando was in what he might call the Joyful Judy mode, with absolutely no intention to bother any lord of the highway or geek of the road. He'd flipped Fifi's new tan ragtop down, her mag wheels were dutifully gleaming, his seat was cranked back nearly like a shrink's couch and his sun-bleached moustachios and receding hairline were flaring in the wind. He didn't much mind about the hairline. English lords and barristers wore wigs, and the brutish Germans just shaved it all off, bald as cue balls and convinced they were utterly, fiendishly sexy.

"Therefore, why bother, I?" He shouted to the wind.

Fifi was round and sleek like a dark and rangy little ocelot. He'd heard rumors that Spyders weren't to be boated into the States anymore, but he'd picked his up on a brief filming assignment in Europe. When he wanted to bring it back to the States, his only other friend on the planet besides Keith, semi-gangster Charlie Manganetti, had gray-listed it into California for him. That was back in the fat times when Brando was a middle-ranking somebody at the studio, and *Caesar had been almost entirely given unto* before the lean years set in...meaning Fifi was nearly paid for before he got canned.

He was zooming north out of the San Fernando Valley, climbing the five-mile upgrade the locals call 'The Grapevine,' when a spot of

14

trouble inadvertently scuttered across his path like a dark tarantula.

He was in the far left fast lane cruising at seventy-something when a lime-green Porsche Targa closed in on Fifi's backside. No road hog or, as he would say, *no dog in a doublet*, Brando hit the right blinker and started to cut over into the next lane.

Unfortunately, the Targa was too impatient for the circumstance. The fellow started right at the same time Brando was making his cut—only two material objects cannot occupy the same space and time without some form of mechanical bending.

Brando had moved in front of *le banana verte*. No big deal, but the green banana had to consider tapping his brakes, a major insult.

The Targa eased up a bit and the black front bumper moved within bare inches of Fifi's rear end. And then the Porsche crossed behind and its driver gunned it to Fifi's left.

Brando sensed a flash of pilot's steel-rim sunglasses and a carrot-colored pate, and the speed felon yelled over at him, "Learn to drive, you asshole!"

"You—you—Ichabod!" Brando yelled back, giving him the Western One-Finger. *That would teach the offender*, Brando thought; Ichabod, son of Phinehas in the Bible, a name which throughout history had been used to describe a person without honor.

The name-calling may have been lost in time beyond recall, but the significance of Brando's emphatic hand gesture was not lost on the driver of the green banana. He pulled close enough to

15

Brando's side to shave Fifi's fender. Brando figured they were going to enjoy a West Coast verbal exchange, or maybe banana-man would surface a pistola and pop him in the cranium, and that might just be a blessing in disguise.

"I ought to run you off the road and beat the crap out of you, you stupid schmuck!" banana-man yelled.

Ahh, no pistol popping! Verbals it was!. Brando grinned, overjoyed to use a small part of his large but incredibly antiquated vocabulary of ridicule and abuse.

"Not manifesting overall cleverness today, are we?" he shouted back over the roaring wind. "Who writes your dialogue—Prince Myshkin?" He was, of course, referring to the idiot in Dostoevski's novel of the same name. Maybe not on the current New York best seller list, but it was the only thing that burbled to mind.

"You stupid prick!" Banana-man replied.

"Cod-licking dribble-dick! " Brando yelled with a victorious note to his voice.

"Talk English, you idiot!"

"My English is more English than your English!" Brando shouted back. "You mundungus buffle-headed bumfiddle! You're an affront to good taste everywhere!"

With that, Brando had to swerve as his foe carried out a mad bomber attempt to buzz off Fifi's left fender. Brando braked, and carrot-top carried over across his lane into the parallel on his right.

"You're dicked in the knob, dildo ding-boy!" Brando shouted, meaning his foe was a crazy, womanish knave of the lowest cut. Banana-man

16

jerked his wheel left to force the Spyder off the road. Brando was prepared to swerve out of the way; but, due to wicked fortune, he hit the brakes at a sandy smear and Fifi's back end went goosey.

In what Brando would call *a milli-tick*, a forest of chrome bumpers and dung-brown Southland hills whipped by with a wondrous tilt-a-world sweep as Fifi la Fiat and her owner did a violent 360. The little roadster skidded out onto the center divide, still doing well over 60 in the dusty, loose gravel.

Brando saw flying dry tumbleweed suspended stop-frame in the air for a moment before they burst through it. Fifi was heading for a steep down-slope that led into a boulder-choked *barranca*. Brando tapped his brakes and waited until the last moment to correct, and played the bite of the rubber in a controlled slide the shape of a shallow "C". They narrowly missed the *barranca* and ended up back in the far left lane on the freeway, still caroming along in the right direction.

"Get a life, you sorry mother-fucker!" came the green banana's distant cry..

Carrot-top was receding into the distance. He had floored his pedal to the metal, as the pseudo truck-talkers all said, this being that loquacious epoch when America was suffering the CB radio virus, and he was speeding away. Brando was left behind, shaking and furious in a wake of his rival's sooty effluvium. In ten seconds Carrot-top was just a chartreuse bug, and in twenty he was a disappearing dot on the horizon.

However, this being the Southern California *Southland* where one's reality easily meanders off

17

the yogurt truck, in another minute, Brando passed him. The driver of the green Porsche had been jerked over by a Black Maria, a little copper-gimcrack smirking behind her dark glasses, her taunting femininity plumping out a starched tan CHP uniform as she handed Carrot-top the unpleasantly numbered slip. Banana-boy glared a pair of degans—that is, dagger-eyes—as Brando raised his finger-salute high, yelled *God Save The Queen's Britches!* and roared on past.

He shifted into fourth and then downshifted into third and second, Fifi's engine rapping off wonderfully as *la Spyder* and her master dove across the many lanes and into the designated turn-off for the shooting range.

He and Fifi zoomed from the freeway through a dust-blown off-ramp leading to a cement and gravel operation, where the tight little imp of a car negotiated a swift left on an unpaved road. They cut back under deep shadows between the tall cement trunks of the freeway. Fifi slid through a series of turns and Brando gunned her into third, dodging and weaving around the bigger potholes.

He fairly rocketed Fifi along, eager to meet his pal Keith, for the devious Lagosi had lured him to this location with a gunnysack lumpy with unregistered widow's guns that he wanted to trade for cold, hard cash.

CHAPTER 2

Of course, Brando knew strangers didn't think much of his unkempt appearance and unusual language. He's not a *stupid* bungle-puss.

"Mayhaps that's why I attract adventure, like new shoes attract dog doo-doo," he told Belle Denver, his lean and lusty chick-a-biddy.

But pretty Belle disagreed.

"You don't attract adventure," she said. "You just get in trouble and that's because you're weird."

"Wench," he replied, smiling in pleasant agreement, "That's about the deepest you've ever plowed."

"Uhh…Who plows what?" she asked, eyeing him suspiciously over the French Designer glasses she'd picked up from a sidewalk vender on Sunset Boulevard. Belle, who had ditched most of grade school and all of high school in favor of her career, was suspicious of anyone who said anything she didn't understand. That the two of them should be an off-and-on again number was one of the world's great wonders.

"You're close to the bone on that one," Brando said, trying again to explain.

"Yeah, I like the bone," she said, affectionately patting him between the thighs.

On the morning that he first met the great footballer, Ripper Brown, Brando showed up at the shooting range in the mountains, and, as anticipated, good buddy Keith and his wife Virginia were waiting in the parking lot.

Keith Lagosi was early film star Bella's distant cousin, and he was also the head of the projection department at the studio from which Brando had recently been flung. The fellow Brando was soon to name *shabby dissembler* scrambled eagerly out of his battered old '75 Charger and yanked a lumpy sack from the back seat.

"Hi there, Arachno-Lover!," Brando yelled. People who worked at that particular studio had their own internal language. Brando gave Keith the Opie-Dopie, a sort of upside-down hang-loose sign that crawled as it went.

The Opie-Dopie was the symbol of the Itsy Bitsy Club, the kid's show that had gathered in a bundle for the studio and extended the celebrity life of Opie the Arachnid. Everybody loved Opie, the animated spider the studio artists had "humanized" over the years until he looked like an eight-legged, eight-eyed sheepdog, big floppy ears, floppy pink tongue, *et al.* In the beginning, there was Opie the Arachnid and Ronnie the Rattler. Imagine, if you can—a great Hollywood studio founded on the epic tales of a spider and a snake.

Keith was sporting one of those cameraman/fisherman vests from Banana Republic, the beige cotton number with fishnet air-flo ventilation in back and about 50 pockets in front. He also was shamelessly flaunting a t-shirt that proclaimed Donald Duck was celebrating the 50th anniversary of his nativity. The fudds at the studio would unhappily consider that consorting with the enemy, which was actually why he wore it.

"Hi, Brando!" he said, passing a friendly finger, "Here's what you can do with your Opie Dopie, pal!"

Virginia grinned from behind the driver's wheel. "Hey there, strong, garbled military type," she said. "How's your adverbs hanging?"

Virginia was a friend, but she had a professional interest as well. She was Captain Alice's counterpoint, a retired civilian psychiatrist who had become a part of Brando's life as a result of his friendship with Keith.

"Great, Ginnie, haven't had a Zeeman in weeks," he said. "Good, good," she nodded.

"How about...ahh..." Brando began. She stayed with him, waiting for the predicate. "...how about hanging nifty while we blast some terrain porkers?"

"What some who?" she asked with a good-natured grin.

"*Operacion Extinction des couchon de terre*," he tried, realizing he was only digging a deeper ditch for himself.

"Shoot some ground hogs," Keith interpreted, coming easily to his rescue. "Operation Extinction of some earth-pigs."

"Yes," Brando repeated gratefully, "shoot some ground pigs.

Ginnie smiled and shook her head. "Naw. Not much meat on a ground hog. London broil's on sale at Ralphs, anyway."

Keith smiled, his friendly troll face lighting up like somebody had pulled a chain on his left ear, "Gin likes her meat without all that lead in it, anyway."

21

"You know how I like my meat, fella." With that, Keith's whither-go-ye gave them a wave and a wicked grin. She popped the clutch and made her departure through the flying gravel, followed by an asymmetrical mushroom cloud of dust.

"There exits a dangerous female of the species," Brando said.

"Yep, good buddy…It's that big old V-8 hemi engine," Keith agreed, his eyes twinkling as she nearly lost it. She pitched around a frightened pale blue Ford pickup truck before righting things and making her way down the potted road.

"There ought to be a law," he continued. "Women don't drive nothin' over four cylinders." He gave Brando a conspiratorial wink, "At least, she don't eat her young. Come on, let's go take over a spot on the range before all the yuppies get here."

Keith easily hoisted the gunnysack over his shoulder. He stood well under six foot, with extra-extra-wide shoulders. Keith was in his 50's, but his heavily muscled arms could match those of a weightlifter.

Brando stepped along briskly at his side.

"That bag has the heft of a bloody arsenal," he said, hurrying to keep up, for he could see Keith was of a mood to *get his shootin' in*. "Custer could have atomized the entire Sioux Nation."

"Joey was a collector," Keith agreed, his somber face showing he was reflecting on those earlier Joey days.

Joey Collato had been the token WOP at Oppie and Ronnie's place, back before the racial quotas, back when the studio hired almost

22

exclusively white folks of Northern European extraction. There was a large contingent of redneck, patriotic Caucasians who liked to bear arms. They were plain and simple rustics likely to have a carton of grenades from Korea under a musty old throw rug in the garage, or perhaps a bazooka and a few loose shells in the basement that had been shipped home from Rommel's Afrika.

Those were the early days of television production, and Joey had been unlucky enough to be one of the first to do a videotape show, back when the film union still ran the lot with an iron fist. Joey's full-color tape remake of the classic old black-and-white Itsy-Bitsy Club was six months on the air when a small band of union men sabotaged the equipment truck. They slashed the cables and set the van ablaze. The loss was set at about a half-million, but the money wasn't really the thing.

Joey was forced to recant his heretic tape tendencies—never mind the cost savings—and he took the Kodak vow, that is, he agreed to shoot on film. In weeks, he had managed to move heaven and earth and was retreaded to shoot on 35mm. But in that brief span, Itsy-Bitsy lost its contract with the network. More humiliating, it was replaced by old cartoon reruns.

Joey didn't lose his position. In those ancient times the studio took care of its own. But he became Poor Old Joey. He moped his way through the seasons, producing paste-up shows extracted from the animation vaults. He would stitch five old cartoons together with some cheap camera-moves-on-stills, a new jingle or two and

23

voice-over narration to produce something like "Opie's Easter Party", a one-hour Sunday Night Special.

And then, late one fine autumnal afternoon when the *Santa Anas* were pumping a clear and scorching breeze off the high desert all the way in from Pear Blossom, Joey's sawbones relayed some bad info: He was suffering from cataracts, high blood pressure and a failing liver. Maybe he ought to sip somewhat slower on the frog wine – that is, gin—if he wanted to live long enough to put up the Christmas tree lights. Each cog reacts to its mortality in its own way; Joey went home, pulled his best madras-plaid swimsuit up over his rotund little Santa-belly and hopped into his Jacuzzi with a few of his favorite pistols on one side and a nearly full bottle of Beefeater's on the other. He had his long-time hither-go-ye in the kitchen chopping up his favorite Italian sausages smothered in big yellow onions, garlic and roasted sweet red peppers. The big-screen TV was rigged so he could watch while he soaked, and he rolled a two-hour montage of his favorite segs from the Itsy-Bitsy Club. He poured himself a big martini. And then another. Life didn't get any better than this. When the second drink was finished he decided not to sit it out until his liver blew, or even hang around for supper. He jammed the muzzle of his old Army-issue .45 in his mouth as far as it would go and blew out the back of his neck.

"Why don't you just assimilate this mess into your own horde?" Brando asked, flipping a hand at the bag full of ordnance.

24

"Hey, Old Pal-aroo," Keith said with his happy grin. "Virginia would kill me if I kept any more guns. Anyway, I promised Joey's widow I'd snag her a few bucks if I could."

The firing range was a ragged string of brick-lined sand squares facing a slight incline. About five hundred yards to the west from where they stood, the slope suddenly turned into a steep upthrust of canyon wall. Along the upgrade, pitted metal circles marked the distance from the shooters in increments from 50 to 250 yards. The splintered sagebrush that tenaciously grew there was blasted and torn.

Keith carefully set down the sack and wandered off to pay their fees. Brando waited a moment and then ambled after him. It was only a little mistake, following after Keith. But thinking back, Brando would have to admit to the sad facts of his life, that one simple innocent thing always seemed to lead to another that was just a touch more sinister. Perhaps if he'd hunched down outside and picked his teeth with a timothy-weed like a baggy britches country boy with manure on his boots, maybe the nuggins of fate would have dribbled some other way. Maybe he'd not have gotten into the altercation that ended up taking a bit of their time, and maybe if Keith and he had moved swiftly throughout the rest of their shooting, maybe then he would never have intersected with the Ripper, and so wouldn't have become embroiled in his affairs and wouldn't be accused of murdering Ripper's lovely blond wife. His world, it seemed, was more often than not made up of what-ifs and maybes.

CHAPTER 3

I don't imagine it matters what year you're reading this, but the year Brando Mahr was living it was Anno Dominus, that is, the year of our Lord, 1984. George Orwell's dire prediction of a Big Brother Society had not come true except in those States of Les Etats Unis where group think was creeping in as political correctness. How easily the unthinking press and swell of humanity is again and again persuaded to give up their individual rights and liberties for the supposed brotherhood of man—a situation that can then be controlled by the amoral few for their own personal gain. It is ever thus. Orwell, it seems, had been right about everything but the date. Today, as you bungle through my words, be assured, Big Brother is coming...he's just stopped by for a mocha frappachino and a zucchini walnut mini-muffin on his way.

Keith and Brando stumped into the cinder block café and bellied up to a glass counter case loaded with boxes of cheap practice slugs, stacks of yellowing paper targets and a few cherry-scented air-wicks in the shape of Dolly Parton before she found Herbalife.

Outside the dusty plate glass window and on down the line, three or four shootists were pinging away. The crack of pistol fire and the familiar acrid gunpowder smell was making Brando edgy. He fished in his pockets for a small metal container of beeswax plugs that he used for target practice. Brando found that, as it said on the label, *Nothing shuts off the buzz like beeswax.* He stuck a few plugs in his ears and started back out the door. But the ancient proprietor, sitting behind the counter, hadn't seen him put in the bees wax.

"Hey, Buster," the old man wheezed, "you gonna need ear plugs to go out there."

Upon later reflection, Brando had to admit he should have simply played the meek dog, but the cracks and crackles and whispers and the sharp reek of gunpowder had him in their spell; and so he wasn't in a jolly, go-fetch mood.

"You cornered a monolith on the ear-moderation franchise, eh Old Soaker?" he asked in a polite way.

This was a burly-man's place, a place where men shot guns, and Brando's remark was enough to turn the shop owner's face sour.

"What kind of fruitin' fairy are you, anyway?" he asked.

"I, myself—I am Chicot the Jester," Brando said with a little half-bow from the waist. This did nothing to improve the old man's mood.

"Who the fuckin' frigg do you think you are, Buster?" he said, his voice rising in an outraged response.

"Phileas Fogg, lately of London," Brando replied in chatty *English* English, even though he had that old familiar sinking feeling that things weren't going very well.

Deja vu, the mighty Titanic that was his persona once again was sliding at 45 degrees into the frosty, dark northern seas.

"Tell me, good fellow," Brando continued, "is this Vienna, Venice, Vinh Binh or

27

Vendelinus—the last of which is a 100-mile walled plain on the face of the moon, actually—and have you seen a big, ornate balloon—"

"Buster, I said—"

Keith did his best to interrupt, but Brando was nearly unstoppable now, a verbal juggernaut, Robin Williams on speed. "—a balloon, yes, something like a giant, pretty party condom, rainbow colored, with what looks like little wigglies round the middle?"

"I'm really not foolin' around here, buddy!" The gun-shop owner was in his late fifties, with clogged arteries and a ten-inch belly overhang. *One of those poor sods,* Brando thought, *unlike myself, on which a receding hairline is clearly unbecoming.*

"And who-who-who are you?," Brando intoned like Radio Reader, "Winnie-The-Pooh?" With that, he flipped a digit to indicate the owner's stomach.

"Jimmy," Keith pleaded, "he has his own earplugs."

But Brando had gone a touch far for the usual Keithian smooth-over. The ugly frown deepened as Jimmy took in Brando's wind-blown and out-of-style Ben Franklin pageboy locks, his tattered fatigues and well-trod yellow-and-black Asics Tigers running shoes.

"You snilching me, buddy?" Brando growled.

"What the fuck does that mean?" Jimmy screamed.

Brando lowered his voice another notch, "Ahh, you *are* snilching me! Giving me the glimp eye, are you?"

Oddly enough, part of Brando was shuddering rage while the other half was coldly looking on, eyeing the spectacle. *If we can possess dual personalities*, he was thinking, *is it possible to have two or more souls--and do we split when we die? And how scrum-diddily-bad would that hurt?*

Faithful yeoman Keith came to Brando's rescue once again. "You're *staring* at him, Jimmy, you know, giving him the *bad eye*."

"Well, I'm not sure he's okay to go out there!"

Keith started to say something, but Brando raised his hand like an eager 6th grader, speaking around him to Jimmy, "I cognize the essence. You can't allow crazies on the line. They might pot any poor sod, even the owner. That wouldn't be thyself, mayhaps?"

Keith threw a twenty-dollar bill on the counter, "Here's for the range."

But coinage wasn't going to stop poor old Jimmy, who was now glaring at Brando like he was the delivery boy from Defecation Unlimited.

Keith bean-bagged his right hand back and forth directly in front of Jimmy's rosy-red face, "Come on, Jimmy, the kid don't mean nothin'. He earned those stripes in Nam."

Brando felt a tug of amusement. A handful of clicks past thirty, he was yet *the kid* to Keith, who was still trying to smooth things over, "Jimmy-boy, weren't you tellin' me you were a little fucked up after you came back from the peninsula?

"Yeah, but-"

29

"Tanked up an' roarin, an' tearin' up Arcadia on your Harley, runnin' red lights at over 110 an' no cop could catch you?"

Jimmy sighed and turned away from Brando. For a moment he stared out the window at nothing on the range and then he took the few steps back toward his strange antagonist.

"Keith, here, he says you got whacked up in the jungle..."

Brando nodded, scuffing his feet on the floor like a kid who had wet his pants, "Yeah. A wee parcel...

"I'm truly sorry about that."

"So you're not going to darken my daylights?"

Jimmy reached into the glass case and handed over a Hershey bar, one of the chunky king-size ones in a silver-and-brown wrapper. "Here," he muttered with an uncertain focus that Brando took for chagrin.

Brando reached out and took it with a sort of silent reverence. A Hershey bar with almonds, his prize for serving. *Remember*, he advised his evil inner self, *a candy bar is better than spittle in the puss or a sharp stick in the orb*.

Keith pushed his friend towards the door. "Let's go shoot guns before you find any more relationships to intensify."

It did feel good to be back outside. The fresh air was a shock wave. Brando shrugged back into a form of near-normalcy. As they walked along, they grumbled about the invasion of Grenada, which Keith and Brando both believed was too kissy-assed a little adventure to be a real invasion.

The explosion that caused the derailment in Brando's brain was, as we have stated earlier, a matter of extremely bad timing. Brando had been occupying the wrong X and Y coordinates in the deep green Buddha-lands at the exact moment when a round from the battleship Missouri found glory. This came about because Brando's never-say-die team of U.S. Army Security Agency lost boys were radio-directional tracking Victor Charlies (that is, Viet Cong or VC) about 20 clicks inland.

That was toward the end of the war and there were VC everywhere. The ASA boys were growing mold in their ears and gasping in the thick ether under the stinking green overhang while some miles out to sea the Mighty Macho Missou was throwing out her chest as she steamed up and down the South China Sea, lobbing shells into the upper stratosphere to loop in on the jungle. A marvel of technology, the fact that a big ship like that can fire shells such a long distance—but for Brando the end result wasn't all that wonderful.

Thinking back, he was able to remember the exact moment when he'd lost his mind. There had been a long whine like an old wife's tale, a marvelous and a unique whistle unrelated to any of his previous exploits. And then there was a grand transmogrification—a sort of pseudo-Zeeman effect in which his entire reality shifted forever.

He was suddenly airborne, flying over the spattered ground-soil, herbage, and the dismembered body parts of his fellows. It wasn't a real Zeeman effect, which is actually the difference in light emitted by atoms when they pass through a magnetic field, but it was close enough. Brando's pseudo-Z expanded in his awareness like a magnificent—if momentary—hallucinatory wave. In that moment he was convinced he was one with God-the-Father and then his consciousness winked into what he later thought of as the great blackness of un-cognization.

Extracting him from the bush must have been one fantastic trick. He was a solid catatonic, his eyeballs glazed over like the photo on the cover of the National Inquirer of The Man Who Saw Medusa.

That was at the very end of American involvement in the war in Southeast Asia. He had been in a coma for seven years, but, in an odd way, he was convinced he had been coming back ever since the explosion. Brando couldn't say he was all the way back, but he felt he was on the right path. You can't keep a good catatonic down.

CHAPTER 4

Keith commandeered their firing position, square number 26 on the far left end of the line. Brando sat in one of the folding chairs provided by management while his friend set up Joey's collection. Some thump-men truly cherish weaponry; Brando had long recognized that his pal Keith was among them. In Elizabethan times, Keith would have swung a halberd in each hand, with two swords stuck on his belt, and maybe a hide-out dagger-blunderbuss hidden in his left boot. Naturally, being ex-military as well, Brando himself was no stranger to guns; there was a time in the hot green wetlands when he'd greased and hugged his M-16 and M-79 like baby-love, his first girlfriend.

Eddie's loot, pulled from the sack and set out in order, was highlighted by a matched set of target model Browning pistols, a .357 magnum, a gallery model Winchester .22 and a .30-.30 with a pretty walnut stock. There was a lot of other minor key weaponry to which Brando didn't pay much heed, specialties like a tiny two-shot hide-out, a small odd-caliber hide-out automatic, an antique black powder ball-and-cap revolver, and other quirky collector's items. It was clear Keith was itching to blow off a few rounds, so Brando nodded he should have at it.

Brando crossed his legs in the lotus position and hummed the theme from the movie The Magnificent Seven while the old top-kick sprayed metal in the direction of the hillside.

After blowing rounds through each piece, Keith would run a brief benediction of merit, cataloguing the salient plus and minus factors. Then he would gently lay the weapon on top of the gunnysack for Brando's reflection. He worked his way through the sack until there was a spread of armaments like they show on the TV news after the lads in blue raid an Israeli mafia dope ring in the San Fernando Valley or some street gang in Pacoima.

"Ta-DAA!" Keith marveled as he revealed one last oddity—a Thompson submachine gun. He revealed the Thompson like the rabbit in the old rabbit-from-the-hat trick. "And last but not least, straight from The Untouchables—your own little piece of history!"

"Lord! Don't you desire to..." Brando's brain scurried about like the Mad Hatter, looking for the word for *keep*. "...maintain that one?"

Keith translated easily, not even batting an eye, "Hey, I already got one."

"You are presuming to activate it here?"

"Naah. Blowin' this baby costs 50 bucks a drum. But it works; take my word for it. I seen Joey fire it."

Brando gingerly selected a .45 from the stack. "Is this the instrument that propelled poor Joey to visit Mahamaya?" In Vedantic philosophy, Mahamaya is the goddess personifying the illusion of the reality of sensory experience. Once Brando had fallen off the tree of knowledge, he'd wandered far and wide through the dim stacks of the UCLA library, picking up bits and shreds of information that his brain could not let go of. It didn't matter whether Keith knew the goddess or not: he got Brando's drift.

"Yep. That's the one," he said.

"So, what's"—Brando's hand swept the pile—"the rate of exchange?"

"Well..." Keith eyed Brando, squinting into the morning sunlight flaring in his face from over Brando's shoulder, "I know you ain't exactly in the chips these days, old pal. Just one or two things, maybe, if you could see your way."

Brando moved over out of the direct line of the sun so he wouldn't have to squint.

"For Joey's widow," Brando said.

Keith nodded, "Yeah."

When Brando was being flung from the Hollywood parapet, Keith was the only one at the studio who surfaced with a life raft—he rigged it so Brando could put on the union badge and employ for him if he wanted, operating projectors. Seeing himself as an up-and-coming producer, Brando had declined the offer, not wanting that radical a shift in his direction, but that didn't mean he didn't feel indebted to Keith.

"If you're out here peddling pea-shooters, Joey's whither-go-ye is wincing for ducats."

"She could use the dough," Keith agreed.

"Your timing is on the jolly nob. A couple of ticks historic, the ninja sisters Bonavita and Agathena and I finished our tell-all doc, Trickery in the Nunnery. For some reason, probably all the blatant ritualistic sex positions outlined, detailed and demonstrated, the show has done well by us, and I've recently received my latest gratuity for services rendered."

He plucked a somewhat worn check from between a condom and his Cognize Productions business card and handed it to Keith.

"What sort of strike force can I accumulate for this?"

Keith's eyes widened when he saw the check. "You just bought the whole shootin' match, good buddy!" He gave Brando a second look, thinking about his finances, "Now wait a minute. You sure about this?"

Brando nodded and pressed the check into his hands, "I comprehend these things, Keith. I'm getting a lumping pennysworth, here. Any dealer would skin me deuce the sum."

"Yeah, but can you afford it?"

"I'm not exactly out of kelter. Good times are approaching the embankment. A porcupine in every pot. Two motor vehicles stacked to every meter. And Joey's old lady has the need.

Keith didn't accept the check until Brando uttered that last, and even then he accepted it reluctantly.

"Come on, Keith," Brando badgered, "before I veer my course. And look, I'm not Mother Theresa here. I like guns. Anything that goes boom in the night and reliably blows holes in things can't be all to the negatory."

Keith pocketed the check and they walked back to the Fiat with the heavy gunnysack across Brando's back.

"Only..." Brando paused and grubbed around in the sack until he found the .45 automatic that Joey had used to kill himself. He butt-forwarded it to Keith, "I can't...I can't....I can't..." He gave up trying to say it and simply stared at Keith, holding the gun out towards him.

"I understand, good buddy," Keith said softly. He accepted the automatic, click-clicked the safety and lost it in one of the pockets in his Banana Republic vest. "I'll take care of it."

CHAPTER 5

As they walked back from the firing range toward *Fifi la Fiat*, Keith rumbled snatches of "Blue Moon" in his own unique manner.

"I thought that was a musical impossibility," Brando said.

"What, Good Buddy?"

"Singing Lunar Blue off-key."

Keith mulled giving Brando a playful swat, but he knew his friend was quick as a wildcat, and, what's more, knew a thousand ways to hurt a person. The old top-kick had already been to wars, and he didn't have anything to gain or prove by sticking up for his vocal accomplishments. He grinned and took Brando's new bag-o-guns and sandwiched it neatly into Fifi's trunk.

"You ain't half as dumb as you let on, Brando. Sometimes I think it's all an act with you."

"What is the grasp of your reach?"

"Behind all that weird language and twisted logic, you're laughing at us."

"From your mouth to Jehovah's auditory sense," Brando replied with a bitter taste in his mouth. *From your lips to God's Ear,* more or less a hard-bitten Jewish request for favors from the Almighty.

"Ah well," Keith said, sensing that he'd gone a little too far. "At least we're both still suckin' oxygen."

"Amen to that," Brando replied with a quiet smile. "And hallelujah."

They were soon lofting back down The Grapevine. While they zipped along, Keith ran over his social calendar. Brando's presence was requested at next year's Sho-West. And, to hunt fat and tame pheasants on a ranch in Central Somewhere. To do lunch at the studio. Fly-fish at Crowley Lake. Skeet shoot back at The Grapevine. Chute out of the rear end of an Air Force reserves airplane some weekend. And to set out for albacore fishing from Point Loma. To which Brando replied no, no, no, no, no, no, maybe and maybe. He had never jumped out of the bumfiddle of an airplane and something about it appealed to him, the idea would he or wouldn't he have a Zeeman in exactly the wrong clutch? And then there was that special *quelle chose* about ocean sport fishing; Brando routinely suffered seasickness, and, in an oddly masochistic way, he enjoyed facing the shallow cousin of the grim reaper (as seasickness was called in the penny novels he'd read.)

Brando was going to drop Keith off at his bungalow residence in La Canada, but as they motored east along the 118, Keith suddenly claimed to have fallen prey to a dusty throat, and persuaded Brando to detour off the motorway into an alehouse he knew on the rim of the Hanson Dam public golf course.

It had been your average, sun-drenched August afternoon, and so when they arrived at the handy pub, the place was clogged with sun-dried duffers intent on hydration. Brando had hoped it would be fairly deserted, because he did not do well in crowded places. He hesitated at the doorway, but the top-kick had already pushed his

39

way inside. He trailed in after Keith, hoping for the best.

The place was packed. A pair of thick-wristed bar-wenches chugged back and forth, manhandling heavy mugs and pitchers of tap beer, and carrying heavy metal platters laden with the simpler mixed intoxicants. Semi-sodden golf duffers jammed around a dozen tables. They were all blathering in a chorus Brando found instantly dense and bothersome, while the overhead TVs blatted and blazed for attention. Brando knew he wasn't going to last long.

He had turned to make his way back outside when he got his first glimpse of the huge black man. Ripper Brown was in his late 40's. He had an enabling bass voice and a big, hearty laugh, and was holding court like a Ghanian king of old. The assembled lot of duffers were snatching up his comments and overdosing on his every word. And when Brando looked his way, the great man appeared to be waving at Keith.

"Hey, hey, HEY!" Keith boomed in his own strong voice, waving back like he'd found his long-lost brother.

Brando smelled the rat and sensed he should be leaving right then and there. But too late, his pal, the devious old war-whacker, had wrapped a big arm around his shoulder and was already speaking in his best Yogi Bear imitation as he dragged them both in the Ripper's direction. "Do you know who that is, BooBoo?"

Brando was feeling the light non-alcoholic buzz that often precedes a Zeeman. Bring it on, he thought grimly. But he wasn't going to let on he was in any difficulty.

40

"Oh, allow me to answer the quiz, Master," Brando said, miming the hunchback in Mel Brooks' horror spoof, Young Frankenstein. "Is it the Black Santa Claus as created by the great ex-Disney animator Phil Mendez? Is it Nebuti, King of the Bahutu? Or perhaps the reincarnation of Othello? No, no? Then mayhaps Hamlet's father's ghost in blackface?"

Brando knew he was on the far side with most of those, but once the Zeeman lurked, he didn't really care. While Keith gave him a blank stare, he mulled happily to himself. Hamlet had rarely if ever been played in blackface. Also, the Bahutus were African Bantus from Burundi and Rwanda and not nearly tall enough to apply to this great person, who would surely be a Zulu warrior.

Keith was flicking the skin on Brando's arm to see if he was still a sentient being. Keith waved his arms in the air, "I'm surprised you didn't get it. What we got here's the Doomsday Machine himself, the incredible Ripper Brown!"

Keith pointed both hands in the ebony giant's direction, like a Barnum & Bailey ringmaster introducing the main act.. Brando whacked his own head with the palm of his hand, feigning astonishment but really trying his best to stave off the oncoming Zeeman.

"Hoan Ho!" he cried, which is Vietnamese for magnificent. "You may flagellate me with wet angel hair pasta, call me a member of the Macaroni Club and express reality as a wonder. Or is that too kinky?"

His reference to the early 1800's club of flashy London dressers was far too arcane for even Keith to grasp. Brando was just trying to be

41

cool—but at the pre-Cambrian level and in spite of his rapidly deteriorating condition he really was impressed. While he'd been feeding leeches in Nam, Ripper Brown had attained fame and presumably fortune as the greatest defensive lineman of all time. He remained the most revered member of the famous Mighty Foremen, the front line that had dominated pro football throughout his fifteen years on the big stage, his mini-eon in the sun.

To Brando, Ripper didn't look much damaged for the struggle. Brando figured he had to top out at a cloud-scraping six-foot-seven. He was so tall he actually had to stoop over so his head wouldn't smack the TV sets hanging over the bar. Though Brando guessed he weighed in at 260, the ex-footballer didn't have a mid-life paunch. If it wasn't for the gray frost in his close-cropped curly hair, he looked like he could still mount the field and bang bumfiddles *avec des infants*.

Brando thought Keith wasn't going to get through the packed crowd, but in another minute he returned with the very big black man in tow. There he was, Ripper Brown in the very shape of his famous self, hulking behind and over Keith like something that had recently been shipped in from Easter Island.

"How ya doin', Pal?" the great one boomed. He extended a pink-palmed paw that was roughly twice the size of Brando's. "Heard a lot about you," he said.

"Ohh..." Brando replied, squeezing the skin on his forehead while he darted Keith a quick glance. "Which of my vices was brought to your attention?"

"Don' be modest, man. Keith here tol' me how you produced that fabulous award winner, your Early Days of Football show."

It was true that Brando had manufactured a cable television sports special. With the help of his violent twin nun friends, he'd kneaded together a cable doc, The Leatherheads: Early Days of the NFL. The nuns didn't know anything about the NFL, but their grammar was impeccable. You may never have heard of an Ace, but movies have Oscars, regular TV has Emmys, and cable has Aces. Their Leatherheads show had won an Ace award. Brando dizzily wondered why the subject had come up. A guy like Ripper Brown must have bigger balls to bounce.

Keith shrugged and gave Brando his Mister Sincere Affection look, "Me an' the Ripper were over at Genios the other day, tossin' a few down, and we got to talking about—" His voice trailed into the crowd walla, and in that moment Brando recognized that he had underestimated his friend, thinking he was too short and squat to be Hermes, Greek god of, among other things, cunning.

A nearby chair became unoccupied and Brando sat down heavily, trying to swat away the halo of colors swarming around his vision. But Mister Football sat down next to him and carried on as if he couldn't tell Brando's world was swimming in rainbows and about to come apart.

"We was talkin'," Ripper continued happily, " 'bout who might be the best person in town to do my life's story."

"Your life story?! You're not—not *decayed* enough to do your life story."

"Oh, I got decay on me," the big man argued. "And a man lives like me is big enough for two or three life stories."

"And you want to get started on the first one..."

"Yep. The Saga of The Great One, The One And Only Ripper Brown, the best Defensive Tackle professional football has ever known!

Brando got the picture that Ripper wandered into hyperbole easily; he was Dorothy tumbled from the yellow brick road and Goofy Yaaa-Haaaa-Hooooiee! Over the waterfall, particularly when the subject was himself.

Football heroes come and go, and it had been over four presidencies since this particular sports thug had hit an offensive lineman in anger. And yet you still saw The Ripper doing bit parts on sit-coms, or being interviewed during an intermission on Monday Nite Football. There he'd be, illuminating the benefits of The Ripper Way, the slant versus the front-on smash, and the merits of quickness against bigness. In short, he seemed to have made that nearly impossible transition from all-pro sports star to big-time personality.

Brando was used to pitches, and even in his present condition he could smell the bait a mile away. Revelation overcame him like a nasty Zeeman or a flash of biblical inspiration. The Ripper may have been genuinely lost in his own greatness, but this was all Keith's doing. Brando glared at his last, best and only friend from the good old studio days. And as he did so his mind was slowly forming the words *ignis fatuus*, another foolish pipe dream, in misty neon above Keith's head.

Then Brando wasn't angry anymore; just saddened at the thought of how easily he and his friends all stomped off into the green, green swamps of self-delusion, chasing after the mischievous imps of their own great ideas and schemes. How could he stay mad at Keith? He, Brando, may be the weird boy out because of his afflictions, but he knew he and Keith were both the same when it came to the Tinseltown games. Hadn't he, Brando Mahr, cast similar sticky webs a hundred times? They only ended up selling one out of every hundred of their dog ideas, that is, if Dame Luck was lifting her skirts in their direction. But still, that was the game they all played.

All that said, speculative project development takes real money, and he was in no financial shape to get involved.

"Spec, Hermes?" Brando sighed.

Keith gave him an innocent look.

"The remuneration, Keith; the moola. Is this to be another of our speculative ventures?"

Keith turned away and redeveloped his intense preoccupation with the TV set where an ethnically predetermined batch of guests was falling into a swimming pool due to the stimulating effects of some glasses of iced tea.

Brando blundered on, "Keith, speak to me. Deutschmarks. Francs. Pound notes. Piasters. River pearls, even."

Keith was no help, so Brando tried a shot across the Ripper's ebony bow. Once again, the words didn't come out quite right. "Mr. Brown," he asked, "what is your outline for reparations?"

45

The Ripper looked over at Keith as if Brando came from an alien race of creatures.

Keith's wide grin slowly faded as he realized his friend's question would have to be answered. And that meant this grand scheme, like so many others, could easily drift back to earth in the manner of a tired hot-air balloon in the gathering coldness of late afternoon.

Keith tried his bright and truthful approach. "Well, sir, Brando, I knew you wasn't doing nothin' special right now, Good Buddy—you said so yourself, and, you know, the Ripper here is a hot property..."

The Ripster nodded happily. And with that, he joined right in, showing he understood a good bit more than he'd let on.

"Hell, Brando, I figure I'll make you a full an' equal partner! No sharecroppin' fur you—you gonna be on a par with the master!"

"A full partner," Brando repeated, at that moment begging for the onset of at least a small Zeeman to carry him away. "You, sir, are too kind." *Where are all the good seizures when you really need them?* "And all this simply for immortalizing your incredible gridiron saga in song and dance as the legend of the nation."

"Well, maybe not song and dance, but the rest is right on!" Ripper's face lit up. He raised his arms, nearly swiping a wagon-wheel chandelier that hung high overhead. The room—nay, the world—wasn't big enough for this man.

"Yeah! I can see you see it!" Ripper boomed. "It gonna be a box office bonanza! The true one-and-only film. See, there's stuff nobody knows about me. Born dirt-poor on the other side of the

Civil Rights Act. Hounded out of the Deep South by nigger-hatin' crackers at the point of a double-barrel! The flash an' glitz of big-time sports scullduggery—an' the inside story of what goes on in the trenches! The spoils of victory!"

"Mighty deeds of sex as well, I wager," Brando muttered.

"You got that one right, Brando! All the lovely ladies, the famous movie stars and gorgeous Motown gals I've loved, uplifted an' left."

"Whoopee!" Keith shouted.

Not needing enthusiasm or affirmation from anybody, Ripper thundered on, "This gonna be a cinematic event! A motion picture movie of epic proportion. The parties. The booze. The drugs. The evil team owners. The nearsighted refs. No stone unturned—The Great Ripper tells it all, jist like it was!"

"One moment, Ripper," Brando said to his new giant. He managed to stand and give himself another hopefully unobtrusive whack in the head. Then he took Keith by the elbow, pushing his thumb in a little at the pressure point. Brando could bring pain with the best of them. It was another of his talents, bestowed on him by the mad gods of war.

"Ow!" Keith said. "That hurts!"

Brando hoped he personally had enough gas left to hike them both around the huge footballer and get them out of the room.

He gave Ripper a neat little nod to facilitate their exit, "Excuse us, Mr. Brown. Keith and I have to palaver regarding the coming of the

47

Iceman and what effect that will have upon his circulatory system."

Ripper didn't budge, but his smile was beatific. "Oh, don't worry about that. We gonna give Keith his agent's fee—that's ten percent of your 50% from you, and ten percent of my 50% from me, completely fair, right down the middle." The huge black man gave Brando his broadly innocent con-man's smile.

"No, not his compensation," Brando confided. "I mean his second coming. The one proceeded by the four wild riders of the Apocalypse."

Rounding the corner of the Ripper, Brando saw daylight in the distance. He managed to throw a Hamilton on the table and one-handed Keith through the crowd. With Brando's hand on the rudder of his friend's elbow, he steered Keith like a water-logged ketch.

"Owww-aggg," Keith said as they went. "My arm's going numb, good buddy."

"Oh, you're a deep one, Keith, a sly, designing napes of a fellow!"

"No, Brando. You've got it all wrong." He had that Barney Rubble look on his face like when Barney's wife caught him with his fist in the applesaurus pie.

Once they were outside, Brando took a deep breath of fresh smoggy air and released his arm. "The least significant but acceptable gesture you might attempt might be come clean before you howl your *mea culpas*."

"Alright, Brando..." He gave Brando his hangdog, Little Mister Poopypants look. "Ripper an' me met at Sho-West." He swung his arm, trying to shake out the sting. "He was signing autographs for some football flick where the professor at this high school with a loser football team discovers some sticky goop that-"

"Get to the point, dissembler."

Keith kicked at the parking lot gravel like it contained something of interest. "Well, Good Buddy and fellow Opie-Doper, we hit it off an' tossed a few brews, and when the Ripper started pouring out his life dream, I thought of you."

"Oh, Lord of the Flies, why me?"

"Jesus, Brando—I'm trying to do you a favor here."

"A project about a busted yesterday's-article won't slip our bumfiddles onto the fine leather sport bucket seats of twin Ferraris, Keith."

"Has-been?! Ripper Brown is the greatest tackle there ever was! That's got to be worth something!"

By now, Brando had made his way half across the parking lot with Keith trailing after. Being Keith, and endowed with amazing army reflexes, he hadn't spilled a drop of his drink. Brando pointed to the unlocked door on the passenger side and climbed in on his own side, twitching as he scrambled across the hot brown leather into the bucket seat. He reached back and pulled the soft-top forward with his right hand, and in ten seconds had the roof pulled up over his head, locked and ready. Keith was still standing outside, his margarita arm out like a hitching post. He leaned sideways so he could stare in at Brando and gestured that he should roll down the glass.

"I gotta go back in there, Good Buddy. Don't worry, Ripper will give me a ride."

There was a long pause during which neither person said anything. Then Keith sighed, "Okay, Brando, it was a set-up. But it's for your own good. It's not like you're terribly busy right now, and this could be very good for you."

Brando tried to interrupt, "I don't cognize how."

"Look, Good Buddy, you don't ever do anything you don't want. You know that. And I didn't promise him anything. Not anything firm." He thought that over. "Except, maybe, you would take one little meeting over at his place...?"

Brando twisted the key in the ignition and his sweet little *Italiano* engine caught on the first burst. Brando worked the throttle a little and gunned the foot pedal. He didn't know what to say. He took his silvery aviator sunglasses from their place on his rear-view mirror and hooked them on, assuming a glittery look of alienation.

"You won't let me down, will you, Little Buddy?" Keith pleaded. That was the role at which he was a complete marvel, playing the loveable Captain on Gilligan's Island. *How could anyone say no to the Captain?*

Brando rumbled out of the lot without answering, but Keith was used to that. As Brando drove off he was grinning and waving like they were about to set forth to sea in the Good Ship Lollipop.

He would phone Brando in a day or two as if nothing had happened and tell him when and where he was supposed to connect with the Ripper. And in the end Brando supposed he would dance to the pipes and show his visage at the engagement. Like Keith had said, it wasn't as if he had studios clamoring at his door and twenty or thirty projects on his agenda, all green-lighted and ready to ignite. Actually, at the moment, he had nothing.

CHAPTER 6

Inside Brando's place of business, the paint was peeling from the thin walls and the wooden floorboards creaked. But he liked his small workspace. He occupied it rent-free in exchange for directing a promotional commercial or two every month or so for KTGA, a local television station. He directed the spots *sub rosa* so the guild wouldn't catch wind and boot him out on his bumfiddle. Everybody does it, he had been told in the greatest confidence—just don't let the iron maiden snap shut on you. Being guilded in the DGA was a big deal to Brando; aside from the annual meeting where they confided what they did with his dues and fees, he felt it was some official acknowledgment of his progress in show biz. And then, there were the health benefits, a big plus to a fellow with his unsteady props.

From his quake-sprung doorway he could hungrily ogle the leggy secretarial wenches as they browsed by on their way to the cafeteria. And he could also see the good-looking wannabee starlets on their sad pilgrimage to and from casting. On one old shelf behind him he had a buzzing blue neon Hamms beer sign from a shoot he'd done for the industrial division of Hanna-Barbera, and there were photo blowups pinned to the wall of himself with stars and personalities like Bill Cosby, Steve McQueen, Jacqueline Bisset, Ali McGraw, George Plimpton and Ray Bradbury—luminaries that he'd shot in commercials and in motion picture featurettes.

Featurettes are the same story over and over, what a struggle it was and how everybody plowed along together like maniac geniuses to achieve an incredible and miraculous movie on time and on budget—which is what they're supposed to do anyway.

On Brando's desk there was a big, moldering lump of an encyclopedia from the pre-army times that his grateful mother gave him when he'd stopped meandering through Learningsville and finally graduated. And a small color photo of a wench he'd known, strummed, and yes, cherished is the word, in Dorothy and Toto's jungle place, somewhere on the other side of the world. The pages of the encyclopedia were worn and tattered, and the Ektachrome of his lost love had migrated through a spectrum shift, the tan of his once-upon-a-time lady's skin and the background blue of one of those rare clear Mekong delta days both shifting toward a murky green. Not the way he remembered either of them...not that he remembered that much.

There was an expensive IBM Selectric and a new Apple 2E computer, both bought and paid for, but there was no window in his office, so Brando usually kept the door propped open. He was grateful, in spite of the limitations of his office; with the big one-lunger air conditioner cranking over the couch, it was passable in the heart of June, which can be the cruelest California month, those days when the morning bay shroud fails long before the dry autumn winds begin to blow.

He leaned back in his battered wooden studio chair, with his Clark Wallaby's propped up on the

53

distressed-by-life wooden studio desk, and touched in a call to his old army chum, semi-crook Charlie Manganetti. He was eager to rag his friend about meeting the great Ripper Brown. Charlie relished pro football almost as much as he adored professional boxers and lifting chunks of money from unsuspecting gulls.

Brando had first met Charlie at the Defense Language School in Monterey, back before Nam and his explosion. Charlie was one of those expressive Sicilians who waded into life, love, food and conversation like a jovial Calydonian boar. Young men, they had argued about Camus and Sarte, football and boxing, woman and women, and he always claimed Brando saved his bumfiddle in Vietnam.

Brando didn't, really, although he was somewhat involved in what happened. It was an innocent and wonderful scam, a worthy fetch on their military masters. The year was early 1965, and Brando was a crypto-linguist, a junior grade spy working for the 3RD Radio Research Unit. He was stationed at Tan Son Nhut, the big air base just west of Saigon. He'd been de-garbling covert Viet Cong messages for nearly a year when Charlie shipped in-country. Charlie had been stationed in the Philippines where they did the same spy stuff to offshore electronics picked up by U.S. destroyers.

When Charlie called, his voice had sounded frightened and tinny through the lines of the antiquated French phone system. He used Brando's nickname from language school, "*Kha*," he said, "I'm in big trouble!" *Kha* meant big brother.

54

Back then, Brando was known as somewhat of a smart-lip rather than the garbled tongue he'd become.

"Charlie!" he'd laughed. "What's the problemo, Mister Romance? Pineapple Girls give you a dose of the big C?"

"Can the jokes, *Kha*! I been loaned to the 3RD, and they're shipping me into the bush!"

"Not to worry, Hondo; I've been there. You just camp out, sort of, and listen to the static through your headphones 'til fungus grows in your ears. Six weeks later you come back, we lay out a few ceremonial girls at the Chez Rene and—"

"No, no, no, NO! I'm not going to die out there! I had a bad dream about this! And you gotta help me!"

"Me?! I'm a lowly Spec.5, Charlie!"

"*Kha*, you got to! That's what friends do!"

To that present day, Brando still didn't know why he'd done what he did next. He'd shrugged into his tropical tans, taken off his nametag and borrowed a jeep from the motor pool. By the time he negotiated a few pot-holed side streets and drove across the sticky-hot tarmac, Charlie's outfit was settling into a big, semi-permanent tent-barracks. Brando strode in like one of the mean, power-tripping son-of-a-bitches you see everywhere in the military.

"Manganetti!" he yelled out of the side of his mouth, "Where the goddam holy hell's Spec. 4 Manganetti?"

Thankfully, no officers were around and Brando's lowly bar-over-eagle outranked everybody in the place. A wide-eyed corporal actually saluted him. "Ah—over there, sir!" he said, while the rest of them kept their noses in their shoe polish. Charlie came, dragging his duffel bag.

Brando barked, "They want you over at the 3RD!"

And then he stalked out of the tent-barracks before anyone could get a good look at him. Once they were out of sight, he swung the jeep around and headed for the main gate. Charlie borrowed a few thousand piasters and the last Brando saw of him, he was heaving his bag into the back seat of a blue-and-cream *Xe-hoi* Taxi.

The splendor, riches, wonder and mystery of the Orient lay before young Charles Manganetti. Joseph Conrad's Orient, centered around the ships, the merchants, the teeming, colorful port of Saigon.

In retrospect, Brando thought the lesson to be learned was that the wonders of the Orient stirred something different in everybody. For Charlie it was fine food and beautiful women. In no time at all, he was pleasantly shacked up with a doe-eyed girl he connected with at the Cherry Bar. He spent the next few weeks dining at the finest restaurants around town with the officers. He frequented the haut French *Tour D'Argent*, *Le Bistro*, *Chez Brodard* cafe, the *Hai Cua* crab house, and Cheap Charlie's Chinese where conscripted beef-in-broccoli, sweet and sour pork, pressed duck, curried shrimp and fried rice were served "American Style" with knives and forks on white linen.

And he actually showed up at the 3rd RRU every pay period. He would read the bulletin board in front of the C.O.'s office, and jaw with some of the lingies he knew from Monterey while he stood in the pay line. They paid him, too, and it was some ticks before anybody caught on that he wasn't assigned duty or even living on the base.

The *merde* finally did hit the fan, and the Commanding Officer of the 3rd furiously pushed for a court-martial. But Charlie managed to have the legalities shifted back to the Philippines, where he successfully pleaded it was just another army screw-up. He got off scot-free, and he never did have to go out into the bush to see if his death-dream would come true or not.

Anyway, that made Brando and Charlie amigos for life, no matter what. And there'd been a what or two since. Charlie prowled around San Jose, where he'd transformed himself into a successful mortgage broker. He'd also seemed involved in some deals that looked a little south of the law. Brando wasn't quite sure just what his friend was into. It seemed better not to ask.

The phone rang a couple of times, and then Charlie himself picked up on it, "Universal Mortgages."

"Hello. Dis is d' loan company," Brando said, pinching his nose shut with his fingers. "You ain't up on your payments, an' for dis very reason we're comin' to repossess your furniture." That was another reason Brando liked telephone conversation. There was less visual distraction and he could play his pretend writing-it-and-talking-it trick at a pace that was almost normal conversation.

Charlie's laugh warmed Brando's heart. He knew who it was right away.

"What you doin', *Kha*?", he asked.

57

"Guess who I just met—Ripper Brown!"

"Naw. You're pullin' my leg."

"Serious. He wants me to carve his life story!"

Charlie was duly impressed. He did his Bayonne street dialect, "Woooow. You still goin' to talk to us peasants?"

"Maybe, maybe not. You got to be *respectful*, as they say."

Charlie laughed again. "Now that ain't my strong point."

"Suppose this was your dish to carve, *Nha*?," Brando quizzed. *Nha* is Vietnamese for house. Charlie was shorter than Keith Lugosi, and wider, too. "How would you conduct your behavior? I mean, would it be The Black Kid From the Deep South Makes Good? My Life as a Pro? From Big Bruises to Satin Bedsheets? Or just plain The Ripper Brown Story?"

Brando could almost feel his friend's pleasure gushing out of the phone. Nothing made Charlie happier than to talk movies, and here they were, discoursing about actually making one. Well, a TV Special, maybe. It was all the same to Charlie. He didn't say a word for a while. Brando waited, knowing his friend would dredge up something worth the effort.

"Well, *Kha*," his voice came over the phone sounding smooth and tentative at the same time, "You could do all those things."

"But…?"

"But like you already know, that's all stuff that's been done before. Why not do something like… The Championship That Never Was?"

"Illuminate, oh master."

"Well, *Kha*—when I think about the Ripper, one season always sticks in my brain. One season, one game, one quarter, and ultimately, I believe it came down to a couple of plays."

"Do not hold me under the *agua*," Brando said.

"It was 1967, 68 or 69—one of those years. The Rams were in the play-offs against somebody like Green Bay or Minnesota—I can't remember, I just remember they were playing in a cold place up north in the Midwest. It was the kind of game the Rams should have won. At least, I always thought so. *But they didn't win, Kha!* They didn't win."

"You're cognizing some crook crossed the Rubicon on a sacred NFL game? Is that even possible?"

Charlie's soft, knowing chuckle came over the phone like he was sitting across from Brando on his rump-sprung casting couch, the couch of a thousand lovings, that spread its ruined frame under the rusted and leaky air conditioner.

"Now, is that what I'm saying to you?" Charlie asked. Brando could visualize him with the phone cradled to one ear as he waved his chunky hands expansively in the empty atmosphere, "*Kha, Kha, Kha*, you know I don't believe in nothing so simplistic. On our beloved sports scene in this great land of ours we have rules, factors and considerations. Weight, velocity, trajectory, gravity and the other assorted forces of nature. You know about it; you're an educated fellow. Man goes against man. They clash. One falls, the other is victorious. Sometimes, surprise—the little slow man beats

59

the big quick one. But now, me—I like to know *why*, that's all, *Kha*."

"You give me magnitudes upon which to cogitate."

"Of course I do. I tell you, when I think of the old Ripper, my mind wanders back to that notorious but forgotten game back in the late 60's. You'd have to go dig in the old newspapers, and interview the players and the coaches and everybody...but I bet there's a hell of a movie in there somewhere!"

What he was saying made for an interesting pastiche, but Brando believed his friend was trying to pass on more than he would or could ever say. There was a whisper here, a hint of something musty and maybe dangerous. *Dead mouse under the house.*

After they hung up, Brando ruminated for all of five minutes before he heard the crunch of her shoes on the gravel. He knew who it was. Earman didn't have to see the doxey wench; Brando could follow her progress as clearly as if she was in his field of fire. It was that quick, impatient step of hers that gave her away. Then the click of her high heels on the short strip of sidewalk, two soft steps in the little patch of grass in front of his steps, and the sharp rapping of her heels on the wooden steps that led to his door. No pantyhose, Brando thought, not hearing the fabric swish on her inner thighs. And then Belle Denver, his favorite wannabee, walked in wearing a skin-tight cotton blouse striped black-and-white like a convict's shirt, a tightly packed black mini-

60

skirt and a pout that was dripping wet with fire engine red lipstick.

"Hi, Wild Thing," she purred. Brando couldn't get serious with Belle, and he'd tried a time or two. They'd been an occasion for over a year, and though they strummed each other at irregular intervals, they never dated. Belle called the shots, and that was the way she wanted it.

In the early days, he'd asked her out so they could get to know each other better. She had responded with a strained, puzzled look and asked him, "Why?"

When he couldn't give her an answer, the wench softly punched his cheek and whispered in that husky Brooklyn dialect of hers, "Look, Tony Tongue-Tied, I got the strong vibration, the more we'd comprehend each about the other, the more we'd find to not like."

Brando figured she was a true whip. On her own turf, she was smart the way a sea vixen is smart. She had a few good moves and steel claws when those failed. She knew who she was and what she wanted. And she didn't like to talk about it. The ultimate consumer, straight out of a Greek legend. So without another word, his hormones went racing off like Goofy, Ya ha ha hooie over the falls. They were a number, of sorts, but even Brando could grasp that their passion storms were hardly the sort of manifestation Ann Landers would categorize as serious or meaningful.

"I didn't get the part," Belle said, explaining the pout.

In thirty seconds she wasn't wearing anything but the shoes and the lipstick, and Keith, Ripper and Charlie were all fading off to another world.

Ever an impatient *ready duchess*, she'd be equally delighted to take it standing or with her clothes on, but it was her one concession to Brando's plea for romance above mechanics. On the other hand, she couldn't find a moment or two to close the door, and he barely had time to turn over the picture on his desk and reach for a Ramses Ram Jet #7 before she was communicating with pego like a warm kitten on a stick. Brando Mahr, consolation prize.

CHAPTER 7

After Belle and her whistles left, Brando stirred but did not shake under a tepid shower in one of the guest star suites. He threw on a faded *Metal Heurlant* t-shirt and a pair of black jeans, then snared a few fish tacos from the studio commissary and wandered back to tidy up his office. But he found himself ignoring the food to stare at the color-drifted old Ektachrome photo of his lost Nam love.

His explosion had taken her out, too...at least, out of his life. That single blast had mushroomed into long-term complications on fronts far beyond his personal physical wreckage. She had needed him, and after his injuries, he was gone.

She never knew what had happened. After they pulled him out of Tarzanland, he was crated and shipped—first to Clark in the PI. And then, once his vital signs came up off of dead zero, he was sent on to Oakland. This meant he was forced to abandon his own little personal world in *thanh-pho* Saigon.

In that city known as *the faded pearl of the Orient*, Brando had led a private personal life, secret far beyond paranoia. He had good reason, for the military has always frowned on lowly nobs with high security clearances fraternizing with the natives. After the blast, nobody thought to ask him questions pertinent to his former life or his lost love. *Understandable. They didn't even know she existed.* And he was in no state to answer.

They air-freighted his once-finely conditioned and trained-to-kill body back to the States. And there it took seven planting seasons and the highly coordinated play of some of the world's finest and most dedicated neuro-scientists to demonstrate there were no scientific answers to common questions like *What is a human being?* and *How do we form ideas?*

In the early days he had performed like a circus bear or some other show animal before panels of glass-eyed prattlers. He came to be known and even quasi-famous in the Scientific American and other journals as patient B.M., the man who couldn't say what he was thinking unless he wrote it down before he said it. Scientific articles were published with him as the marvelous unknown quantity. Captain Alice Padrow ran banks of tests just to make sure he had no new powers like future-vision. Actually, in those confused moments, he did imagine he could visualize the playing cards before they were turned over in front of him. Since he had no way to communicate his incredible abilities, it was a moot point.

Later, he became the marvel who could speak by pretending he was writing it down. That may seem a small and foolish claim to fame; to Brando's rehabilitation it meant a mighty leap.

The jungle blast had not stolen his entire ability to read, though he was piecing words together letter-by-letter and letters word-by-word. So he slowly devoured the first articles written about his condition with a certain inconstant interest, this between extended bouts during which he was inordinately fond of primary colors.

One morning, he discovered the latest scientific paper of interest, which some wag had tacked to the wall over his bunk for a joke, certain Brando would not and could not read it. Brando somehow lurched and staggered through it. He found it encouraging, mostly because it included other test cases of other semi-terminal wretches like him who had responded to stimuli, albeit in inconstant and unpredictable ways.

Brando came to realize the world had other aphastics, though they were mostly created by the rich American diet. Once Captain Alice saw he was interested, she gave him an article on the strange case of G.W., the Kansas stroke victim who could write verbs but had difficulty speaking them. "Why?" Brando asked, giving her a curious stare. She went away shaking her head. She didn't really think he understood it.

And then Brando regressed towards the beautiful saffron island of Catatonia. For weeks he was devoted to the notion that red was surely the most vibrant color God-the-Mother and her concubine live-in, The Holy Ghost, had ever invented. He stared at a red ball for weeks, until Captain Alice took it away from him, mostly out of idle curiosity to see what he would do.

Without his ball, he came out of the red end of the spectrum to read about Mrs. P, another stroke victim who could speak verbs but couldn't write them. And then he had his yellow phase, deciding yellow was probably even more magnificent than red because it was the color of lemons of the Lemon Tree very pretty/ and the

65

lemon flower is sweet/ but the fruit of the poor lemon/ is impossible to eat. Captain Alice got him one from Farmer's Market. The lemon shriveled and turned dull beige before he would relinquish it. And he read about stroke victim L.P. who could name and describe an animal, but not inanimate objects, and J.T., victim of a blow to the head, who could recognize the fender of a Ford Bronco, but couldn't tell a wallaby from a whale. Somewhere in this time, Brando remembered his own Aunt Tillie who, after her first stroke, had begun sprinkling her table-talk with German, a tongue she hadn't spoken since she was a little sprig.

Yet again he had a relapse into green. Green, beautiful vibrant green, the color of trees and grass and that pretty green gemstone with a hardness of eight on the Moh's scale that he couldn't remember the name of...

Finally, running out of colors, he was forced to face the one hard fact of post-combat life, the reality that every cracked vet has to face sooner or later. While he had boodles of sympathy and acres of friendly chatter, there was no actual plan for his recovery. Brando Mahr, known throughout the community as B.M., was a good guinea pig, maybe too good for his own good. After that, Brando developed a secret attitude. He grew suspicious, suspecting that every silly grin that knocked on his door fronted a test that was somehow constructed for the betterment of science and the advancement of careers. There was no plan to get him up and running, no timetable to push him out into the real world. Entire months had passed since he'd fixated on purple and his mental gymnastics were consistently adding to the skimpy body of knowledge on the workings of the sapient mind. He deserved the Good Contributions to Science medal. And yet he was beginning to understand, to cognize, as he would say, that the time was at hand for the patient to heal himself, if it ever was going to happen at all. That's when he got the pass to leave the VA hospital, skipped away and eventually found the menial job that allowed him to bury himself for days at a time in the UCLA library. Let them search the wino and bum crowded streets of Santa Monica; they would never find him deep among his friends, the multi-colored books in the library.

The librarians saw right away that his uncanny ability to remember numbers would be useful; they gave him a job, wheeling the carts to return books to their places deep inside the stacks. They even got him a place to stay, a small low-rent room tacked on behind a garage that was nearby but off campus.

Over the years he spent in the stacks, Brando rebounded to where you wouldn't recognize the glowering, growling gargoyle he'd been. But he wasn't all the way back. He had his killer headaches, and those intermittent moments when the Gordian knot could not be cut and in those times he would see visions and finally fall foaming to the deck of mother earth, the mighty cypress felled.

He felt in his heart that he didn't deserve better than Belle Denver. He was the lowly fool, he was Chicote the jester. At best, he jerked his conversational phrases along like a cerebral one-lunged John Wayne, a pesky Quai Chang Kane, or maybe a spastic, in-the-know Paul Harvey, America's Newscaster; while at his worst he was the just-plain-Chicot-who-couldn't-talk-straight.

Belle had walked out on him dozens of times. He couldn't really blame her. Beyond his communication problems, there was the no-small-matter of the return of the Zeeman. He did have his epileptic fits, particularly when under an excessive dose of adrenaline. If only he could sit by some quiet shore and dribble his life away. But he couldn't. He told himself he wouldn't. He would not.

His seizures were dubbed symptomatic, that is, the result of organic injury, and Jacksonian, in that they began with unusual sensations in one part of the body. Alas, rarely sexual. In his case, there was a peculiar set of sensory impressions that seemed to have been imbedded in his early childhood. *A hot joyful sunlight, a barnyard, the warm, close smells of the barn and the domestic animals.* These were followed by the Zeeman's lovely kirillian glow, emanating from anything on which his gaze fell. When that warning came, he would expect to experience what the psychiatrists call *petit mal*. To the casual gadfly he appeared momentarily distracted. And it was in this moment that Brando, unlike many epileptics, still had a gambler's chance to avoid a major or *grand mal* seizure.

At this point, he could still see the barnyard door for what it was, and be aware that he must not enter that door. Once in, he would be overtaken by the rich smells of hay and animals and manure, become confused and display

68

irrational behavior. There would be flashes of light and color, and he would finally fall to the earth in a state of sheer and utter catatonia.

Yet the interior of the barn was dark and warm and exciting. In those times he felt he must go there. Once he took a hesitating step in that direction, the Zeeman flared. Something must be done to brake his path. And he did it. He smashed his head into the nearest hard object. This was his only cure, and this was why he was not considered by experts and amateurs alike to have a long lifeline. For, unfortunately, the self-saving interruption Brando had chosen—the only one he'd found to stave off a grand mal seizure—was a violent and self-destructive blow to his own head.

CHAPTER 8

You may not have been alive in the 1980's. Some would tell you that you didn't miss much. They didn't even have high def television or text messaging. But back then time itself still ran in the same direction as it does today, and at pretty much the same speed. I keep reminding you this is an 18th century London street penny novel that takes place in Los Angeles in 1984. Impossible, you say...or, at least, one chance in a million. But when you start to think that way, I'd have to agree. You're actually describing the likelihood of Brando's return from the dark swamplands of his once shattered mind. But here we are, four years into the decade of the 1980's.

And so it came to be a late afternoon, three or four days after Brando's conversation with pal Charlie. Brando had muscled the tan ragtop down and was rolling Fifi and her four mag wheels west on the Ventura, *careful to keep the shiny side up*, as the truckers said, as he dodged between the busty chromed behemoths heading in the same direction.

He reminded himself that he had to stay alert when everything else was bigger, heavier and wider than he was. *Must be what it feels like to be a quarterback in the NFL.*

He circled off the freeway at Topanga Canyon Boulevard and after puttering through a few urban blocks began the circling climb over the ridge. Fifi shot through the short, flat space at the top and began negotiating the winding drop into the deltoid system of Topanga Canyon, from where all water drained like poetry to the open arms of the sea.

The radio was blaring the clean and simple second movement from Mozart's 17th, proving to Brando that there was, indeed, a God who loved all of his creations and him, Brando Mahr, in particular.

By the time the canyon flattened into its last few looping curls and made for the salt water, he'd left the valley desert weather far behind. He sensed a smell of kelp and buttered popcorn, and overhead, feathery clouds were emblazoned across the sky like heraldry in a golden postcard sunset. The go/no-go light was electric green at Pacific Coast Highway. He downshifted Fifi into third and they executed a neat right turn. Fifi scooted along with the deep blue Pacific on the left, the darkening and unstable loess and conglomerate cliffs on the right. The red-orange sun was in Brando's eyes and his moustachios were whipping poetically in the wind as he rode along.

Ripper lived in a side-by-side duplex several miles south of the colony, toward the south end of what might be called Malibu proper, though the smarmy film crowd effete called it Topanga Bottoms, the butt of Malibu

But even the Bottoms had its status; after all, if you lived there, you were on the beach. The duplexes were crammed smack together on the ocean side of PCH so the riff and the raff couldn't get down to the sand without trespassing. If you lived there, you could off the highway into your garage, walk through your house shedding your suit and your shoes and walk right out onto your own little wet slab of beach. You bought the house proper, but the land was all 100-year leases, and they went for a million or more...the low-rent end of Malibu, even at that price in the 1980's..

Brando parked Fifi on the cliff side of the highway, under an unstable-looking overhang of ice-plant covered loess. He dodged across four lanes of traffic. He carried his yellow legal pad and a couple of American Hardpoint Wonderwriter felt tip pens. He despised ballpoint pens; he could hear the annoying little scree of the tiny ball rolling around while he was taking notes, and he'd rather write with a sharp stick dipped in his own blood.

The door to Ripper's place was open, and Brando heard the growl and beat of the *Heurlant* music. He gave a last look across the street at Fifi. She looked lonely and vulnerable, snuggled up against the hillside with no place to go if some boozy musical wizard from A&M Records or coke-snorting babe from Paramount lost control of their Bentley or Mustang 5.0. Brando sighed and pushed in through the door, which gave way reluctantly because of the mound of coats and furs stacked behind it.

Once inside, he was surprised to find a pleasant room that was tastefully decorated. There was a huge gray leather sofa and a multi-layered cocktail table of brass and glass. The on-shore breeze coming in through the open floor-to-ceiling windows was brazen enough so that the fire roaring in the brick hearth wasn't all that bad a notion, even for August in Southern California.

Ripper's party wasn't nearly halfway to Sodom or Gomorrah, but there was enough noise and exposed flesh to inspire a mid-sized clerical denunciation . The place was packed with what looked to be a prime slice of the current football in-crowd. There were young duddering rakes, as Brando would call them—both Blacks and Whites—with huge biceps and thighs and the innocent stares of oxen. They mingled with the giants from another era, legendary footballers with the coming stoop of age to their huge frames.

Brando felt the hammer-like beat of the music and the attraction of the milling game—the drop-dead gorgeous foxy duchesses and the cute and fubsey wenches. It was a veritable family of love in bikini bathing suits, in short shorts and halters, in party dresses, all of them blowing the gab and flashing their ivory or gazing haughtily out to sea, funking their cigarettes and sipping their frog's wine—that is, gin, so-called in the London of 200 years ago because it was affected by the French, er, *frogs*—the wenches all with come-ons or beat-its clearly tagged across their mascara.

"Hey, dude, your mouth is hangin' open," a tawny young mammillaria in a hot pink g-string bikini said as she fussed a platter of shrimp *hors d'ouvres* in his direction. She was what Brando thought of as a dimber mort, that is, a leggy beauty, but he was here to work, so he gave her his Mister Serious look.

"And where is the location of the Rip-man?" he queried.

She gave him a pout and drifted away without answering. He didn't blame her. This was a long way from his ordinary production meeting.

73

But he wasn't left to drift for more than a moment before Ripper Brown spotted him. The big man hailed his budding Boswell from a far segment of the room, "Brando! Brando Mahr! Over here, buddy! Hey, everybody, here he is— my biographer!" In another moment he was at Brando's side, his huge arm wrapped around Brando's shoulder, "The writer, the director, the man who's going to tell the story that will set the National Football League on its ear!"

In retrospect, Brando would remember that moment and realize he should have heard the bugle call and retreated. But an intro like that leaves one no exit. He smiled awkwardly and gave a humble little hand-flip to the audience, the salute of a young Truman gesturing from the Cadillac convertible beside the mighty Roosevelt.

"What's the social gathering?" He queried for conversation's sake.

"No special thing, man." Ripper looked baffled for a moment, considering the possibility that other celebs didn't throw parties like this all the time. Then he was in motion again, yelling over the general wash of noise, "Tony—hey, Tony! Come here a minute."

A powerfully built young Black rotated himself away from the wet bar and a platinum blond who was attached to the stem of a strawberry Marguerita and came lumbering over.

"Anthony Noble," Ripper said. "Defensive tackle for the Raiders. This boy's gonna start next year, an' he's gonna be a great one!"

Tony gave them a calculating, shy smile, centering his attention on Ripper. The hero worship was so blatant it was overpowering, but Ripper apparently felt it his just due.

Ripper clapped Tony between his wide shoulder blades. "One of the few and the rare— Tony gonna have a chance at the Ripper's records, he be that good!"

"Stay healthy, Tony," Brando said.

"You got that one right, man," the Ripper added, giving Brando his own thunderous clap on the back and steering him away from Tony in the same gesture. "He's gonna need ten to twelve good solid years, just to get close. You know what the odds against that are in today's NFL?!"

"Not too good…?"

"As-tro-NOM-ical!" Ripper laughed again, clearly stoked that his records were safe for the near term, and probably for all time.

They motored Zeus-like through the crowd's adoration. Ripper sprinkled Brando's introduction around, first upon a Nordic blond dodsey who had played on an episode of one of the Star Trek shows and then to the rake in the silk suit, who— no big surprise—turned into a wreck-chaser, that is, a lawyer, who represented sports stars.

"Where can we discuss events and communicate realities?" Brando asked.

The Ripper passed him a 'Say What?' expression.

"Hic labor est," Brando said, Latin for *We've got work here.*

"Like, huh?" Ripper said.

Brando waved his arms and tried to clarify, "Beyond spice and vigor, we must begin to discuss the salient details of your *saga incredibilious."* Brando thought there was little

75

chance Ripper knew the adjective *bilious*. But mayhaps he had underestimated the big man.

"Ohh." The little word escaped from Ripper's huge frame like a half-forgotten mouse. He nodded, half to himself. Brando thought it was about that moment when the distant drumroll sounded that there might be some process beyond osmosis involved in the gathering of his mighty life-deeds.

"Quieter out on the deck," he said, nodding in agreement.

He ushered Brando past a wall of shelves laden with the trophies of an NFL Super-being. There were game balls, Most Valuable Player plaques and heavy bronze Defensive Player of The Year awards. Ripper had even collected programs from the key games in his career, now framed and gleaming behind clear and dustless plastic.

They moved out to a deck that gave way to a view of the ocean. The fresh evening breeze was ruffling the air. Brando saw the slippery amber orb of the sun was already lost behind the menacing obsidian hulk of Point Dume. A dull red afterglow still hung in the airy elements, themselves thickening with the incoming fog off the now slate-gray ocean. Two people sat on clunky wooden lawn chairs around a redwood table. Overhead, the Red, Green and White of a Cinzano umbrella had dulled to jet black, lesser black and dark grey.

Ripper sank into one of two empty chairs and motioned Brando to the other. He gestured across the table. "This here's my woman—Lani. Elaine Katzin. You got to spell it right. K-A-T-Z-I-N."

Lani nodded once and flashed a quick grin, "Welcome to the circus." She was a Madonna look-alike, probably about 35 years old, Brando couldn't tell her age for sure. He liked her little hard-edged smile. He was a good student of people, and he knew he was looking at Ripper's faithful Desdemona, a rare survivor of the Ripper Wars.

"Lani, get me another drink," Ripper said. It was a flat order, but she didn't take offense.

She jumped up and said, "Scotch and water, right?"

"Right, babe."

She shifted her gaze to Brando, "Anything for you?"

"Maybe an agua. Aqua. Aquifer. Aqueous."

"Enough, already," she grinned. "Sure, we got water." He caught the notion that he amused her, but in a pleasant way. She stopped at the door screen, "With or without ice cubes? We got ice cubes, too."

"Ice cubes would be a magnanimous gesture."

"Of which we have an abundance," she responded. The smile deepened a little. He smiled back, thinking *A little sanity in the madhouse*. It looked like Ripper Brown was a blessed scoundrel; he possessed a doting whither-go-ye who could point out the important substance and shy him away from the mundungous outreach. *Hey, Sweetheart, maybe duck to the left here. Ripper-Honey, look out for the rocks up ahead. Oh shista, Rip, here comes Hastur the Unspeakable and some of his*

Cthulhuthian monster buddies, maybe we better sit this one out.

"This here be Old Loaf," Ripper said, flip-handing to indicate the black giant sitting across the table. At first glance, Old Loaf appeared to be sleeping. He was hunched back in his chair with his eyes half-closed, making like the thousand-year-old turtle. If he moved a millimeter, Brando didn't see it.

"Loaf gonna be able to fill in some of the detail," Ripper added.

All well and good. But Brando caught the drift that Ripper still anticipated his new partner was going to osmose the details of his magnificence in an hour or so. Didn't everybody know all about Ripper Brown?

In the dim remaining light, Loaf himself was little more than a pitch-black outline similar to Point Dume, a looming rock hulk against the deepening gray sky. And then at last his huge hand journeyed across the table and crushed Brando's. Brando thought, if he continued with this project, he was on mandatory for spring-steel exercise handgrips and Chinese iron health balls.

"My pleasure," Loaf's deep bass voice rumbled. Brando caught a faint whiff of half-digested pork, a burp in the wind.

Barry "Loaf" Ludder didn't really need any intros. Any literate sports buff who had followed the general outlines of Pigskin's Progress knew him. As a founding father of the Mighty Foremen, he had played the devastating front line with Ripper for most of their careers. Now he shifted his great body, moving into a band of light coming from the interior of the beach house.

Brando could make out his heavy eyebrows gathering together like two dark bushes. Deep lines of concern thickened across his forehead. His eyes flicked back and forth, from Ripper to Brando and back to Ripper again. Brando sensed Loaf was something less than a portrait of Tranquility. The smell emanating from him was stronger. It was a barnyard smell, no Zeeman this, a true scent from the sty. That it was coming from Loaf he had no question, even before he heard of Loaf's intestinal problems.

"This be the first I hear of this project," Loaf grunted, shaking a thick finger at Brando. "Now jist what type of motion picture is this going to be, boy?"

"I don't know, Loaf," Brando responded. "That's why we've collected here in close proximity."

Brando was in his classic reassurance mode. Also, he thought he could use the moment to reinforce Ripper with the idea that this was going to involve some real work. "We are meeting to illuminate the details.

But Loaf screwed up his lips like he'd been eating sour grapes, "You know that Ripp-boy here got the reputation around the league of being a fat-mouth."

Brando had to wonder what was going on in Loaf's brain. *Was Loaf jealous of his old comrade's ability to cling to the limelight?* Whatever, it didn't seem to bother the Great One.

"Tell it like it is," Ripper said mildly, lifting his glance out to sea where a brace of pelicans coasted like dark little pterodactyls over the blue-black agua. Brando suspected the big man was

79

not so light when almost anyone else questioned his decisions, but it felt to him like Ripper and Loaf were reviewing set positions in an old argument.

Loaf was unwilling to let it go. His voice drifted up a notch into a ripe tenor, "Yeah, Rip, but lots of folks don' want it told like it is."

"Lots-who?" Brando quizzed.

Loaf turned on Brando like an old black bear bothered by a pesky bee, "You got to be careful, young man! Ripper here don't lack for critics—or outright foes, neither! This ain't something you just go into without thinking it through!"

Brando went into the attack mode, Brando-the-Merciless flailing around on the trail of an idea, "I see it; it's Darwin's finches. You have the commencement of an expansive theory. *Nung ma*, who exactly might the enemy be, Loaf?" *Nung ma*, the word 'but' or 'however' in Vietnamese.

Loaf's lips pursed out like cranky balloons that were irritated by the fact they had been puffed up, "Jist about everybody wit' his picture on a bubble gum card, that's who! Use your head, fool; no idol to millions of little kids want it to be known he was takin' amphetamines or hormones or got in jail for hammerin' on a woman or stuff like that. Ripper here, he come right out an' talk about all that stuff!"

"Be not afraid of the truth, my son," Ripper intoned, "for the truth shall set you free."

To Brando, Loaf's fears seemed unfounded. But then, he had to admit, he'd never had a good name to sully. If he had committed youthful indiscretions, who might know how he would feel now, twenty years after the fact? He started to wonder if drugs were at the festering heart of Loaf's concern.

"Did all your comrades seek comfort in amphetamines?" he asked.

Loaf gave him a look that was as congenial as a man swallowing dirt spooned from a chicken coop floor. He started to sputter his denials, but Ripper cut right in before he could get any real words out.

"Oh, yeah, man," the Ripper said. "99.9% of 'em, in our day, whether Ol' Loafer here will own up to it or not. Amphetamines was our pain pills. An' the young players tells me they still use 'em. Only now they got better stuff, so they don't use 'em exclusive. I swear to God, in my playin' days, I'd turn in all my amphetamines for one goddam lousy little bottle of Tylenol."

Loaf half-stood, shifting his weight as if he was a mud turtle with bad knees, getting ready to dart out the door.

"We not goin' to get on wit' shit like this, are we?" he asked. For a huge and rickety old boffer, Brando thought he still had the hulking and dangerous presence of a big man with great reserves of physical strength.

"Why the saber-rattling, Loaf?" Brando asked. "As the Ripper here says, it's old history. Paradise lost. The epic golden-oldie era."

Loaf looked pained, obviously not liking to be summed up in the same chapter with the ancient Etruscans.

But Ripper didn't pay him any attention. He just grinned his big, bittersweet smile and waved a negligent hand.

81

"Sit down, Old Loafer," he said mildly. "We jist talkin', man."

Ripper rotated his body slightly towards Brando and shrugged, his hands outspread in an 'I told you so' gesture. "See?! Wit' the Great and Fantastic Ripper Brown, you got your certified one in a million. It happened; I tell it. You get the *bona fidas*, the inside story, the real dirt, revealed for the first time."

"No other man the fool to be tellin' it...," Loaf muttered under his breath. He wheeled his big frame away from the discussion and footed for the screen door. Loaf was leaving with such urgency that he smacked squarely into Lani, wetting her thin silk blouse with the drinks she was carrying.

"Oh, Loafer," she said, half whiplash and half tease as she set down the drinks and brushed off her blouse. The clinging material made Brando aware she wasn't wearing mammilary support, as he would call it, but, regaining her good humor, she jibed at Loaf with quiet humor, "Now see what you've done! Can't we take you anywhere, Loaf-man?" Her friendly banter wasn't enough to lighten Loaf's mood.

"You better tell that man of yours t' keep his lip zipped!" he growled.

Her smile drifted to the cool side, "Nobody tells the Ripper anything, Loaf. You know that." Brando saw that here was one whither-go-ye, that is, wife, who knew when and how to stick up for her cull. And he also recognized that no darting Thomas, ding-boy or bastardly gullion should ever be confused about whose side she was on.

Loaf wagged a warning digit back at his old teammate, "You gittin' so many enemies, they

82

gonna hafta fight over which one gits t' ditch you in the river!"

Ripper exhaled his big, hearty laugh, "Aww, now, Loafer..." But the Ripper let his sentence die when he saw he was talking to the blank screen door. He looked down at his feet, shaking his head. After a moment, he let out a laugh of another sort. It was little more than a sarcastic cough.

"The sacred brotherhood of the players," he said softly and earnestly. "We don' know nothin', we didn' see nothin', we don't say nothin'—we jist keep rollin' along!" His words turned into another laugh, but this time it was the hacking laugh of a chain-smoker. It broke into a full-fledged, wheezing cough and Lani had to come over and clap him on the back before he finally fell silent.

Lani sighed and shook her head, "Well, done is done, but you better go calm him down, Ripper. We've got enough trouble; you don't want him spreading nonsense to the other players."

Brando tried to make light of it.

"We don't even...We're not even syncopated on what direction our project might take," he protested.

But Ripper had already headed back into the house to flag down his old teammate.

Loaf was gone, but the strange barnyard smell still lingered in the air.

Lani must have spotted the twitch in Brando's nose, "Loaf had cancer. Most of his intestines and stomach are gone. They say he's okay now, but when the poor guy isn't belching at one end he's giving off fumes at the other."

Lani curled into her chair, wrapped a loose-knit shawl around her shoulders, and gave Brando the smile the big fat hell-cat with the long claws presents to the little yellow bird.

"Sooo...you're the big-name writer," she purred.

"Not so immense," Brando said. "My friends and I did a few shows. And I worked for S&S Studio for a few years."

"S&S?" she asked.

"The Spider & The Snake." He gave her the Opie-Dopie Crawl and she responded with a little grin.

"Oh. *That* studio."

He waved his hand at the crowded room on the other side of the screen. "I like your interior decorations. The Oriental portrayal. The dimensional art."

She appreciated that he'd noticed. He suspected it was more often only her sleek bumfiddle that people complimented.

"It's all mine," she confided. "Everything you see in there. You should have seen the place when he finally persuaded me to move in. Bare floors and apple crates and one wall covered with footballs and trophies." She nodded once, taking him in with a more serious glance. The preliminary introductions were over; things were about to get serious.

"You should know where I stand on your project," she said.

"Please elucidate," he said. Up until now there had been little more than Keith's pipe dreams and Ripper's empty ebullience. He was glad there was someone who might be able to take the project seriously.

"The way I see it, this is just another one of Ripper's big schemes," she said. "He thinks big, I'll give him that. But somebody's got to pick up after him, and that somebody is me."

"He's fortunate to have a hook-up with someone maximized for his benefit."

"Exactly." She relaxed a little more and shook a cigarette out of a gold case she held on her lap. "I divide his brainstorms into two categories," she said, smoothing the cigarette. Her long fingers with their perfect maroon oval nails moved nervously, searching in her small purse for her lighter.

"Nearly as I can tell," she continued, "this one goes in the Harmless File. It won't cost us money, of which we have very little." She gave Brando a quick little look, a sparrow eyeing a big sunflower seed or a french fry, "And I presume you can do an outline or something that won't take him away from his schedule of speaking engagements?"

"Affirmative."

"And it's not just a crazy shot in the dark. I mean, you do have some valid contacts in the business?"

"I'm not Louis B. Mayer, but have some hook-ups and connectives, and I do have my name on the leader and tail-end of numerous films and tapes."

She nodded her satisfaction. "Then you can count on my support. What's the story about?"

"I don't have... the barest awareness... of a concept." She waited until Brando wrenched out

85

the entire thought, confirming his earlier excellent opinion of her. She just watched him, not really making any judgment, and he liked that, too. As Brando himself would say, he held the wench or knave in high regard who gave him the chance to fuster through an entire complex sentence on his own, something with a subject and a predicate and mayhaps a dependant clause or two. It was one of his peculiar acid tests for accountability in human affairs.

"Ripper has a million stories," she said. "He's one of the most colorful, quotable bastards ever to play the game."

"How is he with the soul of the matter, and the distinctions?" Brando asked.

"Like what?" She leaned back and looked at the thickening night sky, forgetting her smoke for the moment.

"Like hard facts. Like exactly which, who, how and what transpired when and where."

"You kidding me? He's terrible! His whole life's one of those splashy Leroy Neimans paintings!" She had a good, throaty laugh, "You'll find the Ripper is swimmingly awash with color, but don't look to him for the details!"

She paused and fired up her cigarette. "Of course," she continued, "if you'd done all the drinking and lived all the wild times he's had, you wouldn't be much different, yourself."

"Je d'accord."

"Hmmm?" She lifted her eyebrows.

"I concur," Brando said. "There is no jackpot in arguing over who strummed the most, drank the hardest, doped the highest. Fond memories too easily careen out of control, and, what the

86

hades, there's always some future moment in which to manufacture yourself as a total dipstick-nimrod."

Lani nodded and allowed a heavy stream of smoke to drift from her nasal passages; he reflected her gesture was not unlike the knowing *dimber morts* do during conversation scenes in European flicks.

"He'll tell you the funniest stories, like the night when some of the Rams players invited in a roomful of hookers and swinging groupies for a little party. Well, things got hot 'n juicy, and it should have been okay because they were out of town for an away game and chances were none of the wives would find out. Minneapolis, I think. Only one of the guys got on the phone to his squeeze. This loser calls back to L.A., probably afraid his lady will hear about the wild times from somebody else. See, he wants to get the word in that he personally had no part in the panty-grouping. You know how guilt is..."

Brando nodded that he understood, and she continued..

"But he forgot about the Old Lady's Grapevine. And so, when our soiled little boy scout troop got off the plane at LAX, every married woman on the team was down there at the gate waiting for her man, waving rolling-pins and divorce papers, breathing fire and demanding explanations!"

Ripper's lady smiled and inhaled deeply. The cut of burnt tobacco was sharp and pleasant in the night air, reminding Brando of his father, who had chain-smoked three packs of unfiltered Camels every day and had left for the thereafter with an unhappy yellow stain around his fingers and a pair of cancer-ridden wheezers black as soot.

"Ripper will have you in stitches," Lani said, "the way he tells that story—but he can't tell you what year that was, or exactly what game, or sometimes even who the other players were."

"How do we reconstruct for our purposes— assuming we find we have any?"

"If it's that important, I guess you'll have to interview everybody, maybe go back to old newspapers in the library," she said.

"I'm good at libraries."

She shrugged; it wasn't really her problem, "It's all there, somewhere, I suppose." She puffed smoke into the dimming night atmosphere. "I guess I misunderstood; is this a documentary or a movie?"

"A fair concern. Most-hapsly, we would aim for reality-based drama. But the baseline is, right now I don't—we don't possess a hook. No idea, no high concept, no low concept...no anything."

"And you think you might-maybe-could possibly get a hook?"

"Maybe-might," Brando said. "I'm of a mind to invest some energy and do some digging. But a hundred aphorisms, a thousand fables, ten-thousand parables doth not a single movie make."

She nodded and a faint, bitter smile crossed her lips, "Amen to that. The bastards string you along and string you along, and let you do all the work, and then they hang you up to dry. That's show business. It's the fucking misery game."

She stood and flicked her glowing cigarette butt off the balcony. It struck the dark sand twenty hands below with a little shower of sparks.

"I'll help as much as I can," she said. "I can give you a list of phone numbers of players and coaches you can interview. You can dig up a lot from the microfilm in the library—UCLA or CSUN—they both carry the Times and Herald-Examiner back that far. Rams management likes us—I'll set you up at their office in Orange County so you can go down there and read the play-by-plays and see any films you want."

"Merci beau coup..."

"But none of that solves our problem, does it?"

"Our problem?"

"What the hell the film is all about."

"D'accord," Brando said. "But I've fished these waters before. If there's a sizzle somewhere nearby you can wager Canada I'll hook the steak."

She gazed out to sea for a moment, her elbows resting on the balcony railing. And then she nodded and turned to look Brando firmly in the eye. "I like you, Brando. I'll throw in Alaska, to boot," she said.

CHAPTER 9

So, here we have FOUL, an 18th century London street penny novel that takes place in Los Angeles in 1984. Time travel? No. Mind-travel? Maybe. But, if you're a story-teller, let me warn you, language over the generations is a delightful, dangerous, slippery, shifty little beast that just happens to be the gatekeeper to everything and everywhere.

By the time he'd worked his way through the crowd to the front door, Brando was sure Loaf would be down the highway. But Loaf and Ripper and three or four others were standing around pleasantly buzzing like a group of lucky onlookers who have just seen a high speed Peterbilt truck take out a tiny Toyota Tercel on the Harbor Freeway. This gave Brando that old familiar sinking feeling in the pit of his stomach.

"Oh, man, where you been?" Ripper chortled.

"I didn't know there was entertainment in this sector." Brando replied.

Ripper took Brando's arm and guided him to the road, pointing gleefully across the highway, "Some damn fool parked under Boulder Alley again!"

In the cold orange-yellow of the overhead streetlamp, Brando saw what the excitement was about. The damn fool's car had been crushed in the hood by something that looked like a large meteorite. From his angle, it seemed like the huge boulder stretched from fender to fender. It was sunk halfway into the engine compartment. The front wheels of the unfortunate little *Italiano* speedster were collapsed sideways, like Opie's cartoon flivver after it bounced down the canyon, took a last, hissing whistle of steam and gave up the ghost. The horn bleated in one long, steady wail. All in all, Brando found it a pathetic sight, made even more heart-wrenching by the fact that the oddly impaled automobile was his own.

"Fifi!" he yelled.

Traffic was somewhat thinner than when he had arrived, and he managed to dart across the PCH without incident. In a way it was unreal; while Fifi's splendid haunches retained their original heart-accelerating curves, the damage to her front end was total. Everything behind the direct impact of the boulder looked in perfect working order. The front windshield wasn't even cracked. Brando noticed a piece of paper stuck behind the windshield wiper on the driver's side. It was a small page torn from one of those secretarial spiral-bound note pads. He reached for it, expecting a helpful note from someone who had seen the accident. But it wasn't that kind of message. It said in crude block letters, "STICK TO CARTOONS, DOPIE. YOU'LL LIVE LONGER." Of course, there wasn't any signature.

The big men walked across the street like they owned it and joined Brando.

"Tell me this ain't your car, man," Ripper said.

Brando knew the huge man had ten inches and eighty pounds on him, but at the moment he wasn't in his right mind. There was his beautiful

Fifi crushed like a matchbox toy! And then to be called a cartoon-maker! He couldn't figure which made him more crazed. He snared two fistfuls of Ripper's rope-like knit sweater and yelled up in the general direction of the huge man's face, "Did you converse with anyone about our intentions?!"

Ripper put his hands up, palm forward and backed off like Brando was a rabid terrier. "Well, I—Brando, maybe a few people—you know, advance publicity..."

"Oh, yeah, he did." Loaf sighed knowingly, "He talked about it with that loudmouth smart-ass half-back Bessbone, an' Bess's sidekick, no-good Nelson the scatback. Don' deny it, Ripper, I was right there, I heard you on the phone."

Ripper scuffed at roadside gravel with one of his size 14 Adidas like the little tad caught with his hand in his own codpiece.

"That didn't mean nothin'," he protested in a low voice.

"Man asked you if you tol' anybody." Loaf gave Brando his mournful eye, "Tellin' those two is like tellin' everybody. I mean, those boys are plugged into the pro ball grapevine so good, they spread the juice faster than Action News or the Hollywood Reporter."

Somewhere in the madness of those hazy reddish moments that passed while Loaf was explaining things, Brando realized where and who he was and what he was doing. He took his hands off Ripper's sweater and brushed it once or twice. After all, the man might come to his senses at any moment. But Brando was still mad, and his brushing was more like hard slaps. Ripper could have laid his famous headsmack alongside

92

Brando's ear and rung his bell, but he seemed as stunned as his new filmic biographer.

"So what nefarious secrets do you retain," Brando yelled at him, "that are so critical that somebody would annihilate my motor coach to persuade me to reconsider my production possibilities?!"

The Ripper was still in the conciliatory mode, "Hey, now, Brando, you got insurance, don't you, man?"

"Insurance is not the predicament," Brando yelled, getting crazy all over again and talking in a voice that sounded like he was choking on gravel. In another second or two he was going to tangle with a giant or strangle in his own angst. He pointed at his ruined car, and stared at Ripper. "What is this all about?!"

"I jist don't know, man. I don't know nothin'," the big man said. He rattled his open palms at the sky like he was the world's last honest man, just begging for Jesus' blessing of forgiveness, and his eyes were wide and without guile.

Maybe Ripper honestly didn't know any more than he was saying. But Brando didn't believe it. At that moment, he felt the big footballer reeked innocence, he exuded it like a dog who'd been rolling in fields of innocence. And whatever that blank and friendly exterior hid, Brando could see he wasn't going to talk about it.

CHAPTER 10

Welcome back to FOUL, our Brando Mahr murder mystery picaresque. Picaresque? You know, an episodic tale with a roughish scamp as our protagonist. Samuel Richardson's Pamela. Smollett's Roderick Random. My own inimitable batch of rascals. Loveable, but scandalous rogues, for all that. Scamps, the lot of them.

The tow truck turned out to be one of those flatbeds on which the crumpled machine rides high above the traffic flow like a California road trophy, held up to public view so everyone can see the splendor of the impact. A man in oily blue overhauls tilted the back of the flatbed down and winched the little brown roadster up to where it would sail along at roof level above the traffic, a dead soldier on a shield, displayed above the field of fray.

Brando took plenty of pictures. They had to leave the meteor-like rock in place; no one could figure out how to remove it from the engine compartment. The tow truck sadly lumbered south on the Pacific Coast Highway and up over the the Topanga ridge, returning along the same route Brando had come.

They deposited his crumpled Spyder in the insurance claims yard in the West Valley and the following morning Brando returned with his insurance man, Morrie Scheidt, who took one look and burst out laughing. He laughed long and hard. Brando turned red-faced and felt quivery.

"I fared poorly in the lottery of life," he said.

"Why's that?" Morrie chortled.

"Look, this is not funny. Other motorists get the Good Hands People. I signed up with the Jolly Sadist Group."

Morrie was an apple-cheeked little man with a crown of yellow-white hair shaped to distinction by a small round monk's pate on the back. Before this time, Brando had thought of him as a mild, almost meek tradester. When he had scribbled his John Hancock on the contract, Morrie seemed so pleased to obtain his business that he'd bowed and oiled his way out the door. Now Brando could see Morrie was actually the incarnation of laughing devil, an Indonesian garuda or Trung Hoa gate dog gone ugly and wrong.

"I'm sorry," Morrie said finally, "but it looks so—so absurd!" And then he went on another round of laughter. Brando wondered what indiscretions he had committed in other lives to deserve this. And even then, the devil hadn't yet had his full due; Morrie called some of his fellow-workers so they all could chortle and have a good laugh at Fifi's sad predicament.

After what seemed to Brando like a very long time, partial sanity seeped back into the claims office. The curious loafers wandered off to their cubicles. The show was over. Brando sat warily on the far side of a grey metal desk while Morrie browsed through several issues of the Blue Book, and intermittently punched his calculator.

"Hmmmm," he said. Brando recognized they had reached the throat clearing stage. Trumpet blasts and drum rolls were in order, or perhaps just sly eye winks in the back of the alehouse. This was the commencement of the initial offer.

"What is your assessment, Morrie?" Brando asked, pretending to fall for his ploy like an inexperienced schoolboy.

"Total loss," the little diddler said, shaking his head sadly.

"And...?"

"Well, the good news is, we can give you Blue Book, which would be enough to go out and lay a sizeable down on something new."

"Or...?"

Morrie sat back in his chair and scratched the smooth spot on the back of his head, shrugging and smiling and scratching like Old Man Gepetto was pulling all his strings at once. Brando knew some men felt uncomfortable when they diddled. The bible attributed it to conscience.

"Well, I suppose you could have it rebuilt," Morrie sniffed, "but we really don't recommend that."

"Rebuilt?! Why, you unctuous defrauder— the motor was impacted ten inches into living asphalt!"

"Exactly my point." Morrie gave a smooth little chuckle and a warning finger-wag, "You get them back, and they're neee-vver quite the same."

"My Fifi was of the virginal cherry mode."

"Exactly," Morrie said.

Brando didn't think Morrie comprehended his exact drift, but he didn't think it mattered. Morrie would soon be enlightened.

From Morrie's point of view, he and Brando had reached the pressure-point moment; the little agent quick-smiled his client and did a fast 180

96

with the papers. He pushed them across, pointing with the butt-end of his ballpoint. "If you'll just sign here, I'll have them cut a check while you wait."

Brando shrugged, "*Khong phai, thua ong*...I won't have you diddle me like this. Your resolution is incompatible with my expectations. What's more, it is fraudulent."

"What?!" Little pink spots sprouted on Morrie's cheeks like rosebuds.

"Yes. Redolent of fraud."

The cheery note drained out of Morrie's voice like Strawberry Soda from a tin can with a fresh .22 slug through it.

"I don't get it. What do you mean?" Morrie whined.

"Don't be so clutch-fisted, Morrie. You can't take it with you when you expire. I've decided I want you to reinstate my beloved Fifi Spyder to her former splendor."

"Now wait a minute, my young friend. You're not being reasonable. That car would cost us more to fix than it would to buy a new one."

"Then fire up your imagination and regale me with a better offer."

"We can't do that," Morrie scoffed. "Be reasonable."

"I read the particulars last night," Brando said, tapping the policy. "If I may paraphrase, you have to 'rehabilitate and return the damaged motor vehicle to me in like condition."

Morrie pursed his lips and looked at Brando like his client had trucked in manure on his boots, "You better think it over, my young friend. You know what that would do to your rates?"

97

Brando sighed, "You are an old rat at this, and to be commended. However, I'm fearful I must commune with a higher authority."

Brando pointed across Morrie's desk and he reluctantly pushed his phone over.

"Ahh...Sure—here," he said. Brando could see the look of hesitation cross his face.

Brando glommed a piece of paper from his own pocket, gave it the old false scan, and punched the numbers for the phone in his own office at KTGA. Once he was connected to the answering machine that promised superior writing, production and directing services, he said, "Los Angeles City Hall?" He waited a moment, and then said, "Consumer Fraud Division?"

There was a fast bustle from across the desk, and then Morrie the Rogue snatched the receiver from Brando's hand and gently placed it back on the cradle. Brando hadn't realized he could move that quickly; he had to remind himself that it showed how primary the self-preservation instinct was in all insurance thieves.

Brando stood and unfolded his old army fatigues cap, stored so the bill was folded properly on each edge, and placed it at the appropriate rakish angle on what he saw as his handsome and perceptive cranium.

"And you have 'to provide a car until the damaged motor vehicle is ready,'" he recited. "A car 'of equal capabilities.'"

Morrie thinned his lips and he took on a morose look, and then he grudgingly found a list from deep in one of the drawers and smoothed it on the desk in front of him like the treasure map to the lost gold of Machu Pichu.

"A fine, zippy little Escort," Morrie said.

"Negatory. I haven't just migrated from the cabbage patch."

"Be reasonable, Mahr. I'll even move you up a category—an Olds Cutlass."

"*Non, mon frere.* Cloy from the unsuspecting, if you must; I have you researched." Cloy is an old word that means to steal.

Morrie hesitated, trying to figure it out as his finger ran down a short column.

"You're not really a bundle of laughs here, pal, he said. "Okay, I bump you two categories—a Buick Regal."

"*Khong phai, thua ong.*" This Brando didn't expect him to get. It meant, in Vietnamese, Not to be, honorable one.

"Final offer. Chrysler New Yorker."

Brando shook his head, humming the refrain from the old melodrama Way, Way Down East, No, no, a thousand times No, I'd rather die than say yes.

"Why not?"

"Fifi is a sportser, Morrie," he chided.

Morrie stood and puffed out his little chest in righteous grumpiness. Brando resented the gesture, figuring the little agent wouldn't have tried it if he was dealing with Marlon Brando instead of Brando Mahr.

"We don't have anything else!" Morrie wailed.

Brando jabbed his finger in Morrie's bible before he could slip it away. He stood and leaned over the desk, and his finger traced to a spot near the bottom of the list.

"That one," he said.

The next morning the pre-noon sky was nearly bird's egg blue with the last wisps of inland fog lifting to mingle with the urine-yellow inversion layer. Brando's replacement car, a shiny new maroon Corvette, topped the Sepulveda pass and lofted south into the L.A. basin with Brando himself in the driver's seat. He was shrouded in his World War II pilot's sunglasses made of true darkened glass and had the bill of his olive colored soft-cap pulled low against the rip of the wind. He sported a loose silk shirt from Manila that had a jagged, fugitive-'50's print of bright red, black, yellow, green and blue trapezoids, and he wore a pair of light-weight cotton shorts pressed military style and cutting just above the knees, and his leather Berkies sans socks completed the picture. It was the Brando Mahr version of the casual Sho Biz look.

The engine thundered and Brando was thinking that there was a lot of splendor in Detroit engineering that your average American schmoo took for granted, and that was about when a CHP angled his lightweight Jap imitation Harley across the freeway and rode shotgun on Brando's left rear fender. Traffic cleared, and the Chip pulled alongside, so close Brando could reach out and touch his handlebars. Brando gave him the informal little salute that had served him so well in the military, thinking *We who are about to die salute you and wishing for a glass of rice wine and a white silk scarf with a red spot on it.* But the Chip just grinned and saluted back, his gesture snappy for a man on a machine. And then he peeled off and dove after a yellow Ferrari offender who was clearly doing five more that the rest of the flow.

Brando breathed a sigh of relief. He could only imagine what the officer's outlook might have been if he'd jimmied the trunk and taken a look at the gunnysack of unregistered firearms Brando had accepted from Keith Lagosi and Joey's widow. But that was not to be.

Brando was feeling more buckish and optimistic than he had for a while. He had been out there in the slimoid corporate world of networks and studio skullduggery, fisting the good fight for his own economic survival—and had forgotten there is real evil in the world. But now he knew differently. That boulder through Fifi's hood represented first contact with the aliens, his own personal close encounter—he had been ridiculed and threatened by a note from the forces of darkness. He found something about that intensely satisfying.

The way Brando saw it, that was their— whoever they were—big mistake. Until then, Ear Man & The Hands of Death (as he thought of himself) hadn't even been aware there was another side. Brando had been ready to dump The World of Ripper and get back to the ordinary known universe of talking spiders and snakes, little bulby-nosed blue fellows who lived in a medieval village, heavy-limbed men in multi-colored underwear who beamed green death rays from their eyes and ooze from their fingertips, and awesome purple monsters with a sense of humor who befriended orphans out of some dim moral obligation and ended up saving civilization as we know it. Here's some dialogue from one of

Brando's cartoon scripts, actually produced by a Dutch animation studio for consumption in English speaking countries (including Japan): *Gorgo: Let's go smash some flowers in the park and eat 47th Street! Little Orphan Girl: Oh, Gorgo-Morgo, you're so silly!*

As Brando whisked along, he was propelled by an old familiar feeling. It wasn't courage and it wasn't fear. It was a mood from the Nam, and he accepted the rush like the return of a somewhat scary but treasured sweetheart—after all, the boulder which had come bounding down the side of the hill onto Fifi might turn out to be nothing more than an NFL alumnus idea of a joke—still, he was almost uncomfortably happy, itching to get on with the day. One part of Brando, the part that had convinced itself it was responsible for his survival, was saying *No, babes, you're too damaged and fragile to be stepping in this manure.* But even as the dampening thoughts attempted to smother the threshold of his pleasure, he could feel a certain sprung joy already moving through his veins, and he knew it was too late. Some fool had unwisely crashed a rock on the light and nimble Brandomobile. Now dirges would play in little cottage churches, and there would be joy in hell, for he was about to send a few new customers down.

Brando low-speed zoomed east on the 10 and south on the 5, heading toward Walt's World and the Berry Farm, and after about 20 klicks he slid off the ramp onto Orangethorpe Boulevard.

Driving down Lincoln, Brando turned right into what looked like a quiet residential area. A couple of blocks and another right turn, and he came to an unmarked gate. This could be a very exclusive boy's school or an ivy-walled elephant cemetery, but the mammoth gate guard checked him off his list and put a sticker inside his window that said, "Courtesy of the Los Angeles Rams". The sticker had a picture of a football helmet with curled horns on it. The whole process was instructional; *Yes, you have made it inside the inner sanctum of an NFL team. Now BEHAVE yourself.*

Less than duly intimidated, Brando gunned the Corvette into a parking spot a few ticks ahead of a shiny black Jeep carrying its own little boom-box wave of junk metal music with it like the smell of rotten eggs. The driver was a short, skinny white guy. Brando recognized him as Frankie Hurno, the soccer style kicker from Croatia. Brando remembered seeing a black & white photo of the little rogue on the inside front page of the L.A. Times sport section, rams-horns helmet off and head bowed in teary defeat, after he'd lost a big'un in Pontiac Stadium. Hurno gave Brando the bad eye.

"I saw that parking space first, Butt-brain" he snarled.

"Don't snilch me the evil eye, loser-foot. You visualized it, just as you did before your spineless, wimpy little boot against the Lions."

"Whaaaat is zis?!" Hurno's lips were twisting in a strange, Adriatic way.

These crazed Baltic people, worse than the Welsh and the Scots, always starting wars, Brando thought happily. *It had to be genetic.* He imagined little Hurno in an animated Rays of Death sequence; he would be Rabido Ratley, all

103

beady red eyes with yellow saliva dripping from his fangs.

Brando shrugged the image away. "Having trouble wiz our sssss sound, are we, Fritzie?" Brando pointed his finger at the surly little man like a pistol and fired an imaginary round past his ear. He felt the bully bumfiddle deserved it; he'd read plenty about Hurno's long-running assault on his wife, a once-pretty Czech girl whose bruised and battered visage kept showing up in People magazine.

"Who ze fuck ezz you, buddy?!" Hurno screamed.

"Never dick with an agent, greenhorn dink-balls. We have memories like wart-hogs."

Ahh, Hollywood, Brando thought to himself, *the land where you are who you say you are.* Only naked human greed at its most flagrant allows the possibility for such bizarre and wicked leaps of faith and logic.

Hurno was halfway out of his Jeep, but Brando's bald-assed manufacture necessitated a re-evaluation of the kicker's options. If Brando really was a dealmaker, the splendor might come when he could snap the little kicker's career like dry spaghetti. Hurno slammed his door and sat glowering behind the wheel like a red-cheeked little troll, no doubt with visions of his future, such as it was, going down the bathtub drain because he'd had the misfortune to bad-lip Jake Bigtime in a fricking parking lot over a fracking parking space.

Unwilling to make a bad situation any better, Brando arm-lifted himself out of the Corvette without opening the door and snarled at Hurno,

104

"You blind, crooked-legged little rooster—words fail me." As indeed they had. Brando's mind had gone blank and he didn't know what else to say. He shrugged and walked away.

Brando wondered how long it would take him to figure out that the entire lot was only half filled and there were four score or so empty parking spaces available where he could park his yuppie wonder-wagon.

CHAPTER 11

So here you have an 18th century London street penny picaresque that takes place in 1984. Our roughish hero, one Brando Mahr, has quite literally lost his mind—and found it again in the dusty basement stacks of a great university library. Found it, I might add, a bit scrambled and somewhat the worse for wear. The admirable thing about picaresque heroes—no matter what, they do amble on into the uncertain future with their own good-natured sense of adventure.

It was obvious to Brando Mahr that Archie Richie enjoyed his job as the Rams head public relations baron. When Brando ambled into his office, Archie was ad-libbing the Harry Cohen Hollywood B-movie mogul role with two phones to his head, one for each ear, just like middle-management functionaries playing the same I'm-very-important-and-you're-not role at grubby production studios and indy offices all over town. Brando suspected Archie was putting on an act, though maybe he'd mixed up acting with real life, like Steve McQueen donning the tycoon's personna after The Thomas Crown Affair, the detective's weary ways after Bullitt and the race car driver's carefree Kiss of Death attitude after Le Mans, until one had to wonder if the real Steve was still anywhere inside his own cranium. If there was such a thing as a real Steve, in the first place, Brando thought with a weary smile.

Archie flipped Brando a cheery wave with his elbow and motioned his attention to an ancient lady with the name Gladys hand-stitched in flowers in a silver frame on her desk, and without saying a word somehow managed to communicate that Brando was to be escorted to the ancient tomb where they kept the play-by-plays, and made comfortable so he could do his documentary-drama thing, or whatever it was that had made him famous enough to gain entrance. Lani Kazin had, indeed, come through for the team.

Brando's take was that Gladys could be numbered among those nepotistic secretaries who weren't hired for looks, personality or secretarial skills. She was a crone with true age on her bones, so far past bouncy she was plummeting free-fall through the final notes of Vivaldi's Four Seasons with nary an arresting angel in sight.

A baggy green sweater that looked like it was buttoned on sideways hung from her shoulders and shiny grey polyester pants fell loosely over her bony derriere. Her walk was a desperate hobble from one secure point to the next, and her right hand was hooked in a permanent claw. With her typing skills limited to the ASDFG side of the board, Brando could see she wasn't going to win any awards for Fastest Peck. He was looking at the chairman of the board's mother, the protected one, the secretary who could do no wrong.

When Brando saw the right side of her face was frozen, his heart went out to her. She was one of his chosen, she could do no wrong.

"Madame," Brando said, as she strained to keep up and lead him at the same time, "I've some

107

notion as to the location of the mystical grail. Mayhaps you should *returnes tu la post.*"

"No!" She shouted in his ear, the living half of her face twitching as if vengeful demons struggled to take over. She gasped for air, swallowing it like water, in loud gulps, "You think—I can't—handle myself?"

"No, far to the contrary," Brando said with a slight bow. "In fact, I'm strategically instilled with patience for your assistance." And then he spoke about something he never talked about with anyone, "My face was once...half frozen, like yours."

Her eyes narrowed, and she examined him closely, finally saying, "I can see that."

"What gives me away?"

"I can see it," she insisted, slurring the "s" sound into a "sh". She was probably right. The bunched ganglia on the bottom left side of Brando's chin were somewhat larger than those on the right, giving him a slightly asymmetrical look. "But you was young. Ain't no hope for me."

"I still exercise." Brando did a series of weird glares, frowns, grimaces and winks. "In the mirror, before I go to bed. I must do it or I'll lose it."

"Well, I'll be going to bed soon enough now," she said grimly, turning away from him and resuming her determined lurch. "So it don't matter none, anyhow."

They made their slow way through the doorway of a building that looked deserted and then inched their way down a long hall and into an empty pressroom.

This working room had ten or twelve worker-bee stations with beat-up editor-type chairs—the ones with the arm-rests, as compared to clerk's chairs, which were without. Each heavyweight steel desk had a phone with about a dozen lines on it. The record files, which Gladys was careful to describe as duplicate, took up one entire wall.

Her eyes widened as Brando lifted a decade's worth of Rams history from the files and spread the play-by-plays out on two of the desks. Her breath came in eager wheezes. Brando tried to think about how far it was to the nearest oxygen bottle. There probably would be a lit sign, Life Support Systems. If she cranked herself up one more notch, he figured they were going to need one.

"Honey, you got—a month's worth—of work here," she gasped. Brando could see it was going to be one hades of a relationship, with the both of them such odd conversationalists.

"That's only for eunochs who aren't completely cognizant of that which they seek," he said.

Her sharp, bird-like stare turned on him. She ground her teeth, making a horrible stone-on-stone sound. "You're making—fun of—me."

He shook his head and held out his hands, "I have my own predicament with words and enunciation. I talk like Dopey of the Seven Dwarves. It's a malfunction of the brain."

She thought about it for a second or two, and then nodded. "Like an old half-back—beat up in the—football wars." She looked down at her shoes, one of which was built up two inches

109

higher than the other to accommodate her crippled foot.

Finally she said, "What are—you looking—for?"

Brando liked the old shill, but he was no simpleton or noddy. He shrugged. "I'm not sure, but like the barnyard fowl and the road, I'll be aware of it when I cross it."

To his surprise, she let out an ancient cackle. He thought it was like the laugh-track they'd play if he'd won the Two Weeks in Hawaii on Make A Witch Laugh. He guessed they didn't get many of comedian types in the Ram's inner sanctum. All sweat and no recreation.

He rotated a chair backwards and sat on it, leaning his arms on the backrest. When she stopped wheezing he asked her, "Were you activated in The Ripper Age?"

"Honey—I was here when—Jim Thorpe played!" Brando enjoyed that she was getting in the act, but she nearly had a fit over her own historical horse-play—if she was joking—and he ended up whacking her back and questioning her health.

"I'm—okay," she finally spat out, but her ancient, wrinkled face bloomed more purple than red, not a healthy glow even if it did set off her grey hair. "Don't fuss—with me," she said, pushing Brando away. She settled into a chair with a little sigh, nodded a few times like she was going to drift off, and then her one bright eye snapped open and caught his, "Ripper Brown...Now there was—one wild—S.O.B.!"

110

"He rose to the top naturally, *la creme de la creme*, number one with a bullet, right?" Brando asked.

"Maybe..." She thought about it before she continued, and Brando thought he saw something firm up in her attitude, like she'd spit up an old, unpleasant memory, "Hard-drinkin', high-livin'—angry young—son-of-a-bitch—overpaid—ballplayer. You get tired—of 'em swingin'—their big dicks around here."

"He was a difficulty to handle??"

"Owner, coach, teammates, women—he had trouble—with 'em all!"

Brando stood, holding out his arm to protect her as she lurched to her feet. Her one good eye bored into him. "I'm sorry—I was sharp with you—at first," she said. "I thought you were...well, never mind."

"No," Brando smiled. "I'm as articulate as possible."

"You—born—that way?"

"No. In my youth I was a wonder of communication. Until one time I was playing in the woods and I encountered a force greater than myself. There was a blinding flash of light and an enormous voice told me *Now you're really screwed up, boy!*"

"Vietnam?"

"Aye, madam, m'lady. The very same."

She gave him a brief nod and smiled back, the one half of her face working while the opposite side remained silent as a wooden board. He'd be willing to lay down wages that if they had the time and she the will, he could get that side of her face working again. The human body has

111

enormous unknown potential to regenerate itself. *It's sad*, he thought, *how little homo sapiens does, each for another.*

"Don't get on feelin'—sorry f'yourself," she said, misreading Brando's mood. "None of us— ain't exactly—what we was. I'll leave you—to your—business." And with that, she bobbled out the door like an apple running downstream in a brook.

Brando's ear caught the sound of her step-drag, step-drag, step-drag on the polished asphalt tiles as she worked her way down the long deserted hall. He hoped a kindly someone would push him in front of the MetroLink if he ever deteriorated to that state. He wondered if he could gather courage like the Opey-Dopey Man, Joey Collato, and pull his own trigger. He listened as the uneven rhythm of her step faded, expecting the next sounds would be the metallic click as she opened the big steel door, the lighter rush of outside air and then the sigh of the pneumatic pull as it closed the door behind her, and one final click as the latch caught.

But he knew as clearly as if he was The Shadow, or a mouse in her apron pocket, that she had stopped shy of the outer door. And then there was a clacking as she endeavored to insert a key, and then the metal whispery sound of the key turning followed by the brush of the bottom of the inner door opening, a door without an auto-flex that had to be pulled closed by hand.

Brando took a quick peek out in the hallway, but she was no longer in sight. He shrugged. *No big wonder, here.* The old mopsqueezer probably had some other little chore to perform before she lurched back to her normal playpen.

He stopped what he called ear-fishing and began his long chore of scanning the play-by-plays of over 200 games—every NFL game Ripper ever played in—and then out of the corner of his eye he saw a single tiny LED wink on every phone in the room. *Ho-HO!*, the inquisitive Jack Sprat in him cried, leaping over the candle stick of his observation; the press phones were all wired so that any worker-bee could pick up any other bee's phone, a necessity with wordsmiths coming and going, editors needing to know where their hired guns were, and the deadlines looming like executions. Yet, suppose that the phones here were wired to others elsewhere in the building? And further, wired to the one that Gladys was clutching at this moment to wheeze out an important message to someone? *Could it be a message concerning himself?*

Brando swiveled his chair around, delicately pressed the glowing button and eased the nearest phone off the hook, trying to make like Robert Redford in All The President's Men rather than Harpo Marx in Duck Soup.

He was rewarded to hear the old woman was wheezing on the line, waiting for someone to pick up the hook on the distant end. After ten breathy seconds, a deep and growly voice boomed.

"Yes. What is it?"

"He's—looking   at—the   play-by-plays," Gladys wheezed.

"What the devil for?!"

"What's—to   worry?   A   needle   in—a haystack."

113

"You're not paid to think, Gladys. Get him out of there."

"But Richie—already gave—his okay."

"I'll handle Richie. Have the stupid idiot call me. No—I'll call him!"

Bully-boy slammed down his end, and then Gladys was on the run again. In the back of Brando's consciousness, he followed her progress as she shuffle-stepped and slip-slid her way out of the building, and he knew he should get busy with the play-by-plays, but he sat there, cogitating what this might mean.

He frowned at the phone, unwilling to hang it up. Maybe he had learned as much as he was going to. He hesitated because, although the gruff dodger on the other end had slammed off, there was none of the usual plaintive disconnect beeps, just a vast and waiting silence.

Brando held his breath. He felt tweeked and spy-spooky, twitchy as a refugee from a Len Deighton thriller. Finally, he heard a click on the far end.

"Santa Barbara Tranquility Hotel & Health Resort", an efficient dodsey's voice said in his ear. "How may I connect you?"

"I was disengaged." He managed to mutter.

"To whom were you talking, sir?"

"Ahh—I—cognize not. They called me."

"We would have no way of knowing, sir." She sounded peeved.

He mumbled an apology and set down the phone.

He figured he would have to move quickly. He guestimated the window remaining to his research would be narrow; he had perhaps a few minutes before Bully-Boy squashed some big corporate tomato that would in turn roll downhill to put the kabash on Archie Richie. Even with the expensive high-speed Xerox copying machine resting in the corner of the room, a full scan would be out of the question. He would never be able to replicate all the play-by-plays before the goons came to take him away. *A needle in a haystack*, Gladys had said. But she didn't realize Brando had a metal detector named Charlie Manganetti. *Where had good old Charlie pointed him? The championship that never was.* Brando went about his business

All too soon, he heard the distant door at the far end of the building bang open and the footsteps of two people running down the hall. The sound told him there was a big heavy buffalo and a smaller, panting rascal with slippery shoes who wasn't much into jogging. In another moment the rascal himself swung around the corner. It was Archie Richie, breathless from his off-season of rubber-chicken and dry hotel cake desserts, followed closely by 280 pounds of muscular youth. But by that time Brando had his role figured out; his feet were up on the desk and he was ignoring the stacked-up play-by-plays like a lazy laggard who was putting off carrying out the garbage. A blank yellow note pad lay on his stomach, and he was looking off into space while he pretended to chew on the butt end of his pen.

Archie screeched to a halt, taking in the scene and deciding things maybe weren't as desperate as he'd thought. Brando saw an expression of relief settle on him like fleas hopping on an oily little dog.

"I'm sorry," Archie said, "we've made a terrible mistake."

"What?" Brando boosted back his army soft cap with one finger, "I wore . . .the wrong hat?"

"No," Archie gave him a little strained chuckle. "Hell, I'll give you a Rams cap!"

"What then?" Brando asked.

"I'm terribly sorry, but I just got a call from top management. Apparently somebody turned you in, and, you know, once the bureaucracy gets wind of something like this—well, I thought I could slip you in as a favor to the old Ripper, but these files are officially closed to anyone who doesn't have press credentials."

Brando figured he would be more believable if he protested a little. "I have a director's card issued by the Director's Guild of America," he said. "And I swill grog and dissemble with the best writers in the valley."

Archie gave him another high, nervous whinny, indicating Brando was joking and he only approved of the jocularity to be polite.

"And an Honorable Mention for a story I sent to the Hemingway Short Story contest," Brando added. "Not the humorful Harry's Bar & Grill contest where they make a mockery of Ernie's style. The *vrai essence* in Key West."

That took Archie back a little. "Well, yes, that's very nice, but after all, we—," he said, the we indicating the nervous young hamburger standing in the doorway, "—we can't let just let people into our files every time some old has-been player wants to have his life's story re-told."

116

Brando realized with a note of pride that Archie had seen sufficient to bring his back-up. An intelligent fellow, to recognize he was dealing with Ear Man and The Hands of Death.

Brando attempted nonchalance. He slapped the files with the palm of his hand. He'd taken pains to assure they were in the same order, "Okay-dokey. Want me to replace everything in its proper file?"

"No. Leave it. We have people for that."

"Geez. I didn't even. . .commence." That was an outright lie, and he hoped Archie didn't catch it. Maybe, Brando thought, he hadn't played disappointment broad enough. The big *machers* at the DGA say if you want believable you have to study the method. *Oh, Constantin Stanislavski, where are you when we need you?*

"You wouldn't mind if I—looked through your bag?" Archie asked. It wasn't really a question.

"Realize your dream to fruition." Brando said. He walked over to Richie's muscle-boy backup, looking up at his freckled face and observing the bristle of hay colored hair that stuck out like an electrocuted badger pelt all over the top of his pink head. He tried to imagine what it must be like to hunker down on the line across from a monster like this.

"You're Gordon Creedy, our first round draft pick sensation—The Alabaster Abalone from Alabama," he said. He played it a little fast and easy with 'our'. He calculated it didn't hurt when they thought you were on the team.

The kid hadn't been in the big time long enough to be cool with adulation. His face went

117

red, and he scuffed the floor with one of his big boots. Brando had him in the *aw shucks* mode, but any fool could see they hadn't had enough time to really bond; Brando knew he'd be better not to make a grab for the coveted play-by-plays and attempt a four hundred yard dash down the hall, across the broad lawn and past the burly front gate guard. They might get him...at least, the Alabaster Abalone might.

Archie was embarrassed enough to pass Brando a look saying none of this was his idea, he just got all the dirty jobs. Brando shrugged while Archie gave his bag a quick shuffle-through to make certain he didn't have any fresh, warm stacks of play-by-plays in there.

The Abalone hulked along at Brando's side as they squeezed their way out the door and ambled along the sidewalk with Archie following along close behind. Brando wondered if whistling a happy tune would thicken his cloak of innocence. He tried a few bars from that old show tune "Put on a Happy Face".

The Abalone rumbled, "Uhhh, Mr. Richie, if you don't need me anymore, I got practice."

"Oh, yes, Creedy, you run along—ahh, we'll talk about those press photos later."

The big bonus baby's wide and freckled face went blank, but before he could say anything Archie slapped his back and gave him a little propelling shove in the direction of the weight room.

While Archie and Brando continued to the parking lot, Archie absently hummed the Phantom's theme from Andy Webber's Phantom of the Opera. Brando took that as fitting reply to his whistling joust. One should never assume that a man who works in sports knows nothing of the arts.

"I've got an idea," Archie said, brightening up and snapping his fingers like Robin in the old Adam West series when he figures how to get Batman out of the cryogenic ice without shattering his physique or setting off the dynamite. "Maybe you could hook up with Sports Illustrated or the L.A. Times Sports section and come back to get the stuff you need."

"Aghhh..." Brando waved his suggestion off with one hand. "Why complicate reality? It's a matter of moonshine, a trifle, a nothing." He hoped to give the impression that the entire project was kaput.

"Well, you seemed like you were awfully interested..."

It wasn't that complex a thought, but Brando struggled to get it out, "Ripper, you see, was awfully intense about me being pro-active in his interest."

"I see," the marketing man said, giving Brando a thoughtful nod. "This your car?"

"Rental. Mine's undergoing modifications.

"Looks like *somebody* doesn't like you."

The scurvy somebody of Archie's reflection had scraped a long wavy line in the paint job on the driver's side from the door to the rear taillight, probably with a set of keys. Brando didn't have to think twice about what dog had wet the fireplug. *May the wiffling cur's boots all go wide of the bar*, he silently cursed. He reflected for a moment. Maybe that wasn't strong enough. *And may his kicking foot rot with ringworm.*

119

That should obtain, Brando decided; after all, it wasn't actually his car. He shrugged, "Hard to keep anything secure from frog-spawn and jelly-boned mongrels these days. Lock your daughters in the attic."

Morrie was going to have a royal conniption when he and Budget Rental finally had their little debate over deterioration; if the tred of life continued on its present track, the little shyster might possibly even work up to his own *gran mal* seizure. Brando felt he certainly wasn't going to plunk down gold for a rented carriage; after all, what is the meaning of insurance in the first place? He levitated his bag over the side and carefully slid into the driver's seat.

He extended Archie his business card, the one that said "We Give Good Concept" along with his phone and P.O. box number at KTGA.

"What's this?" Archie asked.

"So you'll be reminded to express me my *nouveau chapeau.*"

"Oh, yeah," Archie laughed, talking like a carnival barker. "I'll make sure you get the whole new fan-pak; we got yer designer t-shirt, we got yer coffee mug, yer famous Ram-Rams waving towel, plus a magnificent decal for your car. Give us about two weeks."

Brando allowed that would be splendiferous and backed out of his parking spot.

And yet he had not gained his retreat through the gates of hades and back to the world of the living. When he handed the Rams gate guard the pass that had allowed him entry, the surly horned one growled, "What you got in the bag?"

"Same fetchings I possessed upon entrance. You wish to peruse?" Brando asked.

The guard checked what he should do with a look over to Archie, who was still monitoring Brando's departure from the sidewalk, and then shook his head. Brando was waved on through with a final frosty glare, just another unwanted infidel cast out of the holy land.

Brando was impressed at how swiftly they become unfriendly in the pros. He was pleased the guard hadn't accepted his offer to paw through his bag. Of course, the fellow wouldn't have found the incriminating evidence there, either. The two inch thick wad of papers Brando had managed to copy before Archie played his end-game card were stuffed in Brando's underpants, where they were fanned out so the bottoms didn't show and were held in situ against his back by his thin Italian leather belt. With the distracting trapezoidal effect of Brando's expensive silk shirt hanging out over his shorts, he had passed muster and slipped out of the gates of hell with his booty.

The Rams had only been involved in two play-off games that meshed with Charlie's description—the first against the Packers in 1967 and second against the Vikings in 1969. And Brando Mahr, amateur searcher of lost hankey-pankey in need of detection, now possessed the complete play-by-plays for both of them.

CHAPTER 12

So, by now you are saying to yourself, 'What gives this wretched and supposedly mystical translato—who pretends to be channeling in from an attic century long past—what gives him the right to pen a modern murder mystery novel? Well, among other things, I did help invent Scotland Yard. No, not in a story of mine. The actual Yard, the thing itself. So don't be rude. I do know an official bobsnort from an imitative whupnagle, if you catch my scent.

As Brando drove onto the lot at KTGA, Harvey Hedlong, the cheery little sentry encased in the gate-guard box, saluted from his customary station at the entrance to the studio. He grinned his big 100-watt smile when he saw the Corvette.

"I see everybody's making it in Hollywood," Harvey kidded. Harvey longed to play himself in the movies, the jovial, round-faced gate guard, so he spoofed all the producers to show off his twinkling blue eyes, freckled face and big trustworthy smile.

"Oh, yeah," Brando grinned, "Requisition my table at Spagos. But I'm gonna brownbag my own lunch, just for today."

Harvey laughed like he was viewing late night comedy, and waved Brando on into the inner sanctum.

Brando had to creep past the enemy territory surrounding Don Parker's office, in order to pick up his mail. He'd almost slipped by when Don's secretary Shirley sang out in that liquid nitrogen voice of hers, the shrill, high napper that Brando was sure could freeze a grape, "Good Morning, Mr. Mahr!"

Naturally, after that air-raid siren warning, Don, himself, poked his head out of his office door.

"Hi there, Brando—say, you busy today?"

"*Non, mon capitain.* not really." It didn't pay to be busy if Brando wanted his free rent.

"I've got a station promo, big guy..."

"No difficulty, sweetheart-babes-pal."

"Stage 6 in a half-hour?" Don shoved a half-dozen pages in Brando's hands. Brando took a long enough look to see it was crazy blue-screen stuff with people sitting in rocking chairs, sofas and Laz-e-Boys spinning out of control through the interstellar reaches of outer space

"Looks...pleasantly reactionary, Don," Brando said.

"Pleasant, pal? No, no, no—it's super dyno! I paid The Luke Group big bucks for these spots!"

"But...? If you've already shot the wad on Luke, why doesn't the brilliant and capable lady capture the oneness, the essence and the reality, herself?"

"She asked for you, Brando."

"Ever ready," Brando said with a little bow, accepting the inevitable. He was pretending enthusiasm, but the inner Mahr wasn't all that joyful, and he hoped Don couldn't see he was faking it.

Luke requested that Brando direct whenever she'd put too much production value in her creations. The Brass Lady would be all jealousy-dimpled smiles if he somehow managed to make her ideas work—but if the spots took a mundungus dump it would be Brando's nibble on the mousetrap.

He tried to dismiss his misgivings while riffling his mail. There was the usual baker's dozen resumes from young whipsters looking for their first big break, a woeful form rejection letter saying he had to go through an agent before his thriller script ON THE EDGE could be pawed by anybody at Paramount, free passes to the exclusive screening of an explicit gay porno flick, Dueling Stallions, and a thick and promising envelope from Lani Katzin.

He tore open the envelope from Ripper's whither-go-ye. There was a short note scribed in a flowing, romantic hand

Hi Big Time—

Here's the phone numbers I promised.

Am I something else, or what?

XO, Lani

He glanced over Lani's list. His quick peruse showed it contained the name, address and phone number of every great footballer, coach and sportswriter from Ripper's era who was still among the living. He decided with approval that *Lani was something else, all right.*

He still had a few spare moments before he had to show up for the shoot, so he loped over to his office, where he elbowed the big square button on his Phone-Mate answering machine while scanning Lani's list of phone numbers. The Phone-Mate contained the usual smorgasbord of communication for a lightweight Hollywood guy. But there was one bit of good news: Keith Lugosi had enlisted his good little buddy for the Oppie & Ronnie annual albacore trip, Brando's presence being requested on board the Coral Sea leaving next Friday from San Diego's Point Loma at 10 p.m.

The answering machine tape continued; A snide and doubting voice from the Director's Guild wanted to know if Brando had accumulated enough points to join the health plan. There was another beep and Belle Denver came on in her husky Mona The Magnificent mode to relate her latest mad and complicated plan: She was leaving for Savannah for a part as the love interest in a highly low-budget movie about a quasi-maniac savior who was breeding giant pirannas in the dark waters of the Okefenokee to resolve the world's famine problems. Pirannas, the throaty *femme fatal* went on to assure him (as if she could sense his questions about the overall concept), were *actualmont* an enormously rich source of protein and could be the answer to Third World Starvation, but being the nasty creatures pirannas are, things start to get a little out of hand when the radiation treatments make them gain an evil and conspiring intelligence bent on the subjugation of humanity. Belle was having her checks sent to Brando, and would he please deposit them in her checking account. Belle wasn't very good with decimal points and zeros, and so Brando handled her checking account, performing the function of a disaster control.

Belle didn't mention whether or not she would miss him, but at least she'd passed on the news before she left town.

He whacked the HOLD button on the Phone Mate. While listening to Belle, he'd been scanning the lists Lani had sent. He stopped because the telephone number that mopsey old Gladys had dialed from the Rams Camp, the Santa Barbara Tranquility Hotel & Health Resort, was also on Lani's list. It appeared to be the contact number for ex-head coach Nathan Paramis, who had led the Rams for a brief period in the early 1960's. It didn't totally wash—after all, the game about which Charlie had ignited his interest had taken place six or seven seasons later, but *balls-on-fire if this wasn't a clue of the first water!*

"A-hah!", Brando said to himself, feeling extraordinarily sleuth-like. He hit the ADVANCE button to continue his answering machine, and that wiffling cur Morrie's stringy little voice came on to notify him that the mechanics were having problems finding another motor for his damn car. *No way to talk about a lady*, Brando thought. There was a scratchy pause while the tape beeped and ran, and Brando guessed that was it for his messages *pour les moment*. His attention wandered from the Phone Mate, figuring the little reel would meander on a tick or two on its own and then screech into an automatic rewind.

He threw the list of names on the table and started for the door. Don would be less than ecstatic if he was late for his *tres importante* tape session. But instead of the Phone-Mate rewinding, there was one last beep and then an unusually flat monologue wanted to know why he *wasn't sticking to his safe little cartoon world.* That stopped Brando in his tracks. *Whoever this mundungus mutton-head was, he just couldn't stop encouraging him to get on with the Ripper expose!*

Brando ambled over to stage two, directed the couch-potato commercial for Don and was free by two in the afternoon.

For most of the drive up to Santa Barbara he played a favorite tape of old, nearly unintelligible Lightnin' Hopkins blues songs. She' lil'-ol'- blin'- bal'- fat - ugly...but she mine. Brando was in his high spirits mode. The shoot had gone smashingly well after he figured out that they needed to slo-spin the camera to give Luke's coach potatoes a little dynamism. The Brass Lady, Luke herself, declared that was exactly the way she had envisioned it, which was why Brando was her favorite director.

She lil' -ol'- blin'- bal'- fat - ugly, but she mine.

He had to decline an invitation to go out and get buffle-headed and probably rotate a slo-spin of his own while joining giblets at her place; Luke was undergoing a brief period of reflection and solitude in her personal life after grinding up three or four intrepid and ridiculous young climbers who unwisely presumed the way to stardom lay through her bedroom.

Gotta have that wo-man, seem lak all th' time. *That Lightnin'—wasn't he some guy!*

The long, curved driveway extended like a yellow brick road from the 101 off ramp to the Tranquility Hotel and Health Resort, and seemed to carry the mixed message of an overgrown yet meticulously groomed tropical garden, not unlike a fundamentalist vision of the garden of paradise on steroids, wild and rampant lushness, properly pruned. Water rushed down rocky rills and orange-gold mottled fish flashed in pools under exotic foliage.

Brando observed that the resort even had an Eve, sort of. As he slowed enough to shove Morrie's Corvette into park, a leggy gimcrack in the Hooters version of a valet costume paraded out from a structure covered with droopy vines. Complete with a low-slung bow tie, the vision of pulchritude looked not unlike a maroon and gold striped Victorian Playboy bunny without the fuzzy tail. *Divinity*, Brando thought, *appears in all shapes and sizes.*

"Your car has a scratch on it, sir," the gimcrack burbled in a husky whisper. He knew they make them say that so you can't go after them for the insurance, but the way she said it was her own device.

He shrugged and drawled, "Driving too dang proximate to one o'them Lucifer Angels.

He was pleased to see she was a fubsey wench, plump and healthy with a smile like dappled sunlight on a spring meadow, juicy red lips like a field of strawberries on a pleasant June day, lips like those which lit Ishtar's face when first sighting her naked Babalonian youths bathing in the Mesopotamian river...well, maybe not like Ishtar. In fact, on closer inspection he saw it was the smile of Saint Theresa looking down on the terminally ill, or perhaps Scrooge smiling on Bob Cratchit somewhat before the appearance of the three illusionary spirits.

"Hah. You're joking, sir," she said with a firm, accusatory tone.

128

He admitted he was. Time to get down to the cold nut of the matter. "Does Nathan Paramis work here?" he asked.

He exited the car and she moved her handsome buttocks across the seat he'd vacated. He had to admit she radiated a magnificent musk in leather. Actually, he thought, she'd radiate a magnificence in anything. "Nathan Paramis *owns* Tranquility," the not-quite-ready duchess bubbled up at him like a frigid snifter of champagne.

"How wonderful for his ego. Is the oracle in session, today? Actually...*taking appointments?"*

She gave him the glance that went for the low end of cool appraisal and the upper end of scorn. "I don't think he'll see you, sir."

"Still, one...must try." He wondered why, when studly, controlled, martial arts master Quai Chang Kane used that exact same line, it always sounded so full of measured wisdom. And, did David Carradine have the same problems communicating when, say, his pasta wasn't *al dente* to his taste at *La Tristatorre Ristorante*?

"Just ask at the desk, sir." She tossed her tawny mane and drove off through the sunlight with an indulgent wave of digits, probably pretending she was Meg Ryan on her way to see dailies or buy a can of cheap caviar for Trilby, her cat.

At least Brando had no trouble witnessing her master. A heavily browed secretary led him directly into the lair and Nathan Paramis turned out to be a gritty, broad-shouldered little gnome of a rascal with a wide, gap-toothed Ernest Borgnine grin. *Maybe,* Brando mused to himself, *there had been some hanky-panky in the Borgnine family*

129

and this was the gnarly little offspring. Mayhaps, after opening remarks, and getting on with each other, he would quiz Nathan to that effect. And mayhaps not, he decided upon eyeing the man a little closer. No fusty old fogram, Nathan had a grip like iron, a fierce-eyed stare, a short-spiked Prince John beard and sprigs of iron-grey curly hair spaced on both sides of the shiny bald spot where once a crew-cut had thrived.

"Come on in!", Nathan boomed as he held onto Brando's hand and dragged him into his cave-like den, which was lined with old black and white photos of his glory days, and the mandatory limp and dusty old game balls magic-markered with dates and unreadable signatures. There was a photo of Nathan in flyer's gear, loitering about with the rest of the lusty young knights in front of a B-29 with a nearly naked lady and lots of lined-up bombs painted in red on the fuselage; Nathan and a maturing gaggle of military knaves standing in front of a Super-Connie with a huge radar dome on top, and Nathan and crew next to a 707 with the same configuration. In this last photo, Brando felt the old bonker bore a striking resemblance to a caricature of an ageing AirBoy, the great cartoon hero maybe squashed a little flat from falling on his head in one of his exploits, but Brando noticed with disappointment that Birdie, the rocket-like sidekick with the flapping wings wasn't in any of the pictures.

"A considerable clutch of...pilot portraits," he said.

"Reserves," Nathan grinned. "A bunch of us like to keep our hand in." He was cheery as a spring goat, but Brando recognized his voice as the same bullyboy that had clammered and cudgeled Gladys over the phone. *You can't fool Ear Man*.

Nathan plopped himself down in the worn black leather of a genuine Eames chair, like he was a young athlete. He kicked his feet over the matching foot stool. He must have been close to seventy if the record books had the right knock on him, but his bulging biceps hinted he still might lift a ton. Brando had scoped him out in one of those Ram alumnus publications he found in the Sports Book Store over on Beverly Boulevard near Cedars Sinai Hospital.

Nathan had finished his college career at Oregon State in time to be a navigator on a superfortress during World War II, then played tackle for the Chicago Bears and Green Bay Packers before finishing up his career with the Rams in Los Angeles. He'd kicked multitudinous butt, a quality approved by management, and upon hanging up his testical-protector, the Rams had retained him as a defensive coach. He coached the defensive line for a few seasons until one incredible morning in September when the head coach went south and Nathan hopped into the limelight. His glory days had been the brief flash of one of those old photographer's bulbs, lasting for a mere eight games—all of which the Rams lost—and then the owner fired him in a new spasm of the same old agony (that is, losing) that had propelled Nathan from the ranks of the relative unknowns in the first place.

"But you don't want to hear my old war stories," the coach chortled, not really believing it. "What can I do for you, my friend?"

131

"Well, I'm proceeding with 'The Life of Ripper Brown'... Who knows, maybe a TV mini-series."

"Ohhhhhh. . ." Nathan's brows knitted and he gave Brando a shrewd gaze. "And you knew I was the coach who discovered Ripper, and thought you'd talk to me first."

"Ho la—non, mon Pere. Actuelmont, Je'n'sai pas that Archie Richie suggested—" Sometimes Brando's defective speech patterns could be a blessing in disguise. Who knows what was about to blather? He himself certainly didn't; he was pianoing it by ear. But guilt can't tolerate a vacuum, and Paramis hopped right in.

"Richie what?!" His grundy, bullyboy voice cracked at Brando like a whip. Brando knew he'd struck a vein of something; he was suddenly on full alert, or at least as close as he could ever get to any sort of mental push-ups.

Brando shaped his response carefully, "Archie Richie couldn't comprehend what manifestation of reality you boys are so—I believe he said antsy—about." That was a lie, if not a complete lie, at least somewhat of a partial manufacture.

Nathan interrupted a half-dozen times before Brando finally achieved full sentence. He struggled to control his surprise and rage. To Brando it looked like the old coach had to hold himself back from running over to the telephone, and to be content with jumping up, stuffing his hands in his pants pockets and pacing to and fro in the room like little Huck trying to forget he really has to take a whiz.

Finally Nathan shook his head angrily and said, "Archie Richie is a fool."

Brando raised his eyebrows like an Elizabethan fop, "Which-haps in what measure or regard?"

"Digging all this old stuff up is bad for football."

"Tay sao?" Nathan probably didn't know the Vietnamese expression for *why?*, or maybe he did, for he plunged straight ahead.

"Even the hint, the stain of impropriety—right or wrong—cannot be tolerated."

"Better to intomb Caesar Augustus if we cannot obfusticate him?" It didn't seem to matter what nonsense Brando blathered out, old Nathan was on a roll.

"Pah!" The old man made a gesture with his thick arms, throwing them in the air and letting them drop. It was clear Brando and other like-thinking radicals were the world's biggest fools.

"You're not really going to continue this project?" he quizzed.

"Well, I'd like to investigate every gilded moment of the Ripster's golden days in great detail...particularly that one, lone, unique and controversial game."

There must be something about guilt and gravity, because the old coach fell for Brando's ploy like a ton of mundungus merde, "Bullroars! Nobody's going to buy a story about a football game that took place 15 seasons ago."

Brando made a mental calibration, stacking football seasons next to cycles of the solar system. Fifteen seasons in the ago was 1969. Assuming the coach did not converse rhetorically, that was somewhat of a bingo.

He graced Nathan with the effect of his lop-sided smile, which now passed for Hollywood sleaze, "Ahh, sir, but I'm on to an amazing reality...a special edition of old bones and bad deeds, my money-boys say I'm going to be the Robin Leech of football."

"Tell me a little more about it...maybe I can help."

"I—" Brando started as if he was going tell him all, and then held up. "Shame on you! Every entrepreneur in Southern California's a producer!"

"What, like I'm going to steal your big idea?"

Brando gave him a serious nod. "Mayhaps I can reveal some few festerings, after I have it cinctured at the Writer's Guild."

"Have it what?"

"Legalized. Formatted. Established." Brando could think of everything but the word *registered*.

Nathan sighed, shaking his head.

"I think you're doomed to failure from the start," he said. "You'll never do anything with a loser like Ripper Brown."

"The Ripster is an invalid object?"

"A sore loser, is what he is. Ripper's a bitter man. He was a great player; he should just leave it at that."

"Bitter? About which parameters, Paramis?" Brando couldn't resist a little word-play, but if the coach got the bad pun, he didn't say anything.

"He blames people a lot. He never won a championship, you know. In this game, if you don't win the Super Bowl, you're not really all that great—at least that's the way a lot of people think. Ripper can't stand that. He always has to be the greatest of the great, but without that SuperBowl ring on his pinkie, he's just another dinged-up lineman who took a few too many shots to the head."

"Who precisely lacks affection for his greatness?"

"Try the entire Rams organization for starters!"

"I can't properly evaluate your gentlemanly but confusing declarations. Why, Archie Ritchie, himself said—"

"Yeah?", Nathan interrupted Brando. "What'd Archie Richie do for you?"

Brando shrugged. "Archie Richie has an immense affection for Ripper, and through the great one, for myself, additionally, too, also."

"Oh, sure, he'd say that—but what did he do for you?"

"He passed across to me entirely every bit and instance of historical evidence I beseeched of him."

"For God's sake, do I have to pull it out of you with a tooth-extractor? WHAT EXACTLY did Archie Richie give you?"

Once in a great while, an entire thought came rippling unpredictably out of Brando like clear water down a fresh mountain stream. And so it happened at this moment:

"The complete play-by-plays," he said, "for the Rams versus the Vikings play-off game in 1969. That's what."

Nathan's face went whiter than if he'd seen the departed spirit of Vince Lombardi reflected in his Perrier, the wavery image of the legendary Packer coach wagging one finger to remind him victory was the only thing. "W-what did you want with those?" he asked. Brando was gratified to see it was someone else's turn to stutter, for a change.

"I suspect you are aware," he said. And he walked out before the coach could deny it.

Outside the hotel, the same proud minx returned his Corvette from the cool subterranean parking grotto. He noticed her tight vest was designed with that push-up effect that gave an added allure to the exposed top four-ninths—or even five-elevenths—of her breasts, raising the normal questions and alarms that one enlightened by the new realities might have, what with the depleted ozone layer, pollutants in the air and lung cancer on the rise among the entire termagant (that is, female) population.

"Does that tan go the entire way to Mandalay?" he asked, gesturing discretely with his fingers.

"What?!" His vain and capricious gilflurt replied in a frightening stentorian tone, like one of those *haut-noveau* commercials for the right deodorant where they insert a gruff lumberjack's voice in a lady's flapper. There, directly before Brando's eyes, his fairy nymphette transmorphed into a spiteful hellcat. He reflected on what a confusing age it was. *Perhaps*, he thought, *she was embarrassed with the weight of her own sexuality, her own unabashed, musky and uncontrollable response to his rakish persona. That's the problem with the boring New Victorians*, he mused, *they are so entirely*

resemblesome of the boring Old Victorians.
Maybe in another few manifestations girls like her
might revert to high lace collars, frumpy grandma
middles and ankle skirts, and then they'd be able
to replace problems like these with a whole new
set. Finger-licking would make a grand return,
and wiffling quasi-perverts would whimper and
slather over bare calves and wrists. *On the other
tit*, he reflected, *he could possibly have
misunderstood her reaction.*

"Never mind," he muttered. "Here's a
Washington."

She took the lone one dollar bill, crumpled it
and threw it at him. It bounced off his lap and
onto the floor between his legs. He shrugged,
thinking she probably wished he'd tipped her a
heavy, jagged-edged ceramic brick.

"You know where you can stuff it, asshole!"
she yelled.

The lopsided grin twitched across his face,
"Don't be so maggotty. I'm not a swindler, a
sharper or a cheat. Give prurient misbehavior half
a chance, my dimber mort, we might even get it
on."

A muscular busboy with the name Reggie
tattooed to his shirt came bounding over.

"This guy bothering you?", he said, spitting
the words like he might not possess a fully formed
larynx.

Brando leaned back to talk past his hulking
shoulders. "You should get to know me, duchess.
I'm no ordinary lubber or awkward gollumpus,
like Reggie here."

137

"I'll scream! I'll cry rape!" She was venturing into hyper-space. Brando reflected that some gills did that in his presence.

Reggie leaned over to grab Brando with what our hero knew to be a pitiful, phlegmatic move, and from his seated position Brando was able to three-finger him hard just below the ribs. Reggie staggered back to sit on his buttocks, doubled over and gasping for breath.

"Don't persist," Brando warned, "or I'll lump you extensively." The minx went wide-eyed and open-mouthed, not her best pose. It was a depressing scene. Brando tossed her a Handi-wipe singles, "Napkin the spittle from your mouth, foolish, glimflashy wench."

With that he drove off, fully aware that it was another sad case of miscommunication on the part of Ear Man and The Hands of Death. *Oh Cupid, Lord of Hearts, where are you when we mortal louts have need of you?*

Once he wheeled away from the Tranquility, his good spirits bobbed back to the surface and he sang along with Lightnin' all the way back to L.A. There's nothing that brightens a Hollywood story developer's spirits like narrowing the search. Brando still didn't have an exact pinpoint concept of what his story was, but he was getting closer. Some thing, perhaps even a perfidious ball-scam, had happened in a professional football game that was performed way back on Saturday, December 27, 1969. *Ahh, a tick in time that lives in infamy!* Whatever it was that had tumbled down upon that event, Brando was of the reflection it was a dark and lurking happenstance, something important enough that a lot of *cognoscenti* didn't want to review the salient details. And he, Brando-on-the-Trail, was going to find out what it was.

CHAPTER 13

Oh, happy days! Brando thought as he ambulated diagonally across the broad, dusty lawns of the University of California in Northridge (CSUN), the campus being so large that a clever and industrious walker could save real time by avoiding the sidewalks. The incredible, sunny aqua sky was whacking him in the eyes and he could imagine the lanky curved thighs and shapely breasts of the collegiate wenches were throwing themselves in front of his leering gaze practically anywhere he looked. He could not but accept that there was a merciful *Deus Maximus* in rewardsville, and that He—that lordly Guy-In-The-Sky—was beaming goodness down on his servant Brando who had been placed upon the savage earth to develop salable television and motion picture productions, claw his way to the top, become incredibly rich with a pad by the surf in Malibu like the Ripper (and a peaceful cabin in the High Sierras), and, with all this in his pockets, *terra firma* would be a better place.

Brando parked Morrie's scratched maroon Corvette on Zelzah Street under the thick shade of a string of gum-dripping Mulberry trees that were in the throes of some unknown and sloppy vegetational impregnation cycle, and he scooted his way across the campus to the house-o-books. He'd circumnavigated the exact same trek many times before when he was researching the documentary on women pioneers, The Ladies

Who Won the West, that he had created with his pals, the ninja nuns.

The library was a gigantic, four-storied Sumarian granary of knowledge designed after a latter-day interpretation of an ancient Persian ruin, but inside the computer retrieval program hummed, the Dewey decimal system kept things in order and the young kids walked around, taking it all for granted.

Brando ambled in past the turnstiles, whiffing a few unintelligible grunts in typical professorly fashion to the kid behind the desk. The youngster said, "Have a nice day, sir," his quavering voice full of hope for a B+ on that agronomy quiz.

CSUN was a community-oriented college; at the library they allowed any buffle-headed ding-boy or drunken hector to enter without an I.D., so long as one hide the bottle of Ripple and wiped the grit off the back of one's pants.

The microfilm was downstairs near the little booths with the Dukane projectors and the spinning slot-shelves that looked like L'eggs pantyhose dispensers but in reality contained the newspaper record of most every wretched deed that had been conducted over the last half century. Brando snatched a single reel from the rotating shelves—L.A. Times, Dec 23-28, 1969—and headed for the machines.

The place wasn't very busy. There were a few grad students and the usual serious grungy grinds wearing down their writing fingers. Brando flopped down in the nearest booth on one of the empty aisles and surreptitiously nudged the entire heavy projector about a foot to the right with his elbow. Being left-handed, with this new

141

configuration he could put his note pad on the left and it worked more conveniently. The traitorous projector made a rubber-squeal noise and he was seriously frowned by a little Indonesian guy safely tucked behind the counter where they ran the show. Brando gave him the glimp eye and the little fellow turned back to the more serious manifestations of his job. *Ear Man and The Hands of Death knew intimidation.*

He threaded the film and rocked-and-rolled madcap and thunderously back through history to the sports page for December 27, and there it was, the headline that banged out, RAMS LET BIG ONE GET AWAY.

Brando saw right away that it was not your typical gridiron contest. The Rams were winning big all the way until the fourth quarter. But as the game wearied into the second half, questionable moments started to materialize on the field of play.

To quote sportswriter Bob Oates's professional evaluation, "This was a game in which some of the big plays in the third and fourth quarters were made by the officials. The penalties could have been well deserved (in which case the Rams fouled themselves out of the championship) or they could have been marginal (in which case the officials took the game out of the hands of the athletes). In either event, the official's interpretation of the rules on all four plays all went against the Rams in the second half."

"Interesting," Brando whispered to himself. *"Tres interesant.."* And now, he thought, if only one Brando Mahr, film guy and investigator

142

extraordinaire could ascertain the significance thereof.

Brando yanked the reel off the Dukane and tiptoed to the rear of the viewing room where he re-slotted it on a different sort of projector that took xerox copies. He copied all the reports and the howling commentaries on the game, which had dead-ended the Rams championship drive for that year, then returned the box back to its proper slot on the shelf. Usually, he would dump the box in the return bin, but by now he was feeling a little paranoid, and so erased his footsteps like Jimmy Chee in a Tony Hillerman novel, walking backward as he dusted away his bootprints with a sprig of spruce.

And when he returned to his booth, there was a fubsey mouse-hair (that is, a warm and sweet brunette) sitting in the booth next to his. *Poor backward dodsey* (that is, girl), Brando thought, seeing she was struggling with the Dukane, trying to load it upside down. *Ahh, Goddess of Love, thank thee for thy blessings, and I will never, never curse thy name again!* He vowed.

"Ahh, may I be the arrow of servitude to the target of your need, miss?" he said.

"This damn thing", she muttered, nearly ripping the film in the process.

"No, here; allow me, *s'il tu plait.*" He manfully took charge, threading the 35mm in the appropriate fashion, and the damsel turned her grateful gaze on him.

"Thank you, Professor. . ."

"Brando...Brando-son Mahr."

"Mindy Carlson." She gave him her hand, and it felt like a handful of milk duds, warm and pliable, in his eager grasp.

He stared deep into her lovely gaze, the old romantics' darts of love ploy, and whispered, "Are you flaunting one of those stage names?"

"Why do you ask?" When the wench laughed, Brando felt the room ignited as if some presence—probably Venus—had brought out candles and Gallo Blush Pink Chablis. The spruce and sprightly wench disported what the DMV categorized as hazel eyes (she had light brown eyes), and soft brown curls highlighted mayhaps from the celestial orb (that is, from sunlight), and the healthy, fubsey body of a cheerleader.

He gave her a wink and his little salute, and went back to his Xerox pages. After all, it takes more than a pleasant little baguette to distract Brando Mahr, award-winning film guy.

Apparently, the four key plays that had piled up against the Rams were: clipping against Bob Brown, pass interference against Jimmy Nettles, piling on by Ram linebacker Jack Pardee, and a Viking safety which was called when Carl Eller either tackled Rams quarterback Roman Gabriel in the end zone or pushed him in from the one yard line. The Rams had been in front the entire game. They were still on top 17-4 in the 4th quarter, and they had 3rd and six on the Minnesota 20 when the game got away from them. Brando thought this was very strange. He was suddenly feeling the need to establish a telephonic link with his crook-buddy Charlie

Manganetti and analyze the shape of the beast (that is, to talk about the game).

And that was when the new lollipop next door sighed and slammed her pencil down against the blank pad in front of her. She'd been aimlessly wandering through July 27, 1976.

"I can't make anything out of this," she sighed.

"I'm not amazed," Brando said. "1976 was somewhat a vinegar year. Flat, hardly full-bodied, and it hasn't aged well."

She gazed at him and her wide eyes were limpid pools of innocence, "You have trouble speaking, don't you?"

"Something bad encountered me...in the war." He'd been waiting since high school English and his third reading of The Sun Also Rises to say something like that to a beautiful, ready duchess (that is, a sexy and willing girl). It felt about the way he thought it might. The gentle haze of a Zeeman began to halo her in a rainbow of light and Brando barely managed to swing an open-handed, stiff *dao* to the right side of his head in time to catch remission. The pain flared across his skull and the vague beginnings of the barnyard sensations faded almost before they began.

"It's nothing," he smiled, trying to be casual as he shook the spots out of his eyes. "I hate mosquitoes."

Her mouth formed a perfectly empathetic "O". She stood, apparently forgetting all about 1976 in the rush of her own sensuality that, Brando had convinced himself, contact with a fellow like himself was nearly certain to evoke.

145

"You've got to replace what you've borrowed," he whispered, pointing to the film on her machine.

"You're kidding," she whispered back in her best conspiratorial tone.

"X-Y co-ordinates on that terrifying-looking oriental gentleman."

She nodded, gazing in the direction he pointed.

"He holds the power," Brando added.

"Ohhhh," she said.

By now he'd finished rewinding her film and placed it in the box. "Come, let us flex our appendages," he suggested. "We can procure carbonated refreshment at the student relaxation complex."

They walked across the grass to the Student Co-op. After a while Mindy asked what he was working on.

"Old sports realities."

"Finding anything interesting?"

"*Oui...et non*. I'm zooming in my focus, but I don't actually comprehend what I'm seeing."

"Gracious, it sounds like a big secret! Anything you can specifically talk about?"

Brando recognized that some dialogue clown or rogue might gainfully work over her lines. He hadn't heard any living person use the word gracious since his great Aunt Rose peeked in the bathroom and saw what a big boy he'd become. He might not be able to employ current verbiage, but he comprehended hucksterism when in contact (knew a phony when he met one).

"A story idea for a cinema epic," he replied.

146

"Ohhh," the gimcrack emoted yet again. *The fubsey wench certainly had that oval-lipped move down right*, Brando thought. Every time she rounded her orifice his temperature bumped up a degree or two. But this time he thought he detected a genuine flicker of interest behind her hazel eyes.

"Yea, verily", he said. "That is my reality. Auteur, filmmaker, ageing boy-genius wonder."

She gave him her best smile, the genuine 100 watt-er. *She really was an article of work*, he said to himself.

"What a small world! I'm an actress, myself."

"By the great-sword Glaymore! What distinctions have you accomplished?" he asked.

"Well, not so much. I'm in drama here at school. I played the lead in My Fair Lady. And I had bit parts in two Roger Corman pictures."

He don't know why, but he caught the vibration she was reading off of cue cards. He realized that didn't say much for his own unpredictability.

"Speaking positions?" he asked.

She scuffed one of her small white tennis shoes on the grass, "Well, in one I screamed before they cut my head off. In the other I said, 'Where shall I put the tray, Mr. Johnson'?"

He stopped, like he'd suddenly had a brainstorm. "You know what?"

She paused, uncertain, not knowing where Brando's struggling conversation was going to take them next. Brando couldn't blame her. As a general rule, neither did he. But she certainly was a gorgeous inspiration standing there with her

147

mouth open in that stunned-beauty pose of hers and the afternoon sun shining halfway through her fitted t-shirt and cling-tight short shorts.

"What?" she asked.

"I'll wager I could procure a commercial for you!" Brando said.

"You could get me a gig?" She stared at him, only half-believing her luck. Not that it was bad fortune, quite the contrary—but Brando, who strongly suspected her motives, figured this wasn't exactly what she'd signed on for.

"Yes...but..." Brando put his finger to his lips, "You'd have to promise not to reveal."

"Not a soul," she nodded uncertainly.

"You see, normally, you'd have to submit to the cow fetch..."

"You mean cattle call."

"Yes. But I'm *le directeur*. And I desire you!"

"I wouldn't tell anyone," she repeated solemnly, this time nodding so Brando would realize how absolutely she had climbed on board his train.

All-in-all, it was not a bad idea. Busy, brassy Luke had already sold Don Parker a whole new set of promos. Brando could see Mindy's healthy thighs in a pair of fresh-pressed tropical shorts, just the hoots of her ample hootinannies peeking from her bush jacket as she swung home from her jungle office on the vine commute, pausing to smash a pesky gorilla in the face with her brief case and shake a boa constrictor from her soft Italian leather-booted foot, at last to sit happily in her tree house condo on her twig couch, sipping a coconut cocktail and enriching her life by watching her television set tuned to KTGA.

It looked to him to be a win-win situation. Mindy would achieve her first commercial, and mayhaps Brando, mutton monger (that is, sex fiend) that he was, would achieve Mindy. Funny, he reflected, to think what bile the evil Nathan Paramis might spew if he suspected Brando planned to join giblets with his fubsy little cheerleader. On the other hand, it was the coach's own fault for selecting bait that was just too good to be ignored. And for Brando's part, he was only following one of the deepest wisdoms imbedded in the ancient culture of his old teachers, the Vietnamese—*Whenever possible, corrupt the enemy.*

CHAPTER 14

Brando sat in his office, feet on his desk next to the fading Ektachrome record of his less-than-joyous experience in Vietnamese fidelity while his crook-pal Charlie Manganetti's heavy New Jersey dockworker's accent rolled inexorably at him over the speaker-phone. Charlie was sounding amused and full of life, "So, *Kha*—you tracked the dirty business to its lair, you Sherlock Holmes, you!"

"Well, I've reconstructed that it's the 1969 playoff game, Rams against the Vikings, that still has the capability to make certain old soldiers of the gridiron nervous," Brando agreed. "I just cannot cultivate any weeds of motivation."

Mindy perked up, listening to his call. She sat primly on the rump-sprung love couch in his office, across the room from him, still wearing her Jungle Jill outfit. The promo shoot had been a smashing success. Ham-handed Luke, who was making jaw fat like Mindy was her own special new discovery, wanted to use her for yet another spot. This new one featured a heavily robed and veiled Moroccan woman who tosses aside the water jug on her head, gradually disrobes as she enters her Moorish home and finally does an erotic dance of the seven veils, wildly flinging off her garments to stand in her bikini sipping a tall Marguerita and enriching her life in front of her television *machina* which is tuned to KTGA.

"You look at the films yet?" Charlie was talking from San Jose, but with his good-humored *persona*, it was as if he was with them in the room.

"Well, no. I was ejaculated from the Rams headquarters," Brando said.

"Yeah, you told me. Who else did you try?"

"The Vikings sniffed wind I was a trouble-maker, so we acquire no friendly hand there."

"What about the NFL?" Charlie asked.

"The varlet gatekeeper at NFL Films boldly spread the inaccuracy that their footage from that game was mysteriously on leave from their vaults."

"There's a way. There's always a way, Kha..." Charlie said. There was a pause on the other end of the line. "I got it! Harold Dunstain! He was the head coach in those years! The guy kept meticulous records. He's sure to have a tape or maybe an old 16 millimeter of that game!"

"Harold Dunstain lies quietly under a tombstone, genius," Brando reminded him.

"I know that, *Kha*. But remember, he went back to coach some college down there, year or two before he died. Long Beach State! I read somewhere they got his football memorabilia, they're gonna build a wing or something in his honor."

"What allows the assumption Long Beach is going to shower me any more respect than the others?"

"I know a guy. . ." He mulled a tick. "Let me work on it."

Brando was starting to feel like Charlie knew more than he was saying "Charlie—do you possess advanced criteria?" he asked.

"What do you mean, *Kha*?"

151

"You have me assuming the *Meleagris gallopava* position, pecking at a trail of maize kernels."

"A melea-what?"

"Wild turkey."

"You don't trust me, *Kha*?" Charlie asked.

"With my very existence, *compadre*. It is simply that I am presently experiencing a desire to cognize what flavor jellybeans are in the can."

"Ahhhh, hey, I got that one. Tell you what; I'll call you right back. Don't go away." Brando caught a definite whiff in Charlie's tone that he suspected his phone was bugged. *Charlie was like that.* He was, after all, a dimber-damber man who was well-wired to a handful of noted scamsters, as well.

Brando punched off on his end and shrugged at Mindy, "Old war buddy."

"Ohhhhh......," she said in that leading way of hers, but Brando wasn't upchucking any more in her direction. They jawed over her look for the upcoming "Casbah" spot for a moment or two, and then his phone rang again. This time he kept it off the voice-box.

"Hi, *Kha*," the voice in the receiver said over a rush of traffic wallah. "I think we can talk now."

"*Excellente, amigo*," Brando replied

"Listen, here's the deal," Charlie said, "at least, the way I see it. Some very important people that I heard the names of here and there happened to get burned bad on that game. In 1969, the Rams were the best team in the league. They were scheduled to go to the SuperBowl, and, who knows, they could have taken all the marbles."

"So you'd be in ecstasy if I exhumed old bones?" Brando asked.

"Well, it ain't that simple, *Kha*. See, nobody got to the root of it the first time, and that was right after it happened. And believe me, a lot of very smart and not particularly nice people was lookin' real close."

"Et?"

"And they couldn't find nothing," Charlie said.

"Et, et?"

"Et tu, Brando Brute." And so now you coincidentally come ambling along, years later, and maybe there's no good in stirrin' up an old mess, not if it don't lead nowheres."

"So you do not wish me to tread the present path."

"Naa, that's not it at all, you *stugatz*. No offense, huh? The thing is, you just got to tread *careful*." The concern in Charlie's voice was obvious.

"I regale that reality on automatic. By the thundering great-sword Glaymore, I'm the gibbering schmoo with his gigg in the *scheiss*!"

"His what, Kha?" Charlie asked.

"Nozzle in the *merde*."

"One more time, Kha," he said patiently.

"Schnoz in the shit."

"Oh." Charlie paused, thinking about it for a moment. "Look—you go forward. Just stay in touch."

"Gratzi, comarade. Anything else?"

"Just remember, the NFL doesn't want any bad publicity. And the people I know certainly don't want it."

153

"That remainders the cod-suckers attempting the kabash," Brando said.

"Exactly. See, they don't want it neither."

Charlie laughed his soft, amused chuckle. "Nothin' you can't handle, *Kha*," he said, and then Brando heard the click as he hung up the phone.

CHAPTER 15

Welcome to FOUL, our 200 year old London street penny novel that takes place in 1984. I wanted to call it MUNDUNGUS, which means pretty much the same thing, but your sad fellow with his name under the title argued nobody would know what that means. Outrageous, what happens with language, don't you think? Ever try to read Chaucer in the original? A bit like stumbling through Krautlander or Frog-speak, that. Well, neither here nor there, is it? On with the picaresque!

Brando promised Mindy that, after the shoot, he'd provide a carriage ride back to the Van Nuys ranch style home she rented with three other young gimcracks all itching to break into show business. But that was not to be.

"Change of plans," she said, shaking her lovelies and trying to express pouty and sad. "I promised Don and Luke I'd have a drink at Carlos & Charlies."

"It's okay," Brando replied. "Us rugged indy development types are accustomed to brutish manners from the maniac, lusty sho-biz power brokers and the greedy and weak-minded who easily fall under their spell. You would be included somewhere in that."

He could see she was trying to figure out if he was calling her brutish, maniac or lusty. She hadn't yet gotten to the greedy and weak-minded part. But, bottom-line, he could see it wasn't going to be a memorable night of joining giblets for the old Brando. He shrugged his disappointment into the background, and gave her his sad, lop-sided smile.

"Okay," he said bravely. "Maybe in some other dimension."

He watched the three of them head for Don's big Mercedes 500, which Don garaged at the KTGA studio between the lines in the special spot with his name plate screwed to the stucco. Brando's spot was in the most distant corner of the most distant parking lot. He felt lucky; at least it wasn't off the lot on the street.

He sighed and puffed out a sad breath, looking at the pinkening sky. No Zeeman this, but true dusk. It was beautiful, the way the feathered trails of the cirrus clouds high above were dimming to a pale, delicate rose color around the western-settling sun. It pleased him that the rays slanting low-angle over the horizon were still bapping one last hit of orange against the tips of the mountains to the north. *California sunsets, the only California gold....*

He ambled alone to his distant parking lot, where he saw that adventure awaited him in the form of two rank knaves. The two were wasting ticks while they sat on the hood of Morrie's maroon Corvette, which looked pearly purple-black in the fading light. One of the rogues was a chubby *fidlam ben*, an ordinary thief straight out of a wasted-youth video. Brando saw that by looks and attitude the sad fellow was portraying sort-of a nasty albino Fat Albert, only he was *multus annis* (that is, many years) beyond the gig.

156

He was shagged out in a cheap imitation leather vest over his T-shirt. A plethora of gold chains tumbled around his portly neck and a dented pork-pie hat perched on his tomato-shaped head. His massy bumfiddle was disguised in a pair of outsized bag-pants. On his girth the fat-boy pants assumed a certain propriety, but the vest nettled Brando. As a general rule, he registered low regard for naugahyde. If animal skin was meant to be of plastic, he thought, the Maker would have slapped it on cows on the Sixth Day.

The other demon bully-boy wasn't much prettier. He had shiny black skin, which was pleasant enough, but he was picking a gold cap on one of his front teeth with a long-bladed buck knife, a deadly little degen that was attached to a dull black handle. That handle appeared to be worn from steady employment. *Not a good sign.*

"Hey," the fat white boy with the pork-pie hat grumbled, "you own this car?"

"Do you think to purchase?" Brando asked.

"Naw, I don't think so, damaged like it is," pork-pie's black friend said, dragging his knife across the hood to leave a fiberglass-beige trail in the maroon paint job, "We just like to report it got a scratch in it."

"Ahh, do I know you? Surely, are you not the Gentleman Usher of the Black Rod."

"Huh?" they said practically as one.

Brando felt a familiar warm rush of adrenaline, the old psycho hard-on that propelled survivors like him through the harsher realities. There is a lot of fancy blather about the uniqueness of being male, but, Brando knew if the truth were told, modern man was not much

157

evolved from the monkeys. *Next thing,* he mused, *the three of them would rip their shirts off and beat their hairy chests.* That was, if he didn't fall over in a frothing trance and piss his pants before that..

"You more properly mean it has a recent scratch," Brando lectured. "The car already possessed an earlier scratch."

"Huh?" Both their mouths were still hanging open from his reference to the Black Rod. It wasn't an ethnic joke. The BR is an English official who keeps the peace in the House of Lords. His ebony wand is used to summon the Commons to the Throne. Brando felt a pang of empathy; he couldn't expect these simple ding-boys to know that.

"Hey, come clean. You didn't sneak on the lot, did you?" he asked.

Gold-tooth recovered first. He passed Brando a grin like bad gas, an evil smile that would have made an earthworm squeal in fright. "Naw, we got passes to Kids Are Fun," he said.

"See?!" He dug in one pocket and fanned out a pinochle hand's worth of orange tickets. The Kids Are Fun show was committed to tape before a live audience they admitted and whipped into an enthusiastic frenzy four evenings a week. Brando knew the studio had suffered crowd control problems in the past.

"What do you think," the thug asked, "are we gonna enjoy the show?"

From Brando's point of view, there was no particular reason to worry; the situation was in check-status. The blathery goons were minor-key

158

and no damage. *Fun and games*. It was a relationship where he could deal.

He was about to bounce back some buffle-headed retort when the thug's heads became gently limed in the familiar and unfortunate hallucinogenic glow of one of his Zeemans. Brando felt the hot sunlight, the farm smells and the inviting darkness of the barndoor a few steps away—and just like that his reality went from every-day to critical. It was one of the occasional fast Zeemans that came on before he could violence himself out of it. His feet and arms were frozen in place. He tried desperately to speak while spittle drooled from the right side of his mouth. All he could force out was a single stuttering syllable, "S-S-Scu-"

Chubby and Gold-tooth gawked at him and then stared at each other in wonder. "What'd you do, man, plug him in a 'lectric socket?"

"No, man, he jist went goofy on us."

"Well, don't look a gift horse. Whack him!"

Eyeing Brando carefully, Gold-tooth considered the knife in his hand, weighing the pleasure of a clean thrust through the ribs against the possibilities of murder one. Even the shining blade of the degen, now silvery in Brando's Zeeman-expanded consciousness, had assumed the beautiful necessity of karmic fate. Brando felt himself take a first, faltering step toward the yawing mouth of the barndoor. He smelled the rich scents of the barn, the odors of straw and manure. He had to disconnect, to jump the track, to disengage, and yet he couldn't!

The left side of his face contorted in a violent spasm.

159

"C-c-c--", he sputtered. He jerked the muscles on that side of his face until his consciousness bathed in the pain and the Zeeman seemed to momentarily weaken. Freed for the briefest milli-tick he managed to say "S'cuse me." And then he rammed his head squarely against the fender of a nearby teal green Ford Explorer.

Brando's eyes blinked open. He was lying on his back in the parking lot. He could feel the blood running through his hair. *That was okay-dokay,* he thought to himself, *you can't stroke the monkey if you're to bypass a major Zeeman.*

"Christ, put him out of his misery," the chubby bully-boy said, his voice emanating from somewhere over Brando. "Why do we have to look at this?"

Brando regained his boots. He felt hollow and empty as he staggered up to the vertical. Gold-tooth's laughter was an echo in his ears.

"Hit him, hit him," Gold-tooth urged. "Or le'me stick him."

But there were no longer any fuzzy halos around the perimeters of Brando's vision. Ear Man had returned. Maybe not 100%, but he was back…and, unfortunately for his assailants, he'd brought the Hands of Death with him.

"Ahh, no," Brando said. "It is my pleasure, really. Allow me to anoint you with the oil of gladness."

Gold-tooth wasn't very careful, considering he was in critical proximity to The Hands of Death. He was just sitting there. But who could lay blame in his court, considering the sorry way Brando seemed to be conducting his affairs, the way he'd rammed his own head into the Ford

160

Explorer, and the way he looked now with the small stream of red blood trickling its way down his face and dripping from his chin.

Gold-tooth couldn't have been impressed. One of his legs lay idly within range and Brando snatched it, pulling hard and then lifting it high like a hunting trophy when Gold-tooth started to slide towards him. Gold-tooth's body came easily across the waxed surface of the Corvette, but from the unlucky trajectory it took once they ran out of automobile hood, it seemed probable he was heading for a bad upside down landing.

Gold-tooth did manage to avoid a crushed skull by craning his head sideways, but there wasn't enough clearance and so the twilight dusk rang out with a nasty cracking sound as his head itself met the hard, bumpy surface of the parking lot asphalt. His little degen clattered to the ground. Never one to believe in appearances, Brando dropped Gold-tooth's leg and followed up with the heel of his left shoe, giving the thug a nasty dowse on the chops. Brando was outfitted in the director's boot of distinction, a pair of softly tooled and treasured Swiss Bally's, but they had hard leather heels, and he heard a soft crunch as the unlucky front half of Gold-tooth's teeth went for individual orbits.

With his degen-wielding friend down for the count, the crummy albino ding-boy wasn't inclined to continue the fisticuffs. But it was too late for choices of that sort.

He was overly guts-and-garbage to be conducting whack-jobs in the first place. And worse for him, Brando was cocked and in range. By the time the fat boy scrambled off the

161

Corvette's hood, his neck was completely in synchronization with the knuckle joints of the first three digits of Brando's left hand. The chubby knave fell over backwards with a *gu-gu-gu-gu* sound, clutching at his throat. And then he instantly sat up, round-eyed and frantically kneading his collapsed windpipe. Brando could sympathize; a wicked shot like that can easily fade you to black.

But Fat boy wasn't fated for end-game, at least at that moment. In about 15 seconds the crummy crony had his gullet properly kneaded and was gasping for air through his dented pipes.

After waiting patiently through what he felt was an appropriate interval, Brando began his informal interrogation.

"Who...interested you in me?" he asked with what he hoped was the proper menace in his voice.

"N-nobody," the albino ding-boy rasped.

No more Zeemans lighted the night sky. Brando-man was back. Too bad for Mister No Answers. Brando flat-kicked his chest, spinning him over on his side. In the olden times, Brando was more applauded by the lurps in his unit for his hand-work, hence the comic appellation Hands of Death. But feet were all right, too. *When opportunity ignites itself, one employs the tools at hand.* The poor, fallen ding-boy rolled on his stomach and flashed the hash, vomiting chunks of fast food on the pavement.

"Come now, don't be a screw-jaws," Brando said. "I'm an old canine at this. I asked who employed you!? *S'il vous plait*, don't make me get nasty."

Fat Boy could see Brando was psyching up to hoop his barrel (that is, continue to beat him up).

"No, wait! Wait," he cried out, throwing up his hands in a weak show of defeat. "This ain't worth it. You don't have to kill me. It was a guy, a guy in a bar. I don't know his name."

Brando gestured, indicating he should complete his confession.

"The Cherry Bar," he said. "On Winnetka Street. In the Valley." Brando gestured again. "We was just supposed to scare you, you know, rough you up a little bit. That's all."

"Allow me to quiz further," Brando said. "This darkman, whose name you don't know, daubed you half up front—the bribe?"

"Darkman? He wasn't no black guy," Fat Boy said.

"It means evil," Brando said. "How much?"

"Five hundred dollars."

"Odds Plut and her nails," Brando swore to himself, mildly disgusted at the cheap daub, "a lousy five hundred." Brando surveyed the two sad fellows silently for a moment.

"When do you make the grab on the remaining portion of your fling money?" he asked.

"We were gonna go right back there."

"You cognize that would no longer be intelligent, considering the hubble-bubble and the outcome," Brando said.

"Yeah, we cognize. You want the money?" He held a thin wad of $50 bills toward Brando. He was crying and his hands were shaking.

163

"Niet," Brando said. "You're catching the cheat, as is. A queer game like leg-breaking involves overhead. You should bill accordingly."

Exerting very little extra pressure, Brando made him describe what their gallows bird (that is, accomplice) looked like. And then he drove away, leaving the would-be degen-dipper lying on the asphalt and his perplexed crummy boy resting against the green Ford Explorer in spot number 23.

Brando knew he'd won the opening round. But, upon calmer reflection, he sensed little reason for joy. Next time they wouldn't send two buffle-headed little sheep to muff a job meant for Mothra and Godzilla.

The way Brando visualized his situation, there was only one option allowing him to slide back into the plus column. He would have to take the commotion to them, whoever they were. He settled the Corvette into the steady traffic pattern and arrowed north on the 101 toward the West Valley, that is, the western end of the San Fernando Valley.

"Westward Ho!" he sang out to nobody in particular.

As he drove, he rubbed at the gash on the top of his head with a Handi-Wipe that reeked of lemon scent. His song related less to the old black-and-white television series and more to Charles Kingsley's potboiler of noble Elizabethan seafarers. He pushed the Corvette, which he'd nicknamed *The Maroon Dog*, as much as he dared, and unfortunately for him the matter between his ears was an undependable wanderer; after a while he stopped singing, but carried the

164

song in his soul until it was inexorably warped and strange.

He sobbed out loud and the sound escaping from his lips became wierd and oriental and then intensified into a heart-wrenching scream as the pain from his head gash and the smell of the Handi-Wipes somehow conjured images of victims with ragged, nail-less fingers and maroon blood flowing like thick and muddy wine. Only the scene had oddly shifted from the halls of Granada to the basement of a police station in the Saigon suburb of Gia Dinh. The torturers were a special Saigon police security unit rather than the beasts of the inquisition. And he, Brando Mahr, had been there, in that crummy moldering basement begging for the life of one of the Le Nguyens. This poor wretch was the much-loved cousin of his lost wife's father's brother. He had not been able to save him, and the family had never forgiven his failure. In their minds, it was simplicity itself; he was their obligatory designated American, he was supposed to carry the weight to fix these things.

He blinked and brought back the reality of the moment. He was grinding his teeth and his foot was pressed hard against the floorboards. The Maroon Dog was screaming up the Cahuenga Pass, still on the 101 and weaving around slower cars and across lanes like it was a derby race or a Disney chase, leaving a roiling boil of startled traffic behind them. Brando sighed and backed off to double-nickles plus ten; the black-and-whites would be up and running and he couldn't handle another speeding ticket, much less explain the bag-o-guns in his trunk. On the other hand, he told himself, making excuses while he tried desperately to clamp a lid on the old Nam reruns, he didn't want to be late for his date at the Cherry Bar, either.

CHAPTER 16

And so we continue with FOUL, our 18th century murder mystery picaresque starring that rogish scamp Brando Mahr in Los Angeles in 1984. Hang on for the duration, as the ride promises to be bumpy, full of devious cunning and a tragic moment or two along the way.

A plastic banner hanging outside the stripjoint declared, "Where The Action Never Stops!" but the inside was hardly attempting to live up to the advertising. A blank-eyed CSUN co-ed, bare hips ornamented with a thin yellow g-string, twisted awkwardly to an old disco cut. A few dazed borachios were scattered at tables around the bar. They eyed the dodsy wench on the low platform with a glum eye, or gazed blank stares into their ale glasses, nobody looking like they were having much fun.

Brando spotted his mark right away. It took no great talent. The man he thought of as his *cunning shaver* was easy to pick out from this motley bunch; he was a study in counterpoint, a tall and pompous gilly gaupus, and he wore a stern and gray-haired dignity that was as out of place as a Jehovah's Witness at a Hell's Angels revival.

He kept sneaking peeks at the slovenly dimber mort in the g-string with long, sideways, frowning glances, in a way that had Brando questioning the depth of his disapproval. Or perhaps, Brando thought, the man might be a born-again Confucian, which is almost the same thing as a decent Christian, although sans Jesus, the saints, the sacraments or the promise of everlasting life-after-death. But he had the same over-all disapproving frown, there was that in common.

Brando angled over and plumped into the worn chair across the Formica from his mark. He set his Polaroid camera on the table top.

"That seat's taken," the man said, his lime-sucking attitude rising to the test.

"Yes, it is," Brando agreed, "I personally am occupying it. Joshua takes Jerico. Giap takes Dien Bien Phu. Knight takes pawn. Can you buck up to the reality?"

The man's eyes widened, thinking Brando might be a rambling nut escaped from the local VA. *Close, but no cigar.*

"Allow me to quote a snatch of old doggerel," Brando said, and without waiting for the man's approval, he chanted, "If wishes were horses, beggars would ride. If turnips were watches, I'd wear one by my side."

"You're an idiot. What are you talking about?" the man asked.

"Wishful thinking," Brando replied. "As in, Geez I wish I was in another state. Which is, if all things are as I cognize, about how you are going to feel in another moment or so.

"What do you want?" the man asked. He shifted uneasily in his chair.

"To chide you, for the first volley." Brando said, presenting his sad lop-sided smile, "This is all on your own head. You could have rented better knuckles, and right now I'd be racing demons or in winged flight."

"You're crazy—I-I don't know what you're talking about."

Brando shook his head. "My good fellow, cognize the real: Your name is Wally. Your knights of the blade blabbed all, even your moniker. And I'm here to demonstrate that you can't transport prime matter such as I to nirvana for a lousy thousand silvers. That is akin to an ant pissing on an elephant, as the saying goes in old Cochin China. A miserable thousand quid. Flush up some respect, here. Goliath weeps in laughter."

Wally started to rise, but Brando waved him down with one of the Browning automatics he'd taken from the bag-o-guns in the trunk of his Corvette. He held the pistol under the table, where it was pointing at Wally's basketball-like tub-o-guts and other important organs.

A dumpling-fleshed lady of the inn dragged herself by to ask the usual questions. It was bad timing, but Brando saw her tired eyes stayed on her order pad. He figured she was used to avoiding hard knocks. She would see what she wanted to see.

"Didn't I visualize you at the U.S.O. dance?" Brando asked, trying for casual.

She ignored his question. "What'll it be?" she asked wearily

No joy in Mudville; mighty Brando had struck out again.

"Miller Lite," he said with a sigh, recognizing when he was whupped

169

She gave Brando her rump and Brando gave his cull the glimp eye. The speaker system started to play Saturday Nite Fever. The dancer renewed her efforts.

For a head cheese, that is, a top fellow, Wally wasn't maintaining his ice very well. Beads of sweat were appearing on his forehead.

Brando could see his man had strayed a long way from the roost, whatever the coordinates. The man clearly wasn't used to this sort of encounter.

"I don't mean to roast you, but this isn't your M.O.S.," he said.

"My w-what?"

"Military Occupational Status, your normal job description. You're a frog out of the agua."

"No—I mean yes," Wally said, the words tumbling out in a rush, "This is really not—I shouldn't be here." Since he'd caught sight of Brando's ready hand-cannon, he was eager to be understood, if nothing else.

"Rommel under Hitler," Brando said encouragingly. "Moses in Egypt. Montezuma under Pizarro. You had no choice."

"Yes." Wally shook his head eagerly.

"Yet, you are the dimber-damber, aren't you?" Brando asked.

"The who?"

"The big ding boy, the head rogue. The one who launched his foot pads upon me."

Wally couldn't make up his mind whether to deny it or not. He looked at Brando for a moment, his eyes on the hitch of his shoulders, calculating the weight and angle of the pistol. Brando reminded himself to make no mistake, the

170

man he faced was no minor ding-boy. This was Hamlet playing the fool.

Wally came to a decision of sorts, sighed and pushed his weight back in the chair. He studied Brando in silence for a moment before he spoke.

"That is incorrect," he said. "I am not the *'dimber damber man'*, or whatever you call it. I am simply the messenger."

"Like to expand on your function?" Brando asked.

"No, I do not."

"I did ask you politely," Brando said gently. "Now's about the last chance to grab that bar of soap and scrub your doodle."

"What?"

"Scrub your mouth. Come clean. Tell the truth."

"No, thank you," Wally replied stiffly.

*Confucianis*t, Brando decided. *Etiquette over improvisation.*

"Then I would ask you to climb out of your jacket," he said.

"My jacket?" Wally raised his eyebrows as if that was impossible.

"Yes. This shapes not into a Noel Coward play; rather, we ruminate old lives and loves in a house of broken dreams in Canoga Park. This is a Mike Hammer chapter. In other words, people easily can get rather badly dinged here. Now give the jacket over to me."

Wally did as he was instructed.

The dish-clout waitress slammed Brando's beer on the table, setting a little foam dribbling down the side of the mug. Brando folded Wally's

171

finely tailored jacket, placing it over his carrying hand. He took a sip of the beer and frowned.

"The Europeans are far advanced in the non-alcoholics," he said to no one in particular.

"Well, they got their share of alcoholics, too," the dodsey waitress replied, dimly staring at the wall behind Brando while she waited for her money.

"Absolutely," he agreed. "Home of weinerschnitzel and the sordid drunk." He passed her a crisp Franklin from Wally's wallet. "Bring us a double decker glass of gin, sans tonic. No, make that a triple. And retain the change." The waitresses eyes lit and she scampered off, as Brando might say, *harum-scarum for the three-bagger of frog's wine.*

Meanwhile, Brando accomplished significant digit-walking through the wallet, feeling every inch the successful cut-purse that he was. The old Domine-Do-Little's full name was Walter Crankshaw, and he was a lawyer, a petty-fogging cursitor from Minnesota.

"Walter," Brando scolded, "You didn't bring me a Vikings T-shirt.

Wally didn't rise to the bait. *He was Galileo, silent before the pope.* Perhaps, Brando considered, *the Crankshaws all presented stiff upper lips when facing the absurd, some sort of genetic trait to go along with their weak chins. Or perhaps Old Wally was just plain poopy-pants scared.* Brando comprehended he, himself, would be as blanched of complexion, were he wearing a similar fate.

When the frog's wine came, Brando smiled his lopsided grin, "Say, what, here's your knock-

172

me-down, you buck-of-the-first-head, you. Hoist away—bottoms to the constellations, Walter."

"Now just a minute here—", Wally started angrily, trying a feeble little verbal counter-attack. Brando gently tapped the tip of the Browning against the bottom of the table, to remind him who was whom.

"Wally-boy," he said, "face the facts. You've reached your *Ultima Thule*. Calm it, or I'll make you sing *Oh Be Joyful* out of the other side of your mouth."

Wally may not have gotten the exact meaning, but he quieted down like a rogue who was considering consequences and his own mortality.

"Now, playboy Wally," Brando said, after his mark had gulped down the big glass of gin, "I want you to remove your pants."

"What? I'm not—"

Brando reached under the table and shoved the pistol in his tummy, "A little less melodrama. This isn't *Gotterdammerung*, either."

The waitress came running from across the room, "Hey, mister, you can't—"

Brando handed her two more of Walter's crisp Benjis, "Go hop the twig to the ladies room for about five minutes. Go—Now!"

She scooped up the money and jogged out of the room, her hopper-arsed hams doing a right-left-right under her pleated black shorty-skirt. The bartender tossed them a funny, half-frightened sneer, but he'd seen big money change hands, and so he took off after her for his piece of the action. Brando could imagine a phone back

173

there and the bartender busily working it. But by this time Walter had slithered out of his pants.

"And the shirt...Wally-boy," Brando said.

Wally unbuttoned his shirt like a reluctant new member of the polar bear franchise, but finally he was splendid and ready, all pink and goose-bumpy in the frigid air conditioning.

"Now get up there and gyrate, baby. Go ahead. Be the buckish wonder."

"You can't be serious!"

"Wally-bear, I'm not requesting the Joeffrey Ballet or the Paris Opera, here. Just ambulate over to the raised dias and hop it up a bit or I'll separate you from your current reality with dispatch, as you stiff upper-lippers are wont to say."

Brando was feeling good about the encounter. Wally and he really seemed to be communicating.

Walter Crankshaw crept up to the little platform, but the dancer shook her head and started to leave. The entire spectacle threatened to shrivel until Brando encouraged the flustered rantipole by stuffing more of the purloined proceeds of Walter Crenshaw's wallet in her chrome yellow G-string. It actually took the rest of Wally's 50's to reassure her it was just a happy prat for the boys at the Odd Fellows Lodge back in Duluth.

A la most Southern *Californiosos* of the 1980's, Brando kept an instant Polaroid in the trunk of his car, mostly to nail reality for insurance purposes. It was always in there, hidden in the guts of the same gym bag with the rest of his potables—the plastic gallon of

Arrowhead water, the Level 25 sunscreen and the Hi-Tek-Ton-Iks earthquake survival kit. He'd transferred that bag—plus his bag-o-guns—to the Corvette after they had dragged the crushed Fiat into the repair joint, and when he'd entered the alehouse he'd thought it a nice plan to bring the dependable fold-down camera with him.

Once Walter was gyrating in reluctant bodily harmonics to the hoot and holler of the musical madness, Brando snapped off a string of Polaroids. There was the staid and stolid Mr. Walter Crankshaw, esq, cavorting with the wary young wench in her sweaty G-string. Brando, ever the D.G.A. certified director, carefully lined up camera angles he felt John Ford or even Steven Speilberg might envy.

He couldn't decide if Wally's Joe Boxer rainbow trout shorts and argyle socks were a colorful accent or a disappointment, but he suspected he'd pinked his foe the limit, circumstances permitting. Some day in the future, those snaps might be worth a pile of Franklins.

Brando mused he might even cause them to be numbered and signed. He considered that stranger things had happened—consider the wild outburst in speculation over tulip bulbs, the so-called Tulip Mania of the 1630's, which burst in Holland and swiftly spread all over Europe, a veritable flowers plague. Some bulbs went for over a grand apiece. Bulb-o-mania, right here on the planet. We could, he reflected, have a rush on Wally-snaps.

"Dance on, Wally-bear..." he said. He left behind an extra snapshot, one of the losers he felt he wouldn't need. He hung Wally's suit over his arm and vamped it for the door.

"Steady she goes," Brando warned, "I'll be watching through the glass to make sure you continue." The essentials all in place, he left at a hasty clip.

The minute Brando hit the fresh air, he fished Wally's car keys from his pants pocket. Wally, he saw, had rented from Thrifty. Brando was pleased to find one of those handy little Thrifty Rental plastic key chains with the license plate and the make and color of the car, which made it easy to select Wally's silver-gray Ford from the nearly deserted parking lot.

The trunk was empty except for Wally's briefcase, which wasn't locked. Inside were assorted legal papers for a corporation, GH Enterprises. From the handy annual report, it looked like GH was a big company that ruled acres of Minnesota timberlands and North Dakota wheat and corn fields, considerable numbers of beef steers and a few dozen racing horses. There was a $20,000 GH Enterprises company check made out Walter Crankshaw and signed three days earlier by a man named George Haslins. *George Haslins.* Brando felt there was something familiar about that name. At any rate, the sum was more to his liking. Even with the rate of inflation being what it was, Brando could visualize himself being bumped off for 20 g's.

Still, there was no time for contemplation. Brando stuffed the check in his pocket and tossed the brief case back in the trunk, leaving everything else as he'd found it. He slammed and locked the trunk and then quick-stepped around

176

the car and threw Walter's suit, keys and wallet in the front seat and locked the car door. Wally-boy could always filch a coat hanger somewhere, and he probably wouldn't want to discuss matters with the local gendarmes unless he had to.

Brando's luck still held. There was nary a black-and-white in sight as he pulled slowly from the parking lot and made his way back to the 101.

He popped Lightnin' Hopkins in the cassette player and wailed along with the old master as he pointed his sleek maroon Detroit dragon back toward his office. He figured that, with things heating up, the studio might be a safer habitat than his ordinary digs, the old coach-house that he rented. The coach-house was a nice enough little brick place in a stand of eucalyptus snugged up against the hills in the mid- San Fernando Valley, but it didn't feature much in the way of security. The Corvette whisked him ably along, and he enjoyed the slap of the cold night air.

Not a bad couple of rounds, he was thinking. They hadn't lanced him hard yet, and he had pinked their footpads and flushed a pair of odd quail—Walter Crankshaw and George Haslins—out of the gnarly copse. What's more, he could guess that at least some of the somebodies who didn't like him lived in far-away Minnesota...the same place where The Inordinately Big Game had thundered across the gridiron to its sad, whimpery and questionable ending back in 1969.

Of course, insurance magnate Morrie Schiedt wasn't going to be overly ecstatic with that new knife gash in the Corvette. But Brando figured that Morrie, in addition to being a clever shaver and a whiffling cur, was an adult player. The balding little insurance agent was going to have to watch his own back, and scratch it too, doubtless.

Brando's giddy optimism lasted long enough for him to get back to his office and curl up on the couch of love and low budget productions. His silk Opie and Ronnie jacket rested lightly over his shoulders as he dozed off into a troubled sleep. Sleep was seldom a joyful time for him; it tended to nightmare scenes and violent happenings, bloody jolts and starts and jagged bits of old Saigon, faded pearl of the Orient.

He knew he wanted to wake and brush his teeth, but he couldn't; he was wrapped in sticky yarn and a giant grinning spider yawed over him, only it had mind-shrink Captain Alice Padrow's face stuck on a fat black body that was all tummy. The spider-lady was triumphantly gesturing with two front legs to where enormous words beginning with the letter "c" marched in rows, strutting their significance before his eyes. *Centrepiece, centric, centrifugal, centrifugal force, centrifuge, centring, centriole, centripetal, centripetal force, centrist...*Padrow had never approved of his reading the dictionary like a bible. *The brain doesn't normally think that way*, she'd said. *You're going to screw yourself up, boy.*

She had a point; the human brain is hard-wired early on to comprehend grammar, not alphabet. It groups verbs, nouns, pronouns, adjectives and the other parts of speech, and then divides them into subgroups, sub-subs and sub-sub-subs. And it further catalogues objects by their perceivable traits.

178

For instance, the ordinary human brain knows a grape is a grape not because it comes under "G" in the dictionary, but because this thing it sees is tasty, a fruit, round, green, purple or red, sweet, of a certain size like a marble, with a firm smooth skin. Basalt goes with the minerals, beans go with the vegetables, and bears go with the animals. None-the-less, the words marched on in Brando's skull, *controvert, contumacious, contumacy, contumely, contuse, contusion, conundrum, conurbation...*

His problem, as he'd come to recognize it back when he was still cottaged in the military junkyard, was that his natural system had been damaged beyond the ability of all the king's men to stick it back together again. In bone-saw lingo, some of the neuron pathways which allowed him to cognize the most common details and objects of reality had been altered or destroyed. He'd been vacationing at the VA facility for several years and by that time his body had mended except for the metal-chew scars. He was running and lifting weights again. And he slowly came to realize that the top half of his brain, the part where he did his thinking, was going to stay knotted up forever unless he made some radical moves. He simply traded away chaos—in return, he got the tyranny of alphabetical order. What he did was borrow a Random House College Dictionary from the captain's bookshelves and started spelling out the words in his bunk. He read by flashlight with a blanket over his head. He kept place with a finger and whispered to himself through the long nights. It wasn't a conscious decision, it was a

179

reflexive retreat into the only source of cognition available, and eventually it brought him back to the light.

Still, there is a price for everything. Now, in his fitful slumber the joyful words shrieked out their names, well into the "d's", *D'Annunzio, dance macabre, danseur, danseuse, Dante, Danton, Danube, Danubian, Danvers, Danville, Danzig, dap, Daphne...* The spider began chanting the words like a roll-call as they passed.

Brando stirred and the words shrilled and then the marching letters animated themselves into a roaring rodeo crowd and Belle Denver was riding his back, naked as the day they had first brushed, laughing and whipping him with a braided silk quirt as she rode. Only Brando wasn't himself, he was some kind of trout with sharp teeth, and he kept trying to snap at her, and the crowd roar became a temple gong ringing louder and louder in his ears and he finally realized it was the telephone, and then he was somehow allowed to wake.

Brando wearily fumbled across the desk for the offending electronic messenger.

"Who requests lip-flap?" he mumbled sleepily.

"Brando, it's me, Keith."

"Did I miss the fishing expedition? Come on, top-kick, it's still darktime in the A.M....by Odds Plut and her nails, it is..."

"Brando, stop blathering and listen up: I'm at Ripper's place. You got to get over here right away."

He groaned, "Oh, no, no, Julio. The great man wants to ramble about his life at this wee peckit?"

"Brando, listen to me! Somebody ransacked his house. The place is a mess, and Lani's missing!"

Brando blinked twice, told Keith he'd be on the next train, and dropped the phone to the floor. He ground the sleep out of his peepers and searched for something joyful in the sunrise, but his previous day's elation had disappeared. Except for Charlie's whispered secrets, he didn't even have the glimmer of a concept yet on the Ripper project. *Not a nickle's worth of joy in sight, and now further complications.* This was getting to be too much for him. *Maybe the bumfiddle rogues were right*, Brando thought ruefully. *Maybe I should go back to animation.*

CHAPTER 17

We continue with FOUL, our brazen and spirited little 18th century picaresque that takes place in 1984. Picaresque? You know, from the Spanish 'picaro'...the adventures of a low-born, roguish fellow who drifts from place to place and from one social milieu to another in an effort to survive. If that isn't our Brando Mahr, then tell me, who is?

Brando allowed The Maroon Dog to coast to a halt in front of the coach house he rented and trotted in for a quick dunk and scrape. He threw on a clean set of jeans and a cotton shirt, hooked his Opie and Ronnie jacket and his army soft cap, and was out the door in 4/4 time.

By now the sun was up, and the early morning here-to-there had coagulated to a slow crawl through the two lane curves of Topanga Pass. It was clog-and-go, but Brando finally edged off the asphalt under Boulder Alley and sprinted across the street to Ripper's pad. It wasn't that he'd forgotten where not to park, but the black-and-white Ford Victorias and the city's clunky detective-brown Plymouths were hogging up the good spots. And, after all, it was Morrie's machine. Brando ducked under the yellow and black crime scene tape and made his way inside.

Ripper's pad was a mess. The sculptured paintings Brando had admired were smashed and pulled off the walls. The art deco glass coffee table was splintered and the oriental furniture was dumped over on the carpets.

Ripper himself paced back and forth like a caged jungle animal. A short, oriental man in a rumpled suit dusted anything he could find for give-away fingerprints, while several uniformed policemen stood around with coffee cups poised, trying not to be obvious that they were surveying the lifestyle of the one and only. Good Buddy Keith was out on the deck trying to calm down Loaf Ludder, who looked angry and upset. Loaf's attitude didn't quite play for Brando, but he couldn't figure exactly why. Anyway, there were urgencies more pressing than the dire and pouty Ludder.

Another man stood in front of Brando. He looked about Brando's age, in his middle-to-late thirties. He had short blond hair and sad grey eyes, and wore a suit that had seen better days. His shirt had the dog-gnaws of age at the collar and the cuffs. His tie was one of those western-motifs with Trigger, Fury or Silver rearing all over it—Brando never could get his horse-heroes straight—and there were pulls in the silk, and soup spots where Brando imagined Trigger might have taken a dump.

"You're Brando Mahr," the man said.

"My name precedes me."

"Don't get smart with me, pal," he said. "It ain't a good idea."

Keith came over and took Brando's arm, "Brando, this is Lieutenant Baker. He's in charge of the—"

Baker impatiently waved him away, "Okay, Mahr, what happened here?"

Brando shrugged, "I just arrived. Re-decorating would be my suspicion."

Something behind Baker's face hardened. "I see how it's going to be. Look, pal, you better get in your head—you're a suspect."

"Not me."

"Says you."

"Who declares otherwise?"

"Well, for one, Ripper's best friend Mr.Ludder over there says you and Ripper were working on a story. Only things weren't going so smooth."

By now, Ripper noticed him and started yelling in his direction, "Brando-man, look at my trophy case!"

"Don't blame me! You're the impresario who was itching to reveal your greatness to the new generation of Ripper Ravers."

"Didn't I warn you about Brando Mahr?" Loaf yelled at Ripper. "But no—you wouldn't listen!"

To Brando, the world was suddenly gone crazy. *Why all the finger-pointing at him?*

"You mind if we take a look in your car?" Lieutenant Baker held out his hand.

"No. Here." Brando confidently lagged him the keys. "Maroon Corvette...across the street." He'd selected the right door again in the game show of life; the Joey bag-o-guns was safely stuffed away in his wall locker at KTGA.

Brando shuffled a few steps and stared out the window. The first rays of sunlight shot sharp glints off the flat plane of the ocean. A middle-aged cull and his whither-go-ye, both somewhat less than average specimens, jogged by in the nude, their various parts jiggling in the normal discomfiting nudist way. The cull stopped suddenly and jabbed into the sand to retrieve something. He studied it for a moment and then tossed whatever it was away. He said something to his dishwipe dodsey and gave an ugly little laugh, and then they both jogged on. Brando found himself thinking how un-pretty casual nudity could be. He wanted to yell at them to surrender themselves to fabric, but the timing wasn't right; Lieutenant Baker was returning through the front door, moving with the swift certainty of a vengeful juggernaut.

"You got almost nothin' in that car." He chewed the reality like Brando had created mischief and evil.

Brando shrugged, "It's a borrowed-for-money vehicle."

"A what?!"

"A rental," Keith interjected.

"Will you shut up?! I'm talking to him!" The lieutenant sneezed on his jacket sleeve and then snorted and yelled at Brando, "How do you explain this?"

He held up a gleaming, unspent bullet. Before leaving the studio, Brando had dunked the gunnysack full of guns in the locker with a sea of running shoes and moldy socks; but he'd apparently overlooked this one round of ammo, leaving it to rattle around on the floor of the trunk. It had the shape and size of a 9mm, probably a round from one of the Brownings. *On the other hand*, he thought, so what? *Bullets can't talk, unless one fires them.*

185

He lifted his shoulders again, Brando Mahr, *insoucient extraordinaire*, "The motor coach is a rental."

Lieutenant Baker watched his every twitch, as if he thought Brando was going to bolt for the door. Brando hunched his frame and turned away from him "You missing particulates, Ripper?"

The big man's peepers flicked around the room like he was taking count for the first time. His look went wide and blank, and then shifted to fury. "My scrapbooks! The bastards stole my scrapbooks!"

The lost career. This seemed to outrage Ripper more than the shattered furniture or his missing girl friend. He plopped down like a big, black Br'ar Rabbit with his huge ebony feet stuck in the tar. He looked ready to burst into tears.

Brando patted Baker's reluctant shoulder and pointed to the beach, where he'd witnessed the ugly joggers. The tide was low, and now, in the better light, he saw it was strewn with soggy bits of paper.

"Perhaps out in the littoral zone," he suggested.

If Baker was grateful, he didn't show it. He pointed a stubby thumb at Brando and threw a grim glance at one of his trusty constables, "Keep an eye on this smart article."

Keith and Lieutenant Baker hurried down to the surf line, where Brando was fairly certain they would find the last scraps from the glorious career of Ripper Brown suspended in the beige-green opacity of the shallow water and half buried in the sand.

"Come, valorous foot pad," Brando said to his appointed guardian. "Should I become dangerous, you can as easily dispatch me from the sand."

"You can't go out there," he said.

"I am Fearless Fosdick," Brando emoted in sonorous tones. "Nobody plugs a dick in the back." He trotted down the wooden stairs from the deck and hustled his bones across the sand to join Keith and the Lieutenant. His escort came snarling and scuffing the sand behind him. Brando figured he wasn't going to catch up; police loafers aren't constructed for beach fun. The first piece of paper Brando retrieved from the sand was a soggy snap of Ripper with a big bronze trophy in his hands.

"Alas, the scrap books," he said, "I knew them well." Nobody else said anything, so he added, *"Sic transit gloria."*

"Gloria who?", Keith wanted to know.

Lieutenant Baker didn't seem all that joyful, but before he could express what he felt, something else caught his fitful glare.

"Hey," he said, shading his beady eyes and pointing one finger out over the water. Brando's curious gaze followed his excited arm motion. About two hundred feet from shore, on the other side of where the surf started in neat little rollers, something was bobbing up and down near the kelp beds. From Brando's point of observation it resembled a sack of potatoes, a curvy lump of bleached driftwood, or a human body floating face down in the water.

Of one thought, Keith and Brando kicked off their shoes and stripped to their shorts. They
187

churned the frigid water like two paddlewheelers and then towed the body back together, each taking an arm and side-stroking like log-laden beavers back in through the surf. The entire morning excursion out and back took less than ten minutes, and the body didn't fight them at all.

They pulled the victim up on the sand and the two policemen took the blue-white limbs from them and quickly turned the body over. *Just like Nam*, Brando was thinking, *always intent on identifying and bagging the remains. We're Americans, boy. We takes care of our own.*

Brando had his clothes back on when an unearthly, high keening wail cracked through the Malibu morning stillness. It was a long, mournful and soul-piercing sound and it came from Ripper Brown, who had given up his funk over his missing scrapbooks long enough to come out on the deck and witness the body lying limp and crumpled on the sand. It was his right to mourn, for the dead person staring with lifeless eyes at the bronze morning sunrise sky was the only person in the world who truly cared for him—his steady, loyal doxey, Lani Kazin.

A chill ran through Brando and he unconsciously slapped the side of his head; but he need not have bothered. There wasn't a blessed Zeeman in sight. He was stuck with real life.

The scene was fogged and caked in horror, like a modern frosted-over still life by Dali. The nude joggers had disappeared and the dull tan beach stretched away in both directions with no one in view as far as Brando could see. The dark blue uniforms of those sworn to protect and serve were back-lit and black in the early-morning

188

glare.   Thunder-faced, Loaf stood silent and spread-legged on the deck. He stared down at them, his face twisted with churned up emotion. The gulls overhead wept their mournful cries at a tiny pale moon that looked like it was permanently pasted in a corner of the metallic gray-blue sky.

For his part, Brando was numb with the feel of the reaper's work radiating from Lani's cold body.   Words formed in his brain, marching across with their own impeccable logic. *What mundungus bumfiddle could count such a foul perfidy in the recognition of his days?*

Brando felt the cold bone of a handcuff snip-snap around his wrist. The other cuff was in the hands of Detective Baker. Baker eyeballed his captive with a tired expression.

"You're going to have to come with me now," he said quietly, the tone of his voice reminding Brando of a rectangular shaped slab of pink and black flecked granite falling in place over a soon-to-be-forgotten grave.

189

CHAPTER 18

How's your suspension of disbelief faring at the moment? Here we have FOUL, claiming to be an 18th century London street penny novel that takes place in 1984. And that's impossible, you say. You've bought in on space aliens, virgin birth, the supremacy of the of the human race over something or other, and why the Meleagris gallopava crossed the road—why is this any different?

Many hours beyond the sad moments at the beach, Brando found himself still detained in one of those stale green cubicles where the city's finest spent their hours wringing confessions from rogues, knaves and rascals. Brando was bleary and mind-tattered from responding to the same quizzings over and over, and his eyes were red-rimmed and aching from sweat and tobacco fumes. With their heavy docket of wrongdoers, the L.A. police department had no spare time or inclination to observe the Surgeon General's reports on primary or secondary smoke.

The table was littered with cups half-filled with cold brown caffeine-water and swimming with cigarette butts. A cardboard Donut King box still sported a few crumbled remains of the morning's sugar splurge. These were stacked on top of last night's empty Domino's Pizza boxes that now reeked of limp bell peppers.

Brando had declined the idea of an attorney to represent his interests, arguing that *he was innocent anyway, so why be concerned?* That

190

seemed okay with them. Lieutenant Baker had accomplished three shifts in his presence, singly and with other sad-eyed people, and now he had returned for the swan song, confident Brando was about to crack and spill the beans.

Brando didn't have his medicine, and there was a good chance it wouldn't have had any effect in the first place. Halfway through this final session, they'd been in the middle of a shouting match when the Zeeman came, softly at first, on little zee feet... and then it gathered force, bunched its shoulder muscles and pounced on him.

Brando froze like a statue, in mid-sentence, while staring at Baker. He tried to sputter out words, and then tipped over of his own weight and crashed down onto the floor. The dark, warm Zeeman opened wide and swallowed him whole.

With no sense of time, he was free to roam as he would. His awareness wandered deep into the warm barn he remembered all too well. He rushed eagerly through the door to the horse stall, only to find himself back in the sixth grade, handing his far-away and sainted mother a group photo, taken a few days before at school. There he was, standing erect and devout in front of a painted faux marble altar at St. Liborius, in the middle of a flock of fellow altar boys all ornate in holiday scarlet toe-length cassocks and lace-trimmed white linen surplices. *Ah, was he ever so pure of heart?*

When he came back to reality, he was still in Baker's lime-green room of interrogations, lying on the floor. Someone had stuffed a wad of toilet paper in his mouth.

He spat out the soggy paper. The red-brown marks on the toilet paper showed that he'd chewed his tongue or his cheek, or maybe both.

"You turned blue in the face," a weary voice said from across the room. "Actual blue. I thought I seen everything, but I never seen that before."

Brando stared through the glare and the pain until he spotted Lieutenant Baker.

"Still on the job, I see," Brando managed to whisper as he wearily dragged himself upright and flopped into a chair. "The devil sends his compliments. I'm to pass along that he's got a spot waiting for your delirious bumfiddle."

"Yeah, yeah, yeah," Baker said. "Tell him to get in line. I already owe my soul to MasterCard."

Brando's head felt like someone had split it down the center with an ax and sprinkled salt inside. He spat and gritted his teeth, "Who stuffed the bum-fodder between my choppers?"

"Blue toilet paper. I did."

"Thanks," Brando nodded. "I could have swallowed my tongue or bitten off the tip. It happens."

The lieutenant cleared his throat, "You have no recollection what happened after you...started having this fit-thing, here?"

Brando shook his head no.

"You were a fuckin' monster. You got rigid and you were shaking and foaming bloody foam from your mouth, and, of course, you peed a big puddle."

Baker had a mouse under his left eye and scratches on one arm, further evidence it had been a bad one.

"You helped me," Brando said.

The lieutenant shrugged, "I done a million things on the force: Delivered babies. People with strokes. Burns. Near drownings. They teach you what to do, but I ain't never done that before."

"I owe you an appreciation," Brando said.

Baker shook it off. His grey eyes hardened, and Brando could see the blocks going up, one by one.

"This ain't good, you know. You're already our chief suspect. Only now we also know you blank out and go crazy. Maybe that's what happened to Lani."

"I am not a menace...to any innocent!"

"Unless they try to help you. Maybe that's what Lani did. She tried to help you. And you killed her. Maybe that ain't murder 1. Manslaughter, maybe."

"Not possible..." But even as Brando spoke, the policeman must have seen the uncertainty in his eyes.

"No way you can deny it. How would you know?"

"I do deny it. I was nowhere....near there."

The lieutenant sighed and settled in for another round, no holds barred. By now Brando's head was raging pain and he was reduced to syllables and to words separated by long pauses.

Baker thought he had a chance to break his suspect. Brando found that grimly amusing. *Welcome, lieutenant, to the timeless world of Mahr, where there is no word for length of time, no sense of duration or the passing of events.*

The interrogation dragged on and on until Baker was routinely answering his own questions and finishing Brando's halting sentences for him. Finally, reduced to Brando's level of thought, he stared straight ahead, like a seer gazing into the past. They were two heavy punchers, spent and listless, arms down, staring at each other across the ring.

"Okay," Baker said with a final weary sigh. "Let's see if we can work together and sum this up. We got two wildly different theories here of what went on last night—yours and mine."

"Only yours...is a theory...*mon Capitain.*"

Baker's gray eyes flicked angrily in Brando's direction. "Yeah. Well, that's what you say. I say the headline reads SPAZZED NAM VET WIGS OUT OVER PRETTY LADY."

"You've seen too many...M-Magnum P.I.'s. I retort, the headline...actually proclaims...BOY-GOD OF INTERROGATION DOESN'T HAVE AN INTERCOURSING CLUE"

"Crap!" Baker shouted, slamming his fists on the table. "You crazies flip out over fly-sweat! It happens all the time. You proved it in here today. That's why they keep most of you fruitcakes locked up in the VA. I used to be against it, keepin' 'em in there....but now, lookin' at what you done, it might be a good thing."

Brando had his head on the table, "Nay, bull-dick, nay. Just because I don't...possess your...elocutionary skills—"

"Bag it, pal. Maybe that con worked for your shrink, but not here. I seen too much to fall for that PTSD syndrome bullshit. You were a killer in Nam—"

"S-soldier!"

"I seen your file. I know what unit you was from. I read the reports on you. Jesus, do you even have any idea how many people you killed—do you remember them?"

Brando felt the cool flatness of the table against his cheek and said nothing. *Baker couldn't be that naïve,* he was thinking. After a moment, Baker became aware that his captive was looking at him with a curious light of interest in his eyes.

"Don't you?", Brando said quietly, not bothering to get vertical. They stared at each other, two duelists saber-locked at the hilt.

Finally an angry twitch crossed Baker's face and he looked away. "Of course," he said, after what seemed like an ocean of ticks.

Brando nodded from his resting position on the table and muttered softly, each word coming in out of the black void and breaking like a wave of pain across his own skull.

"Me, too," he said. I remember every chop, cough, curse, cut, crash and cry...every kick, every kill...every rage, reaction, rent, rift, rip, riposte...every scream, slash, slip, strike, swing and swipe..." His voice drifted on, a weary semi-Gregorian chant, "I remember, I remember, the way it was that soft September...in the rain."

Of course they both knew, the same way Steve Garvey knew his own batting percentage and Nolan Ryan knew his strikeouts. Maybe Baker's hits came while defending the citizenry from crime, but Brando had fought to save democracy and the American way. He wasn't proud of the score, and neither was Baker. The lieutenant was silent and shaken under Brando's sad, crooked smile.

Wrong trail, boy-wonder detective, we're not supposed to be bonding here, Brando thought without saying anything.

Baker took a moment to balance and reload and then he fired again. This time his voice was soft and warm as a friendly con's with a worn and familiar deck and a lot of time on his hands. Brando wasn't fooled; he could see the lieutenant was just trying to construct his house-o-cards, "So you're having a tough time relating in the real world, Brando. You lose your job. You meet this beautiful woman from a world you've never known. She's got everything you've always desired—glamour, fame, money. You pick a time you know Ripper's got a speaking engagement out of town. You go over there, but—wonder of wonders—the lady rebuffs your maggot-mouthed, tongue-tied advances. She thinks you're a dummy. Or a fairy. Or both. And when you can't stand that, you whack her."

"No octane in your gas," Brando said, still eyeing him sideways from the table, "You, yourself are aware...your theory doesn't...hold liquid."

"Yeah, sure—and your story does?!" Baker picked up the yellow legal pad overflowing with his chicken-scratches. By now he had filled all the pages, then filled the backsides of each yellow page and now he was writing in the margins.

He leafed through his manuscript, stopping where he'd drawn arrows or little stars or wavy lines next to items of supposed significance, "Now, your story. One more time, let's see if I can keep all the bullshit straight. You're directing a Jungle Jill commercial for KTGA. You leave the studio at about 6:30 in the evening, for no other reason than you want to. You have no difficulty leaving, even though the gate guard reported that some guests of the studio who were there for a taping happen to see a scuffle in the parking lot. Said scuffle occurs between two known felons currently on parole and some mustachioed fellow with a description that matches up 100% to yourself."

Brando nodded, but didn't add anything.

"And even though we now have one of those two injured felons in Queen of Angels with a very nasty skull fracture, and the other is resting at his mother's home with a big purple bruise on his neck, you don't know anything about that."

Brando nodded again.

"And then you drove for some inexplicable reason way out to the other end of the valley. You go to a dive called the Cherry bar, where you had a drink with a well-dressed man named Walter. You don't even know his last name; you say you just struck up a conversation. At some point, Walter—who now cannot be found anywhere around town—gets drunk, tears off his clothes and dances with a naked go-go girl."

Brando gave him another nod. "Nearly buff," he said. "She had yellow bikini bottoms."

"Yeah, well…You drive back to your office at KTGA, spend the night working on this movie about the life of Ripper Brown, fall asleep on the coach sometime after the night shift leaves the studio—I am assuming between 12 and 2 a.m.—and that's all you know and remember."

197

Brando tossed out another nod.

"Are you sure that's all you want to tell us?" Baker snorted in disgust and slapped his yellow notepad back on the table.

"Affirmative," Brando said. "Those true reflections are the sum of my recollections."

"And what's your theory again about the threats you say were made against you? The scrap of paper on your windshield and the call on your Phone-mate?"

Brando shrugged from his sideways slump over the table, "Some jealous...Hollywood mogul wants to steal...Ripper's epic story."

Baker gave the table a savage slap with the palm of his hand, the sound booming like thunder in Brando's ear, "Do you have any idea how weak that is?"

Brando jerked erect, looking around wildly for a moment to gain his coordinates. After a grand mal, epileptics have minor disconnections, what the doctors call psychomotor epilepsy. As Brando would say, *those bone-saws and medical nip-boys have a name for everything.*

His head was black with pain, his neck ached, and his hand throbbed where he'd hit Fat boy in the neck. *Hand-to-hand physical combat isn't all sweetness and light the way they make it out in the mock 'um rock 'um sock 'um movies, where the heroes are so good they enjoy clever talk before violence.* Brando sported a knotty scar and residual pain in his left knee where some North Vietnamese goomba had bayonetted him years ago. The rusty degen went in right under the kneecap and stuck there. Maybe that was fate, because Brando got to work on him while he was

198

trying to pull it out. But before they could evacuate, Brando's knee had bloated and turned greenish purple and he nearly lost it.

Brando started awake. He'd drifted off again. Lieutenant Baker was still talking, spinning his case like a tired old grey wolf-spider, "You were alone in your office all night."

"That is not illegal. I often work the darkman through. And the studio gate guard...corroborated I was within the walls, *n'est pas?"* Brando asked.

"None of your business, cake. I ask the questions."

Brando blew on the palms of his hands and nodded his assent, then joined his fingers. *This is the church and this is the steeple.* At least the knuckles where he'd hammered fat-boy showed no outer signs of wear and tear. He realized Baker had tracked down the waitress and the bartender at the Cherry Bar, and they had probably verified enough of his story to throw a monkey wrench into the lieutenant's dream-version of what had happened. Also, Brando knew Baker had to admit that even the knighted royalty of the silver screen couldn't simply vaporize in or out of the studio without passing Harvey at the main gate. After-hours, one must scratch the pad and so Brando had signed in with his bona fide John Hancock and he and Baker both knew it. The lieutenant didn't spout any more theories for a few moments. Brando reflected how pleasant the silence was, like the calm after the great black hole implosion. "Anything...else?" he finally asked.

"NOTHING else!" Baker screamed in his face, slamming his hand on the table to give his captive another jolt of pure, raw sound. "Fucking nothing at all else!"

Baker yanked a fat manila envelope with Brando's personal possessions from an old-fashioned rectangular brown plastic briefcase and slapped it down on the table. "But the minute we find anything else, Mister Big-Time Crazy-Head TV Director, your ass is mine!"

And then his face softened, like one of the great stone faces of Rushmore crumbling at the edges under eons of plant rot and acid rain. Brando was witness to his internal struggle, the little, tiny, good cop fighting with the great big bad one. After a while Baker made up his mind.

"Follow me," he said. "We got showers here, towels and stuff. I'll show you where..."

The lieutenant rotated away before Brando could reply, and his captive followed his cool side out the door and down the hall. Brando walked after him without saying another word. He was going to get a free shower from the guardians of the people, and he didn't want to screw it up

200

CHAPTER 19

Just what is a London street penny novel? I imagine it's beginning to gnaw at some of you. Some shallow scholars and envious critics will tell you they were cheap thrillers scribbled by hack writers. They were the people's literature, popular in my day as Stephen King and Marcia Muller are today. Also known as 'penny dreadfuls', 'bloods' and 'shilling shockers.' There was Varney the Vampire, or, The Feast of Blood. You never heard of it? Well, how about Sweeney Todd, the Demon Barber of Fleet Street? On the high end, where things are called literature, my countrymen reveled in roguish heroes like Dafoe's Robinson Caruso and Smollett's Humphrey Clinker...Well, that was that, and this is this:

It was two days later, or as Brando would say, a few ticks of the grim ghoul's glare after his interrogation. Brando found himself at Lani Kazin's funeral, which turned out to be a very busy affair. It seemed as much a gathering place to conduct business as to send off the dearly departed.

Not one or two, but three different sets of gimbal-eyed culls sidled up to conference with Brando. And it was there that he crossed paths with the true ghost of football past. He hadn't planned on being so popular, but then, popularity isn't all it's cracked up to be.

The service itself was a non-denominational reading of bland beatitudes, the typical beautiful but empty Southern California Event-of-the-Joyous-Passing.

All this took place under the lofty, sooted arches of the big limestone Episcopalian church in old Hollywood. The church is located where Highland Avenue takes a jog to avoid the hills and runs north, parallel to the freeway as they both go up and over the Cahuenga Pass.

The service dragged on and on, long by anybody's count. Brando mused that, if he were the deceased, he would have long since gotten up and made his own way to the cemetery. The worshipers seemed to feel they had plenty of time for palavering, and, of course, they were right. Lani wasn't going anywhere.

Brando felt tense and uneasy, as he always did in crowds and social gatherings. The dusty interior of the house of prayer was candle-lit in the proper dim reverence. There was a slanted thin haze filtering through the grimy stained-glass windows. The high altar was smothered in yellow mums and red carnations theatrically spotlighted to present a gaily multi-colored blaze to the congregation. The great hall was filled with an intermittent dull wash of organ music, and the guests had plenty of time to reflect on life and its easy passing.

As nearly as Brando could patch it together, the people who huddled in the pews were divided into their own distinct groups. There were the Hollywood minor key celebs in their origami play outfits. They were the movie players and singers, the shills and ringers who had known Lani in the early days before her first marriage. Next, the jock group, the big-meat football boys and their flashy vixens, who were all now gathered in a rare somber moment around the Ripster. Loaf Ludder was steady-she-goes at the great man's side, though from time to time both men honked their noses and sobbed like lost babes. Brando wasn't impressed by either man's show of sorrow. Loaf seemed pure acting, and as for Ripper Brown, *wasn't it about the proper time that the great Ripper finally recognized the extent of his loss?* Brando thought he was well overdue.

And finally Brando picked out the sharp-eyed louts in blue sprinkled around the church. He figured the poor rascals of the law had shown up simply to mark down who else had made the scene.

The first squinty-eyed cull to invade Brando's space and invoke his attention was the good Lieutenant Baker, himself. He came up to Brando while he was wandering about in back of the church, pacing beneath an arched balcony where the organ played.

"So. You haven't left town yet," the flat and nasty voice from the gimbal-eye came at Brando in a harsh rasp.

"Constable Baker. Why aren't you occupied up front, copying names off the flowers?"

"We got people for that, wise ass."

"Can I assist? Philodendrun. Zimbidium. Petunia."

"Very funny. You got any new wild fabrications to confess?"

"Just that you've attracted sauce-of-the-tomato to your lapel. They say a man who ingests

203

spaghetti for breaksup can flash his hash before high sun."

Baker gave his jacket a brief glance and then tried to scrape the crusty brown spot off his lapel with one of his close-cropped fingernails, "Yeah, well, I don't usually eat at high sun."

"You could have humbugged me," Brando said.

He almost thought he saw a flicker of a smile light the lieutenant's dull face.

"Some day, somebody's gonna squash you *like* a bug, pal," he said.

"It is..." Brando eyed him a long and pregnant snilch, "...highly unlikely."

"Yeah. So I heard." The lieutenant's attention lingered, "I wish I'd been in that parking lot when you did what I think you did to those two punks."

"That's entertainment," Brando said.

Baker nodded and Brando shifted his attention to the backs of all the heads in front of them. He was thinking Baker was a little thick-skulled, but maybe he wasn't a complete cod's head. All the detective mystery books generally agreed the police could be a valuable source of information. The problem, as Brando analyzed it, was persuading them to share. He was going to have to put on a happy face, to try and replace his replacement words with common guy talk. This was a sort of a ploy-on-a-ploy he'd artifacted with Captain Padrow back in his humpty-dumpty days at the VA. The only concern was that the game took real ticks to work through the mental gymnastics, and, generally speaking, the hotdog was cold before he could get it in the bun. *But they would see.* If Baker wouldn't say anything for about thirty ticks, he might even get in the first bite.

Brando calculated he needed to chew the conversation around to the subject of the Los Angeles football team. *Do you cogitate fondly on the male sheep sporting club? No, that wasn't it.* He pondered, compressed, re-composed. *Are you intimate with... No, bad start. Just commence with the pronoun, question understood. Cognize, cognize, cognize!*

"You a...Ram fan?" he blurted out.

"Not since they moved to Anaheim." Baker gave Brando a dour look and didn't say anything more. This was turning out to be more complicated than Brando had anticipated. But, as he would describe it, he necessitated the ploy of gifting Baker information, in order to track his trail. Brando knew his opening hadn't been bad, but he hadn't communicated anything of worth, and now Baker was eyeing him like he was the oddest fish in the basket. Brando tried to think through his next comment. *Does your circle of friends extend to professional coaches? No, too vague. Use the name, use the name! Is your memory purged of one called "The Gritty Greek"? No, no, NO!* Brando wanted to rage out loud. Baker was going to say something, Brando saw his flappers move to form the first word and rushed to cut him off at the pass.

"You—know who Nathan Paramis is?" Brando asked.

"What is this, Twenty Questions? Everybody remembers the Gutsy Greek. What about him?"

Brando felt a flood of blessed relief. He'd actually pointed Baker like a bird dog, foot and tail raised in the classic position. His next words burbled out more easily.

"I have a notion, an odd and passing happenstantial thought—Has the question occurred to you, *How is it that this oaf Paramis, this jongleur, a mere obiter dictum in the Book of Football, ends up the grand meister of a posh resort hotel in Santa Barbara?"*

Baker shrugged, "I don't see what you're gettin' at. He made a killing in real estate, during the go-go years when any fool could turn a dollar."

Brando shook his head on the negatory, "There's a may-happen-stance. But isn't real estate what they mutter when the really big ding-boys cash in and nobody can deduce from whence came the lucre of filth?"

Baker sighed and hitched up his pants, shaking his head like Brando was the last fool pig to the feeding trough of street smarts.

"Brando, Brando...and I thought you were a romantic. Now I see that was all a sham; underneath all your stumbling and shambling around you're just another cynic...like me..." His tired eyes stopped sweeping the backs of the crowd and turned to lock Brando in his gaze, "So why are you telling me this? What's the connection between the Greek and why we're here?"

"I treasured the fond inspiration that you might embark on a course of discovery."

"Now you got me digging out your story for you?!"

206

Brando shrugged, trying a verbal fast-step and coming off like the Hunchback of Notre Dame attempting a major role in Swan Lake, "No, I thought it might apply to this dead-bones ceremony. But, on the other digit, if dreams ever do coalesce, I will parcel out...screen credit."

Brando ambled away, figuring he wouldn't want to be within ear-shot of the lieutenant's response, although, you could never be 100% sure, *the fish might well be on the hook.* He could almost visualize Baker in his warm little bungalow that very darkman, half-believing, half-scoffing as he told his long-suffering whither-go-ye how this crazy sort-of producer-fellow had offered to put his name on a film credit. *That is, if Baker even had a regular dowsey, or any private life at all, for that matter.* Brando observed the lieutenant had the marks of one of the burned out knaves, the sad strivers of the law who'd torched all that personal reality years ago.

Lani's parting service ended with a crash and swell of organ pipes, a powerful set of chords that cried triumph and sweet remembrance to those who listened or cared. From Brando's view, nobody much did. One of the football lugs discretely dug at his nose and as the music ended the various cliques turned to scrabble and lurch for the exits.

Brando was in a thoughtful frame of mind. He tried to drift away, as he would later describe it, *in his own discrete beatitude.* But his progress was interrupted as Ripper turned his attention on his scribe. Loaf was there to envelop Brando's left biceps in one of his hefty ham hands. Brando smelled again the stale belch that oozed from the man, Loaf's own sour *scent des manure*.

"Ripper want we should have a talk," he said.

Brando saw it was chop-talk, like having a dialogue with the last of the Mohegans. He attempted to respond in kind, "We-who, black-man? We him-and-me, or We, him-and-me-and-you?"

"You find out soon enough, smart guy."

So, while the guests were quietly filing out, Loaf yanked Brando along to a small, soundproofed crying-baby repository in the back of the church, easily keeping him in tow like a father half-carrying and half-dragging his prodigal son.

"Are you totally elevated that now's the proper moment for us to talk, Loaf?" Brando asked. "You wouldn't want to interrupt the grieving process."

"Yeah," he said. "Now be the time." There was a note of dark finality in his voice.

He closed the heavy doors behind them, and in another moment Brando was encased in a Mighty Foremen sandwich. Up close, he couldn't help but notice the four of them all had quality muscle tone. They may have arrived in their early 50's, but they were taking excellent care of their germ-sacks the way living legends should. Looking at them, one presumed vast quantities of vitamins and multitudinous suggestions of vigor, *a la* let's go pump iron and run up and down the mountain before lunch.

Brando was in that *let it be* attitude, beyond hope and despair and three degrees left of curiosity. He didn't know what this play was about, but he was fairly convinced they weren't gathered to discuss the spring planting.

Rand Burkle, the ball-boy who made up one half of the white membership of the Mighty Foremen, glowered down at Brando from his great height and rumbled, "Dis the guy, Rip?"

Jeff Raymond, the other white guy, gave Brando his meanest snilch. The gleam from his shaved head matched the frosty glint in his eyes. He topped out at six foot nine and he was a lick-spitting NFL version of Mister Clean. Still, Brando was not impressed. He had a long-standing aversion to Nazi-like tactics.

Ripper nodded, "I'll handle this, man."

"Handle what, Rip?" Brando said, shrugging into his most comradely and affectionate manner. Troublemaker that he knew he was, he was no cod's headed fool; he realized how little it would profit him to rile up the Ripper.

The big man scowled, having none of Brando's Mister Jolly act. *So much for friendship and light.* Brando could see that in the few days since Lani's drowning he'd deteriorated in Ripper's appraisal into some sort of bad guy.

"This puts an end to it, man!" Ripper said, looking around for a bone to break or a face to tear off. It's an approach to living that football people sometimes have difficulty setting aside when they retire, and one with which Brando sympathized.

"What? No more life story?"

"No more, man. . .!"

For some time now, The Ripper Brown Epic had been the last set of electrons riding around Brando's tired and battered neural pathways. At that moment, he didn't care if it ever was produced or not. But he didn't particularly want Ripper to know that. He decided to play *Hollywood miffed.*

"Hey, you were the head cully, here--you approached me, dimber-damber man. Do you cognize, Champ? You were the one who got me involved. You insisted you were committed to this. You said the world needs the Ripper Brown Saga—cognize those words, so recently flopped from your own flapper?"

"Well, I was wrong about that, Brando. The world been gittin' along just fine without the Ripper Brown Saga."

"Yeah, Goofy-Lips," Jeff Raymond chimed in. "It don't need it."

Goofy-Lips! That was going to be a difficult appellation to ignore. The Ripper and his Mighty Foremen were building up a long list of negatives in Brando's heart. He found himself unwilling to allow Ripper to walk without a few scars.

"Oh, yes, Ripper? And so shall we also as easily cast aside and dismiss the memory of the fine lady, the staid gim-crack who kept your roguish life together?" Brando asked.

Loaf burped and grabbed Ripper's arm and attempted to pull him away, "Come on, Ripper. We don' need this."

Rand and Jeff looked like they were ready to thump Brando's choppers or crack his pelvis, whatever kicks or blows old Ripper indicated. But Brando still was looking for more of a reaction from Mister Big Football. *What about Lani? She deserved better than this. Was the*

Ripper an insensitive, cloddish lump of a cull? Brando himself didn't think so. The Ripper was not clever with personal relationships or the foot pads he picked for friends, perhaps, but Brando believed he genuinely had cared for his wife and mourned her loss. The light that was Lani Kazin had been snuffed out, and, his own life would never be the same. Perhaps she had bought her ticket from the boatman while defending the Ripster's possessions, perhaps guarding something in those old trippings and lippings of his that he didn't even know was of worth. And now he didn't want to continue with his ode. *That was understandable, and yet, that didn't smack of pure Ripster. Was he trying to forget her, or was it something else?*

"What about your hussy, Ripper?" Brando asked. "Don't we desire to descend to the heart of the matter to find reality, to gain cognizance of what transpired—for her? Do we not wish justice to weave its course?"

Ripper pulled away from Loaf's grasp and moved his giant frame until he towered over Brando, "I said NO MORE, man!"

In that moment Brando felt foolish as Br'er Rabbit with Br'er Bear, but he also felt he had to push the big man further.

"Ripper Brown," he intoned quietly like a soft-voiced narrator of the links reviewing the significance of an important putt on the 18th hole, "Once a mighty destroyer of runners and quarterbacks, but now an insignificant gnarler running scared as a whupped wussy!"

Doubt not, for a matter of seconds Brando saw his own life was in imminent danger. Ripper

211

swelled large and poisonous like one of those cartoon monster toads that double their size when they get riled. He was going to have to pulverize Brando or suffer a pulmonary stroke. Then he turned and stomped away toward the waiting black stretch-carriage limo. With the two others grasping Brando's arms, Loaf pushed him back against the huge marble baptismal font. The three of them bent him over backwards, shoving his head under the water, where they held it until he went limp.

Fortunately for Brando, they had no billing sheet on Earman and the Hands of Death. Brando had learned his water tricks in Nam—he could hold his breath for the rest of his life, if he had to. More precisely, he could swallow his tongue and die before sucking another bite of air. In fact, he could all-too-easily swallow his tongue. *That would certainly show them,* he thought with a grim humor. *I'll have a fit and kill myself before they get around to it.* Chicot the jester's last attempt at a joke, and no audience to share it.

He may have joked about it after the fact, but he was frightened and alone down there under the holy water, looking for the face he'd seen on a thousand Jesus statues. He was a true reconstructed flattist seeking the rescuing hand to materialize from some other dimension, and yet he suspected that neither the face of Jesus nor the magic hand would ever come. His world turned greyish-green, and the black spots gradually enlarged until they pushed out all the grey. Elizabeth Browning's last words, *The fog rises. Or was it Emily Dickenson? Edna St. Vincent Millhas Nixon? A rose is a rose is a rose, unless*

212

it's a fog. Where was the Zeeman's miraculous glow and that lovely warm barn door when he needed it?

His world stayed black for a long time. When he finally ventured back to known reality, he was alone, propped against a hard stone wall. Holy water was dribbling from a corner of his mouth. A door cracked open and a wrinkled old black rogue ambled in. Brando was beyond fear; he simply gaped with bleary curiosity, the ability to cast a glimp eye totally wrested from his personna by his recent baptism.

The old black man was an aged cock-of-the-walk. He wore a lightweight suit of antique white seersucker, and carried a boater finely woven of tan straw and circled with a thin black band. In his other veined and arthritic hand he grasped a cane of white birch crowned with a golden handle. No aged Domine Du Little, he was tall and lean, and his posture was erect and his eye clear.

Brando's mind wandered. *So that old Disney movie, The Devil & Max Devlin, starring Bill Cosby as the devil, was on the smack after all.* Brando had flustered to the dimension of his reward, his soul fluttering down to hades in the process, and Bealzibub was, indeed, Old Black Joe. *Gone are the days when my heart was young and gay.* There seemed something appropriate about the old black man's calm arrogance.

"The pendragon of darkness," Brando muttered weakly, positive he'd achieved the great divide and ready to join hand with fate, "No pearly gates for me."

"Ahh, no…you be still alive, Brando Mahr" the old black man cackled, raising one ancient,

213

white haired eyebrow. "Though for a time there was some question." He hitched a thumb to indicate those who had left. He was the very paragon of spareness of motion, an age-defying, wrinkled, ebony turtle. Brando opened his eyes wider, perceiving a stained glass rendering of St. Liborius holding out a book with two gallstones on it. Oh, fud, silly me, I'm not dead after all, he thought. Instead, he was drip-drying against the cold marble of the baptismal font, still in the back of the church where Lani's funeral had finished up some time before.

He didn't say anything, afraid nothing but water would bubble out of his mouth, a fairly sure sign that he actually was dead. After a moment, the old black spoke again. "I be Jimmy Teams," he said.

Brando finally found his own voice, "Can't be. That would...carbon-date you at approximately 135 sun cycles."

The old man smiled and his dark eyes twinkled with a hard light. He had the intense peer of a hungry grackling. "I will be 100 in three years, Lord willin'."

"Jimmy Motorfoot Teams?!" Brando was amazed, as if he'd struck upon the mythical griffin or an extinct carrier pigeon.

The old man nodded, "Played wit' Fritz Pollard on the Akron Pros, an' the Milwaukee Badgers."

"I cognize that," Brando said. He was probably one of the few people his age in America who was aware of Motorfoot's long-faded fame. "I did a documentary about the Neanderthal days

214

of the gridiron." He couldn't believe it, *Jimmy Motorfoot Teams!*

"I seen it. You got some stuff wrong." Old Jimmy noted his comment brought out the wrinkle lines on Brando's forehead. "It don't matter, sonny. It was a good show, mostly real good."

What a likeable guy, Brando thought. Almost angelic. *Shows you how little I understand about the real world.*

The old man's smile grew broader, "And, I like the fact you care you got it right or not."

Brando took a closer squint at him, not in awe, but not having anything to say. That close to drowning in a water basin, he was now introduced to a true riparian legend, one of Neanderthal football's founding fathers! Ripper Brown may have been the greatest of the great, but Motorfoot Teams was a page ripped out of the first Chapter of pro football. He'd taken the field when black men had to suit up in the colored church down the block from the stadium, and *piling on the nigger* was just another aspect of the sport. His speed and quickness had made him an audacious and feared runner. In the seasons he was active, he'd added up some impressive running statistics, and his gentle wit and humor had won him allies among those few reporters who were open enough to interview him. After his playing days, he'd hung around football for a multitude of ticks, first as an assistant coach and later as a trainer. Brando knew he'd done a trainer-stint with the Bears, a few seasons with the Rams, and then had gone on to another Mid-west team, maybe Detroit.

"They's two factions right now, powers behind the throne, so to speak," the old man said quietly, his steady voice measured like the tick-tock of a grandfather clock. "The first ones, the control-freaks I calls 'em, they want you squished like a June bug, like that man says to you out there in the church, 'cause you bringin' up old dirt an' stainin' the glory that is football."

"Ahh, squished like a bug...", Brando repeated. The jerry-rigged and hot-wired circuits in his brain were snapping and smoking like crazy as he tried to figure how any of this connected to the old man. *Two factions, Motorfoot had said. Did he mean in pro football? In the NFL? The player's union? Or was he talking about some private group, or maybe two opinions within his own camp? And just who made up his camp in the first place?* No matter where any of this led, one thing was certain - the old man had to have been hovering around, picking up on the conversation between Brando and Baker. Sharp listening....a worthy foe for Earman!

"That dunkin' you in the water was jist horse-play," Old Motorfoot smiled. "Maybe the boys went a little overboard, but that was jist all in good fun...But they's a second group, mostly old-timers like me who cares for the game, maybe 'cause it's close to the religious experience as any of us is likened to get. Course, they mostly ain't as old as me."

Brando resisted the urge to crack that mostly nobody in the world was as old. , Instead, he asked, "And what do they—this second faction—advise?"

"They say know the truth, for the truth will set you free."

"And pray what," Brando asked, "could we look as luminous into the clear pool of life and beauty as the eye can see, is the accurate reflection?"

The smile faded from Jimmy Motorfoot Teams' ancient face. "We ain't heard no more than old whispers." He paused, nodding to himself, "But you doin' one thing right."

"Unwittingly, you have my assurance."

"No, you doin' it. I see you doin' it. Jist keep on going. You keep followin' the money, boy," Motorfoot said in his husky old-gip's whisper. "Stay on that money trail. If nothin' else will, it gonna lead you to the truth. Fact is, you might try followin' it to Minnesota, maybe talk wit' a man named Hazlins."

Motorfoot stepped lightly to the door, and in another moment he had drifted away as quietly as he'd come. Brando noted that, for a really ancient speciman, he manipulated lightly as a ghost.

CHAPTER 20

Brando shivered as he huddled on the little marble step with his back against the baptismal font. He was thinking that, in every crack he poked, there was a hornet that wanted to sting his finger. The problem was, he couldn't figure why all the stingers existed, much less to whom they might belong. After all, the subject was ancient sports news, to say nothing of the players. Since the final whistle was blown on that old play-off game back in 1969, life had witnessed multitudinous rotations of the sun and moon. All the cheers and groans were long trammeled under the relentless march of ever-newer football news, waves of new flesh colliding on the storied green. Entire football dynasties had risen and fallen. Since 1969, rookies had matured, thundered their wrath and then drifted inexorably on like leaves floating down Gridiron River, to become geezer-owners of sports bars, gridiron prognosticators and shills for men's shaving lotions and weight loss programs. *What could be relevant from that ancient match between the Rams and the Vikings that would have motivated a set of wrathful fingers to tighten about Lani's lovely throat?*

Brando took his time getting his boots under him and his frame back to the vertical, and the parking lot was vacant when he finally staggered out of the church. Ripper and his berserker-buddies, as well as the admirable Lieutenant Baker and the ancient Jimmy Teams were

218

nowhere to be found. Brando guessed they'd already slapped stickers to their car windows, lit their lights and were slowly motoring after the casket to the cemetery.

By now it was late morning, and the hot fireball of the sun was licking down his collar. He walked toward the Maroon Dog, absent-mindedly reflecting on the tweep and caw of the birds. He could hear the distant whoosh and honk of the traffic zooming by on nearby Highland Avenue and the even heavier sweep of sojourners overpassing on the uplifting sweep of Freeway in the middle distance. The parking lot was tucked in the hillside behind the church. When empty, it was isolated.

The church itself had been constructed against an olive backdrop of humble scrub-brush hills, the one and only Hollywood Hills. This elegant gray rock chapel must have stood alone like a stern last soldier before the firing squad of silver screen squalor in the old days before the Holiday Inn and a clump of high rises were constructed in a manner that blocked most of the original symbolic gesture.

Brando had filched a little prayer memorial card from the service. One side had a picture of a peaceful, sunlit spring meadow with sheep grazing with lions, and the other outlined the parameters of Lani's life and a California Classic Lite poem about going into air. *Well*, he thought, *she'd certainly performed that dubious accomplishment.*

Brando popped the trunk of the Corvette and slipped the memorial card under the burlap corner of his heavy bag-o-guns, which he'd once again moved into the car. Weapons and poetry, *oh what a beautiful morning, oh what a beautiful day, I got a wonderful feeling.* Under ordinary circumstances, he wouldn't have given the illegality of his cache a second glance; being a True Amurican invested with the God-given right to bear arms and inflict damage on the deserving, he normally carried a loaded Beretta under the seat of Fifi la Fiat, anyway. That small automatic had been *in situ* for years, wrapped in an oilcloth and nearly forgotten. But the way events had been compounding themselves of late, Brando was alternately torn between strapping on every one of Eddie's guns, and burying the gunnysack and everything in it in a deep hole in the ground in the San Bernardino National Forest. For the past few days he'd been shifting the sack around like a nervous Nellie, first to his office, then to his locker at the studio, then to the old coach house where he lived, then back into the trunk of the Corvette.

He was about to shove down the trunk lid when a thick-wheeled white Porsche 911 and a racing red Ferrari cornered the church at max speed for a consecrated parking lot and skidded to a stop a hundred feet or so in front of the Corvette. It was the white half of the Fearsome Foremen. Rand Burkle lunkered out of the 911 while Jeff Raymond unhinged his giant frame enough to shake free of the Ferrari. Between the two of them, they had to weigh over 600 pounds. Brando was about to meet with fifty percent of the Mighty Foremen. Under different circumstances, he might have reveled in the moment, but his interpretation was they hadn't showed up to be interviewed.

"Heidy, Heidy-Ho, it's Wynken and Blynken," Brando said, only half-trying for Mister Nice. *After all, these numb-nutzy ding-boys had nearly drowned him.* "Where's Nod?"

"Look, you fuckin' faggot—We don't like your attitude with our friend Ripper," Jeff said.

"And we're here to beat the living crap out of you," Rand added.

Brando frowned. Jeff was assigning him to the ranks of the homosexuals, perhaps the lowest level of veneration your average footballer could consign to a cull. Brando always found it interesting how many bumfiddles associated his speech with the gay blades.

"I can appreciate your interest in *merde*," Brando said. "Probably a life-long avocation." He began to sing in his musty baratone, "Wynken, Blynken and Nod one night / Sailed off in a wooden shoe—/ Sailed on a river of crystal light / Into a sea of merde." He frowned at his shoes, "Gosh, that doesn't rhyme. It should be A-B, A-B, but"

"You are if we say you are!" Jeff yelled, still trying to get a rise out of his reference to the gay crowd.

"And you are...belly-wiggling invertebrates. A lower form, by Darwinian standards. Cod lickers, too, if the stories are all accurate. Did you know cod is actually an early 18th century word for scrotum?"

The dialogue was definitely not raising itself to higher levels.

221

"Whaaat?!" the mighty twins roared. Brando was sure he hadn't heard such oversized roars since Godzilla spotted Tokyo.

"You sure talk fancy fur a pervert!" Jeff was cracking his knuckles in anticipation.

"A rousing defense for illiteracy, I'm bidden to remark," Brando said.

While they pondered that one, Brando reached in the gunnysack for the Thompson. It was heavier than he expected, but then, his intention was to displace mass—nothing like $E=mc^2$, just a little Bonnie and Clyde type overkill. He gave the two quasi-famous footballers his sweet, lop-sided smile, the one that generally was followed by destruction and mayhem.

"I think when you undertake to play for the NFL, you are representing The American Way," Brando said. "And that suggests that you should buy *les automobile Americain*."

"What's that supposed to mean?" Rand asked, his voice rising in a peevish whine. Clearly, he hadn't seen the Thompson yet. Brando moved around the backside of the Corvette, a few steps to separate the two big men from the direct line between Brando and their cars. The two expensive European beauties were perfectly framed against the bare and famous hills of Hollywood.

The Thompson is a short little mother of a gun. Brando remembered that, according to Keith it had been around since World War I, a little dated in The Modern Uzi Age, but once the common, work-a-day infantryman's portable Gatling. Paratroopers employed it with straight clips that they wrapped around their tummies like girdles in World War II; they had to strap the weapons over their spare chutes with their arms on top so they wouldn't get slugged with a barrel in the chin when they landed. An actual Thompson was a historical item, a museum piece. It was hard to take seriously, which was Jeff's first big mistake.

"Hey, nice movie prop, man," he said.

Rand, who was a touch more intelligent than Mister Clean, didn't say anything. Without bothering to respond, Brando took the stance like he'd seen Elliot Ness on Fox's TV remake of the Untouchables, and cranked the lever to cock the Thompson. This pulled the bolt back so that, assuming everything went according to the Manual of Ancient Weaponry, when he actioned the trigger the bolt would go forward, pick up the first bullet, chamber it and fire. This should cause the expected continuation of commotion with a string of bullets flinging themselves from the muzzle.

Brando pulled the trigger. There was a moment's hesitation, followed by a super-loud *Takka-Takka-Takka-Takka-Takka*, and the short muzzle fairly leapt for the sky like it had a mind of its own. Keith had warned short bursts, so Brando let up before he brought down any *condo owners, condors, coyotes, crows or cumulous clouds*. He saw the results were entirely satisfactory. A ragged line of bullet holes had tattooed itself up the side of the Porsche in a neat little tracking design, and most of the windows were reduced to bright glass pebbles. He made a mental note that fresh .45 bullet holes truly counterpoint a white paint job. It was the sort of knowledge that might come in handy if he were to next direct some carefree car chase crashmagora. He could almost see this hip commuter couple fighting off gangsters as they race the freeway, heading homeward to plop in front of their television sets in order that the beauty and vision of KTGA programming might properly enrich their lives. But Rand Burkle obviously wasn't on the same wavelength.

Rand emitted an outraged war cry and charged Brando like a bully braggadocio. Brando thought the sight was akin to watching the charge of the famous mome wraths outgrabe. He arced the smoking muzzle in Rand's direction. That little social gesture brought Rand up short. He snorted a gnarly little yip and hopped back, raising his hands to the clouds. Meanwhile, Jeff stood there like cheap animation, his bald head gleaming in the sun, obviously trying to huck up proper attitude and maybe a new direction.

Brando swung his famous firearm back on the Porsche and concentrated on the wheels. *Takka-Takka-Takka*, went the Thompson, and the near two tires hissed instantly flat, like somebody'd dropped the vehicle from a winch, the sort of thing you observe in shock absorber commercials and truck tests, *We dropped this truck built right here in Detroit by real Americans from an army transport plane traveling at a speed of 260 miles per hour and an altitude of 10,000 feet to see if it could withstand....*

"How come you're only doing my car?!", Rand screamed.

"Makes sense to me," Brando replied.

224

Holding the Thompson with one hand, he dug in the gunny bag for the ugly little M-79. He had no idea where Joey had scooped up that little baguette, but Brando himself had carnal knowledge of army issue grenade launchers. He leaned the fat barrel across the Thompson while he flipped up the rear sight, aimed it, and then slapped the sight down again. With the target this proximate the projectile-drop would be so negligible he wouldn't have to compensate; he could aim nearly straight across. Of course, at close range there was always some danger of feedback. He cracked the chamber like a shotgun and slipped in a tomato-paste can sized grenade.

"Can you bum brushers still ambulate the dash-40 in ticks approaching 5?" he asked. When nobody responded, he said, "Well, allowing for age and deterioration, how about six ticks?"

"Huh?" Jeff said.

"Ding dong retreat," Brando said. "Motivating arse to the rear." He gestured with the fat-barreled little launcher.

Even Jeff wasn't buffle-headed enough to ask who, how, what, when or why. The two of them took off running like rogues half their age. They were about 100 yards away and scrambling up and over the high fence that separated the lot from Highland Avenue when Jeff's lovely red Ferrari disappeared in an entirely satisfactory orange-red blossom of flame.

Brando barely had the ticks to dive behind the Corvette before he was pestered by the incoming spatter of flying debris. The Italian gas tank went with a secondary whump. There was an even bigger fireball and wisps of flaming whickerbees

225

flew by, followed by little molten lumps trailing black smokers that curled down to settle on the sensitive fiberglass skin of his rented Corvette. Brando observed they were imprinting small black scars that went deeper than the maroon paint job, and once again he gave thanks that the Corvette was Morrie's responsibility. He dumped his weapons in the trunk and slammed the lid. As he hopped back in the 'vette, he noticed a regular field of little black pits scarring the hood, and there was a fist size hole punched in the door on his side, to boot. He had known that fiberglass bodies were subject to all sorts of problems, and now he was witnessing it first-hand.

As he accelerated away from the scene, Brando remembered that Morrie had left a message on his PhoneMate to the effect that his own dear *Fifi la Spyder* was finally fixed and ready to roll. All he had to do, Morrie had said, was come into the body shop where he could hand over the rental and take over his own wheels. Soon he would have his own life back. *Right*, Brando thought. *And boar, bison, camels, elephants, and toads* could fly.

CHAPTER 21

Welcome to another chapter of FOUL, our classic 18th century London street penny novel that takes place in Los Angeles in 1984. Classic? Why is it a classic, you ask? Well, age alone dictates all shilling shockers have to be classics. You certainly wouldn't find Moll Flanders and Humphrey Clinker in new fiction.

The next day the weather turned out to be a bleak and smoggy scorcher. It was a month or so before the dry, hot Santa Anas would blow in from the northeast to scour away the valley's usual acrid yellow layer of scummy air, and everything was still under a thick yellow layer of foul air.

Brando, feeling nearly recovered, had agreed to meet Morrie at Ivan's Auto Body. It was a small enterprise that lurked in one of those crooked and narrow alleys west of Reseda Boulevard, a place crowded with craftsman's shops and semi-legal operatives from Old Mexico. Brando ambled restlessly back and forth in front of Ivan's gate, which was heavily padlocked with a big brass Master Lock. He didn't try to break in. Having witnessed the dramatic TV spot on a cable re-run of This Sporting Life, he recognized that attempts to shoot the mechanism of the Master lock with any weapon this side of a howitzer would fail.

To make matters more difficult, Ivan's two portly dobermans padded silently back and forth like overweight trained killers, their little potbellies swaying as they went, paralleling Brando's every move. Mayhaps Ivan hadn't heard of healthy dog fodder like Chuck Wagon Lean, or maybe, Brando mused, *the man's dogs fattened through nacking on trespassers and rogues.*

Time on his hands, Brando found himself cogitating over Ripper's murdered dodsey. He couldn't get Lani out of his mind. Maybe it was the blank, vacant empty stare on her face as her cold body lay sprawled on her back in the Malibu strand, but Brando doubted that was his problem. He'd seen *la visage de mort* often enough to drive the grim reaper's sidecar. It was more that he kept remembering the gimcrack alive, her confident voice and wry-gimlit survivor's grin. She had nearly performed the impossible; she had stayed afloat in Ripper's turbulent world and still maintained her own identity, to say nothing of her sanity. Brando remembered how she'd lashed out at Loaf in her own man's defense, a quick clawing, sudden and definite. *The lady doth bear arms.* He had met the wench but briefly, yet thought she was a good sample of what to look for after you fall out of favor with the one like the one who married dear old dad, as the Country Western yodels might put it, if they yodel-ey-hee-ed in Brando-speak. He had once committed to a girl who was in some ways like Lani, though dissimilar in race, color and creed. Brando recalled the little encapsulated fairy world the two of them had built between themselves, so far from the bub and hub of the maddening crowd, and how it had tragically ended in compromise, doubt and confusion.

Nam Viet, Nam Viet, Nam Viet. *Tres cher nguoi Nam toi. Bai gia, chet roi. Toi Biet, chu*...Vietnam, Vietnam, Vietnam. *Very dear, my Vietnamese love. Gone forever, dead already, I remember always*...He knew it was better to have cherished and lost, than never to have known love at all. But the loss was so painful that the one could easily come to doubt the other. Brando yanked his mind away. It was all words, ashes in his jarred and jumbled memory. Maybe it never even happened, or took place in a dream world, somewhere over the moonbeam, in the dark shadows on the other side of the barn door.

One of the fat dobermans looked at Brando and whined his pathetic little call for human mastery. Brando pushed his hand through a hole they'd gnawed in the fence and the dog slapped his tongue across it, while the other one sat on his haunches, probably wondering if Brando was good for dog biscuits or a filet with baked potatos and sour cream.

Brando had loitering about the facility for a while, alternately exploring the nether reaches of the alley and entertaining Ivan's canine help, when Morrie made his appearance in a new rental green Olds Cutlass. The car was driven by a wide young varlet bulging out of a cheap sports coat. At the same moment, a scrungy little fellow in a pressed putty-grey mechanics outfit pulled up from the other direction in an antique silver Bentley.

Brando tossed his Mister Friendly wave in their general direction. "*Ho-la*, Morrie!" he said. "I didn't realize you insurance guys rated a chauffeur."

Little Morrie glowered at him, giving him the glimp eye until his second chin appeared destined to split into thirds. Brando could see their relationship had deteriorated. "This is Willie Calther," Morrie replied in a no-nonsense tenor. "He's here to drive back the Corvette."

"Hello, Wide Willie. We'll proceed with our reality one lump at a time," Brando said. "First, I need to monitor your progress on my beloved Fifi."

"What? Come on, Brando, I told you it's fixed...," Morrie said, the note of protest clear in his voice.

"Nothing to see," the tall and wide young bone-break added, doing the old Charles Atlas dynamic tension exercise that made his upper arms look like sides of beef. He ogled Brando like he was roadkill. "Where's the keys to the 'vette, pal?"

Brando took in the new dimension. "Morrie! You've brought me a repo man!"

Morrie shrugged from behind his huge protector. "I've got to bring this business to a conclusion, Mahr."

His tone of voice started Brando mulling the possibility that something wasn't right with poor Fifi. Plain as vanilla ice milk, little gnarler Morrie had been gathering his troops and cranking up his courage for this meeting. He looked sour-faced, like Buster Keaton about to bottoms up a bad shot of *Forni's Alpen Krauter*, a gay 90's health tonic, or maybe the once-pervasive castor oil.

Morrie puffed and postured, "Brando, my company is simply not going to continue to pay

230

for that expensive car for you. I could lose my job." He held out his left hand for the keys.

In another reality Brando felt he might have reverted to mild empathy, but this little Tom Thumb had once sniggered at the sight of his crushed Fiat. Brando swung his attention to the mechanic.

"Come on, Ivan the Terrible," he said. "Let's see the car."

Ivan laughed like someone used to blathering pleasantries. He bore a wide and grimy Russian face, a thick head of greasy black hair, and over the breast pocket of his overalls some fool had stitched the name Ivan.

Brando waved toward the locked fence and Ivan went to work on the Master Lock.

"Let us examine what level of legerdemain you've achieved here, Ivan."

"No," Morrie insisted stubbornly, "keys first."

"Morrie, you punster--you old word pecker-- you're that sure my Fiat has been restored to 100% cherry condition? Come now--there is absolutely no chance of some mechanism, lever or gizmo that is not-quite-proper?" Brando spat the words like a proper Britisher.

"Nothing's fucking wrong with your fucking car!" Morrie shouted. He looked he'd be stamping his foot in another minute.

"Then, the fucking proof is in the pudding, wouldn't you say? What are you afraid of?" Brando asked. "And you do know, I have the right of inspection and approval—or not.

The repo man's massive blond head moved back and forth like a golden retriever watching a

231

tennis match. He was in attendance to perform a plain and simple function, retrieve the company's expensive maroon sportster. But Brando had clouded his otherwise sunny day; the vehicle in question—the Maroon Dog—was nowhere in sight. In fact, Brando had positioned it behind Hoa's Soup Kitchen, a favorite Vietnamese haunt located nearly a mile away on Reseda Boulevard. There's an old oriental proverb, *Wise person never trust insurance man.*

It did not seem likely that either of these yahoos might figure out the location unless they forced a confession from him. And, as Lieutenant Baker would testify, *Brando was a walnut of inordinate tough*, or words to that effect. For twenty seconds they all snilched each other, eyes glaring.

Ivan cracked first. "F' Christ sake, Morrie, let's jist start the car up an' get it over wit'," he said, giving rise within Brando the sad but almost certain knowledge that he came from Brooklyn rather than St. Petersburg. Brando was disappointed; he had been fantasizing a true son of the old Czars detailing his precious Fifi.

The engine turned over on the first crank, that much could be said for Ivan. However, hastening upon the initial start-up event, thick black smoke boiled from the tail pipes for about a half minute. After that, the smoke thinned to a vile grey-black dragon's breath, luckily before any of them was rendered unconscious, and the RPMs settled into an uneven death-rattle.

Brando gestured cut-off with his wrist and slid casually around to the front where he popped the hood. As he'd figured, the poor fools had tried to rebuild his old engine; the gouge marks from the boulder were still much in evidence, even though they'd slopped the engine in a new coat of semi-gloss silver paint. Brando's imagination accelerated wildly. What a commercial for the Italian motorworks—*Engine hit by two-ton boulder, still runs good!* He was tempted to call Ripley's Believe It or Not.

He slammed down the hood, "*Nein*, Morris, mine." He chanted softly in pidgin deutchlander, "*Ein-a klein-a, Morris-a, mine-a.*"

"What's wrong now?" Morris yelped.

"Exclusively to address the most basic problem, Morris, the block is cracked. Where do you imagine all that smoke is coming from—some other dimension?"

There being no other matters to discuss, Brando waved to his plump doberman buddies and turned to make his way back to Reseda Boulevard...only to find the gigantic and youthful footpad had positioned himself as an obstacle in front of the gate.

Muscleboy folded his massive arms and smiled down on Brando like bad radiation. His biceps plumped his jacket sleeves out like *braunschweiger* sausages and his yellow teeth glittered in the golden California sunlight.

"You ain't goin' nowhere, nutcase," he said

"Oh, yes, Wide Willie," Brando said, "and you're the bright boy. You have the wits for three—two fools and a madman."

"I don't know what that means, an' I don't care," the big man said. His voice sank an octave, descending into the warning mode. "Let me say it

233

plain: Just give me the keys to the Corvette an' nobody here gets hurt."

"I feel it only sporting to alert you, Willie-boy" Brando whispered confidentially, "I'm a bit of a bully trap; you know, the soft-looking easy touch, somewhat like Clark Kent."

"You're warning me," Willie said with a scornful little snort, as if he might not have gotten Brando's drift, as the haiku goes in the Spenser novels, by the way, that's Spenser with an "s".

"Affirmative," Brando nodded, slapping the side of his head prematurely to nip any mini-Zeemans in the cranium. "And I might be...a little testy today, upon seeing the failed reincarnation of my beloved Fifi."

"Ohhhh," Willie nodded wisely, as if this made all the difference in the world. But he didn't budge a millimeter.

"You're not going to be the hector and attempt to impede my progress?" Brando asked.

"Attempt, no. I'm gonna do it."

Brando postured angrily, taking the role of the assistant manager of, say, a Sears underwear department losing his rationale. Brando stepped forward one pace and flailed at the ding boy with what looked like a great, foolish roundhouse aimed right to his potato trap. The ding boy routinely and properly stepped forward and extended his left arm to block. Brando could practically imagine his yawn, one hand a fist, the other holding an ale mug. But his wild, looping swing never came into contact with the bigger man's arm. Willie was still waiting for it when Brando took hold of his outstretched fist with both hands, and, employing Willie's own momentum

234

like they teach you in those little Double Bubble wrapper comics on aikedo, rocked on his back and at the same time pulled Willie down onto his waiting feet. As the bigger man rotated over Brando, he snapped his legs straight like a whalebone spring, propelling Willie in an awkward and unreliable somersault that ended abruptly and upside down against the gray undercoated rear fender of an old Ford Maverick.

"Hey, I got cars, here!" Ivan yelled angrily.

Repo bull-boy managed to roll over and get to his knees at about the same time Brando met his face with his right Bally boot, remembering to follow through like the golf instructor always insists. Willie's head jerked back and then his arms and legs splayed out like a clubbed donkey. His massive body whumped to the ground and he lay there, quietly breathing in and out with the true peace of the comatose. Brando was surprised. *A Hefty Bag of that dimension!* As Brando's father—him without a pugnacious bone in his body—always had said, it just goes to show, you never know who has the glass jaw.

Little Morrie was now cringing behind Ivan. Brando reached around the mechanic to tap his insurance man's chest with his index digit.

"Fix my sweet little Fifi proper, Morrie," he warned, intoning like John Wayne calling out the Pilgrim. "Contact me when you have achieved the higher reality."

Instead of exiting the front way, Brando slipped into the back and walked through the lot to survey other samples of Ivan's craftsmanship. On the whole, Brando decided the mechanic seemed to comprehend his legumes. The problem

235

must be his gnarly little insurance man, opting for cheapness over morality. There was a good bit of sloppy licking from fat-dobes I & II, and then Brando let himself out into the adjoining alley. The last time he flicked a look back, Morrie and Ivan were peering at their fallen footpad, who was shaking his big blond head and scanning reality from his horizontal position.

Brando consumed the distance to the Corvette without incident and was soon traversing the 101, dragging along with the rest of the sad-eyed early morning mob. About an hour later, he made his way past the grinning head cully at the studio gate.

He managed to dodge Shirley and snag his mail. He frowned at a rejection of IXTAPA, (his Jeckel-and-Hyde horror script that he'd sent to Universal) It was a wonderful story about a golden Incan mask that bore an ancient curse that would freeze half the wearer's face into evil and make the other half incredibly handsome. It wasn't his day; there was another rejection for A LADY'S LIFE, his historical romance about a moral albeit passionate Scottish lady who travels the Wild West from Sacramento to Estes Park in that more innocent time when General Custer still maintained his curly golden head of hair, the latter script that he'd mailed to a marketing executive friend of his over at Columbia. And last but not least, he was blessed with a special delivery envelope containing a round trip plane ticket to San Jose. It was semi-gangster Charlie Manganetti's cryptic way of communicating he would be overjoyed to entertain Brando's

236

presence. *A sort of a friendly mandate, if you will.*

CHAPTER 22

If you've been following along here, you know we've referred to FOUL as a picaresque, that is a story following the adventures of a low-born rogue. The very first picaresque, it is said, was Satyricon, written by Petronius, the Roman satirist who died in Anno Domino 667. You, being a computer un-buff (buff in my time meaning 'naked', remember) can read in Wikipedia that it was a freaky journey through ancient Rome. However, if you have seen Fellini's Satyricon, based on the original and filmed in 1969, as I have (yes, the dead like good cinema every bit as much as you do), will find an unforgettable view into an ancient civilization that in many ways is as proud, principled and corrupt as your own.

But, enough idle chatter...to horse, to horse:

Charlie was a short and chubby chunk of chum-bait. He looked too soft and crummy to be a real dimber damber man, that is, a real gang leader. He more resembled a cheery, fat-cheeked Benedictine monk than an *ursa minor* of the underworld. His look was made complete with the little round bald spot on the back of his wide head and a moon-like pate that forever wanted to burst into a huge grin.

He was approaching his 40th year, and had perfected a personal manner that made the unknowning lose their wary instincts. In Charlie's presence his friends longed for nothing better than to kick off their go-aheads, put their feet up and listen to a pleasant tale of his latest scamperings in the rogue world of the lawless and the untamed. This disarming charm was probably his best although by far not his only weapon.

Quick of wit and keen of eye, semi-gangster Charlie was on a constant and consistent info-harvest. He was always looking about with that wondering gaze of his, staring at the world with a seemingly innocent, child-like sense of bemused amazement. He seemed interested in every cull and gill's personal habits and their occupations. With a casual glance, he would be guestimating how much, give or take a couple thousand, the average draggle-tail passing by on the street was making. And with a second look he'd be idly appraising how much he might be able to shake loose from same said draggle-tail, and how he might go about performing such an operation. Brando knew about 99% of it was speculation; it was the one percent you had to concern yourself about.

Charlie dabbled in a lot of areas that, generally speaking, only wheedle-people like fortune tellers, snub devils and stock jobbers maintained even a passing interest. He would speculate on why a woman might fall for a particular man. *What was fate, what was cosmic destiny, and what was poor planning. Where the spirit pernicious went when it got drunk, slept or died. Who might win the pennant and the SuperBowl, which warehouses might be best for storing accumulated goods and where to procure a silencer for a .38 Bulldog or an unregistered Uzi.* Things like that.

239

In the 1980's, San Jose still had one of those refreshing airports where you of necessity perambulated down a flight of metal stairs to deplane. When Brando arrived, Charlie was idly cogitating on the far side of the metal detector, hands in his pockets. Charlie was decked in a plain grey pair of dockers and a dark blue short-sleeved shirt open at the neck. The shirt was out over his pants. He was conscious of his weight, and went for the tent look in shirts. Or maybe it was so he could conceal a hard plastic 9mm Glock stuffed in back of his pants. With Charley, you never knew.

"Kha!", the dimber damber man greeted him, and his face lit up in a big smile.

Their paths had first crossed in the mid-60's at language school, at the Defense Language Institute on the Monterey Peninsula. Charlie had returned to Northern California after his war stint, taken the vow with his old gill, and gotten successful in the real estate mortgage business. He exercised domestic reality from a massive but friendly one-story home in Monte Serino Estates, and wheeled about in a dark blue Mercedes 500. That was the entire case for Charlie Manganetti, unless you probed deeper—and, selecting to be his amigo, Brando mostly elected not to.

This time, however, Brando didn't presume their friendship was going to get off with such a light sentence. In his pokings about the nether regions of the NFL he'd been hoping to uncover some nefarious double-dealings worth a hot Hollywood sell, but he'd also been Monster Mashing on a wide variety of toes in his typical clubfoot fashion. Some of these appendages, he suspected, were tied in the traditional *foot bone connected to de shin bone* fashion to pal Charlie's friends of the family. These were a set of dark fish quietly skulking about the deep pool that one would ordinarily go a long way to avoid. *If one would walk a mile for a Camel, how far to avoid maim or mayhem?*

But when Charlie's features lit and he addressed Brando by his Vietnamese name, Brando couldn't think of anything but how splendid it was to be in his friend's company once again. Charlie insisted on carrying Brando's under-the-seat bag, and they ambled to his expensive *Deuchlander* motor car, which he'd parked a few feet from the terminal in an empty carriage-slot in the Hertz Rent-A-Car lot.

In a few ticks, Charlie's sleek Merc was humming over the winding, forested mountain trail to Santa Cruz. He said there was a new culinary enterprise on the ocean pier boardwalk that sported fresh clams, and he suggested they throw it a shot.

It was late morning; as Brando would say, highish in the early sunslide, and so the restaurant was almost without customers. He and Charley accepted a pleasant booth by the wide glass, facing north where they could watch the gulls swoop like little wooden gliders and the rubber-suited surfers stare into the many perils as they rumped their boards, awaiting the perfect ride to the rocky shoreline.

A pleasantly plumped-out young gim-crack with a pink-skinned wreck of a visage came by. She was pushing a fresh oyster cart, and so they had to venture their taste buds on some slippery

241

sea yums. It was apparent the girl had suffered as a burn victim; she looked so reserved and shy that Brando snap-judged it would take eons to cognize friendliness, if one ever could. But Charley, humbuggy as an oyster pry, had her chatty in a few bantering moments. After three or four oysters, she was teasing him about his weight. If there was one matter even his close acquaintances never joshed the dimber damber man about, it was the scales. But this was different; this deformed sprite could say anything to Charlie, he just laughed and went about his humanity, the cunning conner conned.

A second waitress, this one more of the dour dishwipe dowdy variety, buttocks embarrassingly half-clad in a short and frilly red-and-white skirt, brought them mounds of clams and fried baby squid and steaming hot bread. Brando summoned a Moussy, one of the world's finest non-alcoholic ales, and Charlie, who seldom swilled alcohol, requested a Calistoga mineral water. And still, he spoke nothing of the business of the day.

"Mmmmmmmmmmm!" he said, eyes rolling as he injested a clam. When Charlie dined, he was visibly, vocally pleased with *the vittles*. Chefs and waitresses at restaurants that had not lost their sensitivity cherished him without reserve. He was the perfect eater, the ideal of what one should be when one sits down to dine. He understood and appreciated good food, tipped well, and made certain every cull and mort knew how much he was enjoying himself. To Charlie, the great unlocked wonders of life were a good brush (loving) , a good chortle (laugh), a bag-job (scam) well done and a great banquet (great banquet).

242

The clams in question revealed themselves as the sweet New Zealand kind in the green-and-black shells and, claiming the gnaw of stomach worms still bit, Brando and Charlie had another order before they moved on to relevant topics.

Brando rode out his curiosity, the way he always did when hanging out with Charlie. He speculated that any rogue who relished reality with Charlie's gusto had a lot to say to a yahoo mud-lard and peasant beachcomber of life such as Brando fancied himself. Brando was satisfied that he could wait to hear it.

Never the muckworm, Charlie squared accounts for everything they ate. *My town*, he always said, *when you come to my town, I pick up the tab.* He slurped another oyster on the way out, managing to share a last laugh with the oyster wench over the supposed aphrodisiac powers therein and to slip an extra Hamilton down the front of her blouse.

Brando and Charlie strolled casually over the rough and heavy splintered wooden planks of the pier, peeping through the polished glass at the tourist things on sale. It was mostly varnished sea-washed roots, shiny pink-and-white seashells, cheap brass icon bric-a-brac, day-glo t-shirts and other flash pan.

"I'm investing in a ruby mine, *Kha*," Charlie said after a while.

Brando smiled, "Another...shot up the wild goose bum?"

Charlie was infamous for his plunges. Losing money was a joke—so long as he was investing and not being scammed or cheated. *If Billy knew all the money I've blown over the years, she'd go*

243

through the roof! he'd shout to the rooftops in his joyful Bayonne accent.

"Naaa," he chortled. "This one's the real thing. A group of Belgians own the rights to a mine in Burma. It's the second largest ruby mine in the whole fuckin' country, only it hasn't been opened since World War II."

"May Lady Luck ride in your breeches, *mon ami*."

Charlie eyed Brando for a moment, allowing him to comprehend he joketh-ed not. "You want in?" he asked.

"Me?! *Pour quois, moi? Or just...pour quois?*"

"Well, you know, it's a good thing, and we're, like, friends. That's what friends do for friends, *Kha*."

Brando lofted him a more discerning squint. "That isn't the entire potato, the whole enchilada."

"There you go again. Always analyzing the crap out of everything," Charlie said with an accusing laugh.

"I need not remind you that you, not I, are the self-proclaimed philosopher."

Charlie sighed and turned away from the sea to look directly at Brando. "What is it, *Kha?* You hurting for money? You need a score so bad you're going to stay in this Ripper thing?"

"*Khong phai, Mister Nha*," Brando said, shaking his head no. "At first, it was simply Where there's smoke...then, when these assorted knock-heads and ding boys started hassling me, I got interested... you of all people should understand—it was a nip of the old rush, like Nam."

244

"And now?"

"Charlie, I developed an admiration for Lani Kazin. She was quite a gimcrack. I reflect that perhaps, if I hadn't accepted this project, the dimber mort might still be among us."

Charlie's eyes slid away from Brando. He seemed to be watching a well-dressed couple drifting by. Probably wondering how he could get the gilly gaupus's gold Rollex watch. But then he nodded, once, like he'd constructed his decision.

"You want a gelato?"

"Yes."

Brando ordered the double-death chocolate, and Charlie had a lemon creme. They ambled away carrying their paper cups and little plastic spoons, angling out toward the end of the pier where the usual motley assortment of casual fisher-seekers were leaning over their lucky wands, beseeching Neptune and awaiting the strike of fate in the persona of a large sea bass, which, as in all other phases of mortal life, almost never happened.

Charlie sighed and looked directly at his friend for the first time. "So I can't talk you out of your quest for the holy grail?"

"I don't understand. You were the gipper who turned me on to this line of thought. Is it..are your...*familia* acquaintances requesting me to abandon ship?"

"No, not anymore. Kazin's death changed things. I was the one wanted you out."

"*Tai sao, Ong Nha?*" Tai sao means *why* in Vietnamese.

245

"Unhealthy climate, *Ong Kha*," Charlie replied.

"Why did Lani's dying make a difference?"

"In a way, it doesn't. I'm still worried about you." Charlie hesitated before continuing.

"...I guess you got a right to know. In another life, Lani was married to a friend of a friend of an acquaintance of mine. He's an old man now, with piles of money and nothing to do but promote good and avenge evil, that is, to reward his pals and whack his enemies."

"Leroy Kazin...," Brando said softly. Leroy had been a real dimber damber, the top buck of the Jewish mafia. Brando remembered seeing random, hastily-snapped portraits of him that had darkened the front pages of the daily blather-sheets in the late 70's, Leroy's grim smile generally presiding overexposes involving hacksawed bodies that had been deserted in motel bathtubs, and situations that had something to do with strangely ignited warehouses. Charlie didn't rhapsodize, allowing Brando to forge his own progress.

"But he was relegated to the hosgow moon-cycles ago," Brando said.

Charlie shrugged, his expression saying volumes about the penal system in a liberal democracy. They left the fishermen, walking along the boards in silence. The shore birds screamed overhead and nimbly came to light at their feet. They ignored them, walking steadily along, and the birds waddled from their path.

"On another subject," Charlie said abruptly, "I got a VHS of The Big Game."

"And what is your opinion?"

He sighed, shaking his head, "Easy to see the problem everybody's had over the years. I've run it a dozen times, and I still don't know. Sure, the calls are bad calls--"

"All...the calls?" Brando's right eyebrow raised. It was a practiced gesture, awkward and artificial, but Charlie knew him too well to take notice.

"Yeah. All of them," Charlie said. "But there's something more. They're kind-of marginal, funny calls—sloppy is really the word for it. I've seen games called worse, when I could have sworn the fix was on. This is different. Those guys don't seem serious, they're like a bunch of tired clowns staggering around out there."

"The officials?"

"The referees, the Rams players, almost everybody on the field except the Vikings. The last half, particularly the last quarter, is a joke. In the end, it looks to me like the Rams just blew it. I'll give you the tape. You take a look for yourself."

Brando nodded, "That will be to my advantage."

"Thing is, *Kha*, I dug around and found some historical background."

"Old wives tales?"

Charlie looked sourly at the ground and shook his head, "Validation of a couple of old rumors; this won't help you sleep nights. See, after the game in 1969, my acquaintances' friends' friends sent some people out to feel around the territory and see what they could see. After all, Kha, they'd lost a frickin' fortune on a game that was supposed to be a simple fuck-the-duck. But they didn't uncover nothin' and they lost four shooters. That's when the police started to smell meat, and the family backed off."

"Were these shooters foot pads of substance, Nha?" Brando asked. Anyone who could take out four mafia hitmen was someone to be treated with healthy respect.

"They were held in high regard," Charlie said.

"Where were they whacked?"

Charlie frowned, "They weren't, at least not in the ordinary way—and that's the thing that makes me nervous for you, *Kha*. One was hit by lightning while swinging a golf club, one jumped off a 12 story crane, and one got frozen in a meat locker."

"Random cross-overs of the accidental variety."

"Yeah, sure. Cosmic destiny. Only the guy with the golf club never swung one in his life, except maybe to beat somebody's brains in; number two was deathly afraid of anything higher than a bar stool; and there was no reason for the third *piasano* to be makin' like Rocky in that locker."

"Mot, hai, ba," Brando enumerated in Vietnamese. "What about...*bon*?"

"Him, they blew up in his car."

"They-who?"

"They, I-don't-know-who."

"Dynamite?"

Charlie shook his head. "C-4."

"CIA?"

248

"Naaa. *Ep Plastique* shit ain't that hard to come by anymore." Charlie used the Vietnamese name for military explosives. Brando had to smile; it was Charlie watching his back again.

"Well, *Mister Nha*," he said. "Four of Italy's best ding boys consume the big weinerschnitzel, and you ask yourself what are the fricking odds on my crazy old war buddy?"

"Yeah, *Kha,*" Charlie nodded, gazing glumly out across the sluggish pewter agua to where a giant blob of pearly afternoon fog was oozing in towards the pier they were standing on. "That's precisely what I ask myself..."

249

CHAPTER 23

Yes, FOUL is a penny dreadful, but we won't have any of that victim's-heads-in-the-vegetable-soup stuff, here. After all, that's already been done to death, to lay a pun every bit mundungus as a draft of bad gas....

A few days passed, and Brando felt he was no closer to any answers. He'd returned to LA and his humble office space, and had begun toframe-by-frame the tape of Ye Olde Game at his leisure. Finally, late in the day, Keith Lugosi had dropped by and accepted space on the old broken down casting couch of love. Keith seemed pensive and downcast for the person he was, and Brando deduced it was Lani on his mind.

"Nothing you could have done, old fogger," Brando comforted him.

"If I hadn't gotten you involved....I feel rotten about it, good buddy." Keith sighed, staring at the worn wooden floorboards.

"Simple ignorance is our current situation," Brando said. "We still don't cognize any of the inner workings. It could have been a simple robbery. Some crazed drugster, and *elle retourne a la porte, et....*"

Keith shook his head, "Cops say no sign of breaking and entering. She knew whoever it was. She let the person in."

Brando fell silent, mulling the contingencies. After a while, Keith began toying with Brando's

250

producer's three-quarter inch VCR, on loan from KTGA. Brando'd had semi-gangster Charlie's VHS dupe bumped up and printed with visible time code so he could track any particularly revealing sequences. Unfortunately, he hadn't found anything revealing, though he'd riffled back and forth through every fumble and wab in that ancient game.

It was Friday afternoon, and Keith had manifested himself early so Brando wouldn't rum out on the albacore run. Keith rumpled around in Brando's small refrigerator like a camp grounds bear before he finally settled for a Miller's Lite ale that was so aged it suffered bacteria crust from last year's carry-out Chinese. Dried scum apparently didn't bother Keith, the way he wrapped his lips around the aluminum. He just couldn't swill any of that artificial slop that Brando favored. Less Filling, Tastes Great, he didn't give a roaring odds plut. What mattered, it was a real bub, an ale with its nuts on and thingambobs intact.

Now Keith was dicking with the zoom stick on the VCR, employing it to push in and out of scenes like a first-time doodle-head director. In another few moments he'd gyred out the humbug-box and was into slo-mo, fast-forward, and little sparkle wipes in and out of scenes.

All the video humbugs were making Brando sick, so he ignored the screen to concentrate on a list he'd constructed of everybody who was remotely involved in the Ripper Brown conundrum. The list went on for three pages. It was too extensive. He had written down every blaggard from the grounds keeper who fondled

251

the turf on Vikings stadium back when to all sorts of organized crime dabblers and even the commissioner of the NFL, who was, for all he knew, the biggest dimber damber man of them all. Brando was thinking perhaps he wasn't made up of the elements of world class detecting after all; his list felt more like the entry sheet for The Big Time Crime Sweepstakes, just show up to gain admittance. Soon, he thought ruefully, he'd be including all the fans, or at least every rabid spectator with season's box seats.

Mindy Carlson sauntered in the office looking fresh and healthy as Virgo the Virgin, sixth constellation of the Zodiac, holding her ear of corn. Except, of course, Mindy didn't possess any corn; that was just the old Greek image of a Greek Maiden, one saucy breast revealed, that Brando remembered from his time deep in the dank stacks of the UCLA library. Mindy extracted a new videotape from her purse, which was one of those huge, colorfully knit Guadamalan pouches that was bigger than the pocket on a kangaroo with quints. The gimcrack still glowed with her successful role in the Casbah shoot that Brando had directed earlier in the day. She perched on the armrest of the couch behind Keith, who was so busy doodling with his new toy that the poor mad fool hadn't noticed her.

She clutched the fresh videotape prayerfully in both hands, and, eager as a puppy, she kept looking at Keith and then back to Brando and back at Keith again. Brando figured he'd better come up with something. It was difficult watching a grown wench in the whimper mode.

"Keith," he said.   "The lovely Mindy is occupying space in our reality."

That shattered the wide slap-fellow's concentration.   Ever since he'd slathered over Mindy's composite pinned on Brando's bulletin board, the old dog had been a man in love, or at least in heat.   His was one of those innocent, hopeless lusts, the mad desire of the gnarled gatekeeper for the Faerie Queen. Now that he was finally meeting her, Brando was sure he'd be happy on the car ride all the way down to San Diego for their fishing expedition. Keith took a milli-tick to freeze the frame on the tv screen and beamed her his most gallant smile.

Brando saw the randy old skirt chaser was in heaven over his most excellent fortune. If Ginnie could only see him now, she'd want to borrow back the Thompson, if only for a few bursts.

"Hiiiii…., Mindy," Keith smooth-voiced, "I've been dying to meet you. How *are* you?"

Brando was reminded of the tale of the lecherous frog who sighted the lovely, blue-bottomed fly. He was saddened to call any buckish friend a *mutton monger*, but the old tomcat was clearly addicted to wenching. On the other hand, Brando didn't know why he thought Keith was so hopeless and obvious—*hadn't all his own silly arguments about staying close to the enemy been mere shallow excuses to lure the wench to his own bed? Who was the true monger here?   Wasn't he himself trying in his own convoluted way to whisk her alone somewhere so he could maneuver into proximity with what he hoped were her highly removable panties? You know, give her the old bumpity-bump…in fact,*

253

hadn't he decided to invite the spruce wench along on tonight's run for the elusive albacore for just that very reason?

Mindy chose this moment to stretch an exquisite stretch, and then she sidled next to Keith for a bit of world class imploring, "Sweet prince, could you put that children's tape aside for a moment and watch something wonderful and important with me?"

That sort of ploy was wasted on Keith; after all, one is not required to kneed warm putty.

"Hey, anything for you," Keith said in cooing tones that disgusted Brando, because, he told himself, he hated butterscotch. "May I call you Mindy?"

She nodded an adoring sweetcakes look with her long-lashed peepers, and Keith lovingly accepted the video from her digits, which lingered on his shoulder.

"What is it?", Keith asked.

"An educational video," she teased, giving him a pout worthy of Brando's own clever Belle Denver.

Keith's face fell a mite, but there was no huff or bluster. Anything for Mindy Sweetcakes. He reached for the portable switcher, and was about to rewind and eject when Brando saw something fishy on the screen and stopped him.

"Wait--hang arse a tick, Keith!" Brando had to wave to gain his attention back from the dulcet Mindy. "Zoom in on the ref--the one in the backfield, behind and to the left of Gabriel."

"Give me a minute, babes," Keith cooed to Mindy. "Duty calls."

Keith examined the screen and then punched the buttons to Brando's request. In the scene Brando had called out, a referee was decidedly off-balance and goofy-looking in an awkward jerrycummumble that had him on his way to the ground. What interested Brando was that he was almost alone. There wasn't anybody around to bang him over on his bumfiddle.

"Okay, rewind about ten ticks and roll tape," Brando said.

Keith did as he asked. The figures on the screen ran backwards in a sort of fast visual gibberish, locked, and ran forward again in real ticks. Brando snatched the frame number just before the tape started forward and scribbled it on the palm of his hand. As the ball was snapped, the official, who Brando figured was the backfield judge, skipped aside, apparently to stay out of the sweep of the action. But his lumbery feet caught on the turf or simply on each other, and he went ass-over-teakettle in an awkward tumble.

"Clumsy son-of-a-bitch, ain't he?!," Keith laughed.

"Yea. The lout flounders over himself."

"Like a clown," Mindy agreed. "So what?"

Brando didn't know how much to say in front of her. He decided to flumpher it, "So, *rien*. I just related to it as funny."

"Ha Ha funny or suspicious funny?" she asked, frowning like an irate mopsqueezer.

Brando shrugged, "Probably just Ha Ha funny," and catalogued her reaction as odd but not important, the impatience of a hoity-toity who wishes to see her own image up on the screen. He clapped his digits, "Keith, old bluster, remove that

255

sportsman's tape and prepare yourself for an educational treat!

As an actress, Mindy was a hard worker; as the casbah lady of Luke's latest variation of the current KTGA *leitmotif*, she'd allowed the sport of belly dancing to consume her. Or maybe she just visualized a lovely opportunity in the KTGA promos and desired to promote the trend. Doubtful, but...whatever. Lucas had put on a CD of Ravel's Bolero for mood music, and the good wench Mindy had bumped, slithered, wiggled and ground her way through the dance of the seven veils like a hot-winded spring *foehn* roaring north out of Africa to melt the Alps winter snowpack. When the vixen reached the climactic part with but one flimsy veil remaining, she tossed that one aside as well and went over the top *au natural*. Brando was totally cognizant that—as the professional actress she'd proven to be—it was purely in the interests of *cinema verite* that she wasn't wearing anything underneath that last veil.

He'd let the shot run, and as Ravel's beat quickened she had continued to pick up the tempo, gyrating her grace and beauty before the stunned and elated crew. Brando hadn't had the heart to say *Cut*. The tape rolled on and on and on, and her performance was hugely successful. They were running two cameras, so he nailed one on the full shot, while he had the other move in for close-ups. It was the way he'd learned since his early nicks as a filmmaker, the method by which one ascertains the scene would fully work once they got into the editorial room. Brando Mahr, *consummate director*.

It had been some buzzy shoot. The takeup reels were smoking by the time their look-out warned that Don Parker and Shirley were walking over from their office. Brando reluctantly tossed a few of the discarded veils in Mindy's direction and called the wrap. Don was a devout Mormon who blushed when forced to report the bathroom had run out of bumfodder. He would not take well to erotica, so for the Don Parker version they might have to stop at three veils.

It worked out like one of those movies where everything falls together perfectly at the last moment. The make-up lady and the costumer bundled Mindy off and the male members of the crew were innocently standing around smiling at each other and the ceiling and hoping their donkeys didn't show when Don walked in.

"How's the new spot look?" he asked, right on cue.

Brando assumed the lean and haggard look of professionalism and led him by his arm to the coffee machine. Don romanced himself with the thought that he was an inside guy; the truth was, his job involved little more than hiring Luke, saying yes to whatever she thought up and then hot-footing the new spots up to top management. He was normally a decent enough burger, but Brando didn't want him catching any accidental glimpses of Mindy in-the-flesh flashing across the floor monitors.

Luke gave Brando her white-faced look of warning over Don's shoulder, but Brando had reality well in hand. "Don," he smoothied. "What we have captured on tape is so phantasmagorical that we zoomed it into editorial.

You'll be the first to visualize the greatness. Additionally, you'll have your own handcrafted presentation copy yet this very day. I swear by the Brando Mahr Seal of Good Videomaking."

Don nearly broke out in tears, looking like some kid had snitched his Tonka, "Can't I at least see a playback or two?"

Lucas, the clever wench whom history would recall had started the entire torch scene with her randy Bolaro tape, now assumed her faint and apprehensive look. If Don napped stare at Mindy *sans* veils, they were all going to need tickets to the Kids Are Fun show to get in past Harvey at the front gate. But Lucas was a gamer; she sucked it up and tossed him a brave smile.

"Great, Don," she said. "You're gonna love it. Guaranteed. Another Lucas triumph for KTGA. But honest, just give us a couple hours to stick it together.

That was what it took. Don would scale any mountain for Lucas. She was his secret fantasy, a monument of a woman. Every healthy male should retain one in his arsenal of lust and longing.

"No peeking, now," she warned. She gave him a peck on the cheek. He turned crimson and she hustled off to the edit bay to join her sacred and profane tapes.

When Brando retired from the set a few moments later, the cameramen's pulse rates were nearly back to normal. But they all were looking forward to viewing two tapes, the one for air and the high octane collector's edition.

Now Keith popped Mindy's tape in Brando's VCR, and lo!, it turned out to *be les edition especialle!* It was truly a piece to be marvelled. By the time it was over, Keith was nearly too bug-eyed and choked-up with gratitude to cheer. Any other time, and Brando himself would surely have gotten more fully into it. He did let out a whoop or two, but he couldn't really concentrate. He kept seeing the image of that clumsy referee, and hearing Mindy's voice, talking about his pratfall, now just another part of a grainy old sports tape. *Like a clown,* she'd said. That was twice he'd heard the same description. His good friend semi-gangster Charlie Manganetti had said nearly the same thing. *They were fallin' around out there like clowns, Kha!* It was enough to make Brando rethink his earlier premise about for whom the fair Mindy might be working.

"Hey, I got a great idea," Keith said.

"I doubt it," Brando replied.

"No, honest." He turned to Mindy. "We're driving down to San Diego. Why don't you come fishing with us?"

Brando was thinking hades would freeze over first, but that shows you how little he knew of gimcracks in general and Mindy in particular.

"I'd love to," she bubbled. "I wasn't doing anything this weekend, anyhow."

CHAPTER 24

Penny dreadfuls are quite back in style, you know, what with the modern Broadway version of Sweeney Todd, and then Johnny Depp starring in the cinema release. Let's laugh a bit about whether Thomas Prest, the British writer, journalist and musician who wrote the original shilling shocker got his royalties this time around. I know for a fact that he wasn't rewarded a shilling back in the mid-1800s when they first stole his book and made it into a smash hit stage play. I supposition you'd call that 'the first time around.' I'd call it habitual larceny

Brando, loose behind the wheel of the thundering Maroon Dog, pointed his salty crew of two south toward Point Loma. Keith and six fishing poles were jammed in the seat next to him and Mindy sat sideways on the bench seat in back, complaining bitterly all the way. They had the top down and the air conditioning on full blast, but the post-noon atmospherics were uncomfortably hot and the stop-and-go on the 405 South was a junket with which to be reckoned.

Brando hadn't anticipated any better, for it was the beginning of the weekend madness in Paradise South. After endlessly crawling out of L.A only to find themselves barely creeping by John Wayne Airport in Newport, Keith rebelled at the steady diet of Lightnin' Hopkins and switched them over to KTLA country western, insisting on rights as chief navigator. To Mindy, there was no difference between wailing hill-billies and howling blacks. Mayhaps there was no way to keep the wench happy. Brando found solace in the fact that her delicioso gams, crossed and sticking out the side of the Corvette, were a worthy study in his rear-view mirror.

The San Diego sport fishing fleet, thirty to forty boats strong, putters seaward from a single crowded landing within the harbor at Point Loma.

The fray started innocently enough, as they always seem to. Brando and Keith spotted some yuppie-lads from one of the day boats who were getting ready to back their BMW station wagon out of a parking spot. Brando sent Mindy to block traffic from the other side while he put on his turn signal, the blinking light being their official claim to the spot, a custom which is known and understood by fishermen pulling into parking lots worldwide.

As luck would have it, the station wagon pulled out backwards, blocking them just long enough for an old black Chevy Camino truck to bump Mindy's lovely behind and slip into the position from the other side.

"Hey!" she complained, but it did her no good.

The truck contained two burly and unshaven hectors in their late twenties and already going to cabbage seed.

"Get lost, broad," one of them said.

Not much of an example for the rest of humanity, Brando thought, the heat rising to his face. The brace of hectors were wearing dirty old Pendleton wool shirts that looked like high school graduation presents and they had fishing vests

261

pulled over them. The vests were open to accommodate their ample gut bulges. Empty beer cans clanked to the pavement as they climbed out of the truck, and they studiously ignored both Brando and Keith while fumbling with their tackle boxes and poles in the back of their truck.

"Hey, fellows," Keith said in his usual cheery voice, "That's our spot."

"Then why ain't you in it?" one of them growled. The other footpad just smirked.

"There'll be another spot," Mindy said, rubbing her butt with one hand and not bothering to look up from Brando's government publication of West Coast Fishing.

Keith smiled his sweetest, "I just wanted to thank you for saving it for us."

The driver snorted, like he was rooting for grubs.

"Driver dropped the keys in the big left hand pocket on his vest," Keith said quietly to Brando.

"Do you generally converse or hit first?" Brando asked.

Keith shrugged, happy as a ginger-faced noodle with fresh mud on his boots.

"Oh, I generally talk before I beat or strike with the fists," he said. "After all, we are reasonable men."

He opened the door and got out on his side of the Maroon Dog, and strolled over to his side of the Camino truck, playing the curious tourist on his best behavior.

"Hey," Mindy said, honking her alarm, "What are you doing?"

"Don't worry, hon," Keith looked back to assure her, "we got reserved parking."

262

He ambled up to the driver while Brando studied the other sad rum-dubber. Up close, neither of them looked any smaller or any more amiable.

"Gentlemen," Keith said, "We have ourselves a little problem here. The only question is, are you going to move that pile of manure or do I gots to take your keys?" He was still smiling, like one of those amiable quiz show hosts who questions whether you'll try Door A or B.

The driver started to mouth words, but Keith dowsed him in his tub-o-guts before he could say anything. The poor mackerel made a gurgle as he slumped, and in another few ticks, Keith had the keys to the Camino.

"Hey!" The fallen cut-purse's friend let out a delinquent snarl, "You dirty sneak-puncher...!"

He ran around the car, heading for his own doom, and caught his chops on the same clenched fist Keith had employed on the driver. The second rum-dubber went down like he'd been clubbed with an alewife's rolling pin. By this time, Keith's first victim was on his hands and knees, flashing his hash as he barfed a bucket of used suds on the crumbled asphalt.

Keith smiled happily at Brando and whistled a few bars from *Frere Jacques*. He winked and Brando saw the *rouleau* of silver coins he slipped back in his pocket. He dragged the second sorry footpad out of the way, and motioned for the first to crawl over and join his pal.

Keith tossed Brando the keys and doffed his battered old fishing hat. "My good sir—your honors, I believe."

263

Mindy stared in bug-eyed wonder as Brando gunned the Camino out of the coveted space to allow Keith to pull the Corvette in.

Keith peered in the trunk as they took out their tackle boxes.

"Joey's guns gettin' too hot to carry around?" he asked.

"It was weapons or fishing gear."

"What weapons?" Mindy asked. "You carry weapons around in your car?"

"Bats. Hammers," Brando said. "You cognize, Mindy, in case we innocents are beset upon."

They had made their way, *ambulated their course*, as Brando would say, nearly across the parking lot before Keith turned to Brando and flashed his patented little-boy innocent look, "I heard some fancy sports cars got machine-gunned and grenaded to death outside the church after Ripper's funeral."

"One wouldn't doubt such a possibility," Brando shrugged. "Ripper maintains all sorts of weird friendships from his rockem-sockem football life."

"Somebody told the cops the weapon looked like an old Thompson."

"There is something to be said for classic weaponry."

Keith smiled and nodded to himself. Mindy looked like she wanted to know more, but for the likes of her more was not to be had.

Keith led them along the wharf and through a complicated maze of docks. He had been here before and had marked where their boat, The Coral Sea, was docked. Brando didn't glance back at Morrie's rental. Having read the bible not once but many times he had an absolute certainty that the power of a backward glance could turn whole cities into salt, much less something as small and defenseless as a rented Corvette.

CHAPTER 25

The Coral Sea rocked in her moorings. The motion was a gentle remonstrance to the unwary that a series of summer tropical disturbances halfway down Baja were providing choppy seas as far into the northern latitudes as San Luis Obisbo. The stout little vessel fleshed out as a 49 foot double-diesel engine fleet-fisher with a captain's cabin on top. There was a galley in the center of the main deck, a flat place for advanced fishing in back, and sleeping quarters down below. There were notches for thirty fishing poles in the thick wooden rail that ran completely around her from stem to stern. An array of disks and fancy directional antenna sprouted over the captain's cabin; these were the probe instruments, the symbol of man's lust to track the elusive tuna. The biggest of these highly desirable lurkers of the deep hadn't been spotted around San Diego in many a year. Currently even fifty pounds was a rarity. The Japanese, particularly, harvested the ocean, hauling them up in nets that stretched for miles. The flesh had gone inside those flat little cans that were labeled Bumblebee and Chicken-of-the Sea. The practice is *called fishing a thing to death*. Or were you not wondering why Sea Bass costs more than lobster?

As they clambered on board the Coral Sea, Brando's awareness settled on three salty gizzards fiddling with the tracking disks. Something about them seemed not quite right, but he couldn't figure out what. He lightly slapped the side of his head to fend off any lurking Zeeman, and tossed Keith his lop-sided grin.

They were the last fishermen to arrive, but it appeared to be as advertised, a light load. Keith and Brando still found good slots in the pole rack and handy places on deck to stow their tackle boxes.

Brando smelled imminent departure in the air; the game plan of the boats leaving here to stalk the best tasting and most elusive tuna involved a high-speed overnight race one hundred miles straight west to the outer fringes of the warm water current that flowed northward, paralleling the Baja coast. If one can say anything whatsoever about the habits of the whimsical and unreliable Albacore it is that they begin running along the coast in mid-summer, and in a good year the run will continue through September or October. But as both Keith and Brando knew, you wouldn't want to gamble the homestead on it. When a school of albacore finally does make its grand appearance it is as pretty a sight as a pioneer's first glimpse of the plains buffalo; the big fish shooting to the surface in rocketing, ravenous packs that seem to boil the water. They hit a few lucky lines like Leaping Lenas and the rest of them disappear forever back into the mystery of the deep swells. *Why bother?* Well, a good-sized albacore weighs between 25 and 40 pounds. Shaped like tough little barrels, they fight the line like demented moose of the sea. And they are almost all meat. One decent albacore cut in thick coral-pink chunks and packed in the freezer can provide six weeks' worth of steaks. So all you need is a few boils and a lucky hook to make your day.

The captain main job was simply to point his boat directly west, cross the shipping lanes, and go at least a hundred and twenty kliks out to sea. Once in the vicinity of their finny prey, the good sports fishing boat captains all tended to drift their boats ten klicks or so south into Mexican waters, maybe for luck or maybe because the belief was the fishing is superior. Brando had been on boats hauled over by the Mexican Coast Guard, which is why Keith and he had bought Mexican fishing stamps as well as their U.S. licenses.

The anticipation ran high; the Salt Water Report in the sports section of the L.A. Times was recording white-hot albacore runs. Most boats were bringing in two or three lunkers per hootboy, that is several tuna per fisherman. Keith explained the reason they were running light—the Opie Dopie Studio had chartered the boat, and he had arranged matters so that only 20 or so of his good buddies were invited. Of those, he expected no more than 12 or 15 to show up, so there wouldn't be any elbowing or furious shoving at dawn when the thrilling call *Hook Up!* came whistling through the galley.

The overhead sky, a jumble of plum and orange clouds, faded into the deepening grays of early evening. Mindy wandered up on deck. Brando thought she looked *tres delicioso* in a sailor-white pants suit with a red and white striped turtleneck under a white jacket. She accepted a Lite ale and tried to be one of the gang while the rest of them—a grumpy pack of mostly studio union codgers, that is, grips, gaffers, projectionists and editors—sat around and told lies about how great it was when the world was young. Eventually the cracker-barrel chat, as it always did, got around to what everybody did in the Big One and the two dinkers that followed—Korea and Nam.

When his turn came, Keith scratched the old puncture marks on the back of his left ankle. "I still feel it," he said, shaking his head as if it shouldn't be possible. "When the weather's gonna turn wet, my ankle tells me 24 hours before she happens."

"How'd that happenstance occur, Keith?" Brando threw him the soft lob.

Brando always got him rolling about Subic, Inchon or Iwo before the conversation could curl around towards Bien Hoa, Tay Ninh and himself.

"Well," he laughed, "You notice the holes are *in the back* of my leg!" He told it all again, about the night when hordes of Chi Coms had come pouring south across the DMZ. Out-numbered and out-gunned, the American gang of bully-boys had retreated down the length of the Korean peninsula, running for their lives.

Keith had caught 9 slugs in the same leg, a close pattern ripped from one of those reliable little Chinese submachine guns patterned after the old Czech model. He'd been spun forward arse-over-teakettle into a shell crater, a shallow depression that had probably saved his life. After that he'd somehow managed to dodge the Chinese soldiers, stop the bleeding, keep his lower leg from infecting and stay alive for weeks until the tide turned the other way and he was behind friendly lines again.

269

By this time the twin diesel engines on their boat were firing up. After ten minutes, the nimble Coral Sea backed away from the dock and eased across the harbor to the bait bins.

Albacore are notoriously picky eaters, and live three-inch sardines are about the only bait that attracts them. Even at that, the bait has to be new and lively, and has to be gill or nose-hooked so they'd still swim around.

Delicious Mindy wandered around in wide-eyed wonder while the crew dipped big scoops of the wiggling sardines out of the bait bins. The hordes of little fish flashed in the glare of the spotlights that were rigged over the bait bins. Some few escaped and hit the deck before the scoops could be deposited in the small holding tanks on board the Coral Sea.

"There's something totally inhumane about all this," Mindy mused to no one in particular as she watched the unlucky few sardines flopping helplessly on the deck. "These creatures are alive, and yet we treat them like a toy or a game."

Odd, Brando thought, *how wenches wax cow-hearted over life on the grand scale.*

He saw it as the mother instinct gone rampant. He visualized Mother Hemingway pondering her ants on a smoldering stick. She would have carefully lifted them one by one and set them back on the planet. *The civilized man's burden. Odd's Plut*, he cogitated, *bitches had a similar, but reverse, opinion of us poor miserable culls. They thought of men as harsh, cruel and uncaring. Yin and yang, Jack and Gill, how shall I love thee, let me count the ways.* Brando figured the ways added up to less in number and more difficult to achieve in the modern age.

There was a snicker from one of the crew at Mindy's concern for the baitfish. Brando recognized the lackey who cracked chuckle as one of the electronic geniuses who'd been monkeying with the directional gear when they'd boarded. He was an awkward young gilly gaupus with a thin neck, a stringy goat's beard, scraggly black hair and a bad sunburn that had hardened and cracked his lips and turned his face bright red. The typical scruffy boat-side t-shirt and tattered jeans hung from his lean carcass. Brando thought skulkers with delicate skin like that should aim for indoor careers, point towards assistant ownerships of Taco Bells or fancy positions as financial securities salesman. But here the simple gull was, burnt to a crisp and mean as hell.

"No," Mindy told the leering sailor, "I'm serious! All of God's creatures are created equal."

Up until this moment, Brando had no idea Mindy was an enlightened gimcrack. To be honest, he'd been so busy alternately suspecting her of devious affiliations and pondering over ways to lure her into a brushing encounter that he hadn't really considered much else.

"You're probably one of those fuckin' vegetable eaters!", the goat-beard cully jeered across the deck at her. "Meat an' fish ain't good enough for you!"

"I am a vegetarian," she agreed.

Brando glanced at Keith, who lifted his shoulders and passed across the wide grin that meant *the Creator surely loves us for does he not continue to provide bountiful entertainment?*

271

Keith was already slapping the many pockets of his jacket to locate his rouleau of guineas.

"The military flaybottomists did teach you in non-commissioned officer's school to share generously with your comrades at arms, did they not?" Brando asked his old friend. "And, if this sad reparte-alas-comes to fisticuffs, it is my turn, and the hell-born babe—he of the lewd and graceless youth—is mine."

Keith sighed and shrugged his reluctant agreement. "Okay, good buddy."

Goat-beard slung the nets full of bait into various bait bins of their boat with a vicious abandon, conscious Mindy's eyes were on him. He paused to delicately lift a single minnow that had been struggling to reach one of the foot-wide scuppers and the joyous ocean below and fiercely bit the head off the tiny fish.

"They's *bait*, lady," he said with an ugly laugh, the bloody fish-head still hanging from his sun-peeled lips. "Nothin' but bait!" he repeated.

He spat the head in Mindy's general direction and rubbed his hand on his pants. The severed fishhead flew from his lips in a fated arc to light on Mindy's white pants just above the knee where it slowly slid down the fabric, leaving a little red trail as it went. Brando and Keith's favorite gimcrack Mindy took on a shade of gray, no longer resembling the robust and lusty dancer of the seven veils.

Brando slipped between Goat-beard and Mindy.

"Until now," he said gently, "I had presumed they chained all the cut=purse scullery knaves, powder monkeys, mundungus swabbies and duck-fuckers below deck in cages until the hour of need."

"Duck-fucker?!" Goat-beard shrieked like a furious little girl.

"Yes," Brando replied. "You know, the chap on board a seaworthy vessel who takes care of the poultry and the-"

"Listen, mush-mouth," the skinny young man flared, streaming his undiscriminating anger in Brando's direction, "why don't you talk straight English like a real man?"

Brando was thinking that the footy despicable was too dyspeptic for his own benefit or wellness. And this, indeed, proved to be true. Goat-beard's lips were so wind-hardened and brittle that they split like orange slices when Brando caught him full in the visage with the cutting edge of his metacarpus.

The young ducker fell backwards in bowling pin style, but he wasn't down for the count. He scrambled up like a decapod crustacean, that is, a lobster, who was trying to avoid the boiling pot. He rubbed the back of one of his wrists across his bloody potato trap. Then he flailed his fists and advanced, making it necessary for Brando to bludgeon him again, this time with a closed fist to his upper torso.

Brando was impressed; Goat-beard was a tough little badger. The skinny little fellow flipped over like a rubber Opie toy, and then bobbed right back up like he had toaster mechanisms for shoes. But this time, as he waded in with his flying fists flailing like a wanna-be windmill, a lean black man grabbed him from behind. The man lifted him like a bag of coffee

273

beans and slammed him down on the deck. And still the plucky young Goat-beard started to stagger up on his props again. But this time the black man pointed a warning digit in his direction. Goat-beard shuddered all over in his rage but he stayed down on the planks, glaring like Lord Montbatten after the Germans sank that one ship the admiralty gave him to play spy with during World War the Deuce.

"I'm sorry about this, mister," the black man said to Brando. He was in his late forties, and his trim elegance reeked of retired military.

Brando shrugged, "It started of its own accord," he said, "like the first clock."

"More like the Big Bang," the black man laughed. "I saw it from up there." He had a deep, hearty laugh, but Brando detected a false note; in spite of his friendly tack, he didn't think the black man was all that elated.

"Toby here insulted the lady," the black man said. He nodded and pointed to the captain's cabin. "On behalf of the Coral Sea, I am sorry."

"The matter is erased," Brando shrugged.

"No, I insist." The black man waved one hand toward the galley, "A free round of beers all around. Help yourselves from the refrigerator."

A little commotion of cheers and huzzahs went up from the on-lookers. The black man nodded and turned to stare down at Toby. Without further provocation, he launched a vicious kick at Goat-beard's chest. Toby rolled over without a sound, then rolled back and glared up at the black man.

"What'd you do that for?" he gasped. His eyes burned with hate.

"Toby," the black man warned. "This trip was your last chance, remember?"

The glaring light faded from the ducker's expression. Then he block-and-tackled himself to his feet and lurched toward the six foot ladder that led to the captain's cabin. The black man gave Brando and Keith a wry shrug, and headed after Goat-beard.

Most of the cock-a-whoops had already pushed their merry way into the galley to snag their free beers, leaving the cold night air to Mindy, Keith and Brando.

"You guys play a little rough," Mindy said. Brando could see all the red blood cells had drained from her loveliness. "I don't feel so well," she added. "I'm going below." With no further ado, she gave them her cool side.

"Another reaction to evaluate," Brando muttered. The matter of Mindy was what he thought of as *a puzzlement*; if she was an emissary from either Nathan Paramis or Charlie, she wouldn't display such vulnerability, unless her acting was of a somewhat higher caliber than that for which he had previously credited her. *Mayhaps*, Brando thought, *the virgin water of my suspicion is my own unease, rather than any pebbles of blame to be cast in her direction*, his way of thinking he no longer was certain of anything in her regard. Brando tried to review everything that had happened; *Was it because some footpads had hit for two points with a boulder through poor Fifi's hood that he was now going paranoid on the world? On the other digit, the information from Charlie that these were sly, successful scapegallows didn't promote universal peace of mind, either. He would be a buffle head not to admit that a potentially lethal move aimed in his direction could come from almost any angle, whatever moment in time that the unknown dimber damber man and his foot pads calculated as most propitious. They could get to him, and he still didn't even know just exactly who they were.*

After the loveliness of Mindy's backside vanished out of sight below, Keith and Brando stood around hugging beers and attempting nonchalance at her withdrawal. *Time goes by so slowly, and time can do so much,* Keith sang in his customary off-key way. Robbie, the world's oldest, surliest and slowest projectionist, muttered the ancient fisherman's curse, "Woman on a fishing trip--Bah! Always bad luck."

"Albatross, wasn't it, Ancient Mundungus?" Brando said quietly.

Robbie ignored Brando (Keith had warned them beforehand) to stare accusingly at Keith, "We lucky if we gets us a single frickin' hook-up tomorrow. You wait an' see."

"Drink y'er free beer an' shut up, ya old fart," Keith said mildly, not able to guess how nearly true the old domine-do-little's prophesy would be.

The throb from the twin diesels deepened as the Coral Sea slid past the breakwaters and left the harbor. One by one the men lofted their empty beer cans into the immense yellow trash 'n barf can and clunked down the stairs to their bunks below.

"Cockshut Time," Brando said, "that moment of falling sun when fowls go to roust and worms and knaves come out of hiding."

Keith grunted his agreement. "Yeah, good buddy. Time to catch some shuteye." He and Brando silently looked out over the dark, oily swells as the black bulk that was the land's end mass of Southern California drifted into the distance behind them. The string of lights festooning the last westernmost bit of Point Loma faded into a thin, shimmering horizontally flat line which gradually began to dip in and out of the ebony waves and finally disappeared from view. They were at sea.

CHAPTER 26

Time passed. Chunks of reality skudded by while Keith and Brando skulked low against the backside of the cabin to avoid the bitter scotch-cold mist, sitting on the deck with their backs to the outside of the galley. They watched the foam trail away from their stern as the Coral Sea thundered westward toward the elusive albacore.

At least, Keith was watching the foam. Brando was already well into round one of his usual grapple with seasickness, and was desperately gazing off into the distance where the blacker black of the sea met the starry blue-black of the night in some semblance of a horizon. Keith was drinking 16-ounce cans of Coors. Brando was swigging Calistoga Water and eating Saltines.

"Okay," Brando said in a desperate bid to prevent his stomach from rolling over, "Let's try figuring...what we comprehend."

Keith grinned. "I bet you head for the rail in less than a half hour. That's what I comprehend."

"Keith, Odds Plut and her nails—" Brando warned mildly.

"Okay, 15 minutes, then. You look greener n' a parakeet, little buddy, an' it ain't the overhead lights. I bet five bucks you don't last 15 minutes, you're gonna puke your guts out."

Brando admitted he was probably right. They were sitting in the only place on deck where the spray wouldn't hit them, but it was the same area where a nasty little fume swirled from the diesel engines.

Brando was shivering inside a dark blue Beans shell jacket over a dark blue New York Giants sweatshirt that semi-crook Charlie Manganetti had given him. He also wore an old pair of fatigues cut off and unraveling above the knees, no socks and his oldest pair of running shoes. Keith was in a marines sweatshirt with the arms ripped off, dark green Dockers stuffed into a pair of rubber fisherman's boots that came up over his ankles, and an admiral-of-the-sea's baseball cap with scrambled eggs on the bill.

Brando sighed and dug a scrap of paper and a pencil from his back pocket.

"Jimmy Teams advised me to nose along the money trail."

"Old Motorfoot?" Keith gave him a skeptical eye, "He's been dead for years."

"Yea, verily. Except I conversed with the codger after Lani's funeral."

Keith took a big swig of Coors and turned to Brando, his eyes lively with amusement. "What do ya know. Maybe there is something to this spiritual medium thing, good buddy. You hire that famous channeler from Malibu?"

"No, I told you: Motorfoot manifested himself at Lani's last rites. He's a few ticks shy of 100. Before the strange and mysterious destruction of the expensive and elegant European motor carriages that so interested you."

"Ohhhhh....." Keith's eyes went wide, as if he was starting to half-believe Brando.

"Ripper," Brando continued, "possesses very minor-key moolah. I know the aging buck lives

279

beyond his means, his fame necessitating the sacrifice of inordinate spending. His hussy revealed as much to me prior to her demise. Ripper is almost broke all the time."

Keith sobered up a touch. Brando could see his friend was wondering what else Lani had revealed.

"Alternately," Brando continued, "Nathan Paramis revels in gobs of guineas, supposedly accumulated in land dealings. I went to visit him. He is a proper dimber damber, the head dog of a plush get-away for the wealthy up in Santa Barbara." Brando ran his finger down the short list he'd scribbled. "Loaf Ludder resides in South Central, about which he perambulates in an old and rusted Plymouth."

"Not many beans there," Keith agreed.

Brando moved the pencil to draw a line through Loaf's name. Keith looked over at the list, which he was holding against one knee.

"Wait, Brando-If you're lookin' for suspects with money, don't scratch the Loafer."

"Support point?" Brando queried.

"That guy's got every nickel he ever earned. I heard if you stuck his property all together he owns two city blocks. He just drives that battered old car because he's cheap."

"You glomed this in a crystal ball?" Brando asked.

"Nope. Old Clyde told me." Keith quoted Old Clyde with the absolute certainty one might apply to Webster's Unabridged Dictionary. Clyde was the ancient, wrinkled shoe-shine boy at the studio, one of the last holdovers from the dinosaur days before civil rights had made movie mogul shoes a little dingier and people like Clyde a lot poorer. "Clyde told me the Loafer puts all his property in other people's names. He forms corporations, that sort of thing."

"How did you get Old Clyde to discuss such realities?" Brando asked.

Keith gave him his superior grin. "We all brothers under the skin, little buddy."

Brando nodded and put a circle around Loaf's name.

"And that brings us to the last of the heinous fiends—George Haslins, landed gentry, the baron-farmer from Minnesota."

"Who-he, white boy?" Keith asked.

Brando shrugged, "I thought I might defer to you."

"Haslins, Haslins, Haslins...." Keith turned the name over, staring off into the night sky.

With the spots flooding the deck, the sky was nothing but blank, inky space. One would of necessity have to rattle one's bones forward to the bow, which was out of range of the harsh spotlights, to see the billions of starry specks and the gauzy Milky Way strung out overhead.

"There was a referee in the 60's or 70's named Haslins," Keith offered with some hesitation in his voice. "I don't know if this was the guy. He was notorious for his bad calls. They called him "Blind-Eyes" Haslins, or "Old Hassler", names like that. Even the newspapers—and we all know how the newspaper guys was in bed with the team owners—used to mention this guy. He was just too colorful to ignore. Brando, what if this is the same Hazlins?"

"Okay," Brando nodded. "Momentarily, allow us to suppose it represents the reality."

"You say he's got a lot of money?"

Brando nodded, "Yes, I am certain of it.

Keith shrugged. "Then we got three rich guys who used to be in football. Nathan Paramis, Loaf Ludder, and George Haslins. And we got The Ripper, who doesn't have a dime."

"Okay, so maybe Haslins worked that notorious game in the long ago...Los Angeles against Minnesota.. And we know that Loaf and the Ripster played in it. But Paramis was nowhere around...I mean, he wasn't working for the Rams or the Vikings."

"We don't know that," Keith interjected.

"True. So, what have we Sherlocks justly and righteously deduced?"

"I don't rightly know, good buddy." Keith scratched his head. "Like you said, the tea leaves are murky in the bottom of the cup. The inordinately wealthy three are an odd group—an ex-head coach on the Rams, a member of the Mighty Foremen, and a blind-as-a-bat referee."

"On the other digit," Brando reflected, "a lot of NFL people parlay their fame to make their fortunes."

"Well, I'd say we got nothin', good buddy. We ain't no further than the day we started."

Brando was unwilling to let it go. "Wait. Now that I reflect, I am certain Haslins punched his timeclock for that play-off game. I recognize the name from the play-by-plays. And I'll wager it was he who did the drunken dance and fall that we twittered over in my office."

"So you're saying George Haslins ref-ed the game? So what? Nothing illegal about that."

"That was an important game to employ a referee so near-sighted he couldn't see which end was the hippo," Brando said.

"Well, that's true enough. But I think they work on rotation, whenever their name comes up. If it was anything else, I'd say the hound's got yoke on his lips."

"The hound 's got yoke? And you say I talk funny!"

Keith stood and yawned, legs spread wide to brace himself against the rocking motion of the boat.

"One of them old movies about a dog named Egg-Eater," he said. "I find you can get some of your best analogies from old nature flicks."

"I've always felt close to Charlie Tuna, myself," Brando said. "Only the best tuna get to be StarKist."

"Young smart-ass. And here I thought I was helpin' with your cinematographic education.

Keith's empty beer can hit the rim of the plastic trashcan and fell in for two points. He hung out a few more moments, looking off to the side where he could see the running lights of three or four other sports fishing boats. They chugged steadily toward the promised water where the fish were big as pick-up trucks and as plentiful as Friday afternoon on the freeway. Brando could see beyond the small sports fishing boats into the distance where a larger string of running lights marked one of the distant freighters and tankers that were plowing their furrows up and down the coast.

But finally, even Keith headed for his bunk below, and Brando was left with his nausea and the grim knowledge that daybreak was a mere 18,000 ticks or so away. He reached in his knapsack for a carrot and gulped down another swig of Calistoga. He liked to think of himself as a venerable traveler of the seas, a veritable Horatio Hornblower, if the truth be known. And, if you've read the series, you know how Horatio was forced again and again to grapple with his seasickness.

CHAPTER 27

A touch later, as they moved toward high-witch hour, Brando saw something he thought was odd…though not strange enough for him to do more than note it in passing.. He was still awake on the boat, still caught in his queasy nightmares, halfway to flashing his hash. He was telling himself for perhaps the two millionth time that he could handle it. He was used to this routine. After all, He'd been indulging in overnight sport fishing boat trips at least once a year for a decade. The song-and-dance never varied; they would full gallop straight out to sea, *balls out and Beelzebub take the consequences*, burning fuel all night so they could cast their lines at dawn. The same fire drill, tick after tick…but this time something happened to vary that steady routine.

At first, the change was subtle. Operating in the inky black of the Pacific night, the captain—or whichever scuttle-bum had the wheel—cut the throttle back, and shifted the Coral Sea into the stiff breeze, where he held position with the engines throbbing at near-idle. This had never happened before on any fishing trip Brando had been on. The journey was always a full-throttle non-stop dash through the night. But the Coral Sea had broken the routine.

Brando was by himself on deck, alone with his *mal de mare*. He'd thrown a bunch of knapsacks and carry-on bags in a corner, and was huddled under a soggy gray-green blanket in the

285

middle of the pile and against the back of the galley, next to one side of the steps that plunged to the bunks below. This protected him from the sharp cut of the wind and the chilly spray, but it also made him nearly invisible, sunken beneath his protective clump of commandeered duffles.

He was fairly certain none of the other passengers was alerted by the shift in engine noise, at least, nobody came piling up from below to see what was going on. The crew—although Brando hadn't really paid attention to this bunch beyond the skinny one that he'd pummeled—the crew usually consisted of no more than three or four deck-thwackers and a cook who could be anybody from the captain's brother to a do-it-on-the-wing duchess or a full-fledged on-your-back trollop.

With the engines snorting their low-throb pulse, Brando could hear the quiet turnings on the shelf-bunks and a steady snore or two from the sleeping fishermen below. He was surprised to feel a gentle bump as another boat came up alongside. He didn't catch sight of it, but he was 100% certain that was what it was. From the feel of it, the way the two smacked together and the sound, his impression was that this new vessel was much smaller than the Coral Sea.

Shortly after the touch, there was a long rubbing sound, like the rogues were tying up but couldn't pull the slack in time and a wave got the better and pushed them a bit apart. *Ahh so, yes!,* Brando realized he was right, as, a few seconds later, he heard a second, smaller bump.

And with that, the overhead spots clicked off, leaving the Coral Sea in darkness except for the dim illumination of its red and green running lights.

Brando's sight was still adjusted to the harsh glare from the spotlights, and so, for him, this was a plunge into total darkness. He closed his eyes, blinking rapidly to rush whatever night vision he could gain in a few seconds. There was one brief pause and then he heard a creaking door noise from the captain's cabin. That door, he knew, was generally locked on boats like this to keep wandering sots, ribalds and common fishermen in their place.

Another moment passed and then he heard a hoarse whisper in the dark, "Okay. All's clear."

And then several solid citizens came out of the cabin, closed the door and tip-toed down the ladder not ten feet from Brando's position. He heard, rather than saw, the scapegraces as they slipped by, though he did capture faint dead-black images against the blue-black of the sky as they scurried like rats across his line of vision. There were three of them. Brando thought he recognized his goat-bearded fool and the black man. The third jock was medium-sized and light-footed; beyond that, he was just a bulk hurrying past in the night.

Brando waited a few ticks, and then stood and slid a peep around the corner of the galley. By that time the three men had disappeared over the edge. Goat-beard was reaching up to throw off the tie-line. Brando charged through the swinging doors into the empty galley, figuring he might get a better look out a galley window at what was going on without showing himself.

His regret was instantaneous. The galley stank with the grease of a thousand old burgers and the moldy yeast smell of ale slop that had been matted into the rotting carpet. His stomach turned over and he fought the urge to run for the railing and flash his hash over the side. He gritted his teeth and rubbed the fog-dew off one of the windows in time to get a good look at the boat that had been snugged up to the Coral Sea. It was a little 20 foot rubber dinghy, one of those ocean-goers rigged with twin outboards. For a moment, the boat seemed to be drifting away, and then Brando saw the thin trails leading from her stern and heard the low throb of engines that had a different cycle from their own heavy diesels. They were sneaking away! Chief Joseph heading for Canada, Don Juan after a stolen love event, thieves into the night.

Brando rushed out of the galley as, in his mind's eye, the walls had begun to run with a greenish scum. This is the last psychological phase before those prone to seasickness barf their guts, and he barely made it back out into the fresh air. He gulped in huge breaths of the chilly night breeze and cracked open a lime-flavored Calistoga.

By now his eyes had adjusted to the darker conditions, and he could follow the outline of the smaller boat. After a few ticks there was a muffled roar as the engines increased their efforts and the little-sister boat took on serious motion. Shortly thereafter, she was out of sight, swallowed by the inky maws of night, as he thought the old romantic poet William Wordsworth might emote.

What sense should he make of this? He asked himself. The only explanation he could muster was drug-running. They were cruising near the Mexican border, which made it possible. But three rats had crawled off their boat. That didn't smell of dope. Brando's mind raced in circles. *Maybe they were escaped prisoners, or fugitives who had to flee the country.*

At any rate, the Coral Sea hesitated a few brief seconds longer, and then turned back on course and was at cruising speed again. At least, the fishing boat turned back to some course. Brando calculated by the sound and feel of the hull smacking through the troughs of the waves that they were angled on a new bearing.

Mayhaps, Brando pondered, *their captain had selected the earlier course because he wished to meet that smaller boat at a certain location. Or maybe he'd chosen that direction because it was the smoothest for the passengers.* Whatever, Brando was sure they were now traveling in a new direction. On the old course, they'd seem to run along for ten or twelve seconds, drop gently into a trough, and then slide up the next one for another ten or twelve more ticks. Now they were careening through wave and trough with a hard whump-whump-whump as if they were making up for lost time.

Doubly odd, though, that they hadn't flicked the overhead gleamers back on. When one negotiated the night run for tuna, the spotlights were a serious habit, something you wouldn't want to go without. That way every fool, fop and fumbler of the high seas knew of your approach.

Brando returned to his huddle of knapsacks and other baggage, hunching around to find a spot that was warm enough, dry enough and where the air didn't smell like burnt diesel fuel. Unfortunately no such place existed. He sighed and settled in for another long and uncomfortable period, convinced that in another life he'd been a true swine of a human being to deserve such cattle car treatment in this one.

CHAPTER 28

Reality drifted and washed back and forth like a body caught in the surf at Malibu. The time crept by, and Brando hung in a semi-conscious state near sleep. He lost track of how long it was since they had turned onto their new course. He felt dull and queasy as the Coral Sea continued to cut across the oily black seas with an uncomfortable chop, and the diesel fuel continued its assault on the inner lining of his nose.

Only now, with the overhead spots off, the universe was flung out above him from horizon to horizon in an incredible display of starry wonder. The Milky Way, which can never be seen from the San Fernando Valley even after the earthquakes when there's a power-out—because of the quake-dust and hang-over inversion layer—now curled across the night sky like the belly of some mythical ghost-dragon. Brando saw why the ancient Navajo storytellers had told their tale of hum-buggy old Coyote grown impatient with placing the stars at regular intervals in the dome of the heavens and how he snapped the blanket, flinging them in the air. Once or twice Brando saw meteors streak like fiery slash wounds across the sky. And there was Orion standing guard, ready to draw his sharp and deadly degen as he had throughout the ages since the ancient ones first looked skyward.

After a while, Brando noticed the Coral Sea was running on a roughly parallel course with a big freighter. Where the span is long and the subjects to ponder are few, such minor events loom more important than they really are. This may be the reason shepherds sight angels and hermits are overcome by visions of naked dancers, usually, but not always, ladies. The large ocean vessel was riding in closer to them than most, and Brando stared at it in wonder, enjoying the opportunity to appraise its girth and magnitude. After some period he was able to calculate that the Coral Sea wasn't running parallel after all. Of course, that would be rare, as nearly all the ocean traffic runs north-south up and down the coast, putting in at the various ports before heading back across the high seas. Freighters chugged along in shipping lanes, while sports fishing boats zipped in and out from shore perpendicular to them, crossing the shipping lanes on their mad dash to the good deeps where lurked the monster tuna.

At first Brando's nearby ocean vessel was an interesting interruption, but then it made him increasingly uneasy on top of the usual seasickness. He hoped the remaining rattus in the captain's cabin, flush with their successful and presumably lucrative transfer at sea, hadn't abandoned them to auto-pilot and drifted off to slumberland. Brando reminded himself that stranger occurrences happen all the time. He knew the sad sea tale of the captain who was running a sport boat named the Sea Dog with only one crew member so he could pay off the money sharks for a gambling indiscretion. Since running round-the-clock with only one shift was impossible, the hired help would just point it toward Japan, put it on auto and snooze until the alarm clock jangled. By that time the Sea Dog would be more or less at the fishing hole and nobody was the wiser. It worked for a rather extended period, all matters taken into account, until one foggy night when the Sea Dog slammed right into the Maranakara, 226 days out of Yokohama and loaded with shiny new Japanese cars and trucks. The 50 footer was gone with hardly a sucking slurp, and there was nothing left the next morning but a few tackle boxes floating on the oily waves. The Maranakara never varied her majestic course by so much as a degree. The lone survivor, a solitary and much-maligned crewmember who managed to jump from the Sea Dog in a life vest, swore the big ship never even slowed down.

On the other digits, Brando had to consider the possibility these brave men of the salt-sea waves might still be touchy about their recent mid-oceanic rendezvous. He didn't relish pounding on the captain's door and receiving a load of buckshot in the intestines for his fervor.

And so he deliberated. He pondered. He mulled. He gulped another sip of Calastoga water and masticated a few more crackers. And all the while, the giant cargo ship drew closer. Every time Brando looked, it seemed more certain that—if they stayed on their present course, they were going to narrowly shave across the bow of that giant of the seas!

A new supposition poured through Brando like ice water. Suppose Goat-beard and the black man had simply wanted to get off the Coral Sea. *But why might they wish to do that?* The answer came clear as a sharp rap on the head. *Maybe because they knew the Coral Sea was never going to make it back to port.* Brando's mind was spinning. *What fob could the tricky ding-boys use to accomplish their demise if they weren't even on the boat? And could they be such cold scapegallows that they would send nearly twenty mortals to their eternal reward simply to ding one soul?* Another chill swept through Brando's flesh. When Keith and he had first boarded ship, those three had been on the tippy-top, tinkering with the electronics. All the Point Loma boats carried directional radar and electronic guidance systems. Brando's thoughts were charging on like linemen thundering toward a trembly little kicker. Generally, directional devices were employed to steer one away from collisions and safely into port. But most any scurvy gnarler who'd been in navy electronics would also be able to rig a ship so it would do the opposite—that is, automatically intersect another vessel. And if a tub small as the Coral Sea met with one the size of—Brando could make out the name now—the Toyota Maru, the results would be the stuff of comic books, only Superboy could not be counted on to arrive before the fated impact.

Brando leapt to his feet. Time to quit humbugging around, to cease plying idle thought processes and limpid inductive reasoning. Time to manage concrete realities. He dashed up the ladder and slammed his fist on the captain's door. There was no response. He pounded louder, and then jammed his shoulder against the door. It was locked and sturdy.

Brando looked up to see the Toyota Maru now looming monstrously large, Godzilla over

Tokyo. *Oh Great and Holy Maker of the Universe, he'd delayed too long in coming to his conclusions!* He took a short run and slammed his body into the door. It was of stout oak and laughed at him as if he hadn't even tried. He looked around for a fire extinguisher or anything of substance he could throw through a window, but the hangers where the extinguishers were supposed to be, were empty.

He realized this was getting him nowhere. Brando jumped down to the main deck and ran down below, dashing between the sleeping fishermen. He needed Keith, but he didn't want to yell because the old studio codgers would mill around and they'd never get back up on deck.

Brando found Keith on his back in the bunk across from the lovely Mindy, snoring like faithful Rex the Pooch.

He rudely shoved, whispering, "Keith!"

Keith's eyes were instantly wide open, "What?" He was wide awake, as Brando expected. Live through combat and you wake like that.

"Disaster looms!"

The old sword-thwacker followed Brando, running barefoot up the ladder, only to be greeted by the great, rusty hull of the Toyota Maru, which now almost completely filled the horizon.

"Great, suffering, holy Jesus!" he said.

Brando had never been so furious at his own tongue-tied brain, which didn't seem any more capable of operating under stress than it was during normal times.

"Captain's cabin's off-limits!" he yelled, "Maybe all dead!"

295

"We got to break in there!" Keith looked wildly around for a moment, and started pawing through the tackle boxes stacked on deck. They were mostly heavy plastic, and these he threw aside.

"Take the steel and the wooden ones!" he yelled, grabbing two he liked and churning his way up the ladder. Brando found another two and ran after him.

They broke the first wooden one before they even dented the window. Keith cursed and swung one of the metal ones like a mallet, managing to star the glass surface. They kept battering away with few tangible results. There remained but a hundred yards between them and the huge, rusty side of the monster ship. Brando's heart sank—it was a container vessel and the decks were deserted! The big ship hadn't even spotted the Coral Sea, and now that the smaller boat was close under the bow, no able bodied seaman except maybe one contemplating suicide would be looking straight down over the side.

Brando figured they were about to transfer their status from the living to the statistical. He intensified his attack on the window. It was double-thick shatter-proof glass with a layer of resistant plastic in the middle. Slamming the boxes frantically against it, they finally succeeded in puncturing a hole big enough for Keith to plow through.

Keith was the man for explosives and electronic timers; They'd agreed without saying that he had to be the one. He wormed his way in headfirst. His shirt caught on something, and he fell as it ripped. There was a thump and Brando heard him curse again.

"Keith you must activate your plan NOW!"

There was a lurch as they came out of auto-pilot, and as Keith spun the wheel, the Coral Sea swung a bare forty or fifty degrees to her port side, and then a huge spray of water arched over Brando's head.

There was a brief pause and the world hung in balance. Brando counted individual rivets running up and down and sideways on the rusty plates of the huge freighter. *At least*, he thought, *they were continuing to turn—maybe they did have a chance!* And then they were sucked toward the huge ship as if by a mighty breath of air. They hit broadside, the mid-ships section of the Coral Sea just missing the cutting edge of the huge container vessel to crash full-length sideways against her hull a few feet behind the bow.

Brando was flung (as he would later tell it) bumfiddle-over-brisket, across the deck of the Coral Sea to crash into the waist-high steel railing. Their old tub yawed away from the towering steel wall and then tipped back toward it, and in that moment, Brando slid over the side toward the churning water between the two vessels. Now on the seaward side of the rail, he hung desperately between his boat and the giant ship, hung on with both hands, looking down into the black water directly beneath him. He could visualize his guts ground to hamburger between the boats or rolled under the huge ocean-going vessel and chopped into fish-bait by her propellers. *They're bait, lady,*

Goat-beard had said to Mindy, They *ain't nothin' but bait!* *Yes, well,* Brando managed to think, *we are all bait, in the long run.*

The Coral Sea continued her yaw, heeling on her side until Brando thought she was going to roll over. His feet dragged in the dark tickle of the waves before she finally righted herself and he could scramble back through the steel cables to the inner side of the railing and catch his breath on the upper deck.

The Coral Sea wasn't in the shape it had been bare seconds before. On the main deck below, half-dazed landlubbers poured out of the sleeping bay and ran about hupper-scupper and yelling as if the world had gone mad. One geek was tearing at the rubber raft tied to the upper deck, and Robbie, the old-fart projectionist and the last rogue you'd expect, had to be restrained from leaping off the stern and taking his chances at night in the whitecaps. *Ants on a stick,* Brando thought. *Where are you, Mrs Ernesta Hemingway, when we have a need of you?*

Just as matters started to settle down, one of the engines snapped out of sync, taking on its own high-pitched whine and vibrating toward disintegration. The Coral Sea had sheared off one of its twin props. After thirty seconds of grouping around, Keith found the right levers and shut the engine down. Still under their own boost from the single remaining engine, they slowly chafed and chugged and clawed their way, putting distance between themselves and the huge container vessel.

Keith yelled from inside the cabin, "Come around the other way, Brando! I've unlocked the door!"

Brando did as he said, only to realize that, except for Comrade Keith, the captain's cabin was deserted. They had indeed been left to their own fate.

Keith conned one of the codgers into holding the wheel, while he and Brando conducted a hunting expedition, but they found no crew anywhere on board. Goat-beard, the black knight and the third ding-boy had probably overpowered the real captain and crew and had left them for bait somewhere back at the docks.

CHAPTER 29

With one engine down, the Coral Sea lollygagged back to San Diego at something less than one-quarter speed. Keith and Brando sold steering the boat as a novelty, not unlike Tom Sawycr bartered painting the picket fence, way back in those golden-oldie days in Hannibal, Mo. They signed up every foot-wabbler who was interested and each got a 30 second briefing on navigation and a half hour turn behind the wheel.

The dawn of a new day was arriving, and with it, Brando's urge to consume vast quantities of vittles and potables. On the high seas at the first crack of light an odd change occurred in his digestive tract. Once the horizon could be clearly observed, raw celery and bubbly water were out and he would turn ravenous. Keith sauntered into the galley and fried them some bacon and egg sandwiches.

They sat outside near the stern, gravely chewing the greasy bread while they waited for dawn come up like thunder. When it finally arrived, it wasn't really a Kipling event, or a Joseph Mallord William Turner spectacular either. No flaring gold and red painted the sky in noble rapture. Instead, plump scuds of lumpy clouds hung a few hundred feet above the surface of the water, formed in rows like sausages, and these turned somewhat uncooked pink for a few moments before reverting to a lighter gray. A sad excuse for a sunrise, but Brando felt intensely grateful just to experience it.

It was some time later when Brando jerked bolt upright with an important realization.

"Keith, you old pickle! We're inadvertently running at trolling speed!"

"What do you know about that, good buddy!"

They took off at a dogtrot, heading to the racks for their rigs. By the time sun had fully established itself above the horizon, Brando had hooked two medium-sized bonita and Keith had a nice yellowtail. They ended up gaffing their limit even though the fusty pigs who were driving wouldn't slow when they yelled hook up and they had to muscle their fish in against the drag.

The old studio farts had lost their interest in fishing. They took over the galley and opened the brews full around and, as Brando later commented, before the dingus wagged they were chirping merry every one.

After some time, Mindy came up on deck and gave them the gnarly glims, like they should feel bad for feeling so good. She herself was pasty-faced and shaky. Steadfast skirt-luster Keith gallantly gallumphed to the galley for a cup of coffee for her.

"I calculate this certifies your dimber damber doesn't manufacture a hoot whether you suck oxy or not," Brando said, eyeing her suspiciously. He recognized it was an unfeeling approach, but someone was trying to extinguish all that he stood for, and he would have liked a solid confirmation of his notion that she was somehow mixed up in his affairs.

"My who don't what?" she asked.

"You reveal to me."

"I don't know what you're talking about, Brando. I come along with you on a silly fishing trip, we crash into a giant tanker or something, and you blame me?"

"Some lurker missioned you to eyeball me. Mayhaps Charlie. Mayhaps Nathan Paramis."

"I don't know Charlie," she said, "and I don't like or trust Nathan Paramis."

And she didn't volunteer any more information. Brando pretended to glare seaward, but secretly he kept examining her out of the corner of his eye. Once she settled down, she failed to express particular surprise or anger. A little nervous and uncertain, maybe. That she was an instrument in this game, he had no doubt. But just what her role was, he had no idea.

Before long Keith, the old skirt-chaser, returned with Mindy's coffee, proud as General Douglas MacArthur slogging beachward through the balmy bay waters of Luzon.

The hazy sun was starting to break through the low clouds, and this worried Keith. "Figure they'll stop biting, good buddy?"

"Poseidon only knows."

Mindy was adorned in a white cotton halter top and matching brief shorts. The spruce wench had brought a big towel to accompany her.

"Think I'll go sun-bathe on the upper deck," she said. "Maybe it's a little warmer up there."

"Not much chance to catch the rays in Minnesota, I gather?" Brando said, giving it a wild shot. Her face blanched and she turned away, leaving him to kiss her cooler.

"About the same everywhere," Keith shrugged, wishing she'd stay and wearing his disappointment like a clown hat.

"Woolly winter weather," Brando shrugged, "in the land of the Viking sun."

Keith gave his friend a shrewd glance and then went after her. While he was gone, Brando caught a big-eye blue-fin tuna that must have weighed 30 pounds. Keith came back muttering about life in general, but the water and the line and the bait were all still at hand, so they both engaged in piscatory tossles all the way east to the Coronado Islands.

By two in the afternoon they were dragging the Coral Sea into her berth at Point Loma. Keith and Brando were the only two bucks sober enough to dock the boat. Keith managed the steering and Brando tied up the lines with the same knot he employed on his shoes, and before they even had her roped down, the real captain of the Coral Sea and about a dozen reporters swarmed on deck.

The two of them had thought it out beforehand; in the confusion Keith slipped off the stern with their rods, boxes and gunnysacks of fish, and Brando mingled with a larger crowd of anglers from the nearby docking Pacific Queen as they came strolling by.

They made their way up the wooden dock, passing four uniformed policemen and several serious-looking gentlemen in suits and sports coats heading purposefully for the Coral Sea.

Keith looked at his friend with mild reproach, "Hey, little buddy—I noticed you didn't use your own tackle box to bash that window, even though it is made of fine hardwood and would have been an excellent choice."

"Oh, listen to the blather! Your own jewel case is armored steel plate!"

"This is a historical tackle box," Keith said, "full of joyous memories of successful campaigns and forays."

"Rather perish than lose these lurid fish attractors."

"Me, too. I guess that makes us real men."

"El Machosiosos Originales."

Unfortunately, they could smell the Corvette from thirty feet away. The source of their discomfort was a gunnysack full of fish heads and fish guts that had been dumped in the back seat, undoubtedly provided by the same two gunners who had donated their parking spot.

Brando had left the top down, figuring anybody could slit it if they wanted in. He reached in the back seat and got a hand around the vile, dripping sack and, holding it at arm's length, gingerly walked to the nearby garbage bins, from where it probably had come in the first place.

"There were some guys scrubbing down a truck back by the dock," Keith suggested. Brando nodded and headed in that direction. For twenty dollars a young whipster named Manuel brought a new pail of soap water and a rectangular bristle brush to scrub down the leather back seat and the floors. The noxious fishy liquid had seeped into the front compartment as well, so he did the mats for free.

"Nice car," Manuel said. "Go very fast." He held his hand out for the money.

304

"I concur...," Brando said. "Here's an extra Jefferson."

Manuel studied the bills carefully, as if he'd been warned about counterfeiters, and then folded them over twice and put them in his pocket. Once they were safe, a new look of concern came over his face and his brow wrinkled anew.

"I no did that theeng," their young sharpster said, pointing to a nondescript beige wire hanging down from the underside of the dash.

"Just push it back to its former position," Brando said. Then he had a second thought. "No. Better just leave it."

"Okay-dokay." Having tossed a bone at the morality of the misplaced wire, the kid flashed a huge grin, retrieved his pail and brush and wandered off in search of other gainful missions.

"Keith," Brando said, "Though neither of us has walked the straight and reverent path of the snub-devils and the tub-thumpers, here is a supernatural reward."

"How you figure, good buddy?"

"It is a miracle; the sudden and unexplained appearance of a brand-new wire attached to the ignition."

Keith shrugged. "Perhaps when the owner starts the engine, the lights go on and the horn honks."

"This innovation could invalidate the manufacturer's warranty."

"Perhaps I should have a closer look."

"*Jah, Kamerade*, you being so advanced in electronics and all...."

Keith located the relatively small, square packet of C-4 taped under the dash on Brando's side. He wanted to add it to his collection, so he used a pair of needle-nose pliers from his tackle box to disconnect the wires, and then peeled off the tape. He gingerly placed it in the middle of eleven mixed donuts Brando had bought from the Winchell's down the block, his theory being that nothing absorbed shocks like baker's dough. There originally had been 13 donuts, but they had to remove two of their personal favorites so there would be room for the bomb.

"Witnessed the charms of Mindy, lately?" Brando asked, talking around a mouth full of demon's food.

"Nope," Keith said, taping off the bare ends of the wires with some flesh colored bandaids.

"Interesting, how the vixen isn't in any proximity to our intended demise."

"Can't be far—with the sea at her back, her avenues of escape are somewhat limited. I say let's go find her."

They picked her up at a bus stop about three blocks from Fisherman's Wharf. The wench didn't fight or run; she just sighed and got in the back seat.

At the first stoplight, she leaned over the seat and said, "It isn't Paramis. I don't even know Charlie. And it isn't Loaf Ludder, either."

Brando said nothing while calling up his best who done it look

She continued quietly, "You were right about Minnesota. My name isn't Mindy Carlson, it's Mindy Haslins. I'm George Haslins' daughter."

Brando gunned the Corvette across the intersection and jammed a hard right into a Carl's, jr. parking lot. *Mayhaps,* he thought, *with the big happy star smiling down on them, Mindy Haslins would be less inclined to tell tall tales.* Keith just stared at the both of them. Brando could see he still was struggling to maintain his image of Mindy as a goody sent from heaven. Keith's feelings about the fair sex in general flowed strong and wide, but not very deep.

"Okay," Brando probed like something less than a finely sharpened instrument, "Why are you here?"

"Somebody tried to kill dad. They shot through our kitchen window. After that, Dad said he had to talk to you. He sent me to contact you."

"About?"

"He wouldn't say. I still don't know."

"And how did he acquire *my nominus?*"

"I don't know."

"So you decided on your own you'd ferret the truth pertaining to my worthiness before discussing matters with me."

"Yes," she nodded. "Dad isn't at the top of his game anymore. I had to be sure."

"What is the relevance of one Walter Crankshaw?"

"He works for dad, sort-of, as his business manager. I don't trust him."

"Why did you not just bare your heart and soul to silly little *moi* in the first place?"

"You're just in this to get your movie. You don't care who gets hurt."

"Disappointing. After all we've been through together..."

"See? You're never serious. You just joke around. Who knows what you really want?"

307

"The young and the optical. How I long for my own pathetic lost youth, to see once again with such clarity."

"You see?", she said, her voice rising. "You're doing it again! My dad is old and tired. He's bitter about a lot of things." She thought about it for a moment, and then continued, "Worse, he isn't always right in his head, and I don't think he always makes the right decisions. For all I know, you're the one who tried to kill him."

"On what unearthly plane did you come to that notion?" Brando asked. "Do you also have a flat-earth theory?"

"Ripper Brown's wife was murdered, and I heard the police think you did it. I've just been protecting dad."

"Which of our mutual acquaintances is passing out the bon-bon that I snuffed Lani?" Even as he asked, Brando thought he knew the answer.

"Mr. Ludder said so. He's sure you did it."

"Mr. Loaf Ludder, whom you had occasion to meet in Bali during the war?"

"No! Dad has known Mr. Ludder for years! I first knew Loaf as a huge black man who bounced me on my knee when I was just a little kid. He and Nanna still send Christmas cards. And sometimes Dad talks on the phone."

Brando settled his spine against the leather-cushioned seats. When the car was motionless, one could smell the faint odor of rotted fish. Morrie was going to idolize him: *Brando Mahr, the rogue who utterly destroyed the most expensive rental he had ever lent to a customer.*

308

"What do you say, Keith?" Brando asked.

"I think we gotta go to Minnesota."

Keith was like that. This wasn't really his problem, yet the loyal pickle just assumed they were going to solve it together.

"Chances of a gorilla trap."

Keith scratched his ear, looking for a banana, and made an Eep-eep-eep sound. But it was only a half-hearted ploy; Brando could see he was trying to read the menu on the drive-through from across the parking lot.

"I don't think we gots us much choice, good buddy," Keith said. "These guys are pretty good. We gotta act now, 'cause sooner or later they are actually gonna find a way to kill us."

"That will not be easy. We're prime matter, as well."

"Nerves, at least, of steel," Keith agreed.

Brando shrugged, "How about ingesting a Happy Burger before we take further action?"

"The Happy Burger might be a little small, good buddy. Better order me a half-dozen."

CHAPTER 30

Brando had to drop Keith off and clean the fish, so by the time he made his triumphant return to KTGA, it was late, or, as he would say, the sundial leaned toward witching.

As he approached his office, he saw a dim light cast through the shade that was drawn down over the glass panes on the door. From the cold blue flicker, it appeared some entity was playing the VCR. *Could it be,* he wondered, *that the night clean-up crew was watching Arsenio?* Probably not.

He cautiously opened the door, ready to swing his trusty tackle box, and it proved to be Lieutenant Baker, slouched across the sadly rump-sprung couch of love while he eye-balled the tape of the old Vikings-Rams game.

On the screen the enormous Carl Eller, monstrous even in a long-shot that was over a quarter century old, was bearing down on Roman Gabriel with mischief and mayhem in mind. Eller crashed into Gabriel and his momentum pushed the unlucky QB backwards until the referee flung his hands in the air, indicating the infamous touchback.

Baker stared up at Brando, his tired peepers looking even more sunken in the bluish light from the television screen.

"Looks to me like he was pushed in," he said.

When Brando didn't respond, he raised one sandy eyebrow. "This your casting couch?"

Brando shrugged, "Correctamundo. We are an extremely low overhead operation."

"This the tape you're claiming got Lani Kazin murdered?"

Brando nodded. "I suspect some unknown diddlery tied to that game. I can't cross-hair exactly what."

Brando set down his tackle box, leaned the fishing rods in a corner by the refrigerator and snapped on the lamp on his desk. His Eurasian ex-wife smiled enigmatically from the picture on one corner of his desk. That reminder from across the seas gave him the old, familiar rush of bitter feelings. *Maybe*, he thought to himself, *that was why he kept the Ektachrome in view, so he wouldn't go mushy.*

"Why are you parking your bones on my futon?" Brando asked. "Constable, don't you have a sweet little cottage somewhere and a soul-mate who loves you and pines for your return?"

Baker gave him a grim look. The ashes of his life settled to the bottom of his gray eyes. For a long time, he just looked at Brando. Then he said in a dead voice, or rather, speaking like one of the undead, like his body was taken over by another spirit, "I'm investigating a murder. What are you doing here? It's Saturday night."

"I've been fishing, soul-trapper."

"Yeah, you're just a regular Huck Finn. I heard about it."

"How did my heroism come to your attention?" Brando asked.

Baker pulled out a pack of Camels. He plucked one from the package and frowned at the filter in the end. "We got a tip you tried to skip

311

the country, that you were gonna hole up in Mexico."

"Who convinced you of that? Loaf Ludder, I bet."

Baker glared at Brando for a moment.

"I know what you're thinking," Brando said.

"What, fruitcake?"

"You're wondering if it is worth beating me with one of those big cop flashlights to find out how I arrived at the correct conclusion."

"The same source also claims he saw you sneaking around Ripper's house a couple of times before Lani was murdered," Baker said.

Brando nodded. "He certainly is being extraordinarily helpful. I suggest you reward him with one of your Dick Tracy junior investigatory badges."

Baker took the cigarette out of his lips, looked for a moment like he was considering biting the filter off, and then put it back in his pack.

"Oh, yeah. You've got another problem," he said. "Clancy the gate guard ain't so sure no more he saw you the night of the murder."

"His *nom de jour* is Harvey," Brando said. "How hard did you have to browbeat him to achieve an acceptable degree of uncertainty?"

"Hard enough." Baker gave his world-worn shrug, "He ain't so sure he actually saw you, or just somebody in that fancy car of yours."

"We do sign in after hours. My John Henry is in the log."

"If you can call that scrawl a signature."

"Penmanship is not the issue," Brando said. "Anybody could have signed you in."

312

"If so, you would already be carting me away, *mon capitain.*"

On the screen, Gabriel still protested the call, angrily claiming Eller had pushed him backward across the goal line. Half the Rams bench was milling about on the field. Baker stood and pointed the remote and snapped off the video.

He returned his dead eyes stare to Brando, "I find it interesting you don't mention that your little fishing boat slammed into a freighter out there on the high seas. Or that your captain and crew was hijacked the night before and replaced by Manny, Moe and Jack, who somehow managed to disappear in all the confusion."

Brando gave him a faint twitch of the lips that might have passed for a smile in other circumstances. "You now extend your range of jurisdiction to Hawaii?"

"God damn it, you stupid schmuck-you're withholding evidence!" Baker-the-Unemotional was shouting; his chunky face was red and his hands were shaking.

"Why don't you...fold it down," Brando offered. He waved to the sofa, but Baker stood there like a statue. "Come on, occupy the space. I'll even enunciate a *please*."

Brando went to a battered shelf behind his desk and pulled out his thick, hand-bound volume of original Opie and Ronnie cartoon scripts. He reached in the vacant space where the book had been and pulled out his special bottle. It was Glenvarnis Glenlivit, his favorite single malt scotch.

"I generally save this for memorable occasions, like the anniversary of the day I caught my flight out of Saigon, like Icarus heading back for The World and not quite landing properly"

Brando found his own digits were a little shaky from recent events. He remembered that's the way it had manifested in Nam, as well. *You wended your merry way through the job, the bullets buzzing about your brain like bees. You skipped lightly as a virgin in clover over the trip-wires, you were iceman the invincible. It was only later that the euphoria—the puffed up vanity that you're still alive—would let out like a popped balloon.* Then iceman melted to mush and super-lurp was slurpied away, leaving only the wide-eyed little kid who had ventured too far into the black woods and found bristly demons with curved tusks. Yes, foul, intelligent and dangerous razorbacks, babirusa and wart hogs, in every shadow.

Brando pondered this lunk-head footpad-of-the-law Baker. He was considering sympathy as an alternative to inordinate rage. Half of him felt he was going soft-headed, but at the moment he was thinking, *It must be the same reality for him.* This was his Nam; L.A. was his war zone, and it would never quit until he caught the big one between his ribs or retired to live out an endless half-life, wondering when some vicious ding-boys would sprout up from the barren field of his past like a skeleton army and destroy him.

Brando poured three fingers into a glass and the lieutenant reached for it without a word. Brando tipped the same for himself and settled into the lotus position on his chair. The delayed reaction from his adventures on the Coral Sea was about to set in.

He knew what was coming next. Earman and The Hands of Death would now attempt to hang on to their sanity by discussing reality. Conversing in low and casual tones sometimes did help. And so he would take Baker at least part way into his confidence. He took a deep breath, slapped his head to shunt any stray Zeemans and plunged in.

"The game on that tape was an event of some annum past," he said. "The Rams were overwhelmingly scheduled to win by the odds makers, the touts, everybody. For some reason they did not achieve victory."

"So?" Baker asked.

"So, in attempting to uncover that reason, I have already danced from the shadow of death on several occasions. As you cognize, Lani Kazin was not so nimble. These mysterious ding-boys have tried to dispatch me..."

Baker nodded into his drink, "How?"

"Hitting the Toyota Maru was no coincidental circumstance. The Coral Sea was rigged to go for the gold."

The lieutenant gave Brando his skeptical, tired look..

"No fantasy land," Brando said. "I saw the wiring. They rigged the auto-pilot."

He didn't blather on about the C-4 in the Corvette, knowing the policeman would be hard-wired with inhibitions to Keith's keeping it.

"Okay. Go on." Baker had already made his way down his glass, so Brando drafted him another two fingers and a wee poke for himself.

"Okay," Brando said, "but what I pass along to you next is going to require imagination."

Baker giggled at that one, a sour little snort, but still a giggle. "Like it's all been real up to now."

"Pretend. I'm procuring the refreshments."

"Yeah. Okay."

Baker tipped his glass at Brando, who continued, "After that infamous gridiron struggle some *tres importante* individuals with Sicilian last names—I do not know those names—were very upset, having lost enormous money of the wagering caliber. They dispatched four *leftenants*...to see what they could find. All four were respected in their field, but they all bit the bullet in semi-accidental and ingenious ways."

"Ways that remind you of a sports fishing boat accidentally hitting another, larger vessel?" Baker asked.

"Yes, thank you, *mon frere.*"

"I ain't your goddam brother. Who do you suspect?"

"Nathan Paramis. Loaf Ludder."

"What do you think they did?"

"They buffed the dog," Brando said without a moment's hesitation.

"Huh?"

"They filched the coppers. You know, maced the joskin of their quid."

"Huh?"

Brando nodded and took a deep breath, "Be patient with me. This is important. Now, I will attempt again: The rogues somehow kimbawed the outcome of that ancient contest, collected the

316

round sum and then dispatched the inquisitive. But I have uncovered no smoking weaponry."

"I think I follow that. No smoking gun…"

Brando nodded, staring into his empty glass, "So. Shall we ride the paddywagon to the hosgow, or am I a free rogue?"

Brando had been sitting on his hands. They seemed to be about back to normal, the therapeutic effects of unburdening the soul, but now the magic moment was gone. The brief truce was over. Baker stood and Brando saw that the bleak look had come back to his eyes.

"Just don't try to leave town, fruitcake. You wouldn't make it to your seat on the plane."

He started out the door, then waved at the PhoneMate as he turned to face Brando. "Oh, yeah. Morrie says your car is ready and to please pick it up. And some asshole named Levine called to say your IXTAPA is one of the four worst scripts he ever read, the other three being TAMMY, starring Debbie Reynalds, NIGHT OF THE LIVING DEAD and SATURDAY NIGHT FEVER." He stood in the door, staring at Brando.

"So?" Brando stared at his perplexed look.

"So you deal with people like that all the time?"

Brando tossed two hands expansively in the air to indicate his office, the luxury of his surroundings, "This is Hollywood Royale, my *raison d'etre*."

Lieutenant Baker shook his head. "Maybe you need a new *raison, mon frere.*"

And with that, the Lieutenant Baker Answering Service and Sympathy Club closed the door and marched out into the night.

In spite of Baker's harsh warning to sit pretty, Brando had climates to visit and realities to ferret out of dark places. Feeling the way he and Baker did about each other, Brando couldn't work up any remorse or guilt over his coming French leave. Baker's threats would have an effect opposite to their intent. Brando shrugged it off. *Warning a wild hair such as himself in such a manner was little more than daring him to go.*

CHAPTER 31

Brando spent the afternoon at his rented coach house clipping his romantically flowing moustache back into a dull Marlboro Man brush, and drastically slashing his shaggy head of hair into semi-respectability. Some time later, he removed the clip from one of the Brownings and stowed it along with his light-weight hiking boots and a set of frayed fatigues in a fabric overnight suitcase.

He shrugged into the dark blue pinstripe suit and wing tip shoes he used for meetings with the executives he thought of as the network white-collar thieves, finishing off with a white cotton shirt and a bold-patterned power tie that looked like it had fallen off the Andy Warhol garbage truck. He was ready to embark on his mad mission to encounter Old Blindy Hazlins in Minnesota.

He'd been sitting on the steps of his coach house, killing time (he called it murdering reality) by reading George Allen's book The Future Is Now . He'd been reading for quite some time before he analyzed and concluded he'd been frozen out. The original concept had been that Mindy and he would travel to Ivan's to check out the Fiat and then meet Keith at the airport. But there was no Mindy, and he'd waited so long that by the time he got to Ivan's the place was locked and lonely with only the tubby dobermans remaining.

Ivan's, he saw, was surrounded by a 10 foot cyclone fence topped by razor wire. It didn't look electrified, but there is only a measure of certainty in the adventurer's life. The silvery wire was woven around and around through normal barbed wire, so there was no way he was going to clear a space to get over the top. At least that's what he had decided until he saw the sawed-up front right quarter of a fiberglass car body leaning against the outside of Ivan's shed.

In a few minutes, Brando had the curved fiberglass fender draped over one portion of the razor wire on top of the fence and was ruining a great pair of wing-tips on his majestic way up and nearly over. It was at the very top, with his weight in swaying balance and his bare neck two inches from the gleaming wire that he caught his power tie in the wire and lost about two inches from the end of it.

Brando had hoped his pals the dobermans were going to be happy to renew their acquaintanceship, but one of them engaged in a big rip just above the knee in his pants leg before they could re-bond. Dobermans, he realized, must have frighteningly short recall capabilities, or perhaps they were conditioned to think their meat fell out of the sky. *Praise Zeus for Dog Bones!* It took a few rounds of woof-yummies, but Ivan's dog guardians finally quieted and Brando resumed his old pal status again.

His little brown Fiat was proudly squatting in the middle of the lot, waxed and spit-polished like it was the crown jewel of Ivan's royal car collection. Brando inserted his spare key and started the engine. White smoke spanged out of the tailpipes for about a minute, after which it turned greyish. Water dripped from the radiator, the hoses or both. The re-painted sections sported five or six loopy drops and paint runs.

Brando found a discarded MacDonalds french fries carton and ripped it open so he could write on the white inner sides of the cardboard:

> Dear Ivan--
> You're getting closer, but
> not much. This engine runs
> like it has 300,000 miles on it.
> My old one had 74,000. Not
> only that, you've stuck a pre-
> '79 engine in there, which has
> less power. Tell Morrie I said
> he should get serious and
> shake the money tree so you
> can do it right.
> Sincerely,
> Brando Mahr
> P.S. Fix the paint job or I'll shoot
> Hans & Fritz, the Doby-boys.

He stuck the note behind the windshield, and in another few ticks he'd given the dogs a last pet and a shower of yummies and jimmied open Ivan's back door with a mallet, the force of which set off a howling electronic wail. No one came to check, and he slunk away down the alley.

His ticket was reserved in "Will Call" at the Burbank Airport under the name Joseph Lugosi. Keith wasn't in the bar, which meant he was nowhere around. Brando could understand Mindy's absence—but unsteady behavior was very unlike Keith. Brando felt certain something unpleasant had happened to delay him.

People who didn't even know Brando stared until he caught a glimpse of himself reflected in a window. He bought an Opie Arachnid tie at the airport concession stand and threw the old one in the waste basket. He was able to slap a little shine on his shoes and to tape his ripped pants from the inside. While hardly returned to his former glory, once he got the grease stains off his face, he was in at least passable shape.

He was checking his luggage when he had another notion. For a rogue who normally attracted a good deal of casual notice, he hadn't been hassled at all. Maybe Lieutenant Baker's threats had been hollow gestures, but Keith and Mindy were missing and the mysterious ding-boys were out to change his destiny. Since there were no hard-eyed men loitering around the airport lobby, it was conceivable they would be waiting for him at the other end of the line.

Brando discovered a phone located where he could study the flow of passengers headed both to and from airplanes, and he started dialing other airlines. Instead of the flight to Minneapolis, he talked his way onto a plane that brief-stopped in Denver and Chicago, with a connecting flight to Duluth.

It was four hours past high witch at O'Hare airport in Chicago when Brando, trying to stay a step ahead of his own sad ending, thought he might have figured out the next clever design—they would now be waiting for him in Duluth. Brando was sitting in the middle of the dull and vacant mind-wash that fluorescent brightness brings to the weary traveler, slumped over a cup of decaf in the Host coffee shop with his bag at his side, and he was wondering how he'd traveled this far this easily.

These ding-boys were able to live invisibly, like Spanish guerrillas living with their peasant families and swooping out of the hills to rain terror on the huddled Roman centurions. They were successful at killing even expert mafia people and could then slip away unpunished. The patterns of civilization were at their disposal, and doubtless any number of unlimited VISA and MasterCards to boot. Why wouldn't they clunk around until they bumbled upon which of the several evening flights lifting off from Burbank had taken the fictitious Joseph Lugosi back east? They could easily track his path to the Windy City and ferret from some hapless functionary the knowledge that he was booked on the local American Eagle flight to Duluth. Maybe that's where they'd be standing by like innocent schoolgirls in their stiff white blouses and plaid skirts, most likely in Duluth at the baggage carousel. His bag would be spinning around and around with his disassembled Browning in it while some stone killer wrapped regally in a black cashmere overcoat would stick a silencer in his left ear and violate his right to life.

He'd nearly ignored his cooling coffee long enough to walk away from it when Joseph Lugosi was paged to the nearest white phone.

"Yes?" He said into the phone.

"Hey, good buddy, where the hell you been?" It was Keith, resonating happy as a mollusc.

323

"Sorry, old canine. I was unable to synchronize with the schedule."

"Hell, I know you missed the flight. Me and Mindy was on it, waiting for you!" In encoded dialogue, Brando realized that probably meant they weren't.

"I was supposed to join giblets with Mindy."

"No. Didn't you get my call, Mr. Opie Dopie? That must explain it." That probably meant there wasn't a call.

"I cogitate I did not."

"At least you got the tickets Ginger left for you." *Ginger. Who the hades was Ginger?* There was no Ginger. White was black, yes was no, up was down.

"Yeah, I got 'em," Brando said. "So, you're presiding over the Minneapolis concourse right now?"

There was a brief pause, and then Keith said, "Yeah." That meant he wasn't for certain.

"I myself am passengering the 10 o'clock commuter to Duluth," Brando said. "Why don't you rent-a-van and encounter me at baggage?"

"You got it, good buddy!"

Brando terminated the call, relieved to know his allies were still drawing breath and able to use their ATM cards. Only he wasn't relishing a family reunion in Duluth. Keith's whither-go-yee's name was Ginnie, not Ginger. Ginnie, abbreviation for Virginia. And Brando doubted Keith and Mindy were in Minneapolis. Keith and Mindy were in the digits of his thus-far-unseen and invisible enemy.

324

CHAPTER 32

Brando was patiently holding his position at Chicago's O'Hare airport, third in line to surrender his boarding pass. He planned to make his way through the wide sliding door, down the metal steps, out across the asphalt apron and back up the few portable steps onto the small twin-engine prop plane that was to whisk him to Green Bay. That was his plan, at least until the mundungus moment he noticed an ordinary-looking cull he'd seen thrice times earlier. The man had boarded the plane, but then had retraced his steps. *Odd,* Brando thought. And he was now making his way back across the apron to an unknown destination. *Odd's plut and her nails.* That is, very odd, indeed.

With much on his mind, Brando stepped out of line and watched the man, glimming him steadily from a spot well back from the plexiglass. The dithering cull of his attention possessed a medium build and sandy hair. Brando guessed that this may well have been the third ding-boy on the Coral Sea, the only one he hadn't seen clearly.

The fellow of his interest was clean-shaven and maybe in his early 40's. And he bore himself ramrod straight, with a trim military look about the jaw and ears. He didn't dogtrot back to the plane, and he didn't return up the stairs to the lobby, so Brando assumed he was skulking nearby, waiting to be sure his victim had actually boarded.

Since Brando couldn't figure out how his enemies could have retrieved his name electronically and run across the airport to board that particular plane, he had to assume the man had been tailing him from the front.

Brando jogged back the way he'd come, not eager for a probable stone-killer to get ahead of him in the long beige corridors of the airport. On these short-spoke commuter flights, one dragged one's own luggage and stowed it on the plane as they boarded, so he still had his suitcase. He'd field-stripped the Browning and scattered the pieces inside his wash and shave kit, and it had merrily passed through the X-ray machines, which for that day and age were not as stellar as touted.

Brando moved up the pace of his dog-trot. At the first radiating hub in the terminal, he selected a sharp left and moved out snappily, as if intending to board a plane at the end of that long aisle. At the last minute, he shifted gears and slid into the nearest phone booth. He positioned the folding glass until he could see the proper reflections, and waited. He didn't think he would see sandy-hair for another few moments, but you never knew. He dialed reservations and enunciated a whispery bomb threat. No reason ten or twelve people on that prop plane should die on his account.

Sandy-hair didn't show, and so Brando half-ran down to the departing passenger's exit, and hailed a taxi.

"Where you wanna go?" The driver snarled. She was a short old duck-legs with a squashed-in puss. Iron-grey hair scragged every which way

326

from under her cap. A Polish lady—Kolijeski, it said on her I.D. over the meter—and she wore a flat hat with a snap on the bill and a big union pin on the side.

"Down-the-town," Brando said. "The Chicago elipsoid."

"Huh?"

"Circle. The down-the-town Chicago circle."

"Loop," she corrected.

"Yes. Loop. Assume acceleration, *s'il vous plait.*"

The dowdy old gammer pestered Brando's moment with a quizzical frown, but he was grateful to observe she maintained clamped choppers. After they had spun some few blocks away from the airport, he had her deposit him at a nearby Ramada Inn.

"This ain't down-the-town," she complained.

"*Odds Plut and her nails,*" Brando said.

"You shouldn't curse," she said, "and God's not a lady."

Brando raised his eyebrows.

"Chicago University," the old wench said, "Masters degree, English Lit. 1956."

"Cum laude, doubtless," Brando said.

"Summa cum laude."

"I shall pay you as if you drove me down-the-town."

"But I didn't. And, by the way, it's *downtown.*"

"You took me for a loop anyway," Brando said.

"I always told papa that education would pay," she said as she took his money.

Brando left her and walked into the Ramada where he John Hancocked for a room. He also rented a deep green Oldsmobile from National. On both reservations, he left cash deposits and printed his name B. Mah in such a way that they dropped the "R" from Mahr. They didn't argue, they just wanted Brando to go away. He was calculating there could be some sort of computer search. And if his foes didn't have the graciousness to program for variables, he hoped his petty deception might throw them off. If they were any hot-brains at all, he figured they'd probably run Mahr with and without the "h" and with one and two "r's" but it was unlikely they'd drop the "r" entirely. Maybe they couldn't even replicate a proper computer search, but after the talent they'd already shown, Brando wasn't going to gamble. Anybody who knew how to rig directional radar could probably hack an entry into automobile and motel rentals records.

Brando took possession of his motor car, and slid the rented Olds into the adjacent lot of the motel next door. Then he carried his briefcase up to his room on the third and top layer of the Ramada Inn. He stood under a shower, chewed his way through part of a big beef slab and eggs-over-easy breakfast, hung out the Do Not Disturb sign and took the pause that refreshes.

It was Chicago, but the fog didn't come in on little cat's feet as advertised by the great poet Sandburg, so he slept in. He blinked wide at ten, quickly settled his bill for ready green and in minutes was scurrying down the road. He pointed the rented Oldsmobile west on I-90, bound for *Vikingland*. The radio said Alice Walker had won the Pulitzer for The Color Purple. The Return of the Jedi was doing big box office. No mention was made of a boffo new film project liming the life of Ripper Brown. So much for the arts. Brando settled back and let the Oldsmobile do its business. And, after a time, Minnesota slid easily into view.

The address on George Hazlin's check proved to be a mere post office box in Aurora, Minnesota. The map Brando bought at a gas station positioned Aurora near Seven Beaver Lake and the St. Louis River. It seemed to be surrounded by the Superior National Forest except to the south. The Olds was newly minted and wanted to slap its fresh black rubber against the pavement, and he was able to brake outside Megan's Cafe in downtown Aurora before six that afternoon.

There wasn't all that much visual input to the little burg. Brando was in upper Minnesota, smack-dab in an area of pines and lakes, northwest from Lake Superior as the crow flies. The whole town shaped up to be about ten blocks long going north and south and four blocks wide going east and west, with a 4-way stop sign in the middle to control confusion and mass frenzy.

Brando drove slowly down the main drag. There was a sporting goods store, a car U-wash, a post office, a grocery-general store and an auto parts store. Megan's was a storefront cafe in the center of the action, right in the middle of the middle two blocks of Aurora. Gazing thoughtfully at the menu in the window, Brando thought he would try the special.

As he entered, a few bells dinged on strings. Four ancient scoundrels looked up from their various slouching positions around their booth. Brando figured they were probably muttering over the day's moose catch or the anticipated arrival of the winter solstice. A young dark lady of the sonnets with the strong Roman features of a Sauk Indian smartly slapped a menu on the table he'd claimed.

"What's the...?" He couldn't say the rest of whatever it was he wanted to say.

"Come on, Hon, spit it out," the hoity-toit said in the sharp tones of an irate mop squeezer or an agitated harpy. She was apparently not long on pidgin English—or patience, for that matter. Still, hers wasn't the proper approach to *The Reality of Being Brando*; interrupting only twisted his brain in tighter knots.

"The unique of the date?" He was finally able to sputter out his question. "The blue plate original?"

She was around 20 and probably lusted for by every buck within fifty klicks of Aurora, which meant she was sitting on top of her little world, as the country western song says. And she was a heavy chewer of gum, to boot. Pandora's box, gum by Wrigley.

The callow vixen pulled the wad in a long string from her ruby lips. She eyed it for texture before flipping it back in the maws and her attention back to Brando.

"What are you, some English Lord or something?" She passed him a dubious look.

"I suspect there's little chance you'll play Calypso to my Ulysses?" he asked, stringing her along.

330

She gave him her prime glare, "The special is beef stew with French bread."

Ulysses got seven long *annum* on the isle of Ogygia out of his nubile and pliant Calypso before Zeus booted him to the dogs. It didn't look like Brando was going to get seven seconds with his contemporary Pocahontas. *Daughter of the moon, Nakomas,* he recited quietly in one corner of his brain, wondering if Henry Wordsworth Longfellow would approve of his having a lengthy indiscretion with this limber maiden-of-the-pines.

She was tapping her foot impatiently. Brando sighed and concentrated on the food.

"I'll have that special. And a bovine lactate."

"Pardon me...?"

"Milk of a bovine animal of the genus bos, hence the term Ol'Bossy, in short, a cow," Brando said.

"Phhhh! Is there any other kind of milk?" the wench said smugly, attempting total coolness of demeanor. But superior transfiguration slowly slipped from her features and her face flushed bright red when she saw he was fixating on the two frontal lobes swelling her tight sweater.

"Pig," she said.

"You recommend swine?" He gave his menu a puzzled look. "I don't observe it on the scorecard."

"Dirty, dirty pig!" She slammed down his glass of ice water, spilling half of it in the process. Kissing him her cool side, she flounced to the nether regions to procure the appropriate foodstuffs.

331

"Don't expectorate in my stew," he warned after her retreating figure, wagging a threatening finger in her direction.

The locals whooped and hollered and slapped their knees in delight.

"How would ya' know if she did ex-PECT-orate in it, buddy?" one of the Domine Do Littles chortled. "It's stew!" That set off another round of cackles.

Brando saw that in Aurora every dog buffer eavesdrops on everybody else's conversation, hoping someone might say something worth stealing or repeating. The Aurorunians seemed to enjoy it that way. Brando didn't hold the grudge. He'd always figured people acted the same back in Tinseltown.

"Yo, there, Mister-you goin't' shoot y'self a bear?" One of them called over to Brando. The oldest duffer, a long, tall sam swimming in worn bib overhauls and a baseball cap promoting Evergreen Fertilizer, was giving him a grin that was constructed of queer cogs and half empty spaces. Brando decided it was somehow a pleasant face, regardless of missing ivories. The man was a rosy-nosed caricature of his younger self, now wrinkled like an old apple carving. He reminded Brando of a political cartoon by Honore Daumier straight out of a Paris newspaper, circa 1876, an old bird transplanted into the *campagna* of Northeastern Minnesota.

Brando was sporting his fatigues and a favorite soft hat that still had the dull olive staff sergeant's battle stripes sewed on. Under his fatigues jacket, he wore the studio colors—an Opie Dopie T-shirt, the one where Opie has his two front paws over his eyes as he drives his little convertible off a cliff. Brando grinned back and rotated his chair half-sideways so he was nearly a member of the Significant Codgers of Aurora Club.

"Maybe a caribou," he replied. "I might shoot a caribou."

They had a good laugh over that one. Thursday evenings in Aurora, everybody assumes the role of court jester. The four of them were in the late autumn of their years—or maybe winter—and they looked like the very last venture they might attempt was a forage in the woods and a little pot hunting, but Brando figured you could never know for sure. Reality is a funny bitch.

"You was in Nam?", one of them asked.

Brando nodded that he had been.

"My Ronnie died in Nam," the old man said. The mood around the table shifted, America as reflective as it ever gets. The old bird fished in his pocket and drew a wrinkled color photo from his wallet.

Brando slid his chair close enough to take the picture from the old man's shaking hand and have his look. Ronnie was leaning against an olive colored deuce-and-a-half, grinning at whatever buddy was snapping the shot. In the background Brando made out a semi-familiar jagged ridge, somewhere in the Annamese highlands.

He stared at the old man's contribution to U.S. Far Eastern Policy, the Keatsian irony heavy in the atmosphere. *Forever young; Ronnie will be forever young.* Brando hung in there until he could taste the bitter ashes in the fibers of his body, and then handed the picture back. Nobody made any more remarks for a while.

"Where's all the acreage?" Brando finally asked.

They just stared at him. "What acreage?"

"You know, the croplands where you rural gentlemen sprout all the alfalfa, the rutabagas, the marijuana."

Ronnie's dad shrugged, "No farms around here, son. Woods an' mining, that's what we got." He smiled ruefully, "Maybe, like you say, a little maryjane in a clearing in the backwoods, here an' there, though I hear the growin' season's mighty short."

Another old crag nodded, "Early frost's broke a lot of enterprisin' young hearts."

"I'm constructing a story..." Brando fished Walter's card out of his pocket, "...on G.H. Enterprises. *Senior Georges* Haslins" Brando pronounced George 'Hor-hay'.

"Georgie-Porgie?! Somebody ought to do an *expose* on that cheap bastard!" The old man pronounced expose with a silent 'e'.

"What foul deed did George perpetrate?" Brando asked.

The various old foggers around the table snorted foul laughs and shook their heads ruefully, conveying it was a tale of serious mischief.

"That squinty-face son-of-a-bitch come in here and snapped up lots of land rights, that's what he done!"

"Land ownership is not a felony in the home of the brave," Brando said.

"No, but this was in the late 60's, early 70's, maybe. Back then, we all thought the mines was played out in these parts. George was the only man buyin', an' so he squeezed an' squeezed. Got nearly ten cents on the dollar. Folks around here resent it, even today."

"It is my purpose to interview the sting rum."

"The who?"

"The stingy cheapskate."

"You goin' to expose the bastard?" one of the old men asked.

Brando nodded gravely, "That is my intent."

"Be our guest." Ronnie's dad waved in a general southerly direction, "Som'bitch lives about a mile off the highway. When you get past the river, you'll see a weather-beat plank with the letters GH burned in it, mounted on two phone poles."

Another raised a wrinkled hand in warning, "But be careful, he got dogs an' a mighty ready shotgun."

"First," Brando said, "*Melange au bouef.*"

"What's that?"

Brando pointed to the waitress who was bringing his stew under a set of dark eyebrows that seemed knit in anger. "Fried wench over easy," he said.

He got another chortle out of that one. Aurora, where retired miners and habitues of the forest sit down to dip their freshly baked bread in hearty stew and laugh at almost anything. Brando's self-confidence soared. Maybe he was ready for the Catskills or a smaller casino in Vegas. If the aspirants at the Comedy Club over on Sunset could but experience the joy. But he

335

didn't allow it to go to his noggin. And he was careful to stir his stew before sampling it, on the look-out for hunks of used chewing gum.

CHAPTER 33

Brando walked aimlessly around town until the sun slid off the western edge of the world. That night, he steered the Olds out of Aurora, driving about ten miles past the bleached wooden board with the big GH burned in it. He pulled over and slept in the car by the side of the road.

At dawn's light he found more permanent lodging in a nest of tourist cabins. He placed a deposit on a weekly rental. His new home was a rustic log cabin located on the end of the back row of Carl's Cabins, a small clump of shabby bungalows surrounded by woods and located a half mile south of Aurora on the main road.

Stubbly-bearded Carl had ten such scenic cabins to let. The grand scheme featured a musty block-brick community shower-and-toilet complex. There were two signs, Man and Woman, and it was generally anticipated that applicants would select the appropriate sign and hang it from two rusty nails over the door before entering. Brando wanted to keep a low profile, but since Carl still had nine vacancies after he signed on, he couldn't envision much of a problem. At least until the weekend, when, Carl warned Brando, *things could get perky*.

Brando maneuvered the Olds along a weed-grown dirt road behind the cabin and parked it so it wasn't visible from the main road. He walked a hundred yards back to his front door.

337

The interior of the cabin was about as nature had intended it. The floor was buckled with the distant remembrance of rain and snow-melts past, and the peaked ceiling was ornamented with dusty cobwebs.

Brando spent the day wandering through the nearby woods, trying to figure out if he had a plan of action or not. *Was he simply going to drive in and introduce himself to Old Blindy?* That seemed altogether too effortless, and perhaps dangerous, as well. He wandered faint paths through the pines, snacking on some Karmalkorn he'd picked up at a gas station back halfway on the road from Chicago. He threw pebbles in little brooks. He stalked a deer for three hours before spooking the creature. The big buck kicked his heels at Brando and was gone in a flash.

After a night on a lumpy bunk in his cabin, he ambled back along the main road a half-mile to the center of town. Megan's Cafe featured a different waitress on the morning shift, and the SOFA Club (Serious Old Farts of Aurora) had yet to return. The new waitress was in her mid-thirties—blond and pretty.

"What for you, hon?" she said, wiping the table in front of him.

"Pig an' Chicken Extraordinaire any good?"

She grinned at him, "Oh, the Bacon & Eggs Special. Sure. We give you lots."

"Does there exist a real Megan?"

"I'm Gwen. Megan's my nickname."

Brando nodded solemnly. Nothing is more important than a person's name. In Vietnam, the bar-wenches and waitresses all had nicknames like *Hoa*, which means flower, or *Tuyet Lan*,

338

which means Snow White. You have to marry them before they tell you their real name, a drastic solution to a simple problem. Of course, marriage can be a lot simpler over there. You arrive at the Buddhist temple, you proclaim you're married, and you are married. *Same, same,* as they say on the streets of Saigon, *for divorce.* Only that could be a little harder, as you had to persuade the lady back to the temple. Brando had tried the first part once, with the lady whose picture was on his desk back at KTGA, only she was Catholic so they'd gone to the Saigon cathedral and done it proper and official. They'd never gotten around to the divorce. Her family was one of the wealthy corrupt, and when they'd upped stakes for Europe, they'd just swooped in and taken her away. Or maybe she went willingly, time and distance having their habit of blurring realities.

Brando shook his head, coming back to the present. Gwen-Megan was clanking plates around behind the counter.

"Walter Crankshaw ever dine here?" he asked.

"Stiff Wally? Not since he got too big for his britches. Moved his office to Hibbing, about thirty miles west." She brought two pots of coffee to the table, "Regular or Unleaded?"

"Decaf. You don't approve of Walter?"

"Too many airs for me, hon."

"Did you know he is an accomplished dancer and a care-free wastrel of the night?" Brando asked.

"Oh, I don't think so, sweetie. The Walter I know couldn't two-step his way out of a paper bag!"

"Mais, non! I have les evidence. A veritable Gene Kelly, he."   Brando selected a prime Polaroid he had taken at the Wally-hop back in Southern California and placed it in full view on the table. He thought Gwen-Megan would drop her pots. As it was, she barely got them back on the burner.

She hurried over to Brando's side and gingerly picked up the photo, holding it by the edges as if it might give her some disease, "Lord, Lord, Lord, what have we here?!"

"Walter's California night club exhibition. The old buck achieved a highly publicized one-nighter at a place called the Cherry Bar. I doubled as his press agent and photographer."

"Worth its weight in gold, honey!"

Brando shrugged, "It's yours if you want it. You could mayhaps display it on the wall over there with the announcement for the Megan's Maulers bowling squad and the weekly gathering of the Kiwanis crowd."

It was a pretty good deal. Brando traded the picture for a plate loaded with bacon, eggs and hash browns, the browns agitated just a little too brown the way he preferred them. He tried to calculate how long the Legend of Wooly Wally would take to traverse the thirty miles to Hibbing. His best guess was that it would be hours rather than days.

After his early morning feast, Brando ambled along the main street of Aurora, whistling a bluesy bit of what he remembered from an old Harry Belafonte version of "Beale Street." He was Mister Casual, hands in his pockets, strolling along. Soon he found himself in front of Barry's

Up North, the Aurora sporting goods store. Barry was open for business, and Brando opened the screen door and procured for himself the top-of-the-line summer sleeping bag with a mosquito net, a ground cloth, a hunting degen, a good land-traverse compass and one of those collapsible fishing rods with nylon 3 pound test line and some lures. As an afterthought, he threw in a box of 9 mm ammo. Plenty of ammo, he thought, is always a superb indicator for survival under adverse conditions. After all, the Sauk Indians might decide to leave their reservation to reclaim the land.

He placed everything but the compass, the knife and the fishing gear in the trunk of the Olds. Then he ventured into his cabin and strapped on Joey's historical old Bianchi shoulder holster and tucked in the Browning. Joey had been given to wearing baggy suits in his last days, and Brando wondered how many times he'd walked around the studio with this same piece strapped to his chest, looking for the invisible enemies who had destroyed his show and his career.

Brando himself had resisted tailoring his fatigues and so, with his shirt hanging loose over his belt, it was hard to tell he was carrying.

An hour later he was casting along the St. Louis river near the bridge where he could observe the motor traffic heading south. The fish weren't hungry, but at about one in the afternoon Stiff Wally's bright red Jeep tooled south across the bridge. It didn't figure he'd be heading anywhere other than under the bleached board with the big GH burned in it.

Wally was alone in the car. Interesting. That probably meant at least three Charlies were lying in the woods with whatever ingenious killing devices they'd thought up, waiting for Brando to dance in and rescue Keith and Mindy. It also meant Walter's jeep could get in all the way to the house without being stopped.

Brando reeled in his line and moon-walked back to Carl's Cabins, where he destroyed some time by leaning against a pine tree and shaving a stick into a walking cane. He conducted himself in this fashion until the red jeep went flashing by, then set down his knife and trotted along the road toward town. As he expected, the jeep was parked across the street from Megan's.

The bell tinkled as he entered the cafe. In mid-afternoon, it was almost deserted. Megan and her gum chewing assistant were sitting on stools at the counter while a furious Walter Crankshaw towered over them, yelling that he was a respectable man with a wife and family.

Megan had a fresh red mark swelling the left side of her visage, and Brando's Indian princess had blood flowing from her nose. The picture of dancing Wally, which had been featured directly over Megan's little league baseball squad, was gone.

Loss of the photo didn't bother Brando. He'd shot a whole pack. Old Wally was so involved with dominating the wenches he hadn't bothered to check who entered. Brando sauntered past the troubled threesome and pinned another Polaroid where the last one had been, using the same pushpin that was still stuck in the wall.

"In some respects," he said to no one in particular, "this shot is even better. In my opinion, it has a sharper focus, and you'll notice it is a side-angle two-shot. Observe , Wally, how your fascination with the naked young thing in front of you shines like the sweat on your forehead."

"I'm going to kill you!", Wally said, clenching his fists like one of the half-humanoid monkeys in Kubrick's 2001.

Brando didn't bother to say anything. Wally advanced far inside the red zone and Brando shoved the base of the palm of his hand squarely and sharply into his face.

There was one of those noises vaguely resembling the one they make in the chop-socky flicks by slapping a bamboo cane against a table. Sad Wally, the would-be ding-boy, made a noise that was half a gurgle and half a whine as he went over on his back.

While he was squirming around on the floor holding his broken nose with both hands, Brando booted him in the guts. *Walter Crankshaw, the little engine who could not.* Brando wanted to kick him some more, but felt he had to observe a fine line here. Wally rightfully should do penance for bloodying the wenches, but he would do The Brando Mahr Benevolence Society no good if he was laid up in the hospital.

"We might have taken him," Gwen-Megan said, "but he knocked me out with a sugar dispenser." She held a clear plastic bag filled with cracked ice on the side of her face, which had started to balloon and turn purple.

The dark-haired gum-chewer brought Brando a pitcher, and he managed to stop the blood flowing out of Walter's nose by dumping icy water on the aged ding-boy's head.

"Thanks for helping us," the dark haired girl said. "I guess you're not such a smart ass after all."

"You're pretty fantastico, yourself. Perhaps we should get together tonight, to see the sights and explore our new feelings of togetherness."

"I get off at 8. We can park by the lake." She gave him a wicked grin.

"I shall return here so we can go together and you can clarify which shore," he said. "After all, this is the Land 'o Lakes."

Things were moving to the up-slide in Aurora, Minnesota. *If only he could find the time to fully enjoy his new recreational opportunities.*

"Come on, Wally," Brando dragged his fallen prize to the door by the scruff of his shirt, "We've got occupational hazards to face."

They were in Wally's red yuppie-mo-jeep, already spinning south of the bridge, when Brando blundered into a bevy of misgivings. The way he calculated, his Visigoths were very good at extermination, and Wally meant nothing to them. *Wally was less than a peanut, and peanuts were five piasters to the cone.* Brando found himself remembering the Saigon Zoo, where the hordes of little peanut kids, eight or nine years old at the most, would rush you like a flock of pigeons, yelling *"Anh, anh, anh*—choose me!" You were allowed to select your own private host, a little boy or girl who would follow you around with handfuls of peanuts wrapped into old

344

newspaper cones. That way, when you arrived at the monkeys or the elephant cage and needed a peanut, you'd be ready.

But, truth was, nobody was more expendable than a peanut boy.

"Pull over here, Wally-boy" Brando said. When the car slid to a stop on the gravel beside the road, Brando jumped out and slammed the door behind him.

Wally stared morosely across the road, hardly daring to look Brando in the eyes.

"I can go?" Wally asked, still not believing his luck.

"Anywhere in the universe except back to Megan's."

Walter glared at Brando like he was among the soon-to-be-dead, then printed a short strip of rubber on the road as he peeled out and accelerated away. Brando watched as the red Jeep turned off the main road and started down the gravel drive under the GH sign. He pushed the timer on his Casio Chrono. After 41 ticks he saw a flash of light deep among the pines. A split tick later he heard the roar, like a flat PAM! sound in the open forest. An oily black cloud of smoke roiled up over the treetops and tips of flames licked at the base of heaven.

Brando looked both ways and then quickly slipped to the other side of the road. He ran south through the forest along a footpath that paralleled the road. The humidity was intense, and he was sweating by the time he disappeared in the thick willows. The ground was low and marshy, and the deserted and nearly overgrown path meandered around beaver ponds and swampy

345

ground. Staying off the road was slow going, but Brando figured the advantages were significant. He was keeping a low profile and he was still heading toward George Haslins.

He estimated he had traveled nearly half the distance to George's house when the sirens and the police car and an old red fire truck raced south towards the mortal remains of Walter Crankshaw. Brando felt comfortable; he was attempting an old Nguyen Tu Giap ploy. *Use the moment of confusion to attack the enemy.* Brando hoped his enemies hadn't read the same G.I. Joe comics that he had.

CHAPTER 34

The Jeep was lying on its side and burning as furiously as carriages in the Great London Fire—err, of 1666 for those of you who do not know. The flames had jumped to the brush and the firemen were trying to knock the fire down before it could ignite the pines. The Jeep and old Wally had met their collective fate near an uncleared thicket. There was a clot of old, rotted logs and a small waist-high patch of tangled wild grapevines where the vehicle had left the road. *That's where I would have strung the wire,* Brando found himself thinking with a sage little nod.

He moved quietly, crawling from tree to tree until he was well past the scene. When he calculated he was beyond the attention of the firefighters, he returned to the gravel drive and jogged for about 400 paces until a large clearing opened up in front of him.

There was a late model white full-sized Chevy pickup truck parked near a two-story clapboard Victorian house. Although the house had been recently painted, the front lawn hadn't been mowed for weeks and the grass was tall and seedy. Pickets were missing from an old wooden fence that sagged here and there. From Brando's temporary outpost at the rear of a gnarled pine tree, he could make out several lean-to sheds and a garage. These were unpainted, their old boards shiny grey in the sunlight. The garage had no doors. Inside he could see a tractor, a snowplow

347

attachment, and a vacant space for the pickup truck.

If the three men from the Coral Sea were here, they would be employing a car parked near an escape route. Brando darted through the woods in a semi-circle to get to the back of the house. On the far side of a wide, grassy lawn, he found an older, less used road. This looked like it might loop back to the main road. He walked along it for a few yards, following fresh tire tracks. In one spot a branch of a milkweed plant was newly crushed into a tire track. The milky white stuff hadn't yet had time to coagulate. A few feet further, some goldenrods off the edge of the tracks had been broken. Brando figured a car or truck had been through here only a short time before, going a little faster than the road would allow.

Brando dashed in a direct line for the house, setting aside the multitudinous possibilities of ambush as best he could. He cut across the high grassy lawn and felt suddenly full of dread for what might reveal itself inside. He took the back steps with a rush and ran through the open back door and across a summer porch. From there, a door led to the kitchen. He quickly made his way through the high ceiling living room and a small library that was floor to ceiling with books on the NFL, yelling, "Anybody in the domicile?"

Brando took the steps up to the second floor in bounds of three, and that was where he found George Haslins, Old Blindy the Clown-man, the same fellow who had taken the ridiculous tumble to the turf in the Rams-Vikings playoff game. Old Blindy was truly old now, so old he carried the spent and wrinkled frame of an ancient gilly gaupus, but he wasn't going to expire from old age. He was spread-eagled in his bed on a sticky red blob of his own blood. And the large black handle of a broad butcher's degen was pushed up to the hilt in his thin chest.

Brando bent down and reached for the knife, but old George Hazlin's eyes squinted open and his head shook a little. He whispered, "No. Leave it."

Suddenly, Brando's reality assumed new dimensions. He heard four or five popping noises, like champagne corks or incendiary grenades and by the time he turned around, smoke was boiling up the stairway.

Brando knew instantly that he was in serious and perhaps terminal trouble. Ancient, dying George and he were trapped upstairs in a dry old wooden house that had been rigged to go up like a Halloween weenie bake. After dancing around traps for weeks, he'd finally taken the bait, and, all things being equal, this one was going to snap his back. Brando Mahr, victim of accidental fiery death in woods while interviewing old NFL official.

"I'll carry you," Brando said.

"Nooo." The old codger spoke in a raspy, bubbling whisper. "I'm gone, sonny-boy." He paused, sensing what had happened, "They've…fired the house." It was a statement rather than a question.

His eyes narrowed in a myopic squint, his face contorted in an almost superhuman effort to stay conscious while the last of his world unraveled around him, "Who are you?"

"Brando Mahr."

One claw-like hand snatched Brando's wrist and the dying old man pulled his visitor close. "Downstairs library," George hissed. "Their deeds and dogged faith. Get it and go out the cellar..."

His hand slid from Brando's wrist and the grimace faded. No question, Old Blindy had departed for the better place.

Brando rushed to the sink in the adjoining bathroom, soaked a bath towel and splashed water on his fatigues. By now, flames were crackling up the stairwell. Brando figured they'd left an incendiary fire-can at the base of the steps and others at key exit points around the house. It would be neat and professional. The local inspector would never even find the grenade cans unless he comprehended what he was looking for. If there even was a fire inspector out here in the *campagna. Fire started from a spark from the car accident up the road,* the local police report would read. *Good enough,* the editor of the local Daily Blather would nod to himself, sipping his early morning coffee laced with black strap.

Brando told himself it wasn't the time to be bothering with alternate realities. *Just squeeze off one shot at a time,* he thought. Soaked down the way he was, he might live to fight another day. But he had to manufacture his exit at once, before the stairs collapsed. He put on his sunglasses and wrapped the towel around his head and lunged from the bedroom.

He went like damp lightning, but still. the heat was enormous and his wet pants were steaming hot by the time he charged down the flaming stairway and rolled into the living room, which was boiling with turgid black smoke, eager for the first spark to set it off. The flames hadn't yet burst to life, but when they did the whole room was going to pop. Brando could hear crackling from the front and back doors. The mysterious *they* had set off more fire-cans. It didn't matter, he couldn't leave anyway. The enemy would be sitting in the trees, their sights zeroed in on the exits, and eager to gun him down as he flew out a door or window. The old man had said something about the cellar—there had to be a hidden exit.

In those tumultuous moments, Brando was trying to remember every Victorian house he'd ever been in. His grandmother's house back in Illinois, his great-uncle's house in Oregon; it seemed the steps down to the basement were always off the kitchen.

Moving in that house was like walking through the lowest rungs of Dante's hades. Brando stripped off his sunglasses and hugged a wall, heading for the kitchen. He might seer his eyeballs, but with the sunglasses it was too dark to see. The wall along which he felt his way was hot to the touch.

Brando hesitated. Old George had donated one other clue before he died. *Their dogs and deeds and faith--something about dog faith... Christ, he didn't have time for this!* An overhead beam crashed to the ground. Brando froze in the smoke-black room while flames erupted all around him. *Their Deeds And Dogged Faith! That had the odd ring of a title. Of course, a book on the history of the NFL, a book published by the Hall of Fame!* Brando had used it for his documentary and for some of his preliminary research on the Ripper. Why would blind old dog George Haslins evoke a literary discussion on his deathbed?

A heavy glass chandelier in the living room slipped its chain, smashing into the heavy Jacobean oak table under it. Brando changed directions and groped his way toward the library, where the smoke was only whitish grey and there only existed a few yellowish tongues of flame licking the far wall. His mysterious friends had done a good job, igniting the windows and doors. He wasn't going to get out this way, either. He didn't see any way at all that he could leave. For some byzantine reason, George Hazlins, living in an isolated woods, had fastened iron bars on all his lower windows. Brando's mind wandered to the quirkish...*Who knows, maybe to keep inquisitive bears at bay.*

Whatever else he represented, George Haslins was a systematic librarian. Brando scurried frantically around the room, hoping the books were arranged alphabetically by title. They weren't, they were alphabetical by author; luckily, the book Brando wanted was written by Rathet and Smith, and "r" is two up from "t", and the book was actually filed only a shelf off from his original hasty calculations. He snatched it and dove back in the general direction of the kitchen as the entire wall of books collapsed behind him in a burst of fiery sparks.

Even breathing through the towel, Brando's throat was raspy and he was nauseous. He had to fight to keep from flashing his hash. *And he'd always sworn seasickness was the worst torture a cull could endure! It shows you how wrong a mortal could be.* He edged his way back through the living room, the far side of which had become a roaring bonfire, and found one door that opened on a smoke-filled pantry. He located the cellar door, which was solid oak and locked tight as a drum. A ring of keys hung to the left side of the back door. But that was across the kitchen, in an area that was now a massive wall of fire.

Brando was coughing and hacking to clear his lungs and get his breath at the same tick, but there was no good air to be had. He suspected he had less than thirty ticks before he collapsed. He stifled his gagging and got a broom from the pantry to reach across the burning kitchen for the keys.

The metal ring was uncomfortably hot, and he burnt his hand before he could drop the keys on the floor. By now the world was a dull haze, and he was sinking to blackness. The air had become impossible to inhale. He recognized it was time for the court of last resort, the old swallow-the-tongue humbug. When you're a kid playing dead under the craggy apple tree, holding your breath is a game. In Nam playing dead was a rare, seldom-needed, but life-saving gift. One thing Brando knew, he could pass out before taking a breath of air. He squinted and pouted, his face screwed up like a prune, and got on with the job at hand.

He figured the key had to be old. He snatched up the ring of keys with his towel. There were four simple old-fashioned keys and a half-

353

dozen modern brass ones of various shapes and sizes. Fortunately for his stay on the planet, the right one was the second old-fashioned key he tried. The door to his salvation opened, and he threw the book down and tumbled after it, tumbling end over end down a steep stairway into utter blackness.

The floor where he lay was cool, and there was a two-foot layer of good air directly above it. Brando turned on his side and coughed and spit. He had to keep moving. He couldn't stay here. The upper floors were going to collapse on top of him.

He tried to get his bearings. By now his sight had adjusted to the dim light. He could make out a thin light filtering in through several small and grimy windows set high on the walls. They were the type of basement window that swung open halfway, to let in some air. There was no way he could squeeze out through one of them, and even if he did, there would be eager gunners waiting.

Yet Old George had told him to come this way. There had to be an exit. Brando picked up Their Deeds and Dogged Faith and his life-saving towel and started crawling. There were only three rooms; the large main room containing an old coal-burning furnace and a work bench with the usual scatter of do-it-yourselfer's tools. He briefly thought of—and dismissed—the notion of crawling into the furnace. The second room was a coal-room that was half-filled with black anthracite. And the third proved to be a small, musty room that had several kegs in a row on a shelf and a rusty wine press. There was a door at the back of this room. Stacked next to the door on

354

a small shelf were a loaded .38 police special and a flashlight.

The flashlight was old, but still gave a weak orange beam. Brando turned it on and then snapped it off to save the batteries. The pistol had not been properly oiled and was heavily coated with rust. And the door...well, fastidious Old George had made certain it was locked.

If Brando hadn't been so sick, he was sure he would have let out a string of curses that would have embarrassed a Lord of the Seas. But things being what they were, he crawled back across the basement floor and staggered up the steps. The doorknob was hot, and the kitchen behind it was now a wall of flames. Brando wrapped the towel around his left arm and reached around and jerked the key chain from the door. He managed to slam the heavy oak door behind him, and then to scramble back down the steep stairway. Lying on the cellar floor, he saw the layer of breathable air in the basement was now only about six inches off the floor. Honored guest or not, he was definitely running out of welcome at George Hazlin's place.

The last of the old keys proved to be the one that turned the lock. But the door had warped and didn't want to give. Brando tugged and heaved until it reluctantly swung open on rusty hinges, revealing a chest high tunnel that led at a gentle slope down and away into blackness.

The moment of his exit had arrived. Still toting the book, he snapped on the flash and made his wary entrance into the tunnel. The rotten plank floor and walls around him were slimy and dank, and the roof, which was so low he was forced to move along in a crouch, was made of old railroad ties and sawed off chunks of telephone poles. Roots had grown down through the cracks between the roof timbers, and the way was heavy with cobwebs.

Brando slapped at brown spiders with bodies big as quarters. They didn't skip or jitter out of the way, like spiders are supposed to; they moved slowly, with what he was convinced were sullen intentions. He snapped his towel to clear a space in front and then began to push his way through the tunnel overhang. The flashlight dimmed to a dull orange glow. He turned it off. Somewhere ahead in the total darkness he heard small animals slopping and dashing through water. *Rats*, he thought, remembering The Nam. *Rats, rats, rats!*

CHAPTER 35

The more immediate concern of Brando Mahr had nothing to do with spiders or the rats. Rather, it was the tenacious smoke that was now leaking over and under the door and into his tunnel. The flash now refused him even its dim orange glow, so he edged forward slowly, making his own path through the hanging roots in the dark.

After the first few feet forward the angle of the tunnel sloped more steeply downward. Brando couldn't remember any slope around the house, but he had come in from the west, following the long private drive that ran from the main road. He'd made a semi-circle through the woods around the south side of the house to come in the back. So, conceivably, there could be some sort of a gentle down-slope on the north side. No other reason coming to mind, he figured Old George wasn't crazy after all; he knew he had serious enemies, and they might come for him. So he had dug himself a secret escape tunnel.

After twenty feet, Brando was sloshing through a foot of chilly water. After a hundred feet, he had to hold Their Deeds and Dogged Faith over his head, because the water had climbed over his waist. But now he had hope, because there was a jog in the tunnel, and beyond it, a faint glow of light.

Brando edged forward as quickly as he could. The water deepened until there was barely a foot of breathing space under the rough overhead timbers. He moved along the tunnel until he could see the source of the light. It wasn't good news.

There was a chink in the timbers through which fell a shaft of light no wider than a half inch and nearly as long as his hand. Seeing that warm shaft of light nearly drove him insane. For a moment he thought he was doomed to suffocate; because ten feet beyond this chink, the water met the roof of the tunnel.

What if he fell prey to a major Zeeman under here? What if the smells, the sights, the sounds turned from underground rot to barnyard sunlight and the scent of straw and animals? There was an attraction, an appeal that was so strong he could feel part of his mind desperately trying to call up the memory. He shook in fear and anguish, and finally, anger. Brando's last Zeeman--worthless, hopeless, alone, defeated in the dark. *He couldn't let it end like this! At least*, he prayed, *let me go out in a flame and a flare. Let there be fireworks; let the young and innocent gasp and ohhh and ahhh at the explosions!*

There could be no more idle thoughts, no more waiting; he had to interact with reality or he was going to die. He could only go forward, could only dive in the murky water filling the tunnel ahead and see if he could come up on the other side. Who knew what was there? Had Crazy George left an underwater exit? Did the tunnel exit into a lake? Did it bend back up again and come out in sunlight on the other side of a hill? When he got there, if there was a door, would it be locked?

His mind was spinning wildly. He knew he had to regain control. He was shaking violently, and it wasn't entirely from the cold, black water. As he crouched in semi-darkness, hunched over neck-deep in the water, clinging to a copy of Their Deeds and Dogged Faith seemed less and less a priority. He was about to let it sink when he realized that George probably had left something in the book. With his neck turned sideways and using the narrow sliver of light, he fanned through the pages. It helped to calm him down, but there was nothing in the book. No incriminating scraps of paper, no copies of old checks, no tormented letters of confession. Still, he didn't want to let the book go. Brando figured he might be able to stuff it in back of his belt, the same way he'd gotten the copies of the play-by-plays out of the Rams office. It would be a little soggy, but that was life in the big leagues.

As he turned it around in the awkward little space above the water, the book slipped completely out of its paper jacket. Brando was left holding only the jacket and staring at the underside of it, to which a single sheet of paper was attached with yellowed tape. There were four or five paragraphs, neatly typed and notarized in 1975 by one Beth Warren of Nashwauk, Minnesota. Brando read:

> To Whom It May Concern:
> It is not easy to be a referee
> in the National Football League.
> The fans always got on me for
> calls I made. The sports writers
> called me "Old Blind-y" and
> "Bat's Eyes" and the people in
> the stands and on the street

called me worse than that. I guess it don't matter,

only maybe to explain how come I did what I done.

Anyway, it was after a Super Bowl III party in Miami in 1968 when I first met Nathan Paramis. I knew him from before but just as a dirty player you had to watch, and later as a lousy coach. That year Namath had beaten the Colts to make the Jets the champs and we were arguing about some of the calls when Paramis started saying football was all the calls, the stupid, lousy calls. "Yeah", I remember asking, "then why don't they pay us more?"

We met a couple of times after that. There was Nathan and me, and Loaf Ludder from the Rams, and Jimmy Teams, who was working for the Rams as probably the world's oldest trainer. It was always the same; lots of gripes, lots of boilermakers and martinis. Paramis hated Harold Dunstain, the Rams coach who had replaced him and he kept saying he wanted something bad to happen to the rotten S.O.B. I don't know when we got our big idea, somewhere late in the next season for sure. The Rams were a cinch to take everything. But if we could pick a game, and bet our life savings on the other team—and then influence the outcome of that game—we would all be rich.

It's not as easy as I'm saying. We were just ordinary guys, except for maybe Paramis. He kept the needle in while we made excuses and put it off. The Rams were winning, winning, winning, and the odds were getting better and better. Then, when they were upset by Minnesota, Detroit and Baltimore the last three games, he was out of his mind—we could have made our killing without doing anything, just by betting in any one of those games! It came down to the Minnesota playoff game, and this is what we did. Jimmy Teams ground up a huge mess of downers and divied them in three packets. At half time, I slipped one pack in the referee's water, and Loaf dropped the others in the Ram's water cans at each end of their bench.

I got caught at my own game when Willie came up to me with a couple of paper cups.

I had to drink or somebody
would   suspect   something.
Anyway, the game got real
sloppy and now you know why.
I guess I could live without
telling the worst thing I ever
done. I just don't want to die
that way.

George O. Haslins

George had signed his name carefully at the
bottom in ballpoint pen, as had Beth Warren.
That was good enough for Brando. He folded the
book jacket with Old Blind-y's confession in it,
and buttoned it in the top left pocket of his fatigue
shirt. The air was thickening, the Brando Breath-
o-meter acceptability rating was taking a
corresponding plunge. If he couldn't beam out of
there, he was going to choke to death or drown.

He took a tick or two to breathe as deeply as
he could. Deep breathing to fill the blood with
oxygen, but under these conditions it started him
coughing. He was a mighty swimmer and had
good lungs for diving. In the army training they
had habitually thrown his squad in with full
packs, boots and all, to experiment whether they
could come up without needing the corporal with
the hook.

The smoke set Brando's eyes, nose and throat
burning. He cursed a last *Odd's Plut* and dove
underwater, swimming as best he could for the
end of the tunnel. In three strokes, the water
turned from black to a dull grey. Three more and
it was grey-green. Three more, and he banged his
head into the rusty grill that served as George's

362

home-made underwater door. That damn old nutty squint-eyes had thought of everything. No Slithus, no Monster From The Black Lagoon or Aqua-Man turned evil was going to challenge his secret entrance. As expected, the door wouldn't budge in or out.

Where was Brando's underwater sprite, his Ondine, when he needed her? Where was Darryl Hannah, the mermaid from Splash? Wasn't he, Brando Mahr, loyal and true and equally worthy as Tom Hanks? About that time, he would have settled for Rosie O'Donnell in a mu-mu, a mer-lady with real heft who could barrel her way through that gate.

In another moment he wouldn't have enough oxygen to make it back to the shaft of light, where he doubted there was enough good air left, either. Was Old George crazy enough to leave a key down here? Brando scrambled around like a madman, feeling between the dead weeds and accumulated slime on the sides of the door. Yes, he was at least that crazy. It was hanging to the left side of the grill, on a part of the metal doorframe, on a heavy nail that had been welded there. More amazing, the key slid in the keyhole and turned easily.

But salvation wasn't going to be that quick or simple. The journey back from hades is always full of perils. He'd already been without a breath of fresh air for over three minutes and Old George's grill-door itself was wedged shut, logged at the bottom in a decade of muddy debris.

Eyes bulging, Brando planted his boots on the sides of the gate and pulled. The gate came, slowly at first, and then not at all. He tried again,

363

and again, and a third time. He had six inches, then eight, then a foot, then possibly enough. Ominous black specks were floating across his field of vision as he squeezed and clawed his way through and kicked to the surface.

He erupted into the universe under the wooden dock in a small round lake, gasping for sweet air, came up so fast he cracked his skull against the dock, re-opening the old scab from when he'd bashed his head against the car in the KTGA parking lot. He hugged the nearest rotten dock post like it was a lover while the blood ran in his eyes and the black spots danced in front of them. He sucked in the incredible richness of the Minnesota air, feeling luckier than he had at any time since he realized he'd been air-lifted from Vietnam.

CHAPTER 36

Brando's euphoria didn't extend past the first few moments of his new extension on life. One interesting side-effect of surviving places with sing-song names like Da Nang and Tay Ninh is that any little thing will yank you back into the war mode, a sort of intense paranoia that makes it impossible to *think friendly*. And equally hard to get from point A to point B. The enemy is out there, unseen and unheard, and you know to your core that he will continue to come at you. To survive, you must attain a sort of transparent invisibility. You must move swiftly, obliquely and unexpectedly and without allowing chagrin or impatience to grow into frustration. Or elation into carelessness. Be Chameleon Man, with his cloak of colors. Seek *hozgro*, the Navajo sense of balance, the Native American equivalent of the Greek homeostasis. In short, by the time Brando came up out of Old George Hazlin's Hades, he'd gone completely fox-crazy.

He'd displayed this particular brand of insanity before, the surviving lurps all had, for weeks and even months at a time. Dead Eyes, the scribes had typed of men like him, with presumptive, superior pity in their fingertips. Now, for the first time since the war, Brando had reverted to form. He was crazy again. Crazy as a bedbug, crazy as a mad hatter, a march hare, crazy like a fox, crazier than a loon. He could lie in the mud for hours and smile just like a crocodile.

Brando no more, he cognized in his heart he truly was Earman. He was the Hands of Death.

He saw from his vantage point under the pier that a fire engine and police car had rolled in to witness the destruction of George Haslin's house. He ducked underwater when the firemen came running to throw the end of a big canvas hose in the lake. The fire engine was a vintage 1950's pumper, and employed its engine to suck and throw water. Still, the flow was only enough to wet down the surrounding area, and the main fire raged unabated. The firemen and a small bunch of onlookers scurried away from the pond as the roof collapsed in a shower of sparks, sending flames shooting into the late afternoon sky with renewed vigor.

The water surrounding Brando was cold, and it was getting colder the longer he remained in it. Still, he waited until everyone was around the other side of the house before he crept up on the bank and made a squishy run for the trees.

He retrieved his fishing gear, which he'd stowed beside the road after letting poor Walter go to his reward. Some fishermen had a campfire going down by the river, and they allowed him to dry his boots and socks while he had to play the buffoon and endure the usual jokes about the big one that pulled him in. He couldn't take his fatigue shirt off, because then they would have seen the pistol, but he managed to dry George's confession, which seemed to have come through without much damage, all things considered. He re-folded and returned it to his pocket, still encased in the paper jacket from the book.

The sun was just dipping below the pine tree horizon, and darkness gathered a half hour later as he approached the wooded area near Carl's Cabins.

He paused behind a stacked pile of split firewood to reflect on reality, life, truth and justice. Here he was, alone in the northern woods. The three clever ding-boys had tried to snuff him again, and had failed. But the poor bastards didn't know it. They were probably sipping stitch-back ales and toasting each other in the Metropolitan Airport in Minneapolis, having eliminated Walter, George and Brando from their nasty equation. *Or were they?*

For the first time since he'd stirred the pot and brought these strange and clever codders to the surface of the soup, there was a possibility he had the upper hand... *but then why had he pulled to a stop by the side of the road? And why was he sitting behind a woodpile with the mossy green bark of a pine tree rubbing his back, aware of an old, familiar twitch gnawing at his sense of security? Was it just the rats of Nam still able to churn his guts, the knowledge that he never could or would know complete peace again? Or was it something more specific, more here-and-now?*

He fought the urge to jump up and be on his way, to hop in the Olds and drive to the nearest airport. If Keith and Mindy were still alive, they would need him. If they weren't, they would need avenging.

He moved upwind about a hundred paces and sat against another tree, letting his limbs relax, trying to drive all conscious thought from his mind. He relaxed and did nothing. And as it

367

always does, his already overbearing sense of hearing became even more acute. The silent forest became darker and alive with night noises. An owl scratched its feathers, preening with its beak. Something little scampered, and then paused for a moment, listening just as Brando was. The wind lifted and brushed a billion pine needles with a soft sighing swoosh sound. And somewhere off to Brando's left as close as half a football field away something large as a dog, a horse, a cow, a moose or possibly a ding-boy bearing arms and ill intent, was quietly breathing. Each once and again the ding-boy would fuss about a little, the way people do in the woods.

Dropping to his belly, Brando inched forward until he was within 20 running steps of the creature. He heard the creature as it scratched, it grunted, it quietly whispered Oh fuck. It was buffle-headed young Goat-beard.

Brando was about to take the ding-boy out when he felt a prickly sensation between his shoulder-blades, the feeling the known universe around him had opened and was quietly feeling him with a sixth sense. Was it no more than the word association of *goat beard and judas goat?* Brando didn't think so. He ducked around behind the nearest tree as a rifle sang out and a bullet clipped the branches nearby. *Night scope!* The shooter was to Brando's right and maybe 50 yards.

"Christ, almighty! Who the hell is shooting?" Goat-beard yelled. Brando was practically on top of him, and he was thinking *Goat-beard must be a big disappointment to somebody. He had to be*

368

the electronics man; he certainly wasn't any good in a fire fight.

Brando darted forward, dogtrotting *circumbendibus* in a hesitant, zig-zag pattern, doubling sideways, back the other way and then moving forward again. He was on Goat-beard in a rush. The skinny little fellow tried to swing up his rifle, but it was too late. Brando knocked it down with his left hand and slashed at him with the back of his right. It caught Goat-beard a little high, on the cheekbone, but was enough to stagger him backwards a few steps.

Three single shots laced the night, two of them hitting Goat-beard, and then Brando had the dead man's rifle and was putting trees between himself and the shooters. He knew there were at least two shooters. He went fifteen yards at a fast sprint with bullets clipping the branches and trees around him. He dove behind a small log, and came up running back the way he'd come. This time he went three steps and hit the dirt. There were no shots, so either they were reloading, or he'd temporarily lost them.

He took a moment to consider. Goat-beard's rifle didn't have a night scope, so he was going to have to make do without. He had heard three shots, whap, whap-whap! Interesting. Two of them had come from the same weapon. So that made it two night scopes, triangulated in on the Judas Goat's position. Only the luck of the draw had saved his spaghetti, Goat-beard falling in one line of fire and the other guy missing.

Their world was electric green and black, a circular field with a crosshair at the center. On the other hand, ordinary night vision is an interesting

369

phenomenon on its own. In the first place, you can actually sense more than you think you see once you recognize that you're working with shades of black. And second, in the night mode, your peripheral vision actually reads better than if you're looking straight at someone.

Their enhanced visual situation was the opposite of Brando's; a night scope illuminates everything with an unearthly brilliance. The problem is, everything's a brilliant monochrome orange or green in your eye. You've got to distinguish the tiger from the foliage, and the main way to do that is watch for movement.

Brando crawled down into a shallow depression, heading parallel to the shooters, and when he'd gone thirty paces or so, found a position in a stand of poison sumac. It wasn't a place he'd ordinarily choose, because there was nothing to hide behind, nothing that would stop a bullet coming in from any direction. But the vertical lines of the sumac, somewhat similar to the size and shape of a rifle barrel, might give him a momentary edge. He lay in the brush, resting the barrel of the rifle on a branch, and waited.

There's no clarity of thought compared with that when you're being hunted. Samuel Johnson said words to the effect that, *The knowledge that one is to be hanged in the morning concentrates the mind wonderfully.* Lying there listening to the hitch and rustle of his enemies creeping toward him in the woods, Brando started to think about poor Goat-beard and that led his mind to wander on to the intent and purpose of Judas Goats in general…and this one in particular. The rifle lying in front of Brando was a new hunting rifle. He would have anticipated men like these, with their military connections, would be more inclined to use an AR-15, or even the old M-14, if they wanted a heavier bullet. But a hunting rifle with something plugging the barrel would explode as efficiently as a pipe bomb. Brando quietly unwrapped his hands from around the rifle and took his Browning from its holster.

This tightened the game a bit; of necessity he would be forced to allow them to come closer, and they would have a better chance of scope-spotting him, that is, if he remained where he was. Brando decided to move. He set a little block of rotten wood that might look like a head beside the rifle, put his soft cap on the chunk of wood, and slid backwards down the depression. He made his way another twenty yards to a new position. This one, while the same exposed type as the last, was in a bed of what looked like poison oak.

Brando settled in on his stomach, arms forward and with Joey's target Browning gripped in both hands. They were coming…Earman could track them as clearly as two bulls in a bait shop.

When that time Brando would call the moment of joy finally radiated, it was over almost before it began. Brando had been holding a loose bead in the general direction of the closer of his two adversaries. He figured he was within five yards either way. But when his first target took the bait and shot at the rifle and the block of wood, Brando's sights were dead-on his muzzle flash. He corrected two feet to the left and pulled off three shots.

Brando rolled as bullets kicked into his position, hoping to get a tree between himself and the line of fire, then retreated ten yards and dove for cover. But he didn't have to bother. He could hear the sound of the last Hector—Brando's last target was in a semi-panic, running away through the woods.

For a moment he considered going after the bully-boy. He waited until the sound of his footsteps disappeared in the distance, noting that the man dogged it further into the forest rather than towards the road.

That was something to ponder. These weren't the type of lurkers who ever panicked. Ergo, Brando figured he was again being drawn to the light. Instead of pecking the corn, he backtracked to take a look at the damage he had caused. The second man was flung on his back, gazing blankly at the stars through the pines. His wrist revealed no pulse. It was the black lurker who had calmed Goat-beard at the start of their voyage on the Coral Sea. Now he and Goat-beard were both beyond redemption. He had nothing in his pockets except a smooth, round percussion grenade, the kind Brando had hugged to his waist in Nam. No wallet, no I.D. The last ding-boy had taken his rifle and was now quietly waiting somewhere in the deep woods. Brando felt there was every chance he intended to continue the dance.

Brando slipped the grenade in his own pocket and drifted quickly back to Goat-beard's silent form. He didn't have any I.D. either. But there was a needle-nose pliers and a small wind of steel wire in one the pockets of his jacket. Another pocket produced a half-used spool of nylon thread and a variety of clips and fasteners. Brando's guess was Goat-beard had been busy as a bee around Brando's rented cabin, and the Olds was probably wired as well. He made a mental note to tip off the state police and Carl of Carl's Cabins, and maybe the man from Budget Rental as well...or they were all going to have to do their explaining to St. Pete.

After a while, Brando felt restless. The local constables were probably vectoring in on his location by now; they'd already had an edgy day, with a blown-up jeep, a burnt house, and now a spate of wild shooting in the woods. You can't have a fire-fight anywhere near civilization without the phones buzzing. They would show up soon.

So he slunk away as swiftly as he dared, heading in the opposite direction from the remaining ding-boy. He was feeling dull and sick to his guts after the killings. By now, the last footpad would be wondering if Brando was hopping through the woods after him. He would set up a cross-fire ambush, and when the game didn't materialize in his cross-hairs, the gunner would realize Brando wasn't coming after him, and then he'd be looping back.

Keith would have advised him complete the mission then and there; *When you've got 'em on the ropes, good buddy, go for the knock-out!* But Brando had lost interest in any more action. At that moment all he wanted was to get away.

Once he reached the road, he sheathed the Browning and dogtrotted in a steady hobbledygee back toward the St. Francis river, trying to get out of his mind that Megan's was featuring a cold

373

roast beef sandwich with California Medley soup on special, and the gum-snapping Indian wench was warming to his special charisma.

The fishermen he'd met earlier were from Duluth, and they'd said they were pulling up stakes and heading back for the homestead after a few more Blatz around the blaze. With any luck at all, he'd be in time to hitch a ride south with a truckload of tipsy bass-men.

CHAPTER 37

A few days later, Brando propped his feet up on the battered desk in his grubby little office at KTGA, and churned through the messages on his Phone Mate. There was a blithe missive from Keith saying he and Mindy had been released in the High Desert near Pearblossom by two white guys who sounded suspiciously like they had once been members of the Mighty Foremen. That figured; they thought they were doing Loaf a favor. *One for all and all for one, The motto of the Four Numbnuts.* Old mutton monger Keith sounded so cheery that Brando was positive the old hitman had beaten him to the mother lode with Mindy. Of course, the duddering rake wouldn't come right to the point; he'd spend the next 20 years teasing his good little buddy about it. Spruce wench Mindy had used the old lifted-skirt routine to good advantage, and they'd hitch-hiked back to the valley nearly as fast as they could have driven by themselves. Only now Ginny wasn't talking to Keith, and Brando, his good buddy, had to call and explain how this latest adventure was serious stuff, and far more than idle hanky-panky, and how Keith and he were working on a serious and important official project.

There were also four or five calls from Lieutenant Baker and a few from Ripper Brown himself, sounding angrier and more frustrated with each call. Every time Ripper came on the line, it sounded like a low voice from somebody in the background was coaching, and everything the whisperer said seemed to make Ripper one notch madder.

As if that wasn't enough, story chief and cod's head Peri Nockel had sent word from Universal that Brando's sci-fi thriller-romance script, THE REBEL, should make up its mind and be one or the other, that is, thriller or romance. And there was a short message from hinny, his honey-, that is, Belle Denver. Brando automatically turned over the old Vietnam picture on his desk when he heard Belle's throaty whisper. *It was raining a lot,* Belle said. *Southerners were all pigs. Had any checks arrived for her? The picture wasn't going well. They'd had a lot of problems getting the fish to cooperate, the little fanged buggers seemed to have lost their appetites, very bad for the picture. Everybody might have to stay on a few extra weeks.* She didn't say she missed him, but Brando thought he caught a whiff of unhappy and maybe even lonely. Maybe their relationship was moving forward. *Mayhaps,* he thought hopefully, *away-fulness does make the heart grow bemused after all.*

He was re-running all the messages to get to Belle's voice again when the door banged open and Ripper roared in, puffing and blowing like a dark thundercloud and followed by a quietly grim Loaf Ludder.

"Hi, Rip. What's coagulating?" Brando said, trying for casual.

He barely had a moment to snatch the old framed ektachrome photo from his desk before Ripper slammed his forearm across it, scattering books and papers in a fit of wild fury. "I tol' you to leave go of this an' stop messin' wit' the memory of my woman!"

Brando looked from the Ripper to Loaf, who had quietly stepped in behind him.

"You elucidate what?" Brando blinked, hoping he was reflecting the appropriate sincerity and interest.

Brando slammed a newspaper on the desk. The headline screamed in his face, "Slain Ripper Brown Lover Linked To Mob Ties".

Brando spread his arms wide, "Any time a celeb is murdered you have rumors."

"I say you to blame!," Ripper shouted..

Brando shook his head, "It couldn't be me. I've been back in the Midwest."

"Shooooo, nuff...that what he *say*," Loaf intoned softly.

"Ahh, the whispering demon is at your side again." Brando shook his head. "Ask yourself, Old Ripster—why is this black fool constantly gabbling in my ear?

"What you talkin', man?" Ripper asked.

"Don' listen to him, Ripper!" Loaf shouted, but Ripper shoved him back with one great hand and pointed his other in Brando's face.

"I asked what you talkin, man?!"

If there ever was a time Brando's heart cried out for a silver tongue, that was it. As it was, he had to blunder through with the clunker he had. "What is the one glory you wanted in your life?" he asked, and without waiting, gave Ripper the answer. "It was to be a champion—*The Super-Champion of the Football Champions*. You wanted to win the SuperTournament. And I'm sorry to be the one to tell you; your teammate and drinking buddy Loaf here picked your pocket."

"Don' listen, Rip! He's a liar!" Loaf was fairly shrieking in that deep bass voice of his—if a deep bass could shriek. .

Brando shrugged and handed Ripper a copy of George's Haslin's confession. He watched the huge black man's lips move as he worked his way down the page. When he got to Loaf's name in paragraph three, his face twitched, but when he found out what Loaf had done, he let out an enraged cry and dove at his old teammate. The two giants crashed into the back wall and rolled around on the floor, with Loaf trying to fight off Ripper's wild blows.

Brando allowed the Godzillian struggle to continue for some time and then took a Browning from the desk drawer and fired it in the general direction of the ceiling. There was an enormous roar, followed by the fall of a six inch circle of plaster. Ripper and Loaf looked over the edge of the desk at Brando, eyes wide with wonder.

"There's more," Brando said.

"What more could he do to me?!" Ripper shouted, already set to resume his attack.

"...Illuminate him, Loaf," Brando said.

"Uhhh, what you talkin' 'bout, man?"

"Confess how you...ended Lani."

"You don't know I done that!"

Brando tapped the paper with Haslin's confession and shook his head, "I'm afraid it's the gallows for you, old rusty guts. Your motivation? You needed to cover up your old criminal deeds. It's all the men in blue will need. They're already

378

on the way." Brando's argument was a lot weaker than when Lieutenant Columbo snaps the trap on his suspects, but Loaf Ludder didn't know it. He crumpled like a paper bag.

"It was an accident, Ripper," he begged, the words tumbling out faster and faster as he jabbered. "I jist didn't want her givin' this creep all that stuff that might open up the whole can of worms, an' she was laughin' at me like she would do whatever she damn well pleased and I got so mad I jist hit her a little tap and she fell wrong against your Vince Lombardi trophy and…man, I didn't mean to…"

That was as much as he managed to confess before Ripper started slamming punches into him. Loaf just tottered in place, not even covering up, while the blood ran down his face. After a while he started to weave, like he was in a daze. When he finally went down, Ripper went after him, intent on mayhem and murder.

Lieutenant Baker, who had been listening through the paper-thin walls from the office next door, came rushing in and he and Brando managed to pull the big man away before he killed his old teammate Loaf Ludder.

CHAPTER 38

Brando put another little piece of the puzzle together later that night when he called Nathan Paramis to find out if they could meet. There was a significant pause and when Paramis finally spoke, it was in a strange, strangled tongue, as if his vocal cords were tortured by grief and rage.

"Perhaps we can meet on neutral turf," Brando suggested, "Somewhere out in the open."

"Yes. I'd like that," Nathan said in a strangled growl.

"We can meet with or without the long arm of the law—whichever you prefer."

There was a long, unbelieving pause on the other end of the line. "Without," Nathan Paramis finally said.

"Splendimonius. I'll motor up. Tomorrow okay-dokay? Twilight around the spa? You can cognize I'd prefer a hundred or so casual witnesses be present in the neighborhood."

"Yes."

"You'll also employ caution." Brando took a stab in the dark, "You've already abandoned one son to his destiny."

"Yes," Nathan said, his voice a hollow whine. He hung up the phone.

Brando sped the trusty Maroon Dog north along the 101 to Santa Barbara with the wind a-whistle in his ears and the late afternoon sun washing a reddish-golden glow across the sea on his left and rim-lighting the hills that tumbled down to meet the road from his right.

He tossed the keys to one of the wenches, taking the time to admire the way the bushel bubby's ample proportions plumped out her uplift vest, and then he wandered through the huge lobby. The place was a *nouveau Californio* marvel in mauve Italian marble, and it featured strategically placed modern brass lanterns and piles of flowering tropical greens spilling from mossy baskets.

Nathan Paramis was waiting poolside at a round glass table with Mindy Haslins and the third dingboy, the same sly rogue with the sandy hair who had tried to extinguish Brando's reality a healthy minimum of four times. The ground sloped dramatically away from the patio where they met, leaving the deep blue ocean for a view. The red-gold orb was slanting so its light still soaked the tops of the pool-side umbrellas in gold, but there was a softer light cast up into their undersides from candles set in heavy tear-drop crystal globes. Nathan's eyes were dark and sunken hollows, and for once he looked his age.

"My older son Roger," he said with an introductory wave of his hand, "and I believe you already know Mindy." The wench gave Brando a cold nod and Roger extended his right hand. Brando held his palm up and gave Roger a little wave.

"*Ecce Homo*," Brando said. "Behold the villain."

Roger looked like he wanted to take offense, but his father held him back with one hand. Nathan frowned and gave a righteous sigh, "Mr. Mahr, this isn't pleasant or easy for us here. I'd prefer if you'd quit your joking around, say what you've come to say, and get out."

But Brando wasn't going to let him lead the dance. "I'm here to regale the party with Uncle Wiggily bedtime stories." He replied.

"We're too busy for this!" Roger barked angrily.

"Sit, Roger," Brando said, like he was talking to a cur, "Or you'll be scragged, ottomised, and grinning in a glass case."

"What?"

"Must I translate everything? Hanged, anatomised, and your skeleton displayed in a glass case."

"You stupid-" Roger started to stand, but again Nathan waved him back into his chair.

Brando shrugged, "Don't radiate such confidence, Rogie-boy. In the tale I'll spin, you're all dirtier than Adolf Eichmann."

"You only think so..." The father was eyeing Brando closely. "And this isn't a trial."

"I have possession of facts that would hold up in one..."

"Shoore you do...and I'm Uncle Remus." Nathan barked a nervous laugh, and his eyes flickered hot and hard in Brando's direction.

"George Hazlins revealed everything before he expired."

"Bullshit!", Roger snapped, "He was dead by-"

"Dead by what, Roger?" Brando asked. "By the tick you left him?" Roger gritted his teeth and looked the other way. Mindy was staring at him, Clytemnestra aghast at Agamemnon.

382

"You killed my father?" she asked. Whereas before, the dimber mort had been cold and distant, the sweet lass Mindy was undergoing a change, her emotions gradually settling into a smoldering, carbuncular rage. "My father treated you like a son!" she shouted.

"Don't listen to this creep, Mindy", Nathan said, waving a hand as if to dismiss Brando.

"Red stain under your fingernails," Brando taunted. "Out, out, damned spot!"

Brando would later swear by *Odds Plut* that Nathan couldn't resist a look down at his own hands.

"These accusations are meaningless, Mindy," Nathan insisted, pounding the palm of one hand on the table for attention. He pointed at Brando, "Why, he was there! He could have killed your father! He could have done it himself!"

"Then why doth your *fils* play Pontius Pilate, procurator of Judea, still trying to wash his hands..."

"Foolishness," Nathan said, raising his voice again. "Stupidity! I say you're bluffing. You've nothing on us. You never did."

It was the classic tick, the moment when Hercule Poirot, the stinking little Belgian frog detective everybody has underestimated, raises the important contradiction.

"*Au Contraire, mes amis,*" Brando said, "I am in possession of the last confession. It implicates you all in the cleverest sports shenanigan since Persepone ran naked in the Olympics." That would have been an Old Scratch of a rarity, since women didn't compete in the ancient games, and Persepone was the goddess of corn to boot, but nobody even noticed, riveted as they were to the folder Brando waved in their faces. He took out copies of George Haslin's certified document and passed them around the table. He placed an extra copy by an empty chair.

Ever doomed to playing straight man for Chicot the jester, Roger asked, "Who's that one for?"

Brando reached up and tapped the small mike that had been positioned not too artfully in the big umbrella over their table, "For the ancient one. You may reveal yourself, Old Remus. George has fingered you as well."

And with that, the dimber damber of them all, ancient speedster Jimmy Motorfoot Teams, stepped from behind a nearby palm tree, gave Brando a dignified nod and sat at the table.

"How did you know?" he asked, his soft voice barely carrying.

"You described the two dissenting pro football factions at Lani's funeral. You didn't mention there was a third bunch, the renegade family-or families-of daubers, crooks and killers who would pounce on me before anyone else."

And yet, life is not and never has been fair: in what should have been Brando's crowning moment of glory, the first faint wisps of a nasty Zeeman crept in around the edges of his consciousness.

"Reprobate mosquitoes," Brando said, rapping at the side of his face with his left hand. It was a hard rap, and Mindy looked at him oddly. But, stoked as he was, the blow wasn't nearly enough to fend off the oncoming Zeeman.

384

Brando was already drifting towards long ago and far away. He felt the presence of the farmyard, he was drifting towards the inviting, dark opening of the barn door, so close he could see rakes and a shovel leaning against the rough wooden wall inside.

"Let me take him now!" Roger said impatiently.

Concentrate, Brando screamed internally to himself, *You are Brando Mahr, Earman; you are the Hands of Death. You are at the critical moment! You cannot lose control!!*

Motorfoot held up a hand, "No."

Through the aura of rainbow-filtered light Brando saw Motorfoot's palm was soft and pink, though the back was wrinkled leather.

The old man spoke, his voice yawing, and the words seemed to Brando to trickle in from a great distance. "He's talkin' and we listening. We can kill him any time." He spoke with chilling confidence.

Brando whacked his own head harder, this time with the heel of his hand. His ear started ringing but it didn't have any effect at all on the slowly expanding Zeeman.

"The expiration... of your grandson," Brando said calmly as he dared. "Was... unavoidable."

"Great grandson," the old black man said softly, nodding his acknowledgment. The dark opening of his mouth became confused with the barn door in the Zeeman. Brando shook his head, a last hopeless sweep to clear the gathering dark spots that were swelling like mushrooms to blot out his consciousness.

And still, last thoughts raced like cockroaches through his brain, seeking an exit where there was none, and his slowly-freezing mouth spoke calm words, "After all, you did manufacture the circumstance, Motorfoot."

The old man nodded once again, and his eyes narrowed, "I got me many sons, both grand and great."

"Though they be as the grains of sand, will they be blown away in the red--re--rrr..."

And there Brando became stuck, the spittle drooling from the right side of his mouth and running down his chin. He felt the gathering warm ice as the black barn door entrance flowed out to greet him.

"For God's sake-!"

Roger, at the end of his patience, scooped the heavy globe-candle off the table and heaved it across the table at Brando. There was no way he could miss at that short range. The glass caromed off Brando's forehead, directly over his right eye, shattering in a hundred silvery splinters and splattering hot wax across Brando's cheek. A hit like that might have sent a normal person to his higher reward. It did knock Brando over backwards, but the irony was, Roger's throw had the opposite of its intended result—and the real, sweet and dear world came flooding back to Brando instantly and with stunning clarity.

There was even an advantage to the sitting position; Brando's left hand was resting on the beretta in the soft Bianchi holster on the inner side of his calf. Before Roger could reach inside his jacket for his own piece, Brando had his automatic out and pointing. People from the

386

surrounding tables began to move away, not forming a circle or anything—just leaving the premises. There didn't promise to be an excess of tips around the pool for the evening.

"Thank you for the hit, Roger," Brando said, "I feel much refreshed."

With his free hand, he reached up to the table and hefted the glass candleholder nearest to him. He lurched to his feet and faked a throw. Roger flinched left, a pasty smile breaking on his face.

"You wouldn't dare," he muttered, turning entirely away from Brando and shrugging his jacket straight.

He was turning back to face Brando when the throw that was for real caught him just over his ear. He crumpled like a stringless puppet and the others let him be, their eyes on the pistol in Brando's other hand.

"Relax," Brando said. "Cogitate. Peruse the real. I've gathered us here in solemn palaver to determine whether or not we end hostilities before your dowdy dishclouts, sleazy doxies and illegitimate yelpers get mowed down in the crossfire. The females of your noxious clans. So, response?"

"Don' see exactly why we have to do that," Jimmy Teams answered, his soft voice carrying in the warm Santa Barbara air. He tapped the paper in front of him, "George Haslins talkin' 'bout ancient history here. Even if you had a case, statute of limitations done be long gone by now. And we are many to your one."

Brando nodded his agreement, "That's an accurate assessment, old carrion hunter. How did you simple muggery-duggeries acquire such nimbleness at murder, anyway?"

Jimmy shrugged, "At the beginning, we had ourselves the advantage of surprise. Nobody never 'spected us niggers an' bohunks of no capital crimes. Later, we did get awful good at it, like folks do who works real hard at something. Though I always felt we had an aptitude for it. Some people's do, you know. And then, we schooled to make ourselves better. They got training courses in the army. We sent our kids. And, I guess it's a lot like football—practice makes perfect." His voice went on in a pleasant drone, but his old face looked hard as chiseled black granite in the light from the candles. Brando suspected he was playing for time, until their little disturbance conjured up reinforcements.

Brando's gaze swung around the table, reflecting on them one by one. *What an amazing little bunch of dauber cut-throats!* They'd managed to pull off the sports diddle of the century, and then artfully killed and killed and killed again to keep their chummage. And here they were, gathered in force after 25 years, still capable of swift and deadly actions. Of the dirty dozen, he figured only Mindy might not be hard-boiled.

"This is not finished," Jimmy Teams said, spitting each word out with a soft but deadly intensity. He looked like a talking voodoo doll, shrunken, wrinkled, black and ominous. "You kill Nathan's son. You kill my kin. There will be a vengeance for this."

Nathan nodded, "You can count on it, Mahr. A day will come, you will open a door, turn the ignition on in your car, be walking in some grassy meadow, and we'll take you down.

"That's poetic," Brando said. "Thee and me and a grassy meadow. But what are the probabilities?"

"You're a dead man," Nathan said.

"A dead man," Old Motorfoot repeated.

"Mindy?" Brando asked. "Are you in this game or are you out the door?"

She stood suddenly, jerking to her feet as if she'd come from a long way back to present realities. "I loved my father, but he was a crazy old fool! I'll have nothing more to do with this! I'm out!!"

"Mindy-" Nathan started.

"You can all go to hell!" And with that she stormed away from the table.

"We are victims in a play. Our paths are chosen for us," Brando said to them. "I'll be Rosencrantz and you can be Guildenstern. Or you take the other part. It makes no difference." He was just blathering, knowing he needed cool conversation if he was to amble away without committing extreme violence. He moved slowly and held his hands in plain view so his enemies wouldn't mistake his intentions. And then he sang an ancient Vietnamese curse, "Troi, Dut, Nuoc-oi!" which in Vietnamese means Sky, Earth, Water--everything!

"What the hell you talkin' funny for, boy?" Old Motorfoot wasn't so old that he was beyond bemusement. In another world, Brando might have liked him, but in this one, he was responsible for death and destruction.

"In plain *Anglias*, May it be upon your heads!" Brando said, pocketing his Beretta and backing away, step by step until he was next to the six foot high plate glass sheets that provided the guests an uninterrupted view of the Pacific and still shielded them from the stiff onshore evening breezes. Several beefy young thugs in T-shirts bearing the Tranquility Hotel logo were moving in as Brando vaulted the plate glass and half-slid, half-jumped his way down a rocky, steep embankment to the service road below. He arrived in a shower of rocks and debris, his shoulder hitting the road with a painful and ungraceful thump. Brando decided he had to be okay, and so without checking further, hurried across the road and angled on a course he had determined would keep him out of sight until he made the highway.

They were foolish Chicots to let him Texas two-step away from that table, but allow his departure they did. Mayhaps, they had gotten slow and dense with their era of success. Or maybe it was simple over-ego. After all, they had declared Brando dead, and no sod ever pays enough attention to a dead man.

CHAPTER 39

Brando left the Maroon Dog in the parking garage at the Tranquility. After all, once you're a proclaimed dead man, you can't be too careful. He hobbledyged a mile to a pay phone where he beckoned a cab to whisk him to the airport. He rolled lucky and last-manned it up the steps of a whiny little prop-jet heading for San Jose. The doors closed as the final glints of light speckled the sky over the Channel Islands. Brando took a seat and enjoyed some honey-coated peanuts and a tonic water, and the steward-wench smiled a thin smile at his scraped and battered appearance.

The ornate antique gilt clock dinged and donged nine as he entered the lobby to Charlie's office, but the buck was still there, on the phone with a client. Charlie's anterior chamber was awash in Louis XIV, but his personal office was decorated in *Oriental Expensive*. He had assembled a tranquil golden Buddha head on a little square table that had been designed just to show it off, and rare Thanh Le lacquers shone from the walls. An exotic look for a mortgage broker and deals rogue of the finest water.

Charlie's face lit up with his classic huge smile when he saw Brando, "*Kha!* What a wonderful surprise! Give me a moment and I'll be right with you." Then he took a closer look at the huge lump still oozing over Brando's eye and ushered him to the washroom before going back to his phone. Brando washed up as well as he could and returned to sit outside his closed door.

He overheard muffled arguing, but when Charlie emerged a few moments later he was all smiles. He took Brando by the arm.

"You look better, *Kha.* I'm beginning to wonder, aren't we getting a little old for these personal encounters?"

Brando shrugged and said nothing. A long look exchanged between the two of them. *At least we were still here.* Charlie gazed for a moment at the smiling golden Buddha's head, sighed, and then smiled.

"We gotta try a great new place! Vietnamese-Chinese, *Kha.* You won't believe their Pho Cua. I haven't tasted anything like it since the Hai Cua!" The Hai Cua, the Two Crabs Restaurant, had been a favorite hangout in Saigon.

Brando stopped him before he had them steered completely out the door, "First, I propose we need a few moments...for business."

Charlie eyed Brando casually, then his booming laugh came again and he steered his friend back the other way and positioned him in a brownish-maroon leather armchair across from his huge mahogany desk, "Okay, okay, *Kha.* Whatever you want."

He retrieved a club soda and a bottle of deep-red colored Campari from the small refrigerator behind his desk and filled two cut-crystal tumblers.

Brando took a sip of bitters and plunged right in. He explained all the violence and percussion that had rattled his reality since they last talked, and presented Charlie with the original of George's confession. Charlie insisted on all the details, descriptions of where Brando had been and exactly what it felt like, and just how close he'd come to catching The Big One. What it was like on the boat and in the fire and underground with the air running out. Aside from that, he didn't interrupt; he let Brando run on in his own way and only stopped him to clarify when there was something he wanted to get clear.

Brando stressed that Mindy wasn't part of the scam or the subsequent string of snuff attempts, and it was his wish she should be granted sanctuary if not complete diplomatic immunity. There was a quiet period into which you could have dropped a boulder and so Brando repeated his request, and after the second supplication Charlie finally relented with a slight nod and an impatient little click of his teeth. *That was enough, but with Charlie, you had to get it.*

And so Brando's entire recital was conducted, and when it was finished he felt a sense of buoyancy, like the third leg in the 440 relays, the guy who has held his own and now is passing the baton to the kick-man. Charlie seemed to understand how Brando felt. He grinned and lofted a three-fingered sign of the cross in his friend's direction, *"Dominus vobiscum,"* he entoned with the reverence of a venal old altar boy. "Say three Our Fathers and three Hail Marys, my son, and forget about all of this." He rose and slapped Brando on the back, reaching for his coat with the other hand. "You have done well. The church owes you for your good works and many deeds."

"I don't care about that." Brando shook his head. "Do you think the evil doers will escape to paradise?"

393

"You're kidding, of course," Charlie said. For a moment his dark brown eyes seemed like black agates. And then he laughed, his mood shifting easily into another gear. "Now come on, Mister *Kha*, you look like a man who could use some hot *pho cua*, and I know just the place. You know, the Vietnamese egg rolls these guys do are Number 1, G.I., you're gonna love 'em."

CHAPTER 40

And so with high spirits and reckless abandon we come to the final chapter of FOUL, our 18th century London street penny dreadful that takes place on the streets of Los Angeles in 1984. Having been your worthy translator, I would bid you a request. Kindly remind the name below the title that I have channeled him this bit of exercise in return for his promise to pen the unknown tale of how my own bones were ground into dust. By whom, and why, and how I took my revenge. Fare thee well, fair damsels and fellow rogues, one and all! And one last time, to horse:

If Brando's reliably erratic memory served him at all, it was nearly an entire year after his confession to Charlie that Nathan Paramis and his son Roger were lost in a blazing tropical storm while fishing near a few tuna-crowded humps of rock located a hundred and sixty miles southwest of the southern tip of Baja. It is ever a temptation, as all ocean-sporters realize, to drift that far from real land in search of the *fabuloso* 300 pounders, the so-called *freight train tunas* that can tear off a man's arms and leave him just the bloody stumps. Tropical disturbances commonly rear their ugly thunderheads, and the Paramis party must have simultaneously lost their radio, their radar and both engines—and hence, their ability to observe or outrun the storm or even to communicate their predicament.

The L.A. Times printed a teary retrospective on the Gritty Greek featuring old snaps of him as a player and coach, and one of the station's up for license renewal broadcast a public service piece on their nightly news intoning the importance of establishing a checklist for boating safety, old white haired Jerry Dunphy amending his nightly sign-off from, from the mountains to the sea, Good night to an ominous from the mountains to the sea-and beyond!

Lieutenant Baker called, curious as to Brando's feelings on these matters. They chewed it over and managed to find common ground in that they both thought it might represent a loss for somebody somewhere. The Lieutenant did, however, accuse Brando of knowing more than he was revealing. And Brando had to respond that his comments oddly made him reflect on the Thomas Eakins painting "The Gross Clinic", completed when England's empirical sun had still not set, said painting which shows with anatomical clarity an abdominal operation in progress. Brando saw that didn't exactly stop Baker cold, but a whole lot of seconds went by before the Lieutenant could think of whatever the next thing was that was on his mind.

About that same time, Jimmy Motorfoot Teams expired quietly in his sleep, of natural causes it was said. *Well, he was a very old man.* And shortly thereafter, two of Jimmy's grandsons were lost in a fiery ball of flame when the helicopter transporting them from L.A. to Jimmy's desert hide-away for the funeral rites accidentally crashed and burned in the San Bernadino mountains. Authorities said the weather wasn't

396

that bad, and suspected a faulty altimeter. Lieutenant Baker and Brando had a conversation along similar lines to some of their earlier ones, though toward the end, the Lieutenant barked something testy about Brando's theories beginning to strain the laws of probability. And Brando answered that life was that way, and, if the Lieutenant was starting to feel sorry for himself, he should reflect on The Agony in Gethsemane.

Still later, tragedy struck the ill-fated Teams clan again when some of them ingested poisoned food at the annual family reunion. Undercooked chicken was blamed for the illness, which left seventeen of the youngest and most active males in the family dead. It could not be explained why the young strumpets only became ill while the culls passed to eternity, though a local wenchist radio talk show host stridently presented as scientific fact that wenchly bodies are naturally more immune to many things which strike down duddering rakes. Brando told Lieutenant Baker he suspected the Motorfoot clan probably should have stuck with Kentucky Fried or maybe asked for his own recipe for stuffed carrier pigeons, and the minion of law and order yelled some fairly harsh personal invectives. *Entirely rude, that!* It might have felt good for the Lieutenant to vent but Brando didn't think he really meant everything he said. Brando reminded him that they had joined forces very well together in the past, *n'est pas?* and he looked forward *avec joi et anticipation* to continuing their relationship, maybe even into the next century. In fact, he was anticipating his friend, being on the police force, might have the inside track on some hot expose that they could take to the networks. Brando told Baker he was willing to share tit for tat, having some research on the Bogomils, a Balkan religious community with some hip theories on both pacifism and the Eastern Orthodox church as the house of Satan. After Brando presented his offer, there was a click and a buzz on the other end of the line, leading him to suspect they may have had a faulty connection of one sort or another, if not phonic then in their relationship.

He heard nothing at all about Mindy, which he accepted as a positive sign.

He was in his office, shoes to the desk, trying on the Ram's hat from the fan pack Archie Richie had sent over, when he heard high heels crunching on the gravel outside with a quick, impatient step that Earman hadn't heard in a while. Then there was the click of the vixen's shoes on the short patch of sidewalk, two soft steps in the little plot of grass in front of Brando's office steps, and then her step on the wooden steps in front of his door. *No pantyhose*, he thought happily, not hearing the fabric swish on her inner thighs. And then Belle Denver walked in wearing a tight red dress and her classic sexy pout.

"Did you get any checks for me?" she demanded.

"No. Not a dime."

She burst into tears, "Those dirty, rotten, awful *fish people…!*

Brando found a Diet RC Cola in the back of the fridge and popped it for her. The gilflurty scamp of a wench sat on his lap and poured out the whole sad story. The producer had skimmed too much off the top, and there wasn't enough moola to finish the principal photography. It had rained nearly the entire time, and the film's treasurer, who was also the driver-cook and grip, kept promising she'd get paid the following week. Every one of the amazing toothed fish had gone belly-up, and the production died from pretty much the same disease, whatever it was.

"Did you miss me, Belle?" he asked.

Brando's prodigal gimcrack looked at him for a moment, startled by the thought and maybe frightened of what she might say. Or maybe it was just Brando's lust-kindled imagination.

Mayhaps, it was the brand-new Rams hat with the horns, tilted sideways on his head. Or the fresh Rams T-shirt, XXL, hanging on his incredible athlete's frame. Brando knew some wenches went crazy over a cull in uniform. Or maybe it was simply the well-known and notorious lure of the male thingambobs.

"I could really get buff with a football man," she said in her husky whisper, teasing him with a few of the words she'd picked up hanging out with the Brandoman, "let's brush."

"You word-pecker, you," he replied fondly before the able wench smothered him in teary mouth-hugs. As always with Belle, he nearly didn't have time to link to his supply of Ramses Ram Jet #7s. They didn't make it to the couch of passion, but somewhere in the middle of rolling around on the floor, Brando wrung from the greedy wench the promise she'd go see a movie with him at the Director's Guild, and maybe even dinner after. *After all*, he argued persuasively, *where else could she be openly snilched by over 500 hungry directors?*

A week later they loped to the DGA screening in his new black late-model Alfa-Romeo sportster. Belle was wearing a sleek silvery nothing that pandered to her every definition. By this time, Morrie had admitted to his errant earlier direction on poor old Fifi, and gave Brando a final offer he couldn't refuse. Brando had picked up his check, tossed across the keys to the maroon Corvette and described where Morrie and his repo footpad could find the sad wheeled beast.

Brando didn't want to be anywhere in proximity when they saw the sorry condition in which he had left the Maroon Dog. All those scrapes and burns in the fiberglass, and that fishy smell never did go completely away. On the dexter fist, Morrie being an insurance agent, Brando was fairly elevated that dinked motor vehicle was safely under the umbrella. But *Odds Plut and her nails*, on the sinister digits, if Morrie didn't strike him as a sad dauber somewhat below the best physical and mental plane. And, as Brando always read in those old penny novels, a simple ding-boy never can tell when one more of life's little shocks will be enough to send him over the edge and flying up to the Big Dimber Damber in the Sky.

THE END

400

ABOUT THE AUTHOR

During the Vietnam War, John Klawitter was a military intelligence spy with a Top Secret CODEWORD clearance. He worked at a SE Asia branch of the National Security Agency's so-called 'Puzzle Palace'. Back stateside and having been awarded an Honorable Discharge and an Expeditionary Forces medal, he became a do-it-yourself filmmaker and won many awards, including an EMMY, for his political documentary work. Advancing over the years as a Hollywood writer, producer and Directors Guild of America director, as well as a member of ASCAP and The Authors Guild, he has authored over a dozen novels and non-fiction books, including the highly regarded HEADSLAP: The Life & Times of Deacon Jones, HOLLYWOOD HAVOC: The Trouble With Fat Boy (EPIC Author's Award 2009 for Best Action-Thriller Novel), and TINSEL WILDERNESS (EPIC Author's Award 2009 for Best Non-Fiction Book). His trade paperbacks are available from Amazon, B&N and the rest of the usual suspects.

E-books of his titles are available in all formats from www.doubledragonbooks.com.

Information on upcoming novels and film projects available at www.johnklawitter.com, www.headslap.com or www.doublespin.com